J-Pop Love Song
By
Shiree McCarver

Other Books by Shiree McCarver
The Lord and the Scorpion
A Satyr's Tale: Selby and Darius
A Satyr's Tale: Zaza and Sylus
Forever Moonlight

Parker Publishing LLC

Lotus Blossom is an imprint of Parker Publishing LLC.

Copyright © 2008 by Shiree McCarver
Published by Parker Publishing LLC
12523 Limonite Ave., Ste. #440-438
Mira Loma, California 91752
www.parker-publishing.com

All rights reserved. This book is protected under the copyright laws of the United States of America. No part of this publication may be reproduced, stored in a retrieval system, or transmitted in any form or by any means—electronic, mechanical, photocopying, recording, or otherwise—without the prior written permission of the publisher.

This book is a work of fiction. Characters, names, locations, events and incidents (in either a contemporary and/or historical setting) are products of the author's imagination and are being used in an imaginative manner as part of this work of fiction. Any resemblance to actual events, locations, settings, or persons, living or dead, is entirely coincidental.

ISBN: 978-1-60043-056-5
First Edition

Manufactured in the United States of America

Cover Design by Jaxadora Design

Dedication and Acknowledgements

    I want to thank Kay Gwalthney for introducing me to the culture of Asian men. I had no idea what I've been missing and now I'm in love. Also, a big thank you to my editor, Kymberlyn Reed, for her support in helping to make this book possible.
    Domo arigato. Thank you very much, Takuya Kimura, Kaneshiro Takeshi, the music of GACKT, HYDE, Hideaki Takizawa, Kazuya Kamenashi, Akanishi Jin, and countless of other Japanese Artists, for enlightening my imagination with their hardworking talents. Because of you this book was possible and my character, KANE, was born.

J-Pop Love Song
By
Shiree McCarver

Chapter One

Los Angeles, CA

STRIDING INTO HER high-rise office, Charlene threw the files onto the cognac colored desk. She was tired and frustrated from her meeting with the producers and director of her Japanese debut drama, *Blu's Diary*.

If she had to do one more rewrite on the movie's script, she would scream. Still, no amount of rewrite pissed her off more than the producers' latest jab at her patience. They wanted a different Asian actor to play the title role. Some twenty-something, Japanese pop star looking to bring his creative talents into the United States and use *her* televised mini-series to do it. All they were concerned about was his ability to guarantee good rating numbers. What about what was best for her character, the domineering rock star, Blu?

This went against everything Charlene had envisioned when they contracted her novel to make into the first Japanese drama series to be done in both English and Japanese and to air simultaneously in both countries. They lied. There was no way the Japanese *artiste* they chose was powerful enough vocally to pull off the original songs she wrote for her tragic hero. She had anticipated a much older and more experienced actor. Now, she would have to settle for some spoiled rich kid with looks and connections.

"You okay, Charlie?"

A deep male voice cut through her thoughts. Charlene turned with a start to find her International Manager, Abe Goda standing in the entrance.

"Abe, you promised me this wouldn't happen!" She started in on him immediately, her own frustrations uppermost in her mind. "I can't believe you're allowing them to pull this stunt on me at the last minute. What happened to the actors that I've wasted months researching? What the blazing hell was that all about if they already made their choice?"

He pushed his hands deep into his pockets with a resigned sigh. "I'm truly sorry that you had to find out this way. I had hoped to get to you first, but I had sincerely anticipated changing their minds before you found out."

"You should have tried harder."

"Charlie, I do see the logic in employing a well-known Japanese name in the music industry; it makes good business sense. People will not only tune in to see Kane in his first serious drama, but the soundtrack will certainly fly off the shelves. Isn't that important also, to have your music appreciated?"

"The tracks I wrote for this project are the best I've done yet, not to mention, the first new songs I've written since my husband died." Charlene defended her skills with all the fierce tenacity of a mother defending her child. "I assure you the music will promote itself no matter who *I* choose to sing them!"

"I can't believe you let them walk all over me in that meeting. *Damn it!* This should have been *my* decision."

"I understand how you feel Charlie and no one purposely doubts your abilities. Nonetheless, until you can completely produce your own films, you have to understand this is how negotiations are conducted not only in the States, but in Japan also," Abe reasoned. "These investors especially want a sure thing considering this script is dealing with such a taboo subject as an interracial relationship between a Japanese male and an African-American female."

She had to give Abe that one. "True," Charlene grudgingly agreed. "It's my first internationally distributed film and if it hadn't been for your connections and support, I wouldn't have gotten this far with these eastern producers."

Abe smiled in understanding knowing that hadn't been easy for her.

"Still," She waved her forefinger at him. "I'm not an idiot, the only reason they chose to produce *Blu's Diary* is that it's a long standing bestseller in the States and also over the past 3 years has received an unprecedented record of a 150 million yen in sales."

"Your point, Charlie?"

"My *point* is it showed them there is an audience for these types of love stories and they realized they needed to swipe it up before someone else did. That alone should give me more leeway in making decisions around here!"

"But you can't guarantee your name alone can pull in the ratings in Japan, Charlie. You also forget that on its *début*, your book was protested in Japan. It brought you to everyone's attention and the Japanese youth love controversy, so they rushed out to purchase it because of the hype. After that, critics took notice and realized you had a really touching story and you did it in a way that wasn't ridiculing or disrespecting Japanese culture. Still, you know these things take time."

Abe continued to reason. "The second selling point," he hesitated. "Is your history during the time you lived in Japan. The local media knew if they openly spoke about your book, then they would also have an excuse to bring up the scandal that forced you to return to the states."

Charlene remained silent. She closed her eyes and rubbed her temple. Would that always come back to haunt her? As long as she couldn't stay away from the country and culture she'd fallen in love with, the pain would always be there.

"Exactly." Abe stated, seeing her silence as a form of agreement.

"Okay, but I genuinely believed the investors liked my idea about causing a media buzz by going from city to city in search for the next big Japanese star."

"The idea was excellent; the increased expense to pull off such a venture was not. You don't have the available budget, sweetheart." In his usual calm and soothing way he added, "I do understand you're upset Charlie, but you have to understand where these gentlemen are coming from. They are investing a huge amount of capital into this project." He removed his hand from his pocket and pushed his gold-rimmed glasses up onto the bridge of his nose. "And it gives them the right to have whomever they want to play the lead."

J-Pop Love Song

"Maybe I should use my own personal resources to make sure that I get what I want and what's best for the script."

"Charlie, now you're deliberately being a hefty pain in my ass." Abe shook his head and muttered softly under his breath before replying to her statement. "Simply put, you *do not* have the right to tell them who should be in this drama." Abe rubbed his chin. "As far as applying your personal funds, I cannot and will not agree to that. It's a huge risk that you simply cannot afford to take, at least a quarter of a million if not more, and in the end Kane will still play Blu."

"As my manager, I can't believe you're convincing me to do this," Charlene grumbled.

"As your *manager*," Abe put additional stress on the last word. "I'm simply looking out for your best interests. I'm not as close to this project as you are, so therefore I am as they say, detached. Not to mention, my dear Charlie-chan that it's an excellent idea." He paused. "Think of the bigger picture, Charlie, of the bridge between cultures. In the end you will be saying, 'Abe, you're a genius' as usual."

She softened a little and gave her manager a half smile. As always, Abe knew the right things to say, and he was just as good dealing with other people as he was with her. Still, it rankled a bit. *Blu's Diary* wasn't like her other works, this one was personal.

Abe closed the space between them and towered over her. "Charlene, you'll be the first African-American woman to have her film produced and directed by several well-known Japanese filmmakers in the business. Having a highly recognized Japanese leading man and a popular African American leading female to be premiered on Japanese and American television is a major accomplishment. Do you eventually want to ruin this opportunity for more Black writers and actors over what…creative differences?"

"What if my movie flops because they cast some pretty boy who couldn't act his way out of a wet paper bag? I'm finished, that's what? I've worked too many years rebuilding my name and reputation and you're telling me to ride it all on some spoiled pop idol!"

"Come on, Charlie. Do you really think I would sit back and let him or anyone else ruin the reputation, *WE*, have built?" Abe's temper flared, something that seldom happened, which gave her pause. Abe didn't yell. He was Japanese to the core, and he took pride in his ability to defuse situations without being overly emotional. "I've put my ass on the line for this too," he reminded her harshly.

"Abe…"

"No, Charlene, *you* listen for a moment," he interrupted. "*I'm* the one who brought your novel to the attention of the financiers and *I'm* the one that convinced them to allow us to film it and air it in *my* country. *They* are the ones who made it possible and as much as it behooves us we owe them. What part of this situation did you not understand going in?"

His dark eyes took in her face as he continued, "I know you want the best showcase for your work, but, Charlie, they should at least be allowed a chance to recoup their investment and Kane is the security blanket they want to green-light the project."

The throbbing vein in the middle of her forehead felt like a thousand jackhammers.

"Give me the word right now and I will trash the entire project if that is what you want me to do." Abe placed his hands on her shoulders with a deep sigh. "Do you really want that or are you trying to sabotage your dreams again? You can't live in the past. It's not success that killed your husband. It was his only foolishness."

She glared at him. "Don't bring that up again, I'm not in the mood for you to play analyst tonight."

"Okay, then can you at least hold your judgment until you actually meet the guy in person?"

"Why should I meet him? They've already made their choice in the matter."

"Charlie—" Abe massaged the back of his neck.

"Abe, look, I'm not completely clueless about this young man," she interrupted releasing a long breath, hoping it would help the tension subside. "I know who Kane is and I even have a couple of his CD's, but he is a Japanese *pop star* and my character, Blu, is a Japanese *rock icon* who was an orphaned street kid who hustled his way to stardom through sex and blackmail. Blu has to be edgy, not squeaky-clean."

"I know this." Abe folded his arms across his wide chest.

"Yeah, so tell me how the hell he's going to pull this off with his reputation? What does he know about growing up unloved on the streets of Osaka or doing what Blu did to survive?"

"How do you know Kane can't handle the role Charlie?"

"Hmm, for starters, that squeaky-clean image will make it impossible for the Asian public to separate the pop sensation from my jaded rock star."

"Again, it's not just your film or your dream, Charlene," Abe reminded her frankly. "I assume you're judging Kane solely on his public persona. Shouldn't you hold judgment until you've met him face to face? He—"

"I don't *want* to meet him," she interrupted stubbornly. "He's just another Japanese guy with a handsome face and a bunch of squealing fan girls who worship the ground he treads on."

Abe raised an eyebrow in that "are-you kidding" way that infuriated her. "Excuse me, you did say you own *all* of his CD's?"

"Don't look at me that way. I said I had a *couple*, not 'all'!'," she blurted, scarcely aware of the volume of her own voice. "I believe this kid has *sugoi*— awesome talent for writing songs and a great voice as cute as he is, but it's not going to be enough."

"That "kid" is twenty-four by the way," Abe pointed out ironically. "You know, it's not like you to judge a person before meeting them. Why is the thought of Kane playing Blu rubbing you the wrong way?"

Charlene glanced out onto the glimmering night of Los Angeles. "Let's just say I'm familiar with the type—handsome and rich Asian men who get bored and want to stir things up a bit."

"*You*, of all individuals, stereotyping and judging someone?"

She cut him a glance that would have melted a weaker man, but not her trusted friend and agent; he knew about all the closets that housed her skeletons.

Still, Charlene was more than sure that Kane would be far from the last of their demands.

Her face took on a faraway look. "Trust me, everything Jason touches he ruins it with his selfishness."

"Jason?" He asked cautiously. "So that's what this is all about. Something about Kane reminds you of Jason."

A soft gasp escaped her. She hadn't meant for that to get out. Charlene knew in her heart Abe was right. She was making hasty judgments based on nothing but her personal baggage.

"Abe, if you don't mind I need to be alone." Her words were shakier than she would have liked.

His dark eyes shimmering with worry, but always the gentleman, he said, "You understand I'm here for you no matter what, Charlie."

"I know." She forced a smile to alleviate his concern. "I'm just feeling a bit overwhelmed by it all, but I'll be fine after I get some much needed rest."

"Are you sure? We can have dinner at that authentic Japanese restaurant you like so well." Abe winked. "I'll even allow you to practice your Japanese with the waiter and order for the both of us. As a matter of fact, I'm feeling so generous I'll even let *you* pay for the meal."

"Whoa," Charlene chuckled, some of the oppressiveness she felt lifting a little. "Now, I know you're feeling sorry for me because not once in the eight years we've known one another, have you ever allowed me to pay for a meal."

"Hey, a sharp man understands when to set pride aside." His thin lips spread into an easy smile.

"I don't need practice with my Japanese anyway; there are just some things one never forgets, thank you. Now go, I need to think about those rewrites they requested me to do with Kane in mind."

"So you've changed your mind about him." Abe took in the stubborn set of her lips before the last word was out of his mouth and realized she hadn't quite conceded.

"I didn't say that," she retorted. "I just need to be prepared just in case they don't see reason."

"Of course. Still, I have all the faith in the world in you, Charlie. *Oyasumi-nasai*."

Charlene removed the stylish Misook jacket and placed it on the back of her office chair before taking a seat behind the desk. With a swishing sound of silk stockings, she kicked off her heels and crossed her legs. It had been a long and tiring day of meeting after meeting, and she was finally able to release a deep sigh of relief that it was over.

Yawning, she looked at the clock on her desk. It was almost nine-thirty. *I should take my butt home!* Not that she had anything to rush home for and she did keep rock star hours, even if she didn't live the rock star lifestyle. Another aspect of her past that hadn't changed.

She flipped through the stack on her desk and saw there were at least twenty pages of rewrites to do before turning in for the night. Charlene figured she might as well work from home, where she could be comfortable. Feeling bitchy, she started to pick up the telephone and call Sharon, her assistant to meet her at the house, then changed her mind. No, she wouldn't be that bitchy just because she didn't have a personal life, it didn't mean Sharon didn't either. At that moment, Charlene wondered how many of her readers would be surprised that in spite of the hot stories she wrote, she was actually sleeping with a laptop and an array of reference books. Most of the time, she didn't even bother to remove them from the bed as she nodded off to sleep.

The phone rang. Instantly startled, she waited for the service to pick it up. The shrill grew more persistent as she continued to wait for the service to pick up. It took another five rings before she realized Sharon must have forgotten to transfer calls to the answering service.

Cursing under her breath she picked up the receiver. "Hello, Charlene Alfred, here."

"Why are you against my playing Blu?" His directness was surprising, since the Japanese tended to be anything but. Even though he had an accent, his English was clear enough for her to hear he was genuinely pissed.

"Kane, I presume."

"You presume correctly."

"Well calling me like this isn't helping your case any."

"What will? You see, I want this part *Alfred-san*," he said. "I know I can play this man exactly as you have created him. Do you know how rare it is for a manuscript to come along from your Hollywood that doesn't stereotype the Asian male?"

"As a matter of fact I do." Charlene said with a bit more asperity than she intended. Who was he to school *her* on Hollywood's penchant for stereotyping?

Though Kane was not the enemy and in all fairness, he would be a fool to pass up a role like Blu, Charlene didn't like having her creative wings clipped just because someone had more clout than she did. This was her baby and she wanted to see it done right.

"I apologize for being so rude to you, Mr. Kane, but it's been a long day and I really need to get home."

"I suspect your husband is waiting for you."

Her eyebrows lifted in surprise. Was he fishing for information in regards to her personal life?

"You'd suspect wrong, but it is too late here to be calling," she reminded him once again.

"Forgive me for disturbing you at such a late hour. It's morning here and after my manager called and told me you had doubts about me…I want to know why."

Charlene heard the genuine sincerity in his voice and sighed deeply. He deserved her objective opinion. "Look, I've heard you sing and I've seen your live performances. You are very talented."

"Thank you." She could hear the wryness in his tone.

"But you only appeal to hormonal teen girls. I just don't see the rawness in you that my character needs to possess."

"Please, allow me to be as straightforward as you have been, Alfred-san. First, you know nothing about me as a *man*. What you have seen is a well-orchestrated persona created by my management team. My long term contract with Takusa Entertainment Group is coming up for renewal and finally I have the

J-Pop Love Song

possibility of becoming the musician and actor I've always wanted to be."

"I understand what you're saying," and she did sympathize with him. "But the problem is still your image. If you fail to sway the viewers, then it will all be for nothing."

"I *know* I can play the part convincingly." Charlene heard the passion and desire in his tone and surprisingly it warmed her. Still, that wasn't enough.

"Mr. Kane, I don't want to risk a backlash of angry Japanese boycotting the film because their non-threatening pop icon is portraying a boozing uninhibited musical genius."

"Look, Charlene, I will not let that happen to you or your film," he assured her.

A brief chill ran though her body as he spoke her name. A strange since of familiarity made her close her eyes in memory. *Jason*. Charlene shook her head and realized she was too exhausted to be having this conversation.

"*Tsukareta*," she whispered rubbing her temples. "Mr. Kane, I don't want the story to be ignored because of the media frenzy surrounding you and with that being said, I seriously think we should be ending this discussion."

"I know *you're* tired and I humbly apologize for being a pest. However, I believe, regardless of the crude side of Blu, I can add a vulnerability to his dominating character, make his unfortunate decisions understood and forgiven."

"Mr. Kane—"

"Just call me, Kane."

Charlene was at the end of her patience. "Whatever!"

"I know what I'm talking about. In our culture when one sees you are sincerely repentant of your behavior, it can be forgiven graciously and without regret."

He was correct. That had been her main concern and the concern of the producers, even though she had rewritten several scenes in consideration of the cultural differences of what the Japanese found acceptable.

She tried a new tactic. "I read that you were born into a wealthy family which tells me you have no idea how to portray Blu. I'm not looking for someone who can act this part, but someone who may have *lived* this part in some way."

"You are shouting at me"

Was that humor she heard in his voice?

"I...I'm not yelling," she said defensively before realizing she was indeed speaking loudly. In her family if you weren't loud, your point of view got lost in the pool of forceful personalities. "I'm just—"

"Excited about the script and the music you've written for *Blu's Diary*." He completed the sentence. "I understand the passion and the message of your story. That's why I want to do it and I'm not going to give up so easily."

"So then you understand what this project means to me, how proud I am about it."

"As you should be, Charlene." He said softly. "I read *Blu's Diary* on a train ride between engagements three years ago and I never forgot it. There was something about Blu that felt familiar to me and I genuinely believe if this book were to become a movie, it would be a sign for me to change the course of my career."

"A *sign?*"

"When I heard Blu's Diary was being adapted into a film I knew this was the sign I've been waiting for because I believe working on this film is going to change my life completely."

Charlene couldn't deny she was touched by his words and surprised that he had actually read her book. Knowing he spent three years contemplating the possibility stunned her. Oddly, she felt more relaxed as she slid down in the chair and crossed her feet on the desk.

"I must admit that your reading my book caught me by surprise." She grinned in the phone as if he could see her and caught herself. The smile disappeared.

"No, thank you for being a wonderful writer. I've kept up with your career since I was seventeen and actually, I've read all seven of your books. *Blu's Diary* was my favorite because your lead was Asian and I was pleased."

"I don't get too many guys admitting they read my stuff. Not straight guys anyway," she chuckled. "You *are* straight, aren't you?" Charlene couldn't believe she asked him that question.

"As opposed to being crooked, you mean."

"No, I meant...never mind what I meant." What did it matter if he was gay or not? It wasn't any of her business. "I'm sorry, I shouldn't have asked that."

"I was teasing. I don't mind, ask me anything," he assured her. "Regardless of any fan-based rumors you have heard romantically linking me to men I have collaborated with or members of my band," he laughed. "I am not gay."

"It's hard to tell these days, though it would have no bearing on this role if the actor was or was not. Are you dating anyone?" *Damn, where did that come from?* She placed a hand over her big mouth.

He appeared to be hesitant in answering since he wasn't as quick to reply as he was before. "Dating...mmm...no," he finally answered. "However, there is someone I am *very* interested in."

Charlene didn't even want to consider just why his answer disappointed her. Why wouldn't a man as sexy and as popular as Kane *not* be involved with someone?

"As a loyal reader do you have any recommendations for future books?" she asked.

"Well, since you asked, more with Asian males, Japanese in particular because they seem to make us the least approachable of the Asian culture and it isn't true." Charlene agreed with that assessment, her experience in that country as proof. "Also, there aren't enough writers utilizing Asian males as romantic leads. I suppose because most see us as technical sidekicks to the hero, or martial-arts wielding strongmen. In *Blu's Diary* you showed that we could be as passionate, loving and screwed-up as any other man," he pointed out seriously.

"I confess that I was hesitant to write Blu as Asian. I didn't want to offend anyone because some of his actions were questionable, though some of it was from my personal experiences while living in Japan. When in doubt I asked Abe Goda, my manager. He helped me big time to keep Blu's reaction in certain situations as realistic as possible. However, in the end it's still a fictional piece."

"Who did you model Corinne, the female lead, after? I fell in love with her from the moment she walked into Blu's life during high school. She felt very real

J-Pop Love Song   15

to me. Even after Blu abandoned her to chase his ambitions, she was his biggest supporter. Her protectiveness of Blu and her desire to generously give her love to him unconditionally touched something in me that I can't explain."

Charlene was thankful he couldn't see her face as her cheeks stained red at his compliment.

"Let's just say Corrine is someone I know very well."

"I see." Kane paused before asking. "Is there a man in your life that you've modeled Blue's character from?"

"There was," she spoke with as reasonable a voice she could manage. "But, he died several years ago."

"I'm sorry." He spoke in a gentle tone. "Unlike *Blu's Diary* it seems your real life characters didn't have the happy ending that you wrote of."

"Nobody wants a romance to be *that* real." She laughed. "All romances have to have a happy ending, don't they?"

"In a Japanese love story? You have to be kidding. It would be surprising if one of the lovers *didn't* die."

Charlene exhaled a long sigh in agreement. "True. As far as my readers are concerned they *demand* a happy ending and…" Her smile faded as sadness gripped at her heart. "I wish every day of my life that I could have written a better ending for the man I used as my inspiration."

Kane's next words shocked her to the core. "You're Corrine aren't you, and Blu is Jason James."

Damn boy was too intuitive for his own good.

Charlene held the telephone to her ear as an awkward silence stretched between them. To make such a confession would be to revealing into a part of her life that she had chosen to exorcise in the telling novel.

But she was even less ready to hear, "Meet with me."

"What did you say?" Her voice squeaked.

"I will make all the arrangements. Come to Japan. I want you to spend some time with me, live in my world and get to know the *real* me, not the image. I definitely want you to know things about me that no interviews, demos, headshots—"

"Or life-size posters," she threw in.

To her surprise he laughed. "Let me guess; shirtless, jeans, and in a downpour?"

You forgot sexy and wet. "Yes, that's the one."

"*Bibitta*! How on earth could my manager send something like that to a potential employer?" He laughed aloud. "I apologize for him. Takusa-san forgets everyone isn't an enthusiastic fan of my music. If it embarrasses you to have it, just throw it out, he won't know."

She could hear that he was truly embarrassed and she found it unexpected and endearing. She would have thought any man who had thousands of women screaming over him since age twelve would possess an ego the size of Texas.

"I gave it to my assistant's niece," she lied to save him further embarrassment. Her eyes trailed to the poster they were discussing framed and leaning against the wall where her assistant Sharon had placed it upon its arrival. "Also, I didn't say I wasn't a fan."

Silence yawned and she realized she caught him off guard with her honesty.

"Will you come to Japan as my guest?"

Was that hope she heard in his voice?

"I...I don't know this is a bit—"

"*Onegai-shimasu*, please, what do you have to lose?" He cajoled. It was obvious Kane was used to getting his way. "At the most, you get an all expense paid holiday to Japan and since I'm in the midst of touring, I can show you a more personal side to a few other places beside Tokyo."

He really was making the offer irresistible, she thought. "I don't know if I can get away at this time."

"What about next month?"

"That is only two weeks away."

"You're going to have to let them know soon if you are going to go along with them hiring me aren't you?" he questioned. "So I will make you a deal. If after spending some time with me you still feel I can't do justice to Blu, I will withdraw myself from the running. That way there will be no bad feeling between you and the producers."

"You would do that for me even though I can tell you want this very much?"

"I am a man of my word. If I must wait to see you, may I call you again, Charlene? *Onegai-shimasu! Onegai-shimasu!*"

He pleaded playfully, a gentle reminder for her that he was only twenty-four.

"Oh now you're showing some manners by asking can you call me when you shouldn't have phoned me in the first place. Not to mention you're calling me by my given name before we've even met. What are they teaching the youth of Japan these days?" Charlene fingered a micro-braid resting on her shoulder, a smile on her lips.

"Sorry, but most of my schooling was done in a boarding school outside of Japan. But, I can make sure not to overstep. I can call you Alfred-san instead of Charlene, and I apologize for being forward in my call, but not in the purpose."

"I can't fault a man for being aggressive in business."

"I'll remember that."

The huskiness lingered in his tone and her eyes clouded with visions of the past.

"About my coming to Japan..."

"The offer is open and there is no obligation, but remember I'm a fan and I bought all your books without a discount." Charlene found herself smiling again. "Oh, no pressure at all."

"Honestly, if you don't want to meet, allow me to take this time and apologize for my manager. If I can't get the role of Blu because you don't believe I'm capable, then I don't want it at all."

Charlene's lips tightened, how could she not accept his request. He was already proving to be more than she had expected and completely different from her imagined perception. This alone made her curious to know more about him.

She heard him clear his throat. Her fingers twirled the braid in her hand nervously.

"Can I ask you something, personal?" Charlene licked her lips wondering why she was allowing him to get to her. Hadn't she already made her decision in regards to Kane's abilities to go from being Japan's darling to playing this dark role, so unlike his persona.

"Yes." He answered without hesitation.

"Are you prepared for how much this career move could change your life, as you know it? Are you prepared for your fans to be appalled and the feedback to be none to positive because of its content?"

"I have walked the path that others have chosen for me for so long I'm not sure who I am any more. Don't get me wrong; I'm grateful and very fortunate to be so well received all over the world. Nevertheless, I can't live under the same restrictions that were given to me when I was a twelve year old boy."

Charlene could hear the frustration weighing heavy in his deep voice.

"I'm a man and I have mental and physical needs. Yet, because of my contractual obligations, I must remain unattached in the public eye."

"Is there someone in particular that has caused you to want to change the way things have been going? Is that your motivation for wanting to do this project and change your image?" Charlene realized that question was too personal and had nothing to do with anything. Yet, she had an opportunity so few received in a lifetime. The ability to speak one on one with an entertainer they had only admired from afar, through their craft.

"I admit recently I have found myself intrigued by a particular woman, but it's not the only motivation I have for wanting to do *Blu's Diary*."

"Thank you for your honesty."

"I will be twenty-five in a couple of months and I find myself thinking of things that other men my age think of, such as a future with some one I can love openly and they love me openly in return."

He released a long sigh and she could almost picture him running a frustrated hand through his dark hair. She smiled remember how impulsive and alive she felt at twenty-five and understood he should have the right to have the same freedom, regardless of public opinions. Times have changed and the young generation was more accepting of the fact that entertainment figures wanted to be sexual and have a family too.

"I know I must really sound pathetic, since I do live a charmed life. Right now I must seem very ungrateful for all the things I have been blessed with…"

"No…please, I understand what you're saying." Charlene intervened. "You need someone to love. What is that saying? 'What good is success without someone to share it with?'"

"Exactly."

She could tell from the way he said that one word that he was smiling again and it made her smile too.

"I'm flattered that you would choose my movie to be the beginning of an entirely new life for you." She said sincerely.

"*Blu's Diary* has all the elements I need to break from this pop mode into the rock mode, which will give me more creative and personal freedom. I'm willing to do whatever is necessary to make it a success for…the both of us."

The intimacy of his chosen words should of shocked her, yet he'd implied them before and each time it caused a quivering response in a place Charlene didn't want to explore further.

"You…you know you took a chance of pissing me off, by calling me this way." Charlie commented. "I will admit it took guts and it seems like a ballsy thing that Blu would do to get the gig he wanted."

"Excuse me, what did you say about my...balls?"

Charlie grimaced, blushed and smiled into the phone at his deliberate misunderstanding because his English was flawless. Another unexpected quality he possessed.

"I'm teasing you." He saved her from further embarrassment. "I understood what you were saying." Kane chuckled. "But, you're smiling, aren't you?"

Did he have such a sexy voice at the beginning of this conversation or was she imagining it had deepened even more. Charlie cleared her throat staring once more at the poster of Kane. Her fingers smoothed over the soft material of her skirt from the top of her thigh to the hem. He really was sexy, mysterious and...young. She hurriedly removed her hand from the trail it was taking up her inner thigh.

Her breath came hot and heavy as she fought off the sensations of longing that started at her feminine core. It had been so long, and there was something about his voice that...

"Charlene? I hear you breathing, so I know you are still there. Will you come to Japan?"

Admittedly, he peaked more than her curiosity for she wanted to see him in his element. It would give her the opportunity to see life through the eyes of a pop star and who knows, it could be research for a future novel."

"Okay," she said softly.

"Okay..."

"I will come to Japan and meet you."

"*Honto-ni*, really? Awesome!"

Charlene cringed at the sound of anticipation in his voice. What was she doing? She didn't want to give him false hope. Still, she couldn't help but feel thrilled by his excitement.

"I haven't said you got the part."

"No, but you will." He assured her. "May I have your cell number too?"

"My cell number?"

"Yes, so I can call you from my private line and you will have my number." He reasoned. "As soon as you can free your calendar, call me, and I will take care of everything personally."

"I don't...that won't be necessary, you can reach me at this number and leave any messages with my assistant, Sharon, if I'm not in."

"I understand. How about I do this the old fashion way and I just tell you my private number and you can call me, whenever."

Was that disappointment she heard in his voice?

"That probably will be best." Charlene stated writing down the phone number he supplied on the inside of his file lying on top of her desk. "I'll get back with you as soon as I can clear my schedule."

"I'll be waiting." He paused as if he wanted to say more, but all he said was, "*Sayonara*, Charlene."

"Good bye, Kane."

She held the phone long after the line went dead, her mind deep in thought.

Chapter Two

CHARLENE FRESHLY SHOWERED and towel drying her shoulder length braids ran out of the bathroom into the bedroom, she snatched up her ringing home phone resting on the bedside table.

"Hello, Charlie here," she breathlessly said.

"Charlie? I like that."

"Kane?" She placed the towel over her nakedness as if he could see her through the phone.

"I know I promised that I would wait for your call, but it's been two weeks and I was worried you might have talked yourself out of coming here," the smoky voice said, and her heart skipped a beat.

"Well—"

"I'm still getting adjusted to our time difference. Did I wake you?"

"No, I just stepped out of the shower."

There was silence.

Charlene rolled and closed her eyes. *Why did she tell him that?* "How did you get my home number?"

Dead silence stretched between him. She could hear him breathing so she knew he was still there.

"Hello?" She prompted.

"I...err...saw it in my managers address book. I hope you don't mind."

"No, I should have called you, by now." Sitting down on the edge of the four-poster canopy bed, she continued to explain. "I apologize; I forgot to have my assistant contact you with an update. I'm having a minor family emergency and it's delayed my making plans to leave the country at the promised time."

"Are you okay? Your family?"

He seemed sincere. She swallowed deeply and answered.

"Yes, I'm fine, but my mother fell off a ladder, her foot got caught and she broke her ankle. She will heal, but I've been helping out with their business until my sister finishes her finals and returns home to help."

"What business are your parents in?"

"After my sister and brother moved out, they retired from their careers and turned our family home into a Bed and Breakfast." Charlene leaned back on the mattress, her legs swinging off the side of the bed.

"What did they do before retiring?"

The rich timber of his voice in her ear was oddly comforting and she responded matter-of-factly.

"My dad is a heart surgeon and my mother is a lawyer."

"Very ambitious and admirable professions."

"My parents are amazing." She smiled. "They encouraged us to make high goals for ourselves, then reach higher and make the choices that will keep you fulfilled for years to come, just in case you get stuck doing it." I love them most for understanding that my dream to be in the entertainment field is what I want, even though they had hoped for something they considered more secure."

"It must be satisfying to go after your dreams with the full support of your family." Kane said and the envy was evident in his voice.

"Wasn't your parents supportive of you?"

"My mother did. She gave me my first guitar when I was four and because I had this ability of playing exactly what I heard without lessons, she introduce me to the piano when I was six and this time with a tutor. She said she didn't want me playing instruments without the ability to read and write music." He paused. "I have her to thank for giving me something to fall on, without those skills I probably would have ended up homeless in the streets, but instead my skills afforded my father the opportunity to unload me on to my manager Takusa-san and the best English boarding schools."

"Your mother allowed your father to do that to you? How old were you? Why would he do that to you?" Charlene asked surprised by his admission.

"My mother died when I was ten. I was twelve when my father sent me away and I guess it was because I didn't appreciate my new step-mother, who had been my father's mistress." Kane answered bitterly.

Charlene heart opened to him and she wished she were there to hold him. That was one disadvantage of communication over the telephone. She didn't have the words to let him know how sincere she felt about what happened to him and "I'm sorry" didn't seem to be enough. She chose to not say anything.

"I want to hear more about your life with your family," he broke the silence.

"Well, even though my father was supportive he wasn't happy with my choices." Charlene laughed. "You should have seen his face when I chose music journalism. My goal was to group both my loves together. When I told my father he asked me, 'what are you going to do, sing to the people when you interview them?'" she said in her best deep "father" voice.

Kane laughed. Knowing she could make him laugh made Charlene feel warm all over.

"That was his way of joking with you, of course."

"Oh yeah, he knew, but I must have changed my mind twenty times before I finally graduated with my Bachelors in music. The only thing that kept me from going crazy in school and trying to maintain a long distant relationship with my boyfriend at that time was reading romance novels."

"Now you write them," he commented.

"Oh man, reading them drove me to want to make some additions to my career. I became so frustrated when I read book after book of women living 'happily ever after' and none of them looked like me, I added more courses and received a Fine Arts degree in writing. In hopes that I could not only change the romance writing industry I wanted to change the movie industry too, so I went

J-Pop Love Song

back and took some courses of screenwriting."

"I thought I was an overachiever." He chuckled.

"Well, I didn't say I made the honor roll, I was happy with passing. Dad wasn't, he wanted me to make honors, but I just wanted to get started doing my music professionally and sell my short stories." Charlene sighed. "I was sick to death of school."

"You mention your father more than you do your mother."

"Do I?" A frown light puckered her eyebrows. "I suppose it's because my mother set her career aside for the sake of the family. She was there when you needed nurturing and she was the cushion between us and dad's temper."

"Your father was abusive."

She heard a note of anger in his voice and said quickly. "No...no, my father is a sweetheart with the voice of a drill sergeant. He was the disciplinary, but not cruel. I think his military career background causes him to run his house like a barrack, but he has chilled out a lot since I was a kid," she said reflectively. "I suppose having the twins late in life did that?"

"Your brother and sister."

"Yes, brats the both of them. Jaycee and Kayla. I tell you when you are twenty years old and find out your parents are still *doing it* because your mother is forty-two and pregnant again, it can require therapy," she murmured satirically.

"I did therapy, but I didn't take it serious." Kane laughed. "After a stint in a mental ward for a few months with a few of those doctors, I actually thought I was the only sane one in the place."

"Kane..." Her voice died away.

"No big deal. Really, it was just a warning from my father that I should do as I was told or my life could get so much worse." His voice, though nonchalant, was husky with emotions. "After you got into writing screenplays, what happened?" He changed the subject.

Charlene swallowed back the tears that tightened the back of her throat. "I...I was fortunate enough to get a job on a television drama as a writer for the experience. I was writing songs for my boyfriend's band and started pulling in enough royalties that I could stay at home and write full time. Soon I was making enough to produce my own independent films that went to television, so even if they didn't have much commercialism I was gaining experience."

"Now, you are an award winning composer, best-selling author doing your first international featured film. You should be proud," he commented. "And happy. Are you happy, Charlene?"

"Trust me, coming to this point in my life didn't come easy and after an incident that I don't care to discuss, I didn't think I would ever be able to move forward." She rattled off nervously.

"But are you happy?" he asked again.

Charlene paused to think about it. Was she happy? She should be, but for some reason she wasn't as happy as she had been, once. Even then, when things weren't the best it could be, she had been happy but now...

"Charlene?"

"Yes, I'm happy," she lied softly. "Why wouldn't I be? As you pointed out, my life is...good. I have a family that loves me, my best friend, Sharon is the best and oh yeah, Abe, is my lifeline."

"Abe?"

"Goda-kun, that's Abe. He is one of my managers, my main manager and close friend. I have much to thank him for, he saved my life," she confessed, her voice softening.

A light frown marred her features as she questioned why she was telling him all of her business. She wasn't one to open up easily, but for some reason it felt easy doing so with him.

"I see," he said in a rush of breath. There was a seemingly long pause before he asked, "This Goda-kun is your boyfriend?" He spoke so softly she wondered if she'd heard him correctly.

Charlene started to explain, but she realized to do so would open a door for more questions about her past that she didn't want to discuss with someone she was just getting to know.

"Enough of me. I read that you come from an elite family of businessmen and real estate moguls. So I would have thought your father would have pushed to groom you for the family business, as usually the case in Japan."

"That's true and my father wanted me to be an exact clone of him." He paused. "I suppose I would have considered it, but I would have had to respect the man to want to emulate him. Besides, I was more like my mother, "a born dreamer with illusions of foolishness" so my father says."

"You know you are so much more than that, don't you, Kane. My God, you're deemed a musical genius in our business, your ability to play so many instruments modern and traditional and at such an early age will go down in the history books of talented musicians, trust me."

"*Domo arigato gozaimas*," his voice faded to a hushed stillness.

When he remained quiet she continued, "No reason to thank me. You should be proud of the countless songs that you've written. As well, the numerous awards you've received from all over the world and all of this, under the age of thirty. And you're young enough to even achieve much more." Charlene said passionately feeling a sense of dissociation to be lying partially naked across her bed soothing the ego of an International Pop Star. "Your father should be proud."

"Yeah, well, he has my older brother." Kane let out a long, audible sigh.

"I see."

"Ryugo is very much like my father and my father is contented as long as he has him and my younger sister Kotomi. I stopped trying to make him proud years ago."

She realized there was nothing she could say that would ease the mental anguish Kane's father must have inflicted on him and at such a young age. She wasn't able to justify another person's actions. She couldn't imagine a parent disassociating themselves from their own blood. That would never happen in her family, no matter what they do. There parents would be displeased by their actions, but never stop being their parents. However, this was something Kane and his father would have to want to work out between them.

Charlene couldn't possibly give him advice when she didn't even know all the facts; all she really knew about Kane up until now, rested in a file upon her desk. A file of press releases, news clippings, and photos of a young man that

J-Pop Love Song

seemed to own the love of the world in his hands. None of this told her about Kane's more personal or human side. Yet, as he spoke to her she could hear the same insecurities that everyone experienced at one time or the other.

What Charlene found stranger than her curiosity about him, was his willingness to share such personal information with her.

"Kane—"

"Can we discuss something else?" Kane interrupted, clearly feeling uncomfortable after his admission."

"Kane, are you okay?"

Stillness settled between them until his soothing voice cut the silence. "Charlene, do you want to know what isn't written under my list of accomplishments? I'm a compulsive perfectionist, an overachiever, and I intend to work hard to please others in order to overcompensate for my lack of social skills."

"Kane—"

"I suppose I should be use to being alone by now." He continued as if he hadn't heard her say his name. "The last time I ever truly felt loved for who I truly am was with my mother," he explained. "It seems that everyone else wants something from me."

"I'm sorry."

"Yeah me too. I shouldn't have disturbed you at home but I truly didn't have anyone I wanted to talk to but you. Today is the anniversary of my mother's death. I went to visit her grave, my father was there, and he brought *her*, his wife, with him. I don't even know how he could do such a thing." His voice was cold and exact. "Didn't the bastard hurt my mother enough when she was alive? Why shame her memory by bringing that woman? Hell, why did he bother coming at all, it wasn't like he loved her!"

"Kane." Charlene closed her eyes for a moment. She felt as if his pain was her own. "Don't worry yourself trying to figure out your father, would it make a difference if his reasons were good ones?"

"There is no good reason to betray the woman you love and ruin an otherwise happy home." He grounded the words out between his teeth.

"I know you have every right to resent your father, but your mother died some years ago. I have this odd feeling that something else is going on with you and it has nothing to do with your family." She rested the forearm over her eyes. "Do you want to talk about it?"

"Am I that obvious?"

"No, it's not that…it's just, well…I don't know *how* I know, I just do," Charlene replied. "Am I wrong?"

"No, you're not wrong," Kane admitted. "I'm worried because I'm in trouble. I haven't been able to write a new song in over a year. And a new single was supposed to be released three months ago and I have nothing!"

She snapped her mouth shut, stunned by his admittance. She completely understood how he was feeling.

"It happens Kane, and it's not unusual or even something to really be concerned about because before you know it, you will find your muse again. I went through the same thing after…" her voice trailed off into silence.

"After what?" he urged her to continue.

"After I...I lost someone I loved very much. For awhile I couldn't seem to function or even think properly." She answered truthfully. "I did well to remember to get up in the morning, or bathe and comb my hair. Music and writing are my great ways of healing but at that time it was the last thing I wanted to deal with."

"Is this the situation that you said your manager, Abe Goda, help you to deal with?"

She was surprised that he remembered. "Yes."

"Charlene, I know that your husband was a highly successful Japanese rock musician and he committed suicide."

She held the phone tightly in silence against her ear, her heart pounding.

"I know that had to be hard on you."

"You couldn't possibly know how..." her voice broke off in mid sentence.

"My mother took her life. I know the situations aren't the same, but our pain is," he said.

She covered her mouth and swallowed deeply once again caught off guard by this unpredictable man.

"*Baka-janai!*" He moaned. "How can I be so stupid? I'm sorry Charlene, I'm really pushing it by calling you again. Calling you at your home makes it even worse. To top my shame I tell you all *my problems*. Forgive me for disturbing you." He moaned again, sounding like a wayward boy that caught doing something naughty.

"Kane, it's okay, really. I'm glad you felt comfortable enough to call and speak with me. My life isn't a secret. Everything you said is true. So don't beat yourself up about it." Charlene couldn't stop the chill that ran up the length of her spine as memories of another conversation she had with a disheartened musical genius.

She closed her eyes and swallowed a sob as tears burned in the back of her eyes.

"Then can I ask you something?"

"Can I stop you?"

"Of course."

She wanted to say no, but then there was no telling what he had already read about her, so wouldn't it be best if she was the one to answer any questions he may have about that time in her life?

"Charlene, you don't have to," he said softly.

"What did you want to ask me?"

"I have read articles that hint of you and your manager as being lovers."

She had to laugh. "I would think you being an entertainer that has been romantically tied to male members of your band, your male stylist and let me see the last pop sensation you did a duet with. So you tell me, is all that information true about you?"

"That's a loud and clear, NO," he murmured satirically.

She giggled. "I love Abe, but he is my best friend and confidant. I wouldn't trade that in for a relationship."

"Well, I'm glad to hear that."

J-Pop Love Song

Charlene rested quietly while holding the phone and listening to his steady breathing. Some of her sadness evaporated, leaving her strangely flattered by his interest.

"You've become very quiet," he said in a low, composed voice. "I hope my forwardness—"

"No...no, I'm just a bit surprised at how much we covered in this short time." She responded quickly.

"Actually, we've been on here for a little over two hours."

"What!" Charlene looked at the clock it was 2:10 am. She didn't remember the last time she talked on the phone with anyone this long. Yes she did. It was with Jason. They use to speak like this on the phone until one or the other fell asleep when he was on the road and she couldn't be with him.

"Sorry, I know I should have said something especially since I know it's late there, but this was the only time I didn't have something scheduled."

"No problem, but I really need to go to sleep I got to be at my parents in four hours to help dad with breakfast for the guest."

"I understand." His disappointment was clear. She smiled.

He had no idea how sexy his voice sounded. She was a heartbeat away from saying, "Talk nasty to momma so she can relieve some stress, Baby Boy". Of course she didn't.

In spite of this need to get phone nasty with the gorgeous Kane, Charlene kept it clean and said, "I need another two weeks to wrap up things here and then I will come to Tokyo. I'm very interested in seeing you move and perform live."

"Hai!"

"Kane, don't just say 'yes'." She rolled her eyes. "I need you to get serious, if you want this part you have to show me you can do it. I'm going to be brutally honest so if you don't have what it takes to play Blu, I'm going to let you know it."

"I don't expect anything less, Charlene," he assured her.

'When I get there be prepared to sing; no perform, a few of the songs from the arrangements I wrote for the film."

"I already have," he answered with staid calmness.

Her smile broadened in approval. "Thank you, Kane."

"For what? I'm the one who should be thank you for giving me this opportunity."

She could tell from the sound of his voice he was smiling too.

"Nevertheless, thank you for calling to check on me and for speaking so honestly about yourself."

"Thank you Charlene, for listening and for doing the same."

"I want you to know as much as I think you are a great guy, I must choose who will be best portraying my character." She countered.

"I know," he spoke in an odd gentle tone, that wasn't lost to her over the phone. "It's not why I was so open with you. As a matter of fact, I don't know why I shared so much about myself with you, I think it's because I feel that if you could write such soulful songs you must understand some of what I'm going through."

"I do," she spoke softly.

"Charlene?"

"What?"

"Do you mind if I call you again? At home I mean."

"If you want." She felt a warm glow flow through her. Even though she couldn't see him, she pictured his full lips parting in a smile.

"*Mata kakeru-ne*. I'll call you again," he stated.

"*Makaseru*. It's up to you." Charlene replaced the phone on its charger with a deep sigh.

Turning onto her side, she pulled her legs up to her chest in a fetal position. Feeling lonely, naked and vulnerable her lashes fluttered, settled, and locked on the gilded picture frame on her bedside table. She looked at the face of her husband, Jason. Forever he was half-smiling in that sexy way of his while the serenity of their lovemaking still smoldering in his drowsy almond shaped brown eyes.

Charlene loved the way he looked after making love. She remembered how he laughed and hid behind his hands to block the camera shot. She told him to give her that multi-thousand dollar come hither look he gave his fans. He laughed and told her only if she could sign a contract for none stop blowjobs. That was her Jason, always laughing and coarse.

Her burning eyes grazed over his dyed auburn locks of hair and reflectively her fingertips twitched as she remembered the silky thick textures as she pushed it off his face when he was on top of her. His full mouth was rosy red from her ardent kisses. As imperfect as he was, she never could imagine choosing to spend her life with anyone else.

He was beautiful…he was soul mate. After she took his picture, he had held his arms wide, she fell into them, and he made love to her until she was mindless. They were so in tune with each other their breathing was coordinated. She figure that is why when he died, she felt that any moment without him she'd stop breathing and went through panic attacks.

Charlene remembered the secure strength of his arms and she remembered when depression hit Jason he would linger on the dark side and not even her love was enough to keep him grounded. Now she wondered how arms that felt so strong holding her could belong to a man so weak in many other ways.

She couldn't believe that after all these years his death was still so raw in her heart. Tears fell silently from her eyes.

Juno-kun, why did you choose to leave me?

Charlene read the email from Kane for a second time. Since the day he'd surprised her with a phone call to her home phone, he'd been persistent in calling her every night before she turned in for bed. No matter what city he was touring in she could depend on her phone to ring at 9:00 pm every evening like clock work. Then came the emails, telling her of his day, the interviews and how his concert went along with pictures. Even though it was a few days away from her visit, she looked forward to his phone calls and emails. In fact, she felt spoiled by the attention he was bestowing on her. Of course, it all could be because he wanted the lead in the movie badly, but than again, he already had that because

J-Pop Love Song

her producers weren't budging.

She wondered if he had been sincere, that if she didn't want him to play Blu he would withdraw from the running. There was only one way to know for sure and that was to tell him she didn't want him to play the part, but she couldn't do that now, because she wasn't so sure he wouldn't be good in the role.

In the past week, she had found so many similarities between him and her deceased husband Jason that it was disconcerting. On the other hand, maybe it wasn't a similarity with Jason at all. It was possible Kane was playing the part of Blu in the real world to convince her that he was capable and because she immolated Blu after Jason, they seemed eerily similar.

"Okay Charlie, give over. You've been looking at that computer screen grinning for about fifteen minutes. Let me see what you're staring at." Sharon came into the office placing a cup of Charlene's favorite mint tea on the desk in front of her.

Charlene jumped at the sound of her assistant's voice. A spread of heat stained her brown cheeks.

"It's nothing," she said hitting the exit button and clearing the screen of Kane's latest email.

"Nothing? If it was nothing, why did you just clear the screen?" Sharon placed her hands on her slim hips.

"Have you seen my itinerary of book signing events for the next three months after I return from Japan?" Charlene made busy adjusting and shuffling the papers lining her desk.

"Yes, it's where it's always been; on the computer in the file marked itinerary." Sharon said sarcastically. "So I don't know why you are pretending to look on your desk, you don't print off your schedule you transfer it to your cell phone calendar."

Charlene glanced up at the slim sleek blond with not only beauty and boobs but also brains and attitude straight out of the Bronx. She was an asset that kept her on time and her work thoroughly edited. Not only was Sharon Lupon her jackpot assistant, she was also her best friend and for that reason alone, Sharon had no problems calling it as she saw it.

"You've met a man."

"Share, don't even go there. I'm not seeing anyone now, or ever." Charlene said defensively.

"Yeah, uh huh." Sharon agreed before saying. "So what's his name, what does he do and do I know him?"

"Who is who?" Charlene's lashes fluttered.

"See, I know when you're lying because you blink three times in quick succession."

"I do not!"

"See, you did it again. You might as well tell me the truth, Charlie, 'cause you know I'll find out once I get to snooping in your business."

Charlene smiled because Sharon was an ace hacker when it came to computers and it wouldn't take her any time at all to crack her latest password. What could be the harm in telling her, it wasn't as if she were interested in Kane romantically. He was fifteen years her junior, for God's sake!

"Okay, it's no big deal. As you know I will be leaving the day after tomorrow to meet Kane and for the past week we have been talking on the phone and emailing one another." Charlene confessed. "I was reading email from him as you walked in."

"I see." Sharon stated.

"See what? There isn't anything to see!" She screeched. "We are just discussing business. It's nothing romantic, besides he is too young to even consider such a thing."

"Well—"

"Well what? See your dirty mind already going to the gutter, Share. That is why I didn't want to say anything because I knew you would blow it all out of proportion."

"Damn girl, for you not to be feeling anything romantically, you sure are twisted tight. I haven't even said anything and you're defending yourself." Sharon shook her head.

"Romancing a twenty something young man is out of the question. Besides there is no way someone like him would be interested in someone like me."

"That's the second time you mentioned your age difference. Are you trying to convince me or yourself, that this could be a problem?" Sharon asked dropping into the guest chair sitting in front of Charlene's desk.

"Have you always been this way?" Charlene asked.

"What way?"

"A pain in my ass."

Sharon ruby red lips spread into a wide smile revealing a stunning white smile. She crossed one leg over the other and adjusted her short skirt before answering.

"Yup."

"Why haven't I fired you?"

"Because without me you would never get anything completed," Sharon said without looking in her direction, her eyes transfixed on her manicured nails.

Charlene laughed. This was a familiar routine between them and it was easier then having to explain her strange growing attachment to Kane.

"You can sit there cool as you please, Charlie, but I know you're interested in Kane."

Charlene closed her mouth tightly as Sharon held up her palm to halt whatever denial she was preparing.

"You know it's cool to be hot for him. He is fine as hell, and I would sleep with him if given the chance. You know it's okay to have sex for sex sake. Trust me when you're going at it like rabbits, you can't tell the difference between love and a good fuck."

"Do you always have to be so crude?" Charlie rolled her eyes heavenward.

"Do you always have to be such a prude?" Sharon countered.

She didn't say anything. What could she say? It was true in some ways she could be considered prudish, she could still count her ex-lovers on one hand and she never slept with a man until they dated at least two months. That was until she met Jason James.

The instant she met Jason, the world went into a state of overdrive. He was powerful, charismatic, and had more dimensions than anyone she'd ever met. As she looked back on their time together, she realized that with him she never had the chance to stop and take a breath.

"You're thinking about Jason aren't you?" Sharon's voice broke into her deep thoughts.

"How can I not? Working on this script keeps him in my mind constantly. I had hoped once I wrote Blu's Diary I could purge myself of all the pain and memories. It almost worked until it was chosen to be made into a film and now there isn't a day that can go by that I don't think about Jason."

"Charlie, you know the only similarities between Kane and Jason are they both are Asian. Jason was hard rock and he lived his life like one. From what I read about Kane he seems to come from a pretty stable background, again unlike Jason."

Charlene realized Sharon wasn't telling her anything she hadn't said to herself already. Yet, it didn't change the fact that in spite of their differences there were also similarities between the two men.

"I know, but still when Kane speaks, I find myself gravitating towards him. He has the same addictive energy that Jason had. Also we can speak for hours about everything and he never bores me."

Sharon smiled. "You're falling, girl."

Charlene's heart skipped a beat. There was no point in denying it. She was attracted to Kane. Not only was he strikingly attractive: the pale golden skin, black hair, and dark, piercing eyes with foolishly long lashes. Hmm...the one thing that enticed her most were those wonderfully proportioned lips with the most delectable pout she'd ever seen on a man.

"I have a crush, that's all." Charlene admitted. "I'm sure once I meet him and spend some time with him, the illusion will be gone and so will my attraction."

"If you say so." Sharon left brow lifted a fraction, her doubt obvious.

"Oh please, Share, after the first day in his company I'll be ready to fly back home. Talking on the phone and emailing is one thing. However spending time with an immature twenty-five year old will be a rude awakening I'm sure."

"Charlie, stop over thinking everything. Enjoy your trip to Japan. Enjoy Kane's company for what it is and nothing more. I will hold down things here. Just have fun." Sharon pushed herself up from the chair and made her way towards the door before asking, "Are you going to take the contracts with you so that Kane's manager can look them over?"

"I haven't said Kane has the part yet." Charlene's voice was cool and dismissive.

"Yeah, whatever you say. I'll pack the contracts."

"Sharon Lupon, you're fired!" Charlene yelled at her assistant's retreating frame.

"You're so funny and you're falling for him!" Sharon yelled back, her voice filled with laughter.

"One day I'm going to fire her ass for real," Charlene mumbled opening her laptop to finish reading the email from Kane.

Chapter Three

KANE'S ASSISTANT HAD arranged for Charlene to be picked up from her apartment by a chauffeur-driven car to the airport.

She was casually dressed in a peach cashmere sweater, black jeans and heeled boots. All her luggage was in the trunk accept for her purse, briefcase and laptop. As the arrived at LAX, she was surprised to find herself being ushered by a hired bodyguard through the airport into a private VIP lounge to await her flight.

The bodyguard exited the lounge and thankful for a moment without him on her heels, Charlene eased down into one of the oversized lounge chairs and accepted a glass of champagne from a proffered tray.

She waited for the liquid courage to soothe her frazzled nerves. She hadn't been able to eat breakfast before leaving, because of the choking fear that welled up inside her. Of course, flying wasn't something that terrified her to the point of not flying at all, but taking off and landing is what she dreaded the most.

It has been sixteen years since she had lived in Japan. She spent her childhood living in Yokosuka Japan because of her father a military medical doctor. She was born in Hawaii, raised in Japan and after graduating from Nile C. Kinnick High School in Yokosuka her family transferred back to the States to Los Angeles California where her father retired from the military and became a surgeon for a local hospital.

During Charlene's first year of college, her mother finished law school and opened her own practice, but her career was short lived because in Charlene's junior year of college her aging mother was surprised to find she could still get pregnant and gave up the stress of her practice due to a difficult pregnancy. Going into her senior year of college her baby sister and brother were born; twins, Kayla and Jaycee.

Charlene tried not to think about being old enough to be the mother to her own brother and sister. It was embarrassing enough that she couldn't visit home and hang out with her friends without the twins tagging along. Often she had to explain to people who didn't know her that they weren't her children. It didn't help that the twins made life harder on her. Every time they were out and a guy would flirt with her, they would wrap their arms around her hips and call her mommy.

She smiled at the memory. It was humorous now that they both were grown and in their prospective colleges, she could look back on those times with

J-Pop Love Song

fondness. Yet, it wasn't an easy transition when there's a twenty-year age difference between siblings.

♪

Kane entered the lounge and came to an abrupt halt in the doorway as his gaze fell on Charlene Alfred sitting quietly in a corner. There was a reflective smile on her full lips. It brought a smile to his mouth. He had seen pictures of her on her many fan based websites and there was a black and white headshot on the back of her books, but none did justice to the real woman in the flesh.

Her deep brown skin appeared flawless from this distance. Classic cheekbones, perfect proportioned features and those sultry dark eyes. She was enough to tempt a man into doing something foolish, like taking her by the hand pulling her from the seat and testing to see if her lips were as soft as they looked.

Kane shook his head as the fantasy in his mind turned explicit. He has spent his life around women that wanted him for numerous reasons; none were because they found him an interesting person, as much as they found what he did for a living interesting. The few encounters he had were discreet and terminated by his management team as quickly as they begin. It was impossible for any woman to have a relationship with him and keep it entirely to herself.

He learned early on, part of the attraction for being with him was being able to tell others they were seeing one of Japan's leading entertainers, he almost lost his career just because he was caught walking into a hotel with one of his band members, girlfriend. It didn't matter that the band member had walked in first. All they needed was the illusion of impropriety and it nearly ruined him in the public's eye.

For him relationships have always been a joke. He would actually take bets on how long it would take the female he was interested in to dump him once the management team yanked her aside and shove a confidentiality contract in her face before he could even ask her out on a real date. They'd escaped as quickly as they could.

Therefore, the only sexual contact Kane had had with a woman in his twenty-four years was with paid hostesses. His first sexual experience took place when his personal manager hired a hostess to celebrate his twenty-first birthday along with his first and last night of drunkenness. That was a memorable night: ten minutes of sex and sixteen hours of feeling like shit.

His lovemaking abilities has gotten better, but he often wondered if there would be a difference between having sex with someone that was being paid and making love to someone that actually wanted to be with him because they didn't want to be with anyone else? The hands shoved into the Levi low-rise denim pockets knotted into fists of frustration.

Kane's contract would expire on his twenty-fifth birthday and he would be free of Takusa Entertainment Group. He had an idea of what direction he wanted to take his career but in order to make it work he had to surround himself with the right people. Charlene was one of those people at the top of his list that he had always wanted to work with musically. Her getting a movie deal for one of her novels was an added bonus.

He had expected her to be attractive, but he had no idea until now just how beautiful she was. Kane had a sudden urge to rush across the room and sink to his knees before her. He wanted to bury his nose against the side of her neck and know what she smelled like. Would she be powdery soft or pungently floral? Was she the type that enjoyed being nibbled behind an earlobe in which a set of small diamond studs and a silver loop was embedded or would she find it irritating?

Gee. What was he thinking? This was not some potential date to fantasize about, this was a potential employer and she was older and more experienced. It probably wouldn't even occur to her to see him as anything more than just another portfolio among the hundreds she probably go through everyday.

He rolled his shoulders under the washed leather-racing jacket and removed his hands from his pockets to make room for the semi-erection his meandering thoughts had aroused while gazing at Charlene Alfred.

Kane's dark eyebrows arched mischievously as he drew in closer and saw Charlene leafing through his portfolio pictures in the briefcase on her lap. His mouth curved into an unconscious smile.

"I hope the real thing can stand up to the photographers artistic skills." At the sound of his voice, the heavy lashes that shadowed her cheeks flew up. She lifted her head and her mouth dropped wide in obvious surprise.

"Kane!"

His dark eyes hypnotically stared down into hers. "What do you think," he asked softly. "Do I do those publicity photos justice or were the photographers being kind?"

She snapped her mouth shut, apparently stunned by his forward behavior before she rewarded him with an impish grin and said, "I thought they did a lot of airbrushing. However, now I see I was wrong."

New and unexpected warmth surged through him at her compliment. Embarrassed he was the first to look away. Obviously, he had a lot to learn about older women. She hadn't shied away from his open flirtation but met him head on with a little flirting of her own. He liked it and felt as comfortable meeting her in person as he had while speaking with her on the telephone.

"*Ohayoo gozaimasu!*" He grinned. "I'm sorry to have you meet me here so early in the morning, but in order for me to meet you here personally, I had to make sure I returned for a radio interview on time."

"Good morning, to you too." Charlene returned his greeting, tucking his pictures back in her briefcase and zipping it shut. "I must say this is a pleasant surprise. I hadn't expected you to fly all the way here just to turn around and fly with me to Japan."

"I told you I was handling our meeting personally, with the acceptation of my assistant calling you to confirm the time for the driver to pick you up. I hope your ride here was comfortable."

He took a seat in the empty chair beside her.

She nodded her head. "Quite comfortable, however I don't have any problems making my way through airports, so the bodyguard escort was unnecessary." She smiled at him and added, "That's the good thing about being a writer and composer, you can maintain a fairly anonymous lifestyle."

Kane's cleared his throat somewhat embarrassed that he had made the assumption she would be mobbed at airports like he was. In Japan, he only

J-Pop Love Song

needed one good bodyguard, since the media and fans were usually content with pictures from a respectable distance. When visiting Taiwan and Hong Kong, he had to have an entourage of guards surrounding him to keep the paparazzi and fans from crushing him.

"An anonymous lifestyle," he said smoothly, with no expression on his face. "I envy you being able to do what you love, yet being able to live normally."

Charlene sat aside her briefcase. "You know, it would be a shame if you hadn't shared your talent with the world."

"Do you really believe that or are you just being nice?"

Charlene spoke with quiet firmness. "The one thing you will learn about me is I don't say *anything* just to be nice; especially when it comes to talent."

Kane's eyes bathed her in admiration. "I will try to remember that."

Every time her gaze met his, he felt a strange feeling in his stomach. He liked her; the way she spoke her mind. Even after hours on the phone until she started to nod off on him, he felt there was so much more she could tell him about her life.

The one subject he wanted to discuss was her highly publicized marriage to rock star Jason James.

Kane felt her hand on his and realized she was speaking to him.

"Are you okay?"

"Um...A bit jet lagged but I'll be okay," he stumbled over an explanation. "I'm sorry what were you saying?"

She removed her hand but he could still feel the soft warmth of her touch.

"I was saying that you never did tell me what time my flight was supposed to leave. I guessed my plane tickets would be waiting here, since I didn't receive them with the itinerary you sent."

Sitting closely, he found her facial bones were delicately carved, her mouth fuller than he thought from across the room. Her skin seemed to glow with deep gold undertones. His fingertips itched to reach out and touch her face, to see if she was as soft as she looked.

"Kane. You're doing it again." Her warm brown eyes gazed at him with amusement.

"I was listening this time."

"Maybe, but you're staring." She said, raising a hand to her cheek. "Do I have something on my face or lipstick on my teeth?"

Seizing the opportunity, he reached out and caressed the corner of her mouth with the padding of his thumb. She lowered her thick, black lashes and grew very still under his touch. He was happy that she hadn't shied away from his touch. Her skin was as soft as he suspected. Not even one wrinkle marred her features; it was hard to believe she was fifteen years older than he was.

Her eyes caught and held his. "What is it?"

Clearing his throat, Kane withdrew his hand quickly and stood up pushing his hands deep into his pockets. "You...uh... a little smudge by your lips," he lied.

"Thank you." She mumbled and rose fluidly from the chair.

His smile widened. At 5'8", he found himself coming up short to non-Asian women, but Charlene was perfect. As she turned to grab her purse from the chair he caught a nice glimpse of her rounded buttocks, and he truly liked what he saw.

"Let me." Kane removed his hands from his pocket and rushed forward lifting her soft leather briefcase and laptop bag from the floor beside the chair.

"Thank you." She smiled up at him. "You never did say what flight we were taking. Do we still have time to grab a bite to eat? They have some finger foods here, but I'm not one for caviar style appetizers and champagne at six in the morning."

Kane chuckled. "You're more a coffee woman?"

"Nope, herbal teas. Especially mint tea," she replied. "I have my own specially blended brand with me and all I need to do is find some hot water."

"I think I can handle that and I can also offer you a more substantial breakfast." He placed a hand on the small of her back and ushered her out the VIP lounge ahead of him.

Once more, he found his eyes admiring the way her black jeans hugged her firm bottom and looked away as she turned to see what was keeping him. He caught up with her and shortened his longer stride to walk by her side. They continued to walk in companionable silence until she realized they were heading into a more private sector of the airport.

"I've never been in this part before."

"It leads to the private runway strip where my jet is awaiting us."

"You flew all the way here on a private plane? I know you're trying to impress me but stuff like this isn't going to make me—"

"That wasn't my intention at all, Charlene. This is the best way for me to travel because it's a nightmare being booked on a flight that happens to have an Asian high school girls volley ball team aboard."

Charlene laughed aloud. "Ah, so it's the voice of experience."

"It is and I don't want to talk about it." He cut a side-glance at her and saw the curiosity on her face. "What I will say is, it's very hard to open an airplane door open when four people are stuffed inside."

"Kane, you didn't!"

"No, I didn't, at least not what you're thinking." He gave her a wicked grin. "If I had done that than it would have been so worth it."

Charlene gave him a disapproving look until he explained.

"I was coming out of the toilet when I was rushed by four overanxious female fans." He was laughing at the same time. "Any other time, it would be a nineteen-year-old male's dream come true. However, for me, trapped in an insufferably small space with four touchy-feely sixteen-year-olds equipped with camera phones, it was a nightmare."

Charlene continued to giggle and he shook his head with a mock-serious expression.

"Yeah, I can laugh now," He smiled, "But at the time I could see the authorities waiting for me when the plane landed. Can you imagine the headlines? *Pop star Kane inducting a group of under aged girls into the mile high club.*"

"How did you get out of the bathroom?"

"My bodyguard, Alfred-san, came to check on me after I was gone for a bit. I swear that was the longest four minutes of my life."

"Only four minutes!" Charlene giggled and playfully punched him in the

J-Pop Love Song

shoulder. "I thought you were in there for a long time being squished to death."

Laughingly grasping her wrist he said, "Oh, so you think four minutes isn't long? How about I get four of my bodyguards to crowd you into the plane's bathroom and we can see how you like it?" he said playfully opening an exit door that led out to the concrete runway.

"I don't know, I'm not a public figure and if they are cute, it may not be a bad thing," she teasingly replied, skipping away from him towards his awaiting plane.

"I can't believe you said that," he yelled after her, hoisting the dislodged shoulder strap back up. "Since you have so much energy maybe you should carry your laptop case."

Charlene laughingly shook her head without looking back at him.

Kane liked this more playful side of Charlene and looked forward to spending time with her. The only way he knew that would be possible was if the media assumed she was there to finalize the role of Blu. Problem was that he didn't know how Charlene would feel about that considering her initial opposition.

Waiting patiently at the entrance of the plane stood his two regular Japanese pilots and a six-foot-four African American bodyguard along with a couple of LAX employees, who had been waiting for autographs.

Settling on the comfortable leather sofa and buckling in for take off Charlene smiled at him and said, "I see I'm not your only fan in the United States."

"Don't let that fool you, they probably want to sell the items on one of those online auction places." He grinned impishly. "I believe that is the second time you implied you were a fan of mine. If that is true what is your favorite song?"

"Oh, that's difficult to say." She played coy with him, but her answer was a surprise.

"I like several but if I have to choose one, it would be *Cherry Blossom Holiday*."

"Are you serious? I think that was on my second CD." For some strange reason Kane was hoping to catch her in a lie, considering it was his first big hit and released as a single before being released on his first CD. If she were truly a fan, she would know this bit of J-pop trivia.

"No, actually it was your *first* CD, but before that it was picked up by a Japanese television drama and released as a single, which is how I discovered your music. After hearing *Cherry Blossom Holiday* for eleven episodes it just seemed to linger in my head and I found myself singing it all the time."

"You know, I think the drama got better reviews than I did for that CD."

"Yeah, well probably because that was the only good song on it," she said bluntly and paused. "I'm sorry, that was rude."

Kane grimaced but could not deny it. He'd only been seventeen years old, singing about losing love and passion and had no clue what the songs were about until he started writing his own music.

"No, you're right. Back when I started, I just sang what was put in front of me. Not much has changed except I write my own stuff."

Charlene shrugged. "Your last CD had a lot of feeling in it, but for some reason it seemed very sad." She downcast her eyes and he marveled at how long her eyelashes were.

Her honesty was obviously as genuine as her beauty. He was flattered that she honestly appeared to be a fan. All the dreams he had been having for so long had been turned into music. Unfortunately, his dreams did leave him lonely, sad and frustrated.

"You still don't think I'm capable of playing Blu."

"I think you're capable," Charlene replied softly. "I just don't think you have enough personal experience to do some of the scenes."

"Such as?"

"Your experience with women for one," Charlene answered bluntly. "We don't have enough money to spend trying to get the perfect onscreen kiss."

She might have been teasing him or testing him, but Kane wasn't as inexperienced as she thought. "Maybe we should find out for the sake of the film, of course." His voice thickened and instinctively he leaned forward, her sweet moist lips beckoning him to kiss her.

A deep voice interrupted the perfect moment. "Excuse me. Kane-sama, as soon as we are cleared breakfast will be served."

"Stuart-san, perfect timing as usual," he groaned, leaning back in his chair, regaining control of the emotions that surfaced from being in close proximity with the one woman he felt a strange kinship with. Disappointment and relief swept through him. In spite of wanting to explore his attraction to Charlene, he didn't want to ruin any developing friendship between them by making unwanted advances.

Still, all he could think about was how he was feeling and what he wanted. How stupid could he be? Maybe she was right. Maybe he wasn't ready for the role of Blu.

Chapter Four

AFTER ENJOYING A COMPANIONABLE, very English breakfast of fresh strawberries with clotted cream, flaky croissants, Cumberland sausages, and a dizzying choice of nearly every cereal imaginable both realized they each had a fondness for sugar.

"In about fifteen minutes we are going to be bouncing off the walls from all this sugar." Charlene chuckled and sipped at the freshly squeezed orange juice with plenty of pulp. Kane laughingly said, "I don't know about you, but I can handle my sugar. Besides I'm already hyper so no one can tell the difference."

"Well, I'm warning you I can't eat like this every morning." She looked down and patted her satisfied stomach. "Since I hit age thirty-five, everything seems to go to my lower half."

"From what I can see it appears to be going to all the right places."

His dark, intelligent and expressive eyes crinkled to near slits as he smiled at her playfully.

"Hey there, watch it now," she said giggling like a giddy schoolgirl. "I'm old enough to be—"

"You can't say my mother, because my mother was twenty-three when I was born and there is only a fifteen year difference between us."

"Only fifteen years?" She gulped, not wanting to think about *that*. "Fifteen years can mean a lot. Besides, I wasn't going to say that, because I wasn't even sexually active at fifteen." Charlene shot a warning brow at him when he started to say something; he quickly slammed his mouth closed. "I was going to say, old enough to be your baby sitter."

He shrugged and threw her an assessing look. "Charlene, please try to remember I'm neither underage nor am in need of a baby sitter."

I'm looking at you right now and I want to baby you all right. Oh yes, right there, baby...oh fuck me, baby...baby, love me...yeah... that's more like it.... Charlene thought scandalously as she sipped from her glass of juice beneath lowered lids.

She and Kane were beginning to tread on dangerous ground with all the flirtation. This was a business trip, not a sexual escapade. As she watched Kane's face grow from playful to serious, she realized he was about to say something that should remain unsaid.

"Stuart!" she blurted out as Kane's friend and bodyguard, Stuart Johnson, affectionately called, *Stu-san* by those who knew him interrupted the tension between them. "Thank you so much, breakfast was wonderful."

Stuart beamed a wide white smile and nodded his shaved head and it caused Charlene to pause and take a second look at the dark-skinned man. It hadn't gone amiss that he was fine. She could see that when he was standing beside the plane, but his beautiful smile eased the harshness of his otherwise too stern face.

He looked to be more her age, a bit taller than she preferred considering her short stature, but workable in 4-inch heels. He had broad shoulders and the tightest ass she'd ever seen in a pair of tailored jeans. The jeans should have been outlawed for "fitting" too well. Charlene also noticed he seemed as blessed in the front as he did from the back.

"Stu-san, leave the rest of that and let's go over the map of the concert hall so I will have an idea of the security entrances and exits that I'm allowed to use." Kane said brusquely, causing her to look from Stuart to him.

He turned in the swiveled chair with stilted movements and stood crossing over to the opposite side of the plane to flop down on the black leather sofa. He had removed his jacket and she could see the tension of the muscles in his shoulders bunching beneath his shirt.

Even Stuart was taken aback at Kane's sudden coolness. It was at that moment Charlene realized the relationship between Kane and Stuart was more like brothers than employee and employer for Stuart grinned and winked at Charlene.

"What's with you, man? I'll be over there after I clear this table," Stuart replied in fluent Japanese, unaware Charlene was just as fluent until she winked at him. He shook his head and took the tray of food and dirty dishes away.

Charlene spared a glance at Kane and she couldn't believe what she was seeing. Looking at Kane's face, she would swear he was jealous. His thick eyebrows were pulled into a tight frown, a muscle ticked angrily at his jaw, and his naturally full mouth was actually puckered in the most childishly adorable pout she'd ever seen on a man. At that moment she didn't know what she wanted to do more, chastise him for his immature behavior or kiss him because she found it rather endearing.

He caught her looking at him and the meaning of his gaze was more than clear as his face softened in silent expectation. Charlene fought an overwhelming need to close the space between them. As if he knew what she was thinking, he slowly stood and took a step forward.

"Okay, Kane-sama, I'm ready if you are." Stuart ducked through the connecting doorway reentering Kane's private quarters.

The spell was broken as Kane sat down once more and turned his attention to Stuart. As they discussed security for the next show, Charlene took the chance to move to a more comfortable chair and remove her laptop. Of course, she wasn't interested in anything on the computer screen; she just needed to appear busy while her mind went over the past three hours in Kane's presence.

Great, if she was this frazzled after a few hours how was she going to handle being around him for the next two weeks?

She'd met plenty of famous people who looked nothing like their artistically altered photos. Unfortunately for her, Kane was as beautiful and flawless in person as he was in his music videos and pictures.

J-Pop Love Song

The only redeeming factor that kept him from appearing too perfect was a small space between his two top front teeth, and his bottom teeth which were slightly crooked.

Charlene found she liked Kane's flawed smile. It humanized him.

Still, she had to force herself to not gawk at him like some star-struck teenager. He was taller than she had expected and as thin as she suspected. Not lean in that heroin-chic rock star ways, but more of an athletic well-muscled and beautifully proportioned body.

Charlene felt a twinge of guilt for allowing herself to dwell on such thoughts. Sure she found him desirable. He was her type, and he was eliciting some interesting vibes of his own.

Great, she was going cougar. Sharon would love that. Here she was a forty year-old woman with the rampaging libido of a twenty-year-old male; scientifically speaking that would make her younger than him. Charlene cursed softly, annoyed with herself. She raised her eyes from the laptop only to find Kane and Stuart looking at her with questioning eyes.

She faked a grin. "Don't you just hate it when junk emails creep into your mailbox?" Both of the men shook their heads and returned to their discussion without a reply. She rolled her eyes at them and made a face behind the screen before returning to her thoughts.

Okay truth time. Kane was a hottie and she was attracted to him, but she had sworn after Jason to never get involved with another musician. It didn't matter what age or nationality they were, all of them were toxic and seemed to suffer from some form of artistic something or the other.

And what the hell was with the pouting lip thing Kane did when something irritated him? A grown man pouting like a child looked ridiculous. On Kane, it looked adorable, huggable and completely kissable.

She released a loud groan.

"Charlene, *nanka nomu*?"

"No, thank you, I still have the remainder of my orange juice."

"There is a mini-fridge over there next to where you are sitting." He added, "There is something stronger if you would like to add a little spirit to that juice."

She heard something that sounded like little boys snickering. Both grinned ear to ear. No shock they were such good friends. Both were absolute simpletons.

"At 10:30 in the morning? I don't think so," she replied.

"That is good to hear." Kane stated. "Now, might I ask what's bothering you? Are you bored already? Stu-san and I can discuss this at a later time, if you need me to entertain you."

"Oh, you are a comedian early in the morning, I see." Charlene arched an eyebrow. "By the way, have I told you that your command of the English language is exceptional?"

Kane inclined his head in a small gesture of thanks. "Courtesy of an English boarding school."

"Ah, that explains the very English breakfast."

"And the bit of sugary American cereal."

Charlene nodded back at him without speaking.

"Is that why you were groaning? Those three doses of sugar in a box," he asked teasingly.

"Oh, please, I had half a box and would have finished it if you hadn't taken that one too."

"*Hey*, that is not true." Kane laughed. "It's the other way around and you know it."

A throat cleared and they both turned their attention to Stuart who had been sitting quietly during their playful banter. "I hate to disturb you two kids from fighting over cereal, which I don't know why since there were plenty—"

"Not the kind with the marshmallows," Charlene and Kane piped in together interrupting whatever he was about to say. They looked at each other and burst out laughing.

Charlene didn't know what was wrong with her but, admittedly, she was acting a bit childish. It had to be the high altitude mixed with the sugar rush. At least that was the story she was telling if anyone asked.

With a long parental stare from Stuart who was now shaking his head at the both of them, she sobered quickly.

"You know when you're flying in a plane it sort of makes you feel like you're..." her voice trailed off. Stuart wasn't buying it and neither was Kane who was still laughing his ass off.

"Kane, will you chill?" Stuart turned that stare on the younger man. "Would you like to take this up later?"

"Yes," Kane managed with a snort.

"No, please." Charlene piped in wiping the grin off her face. "I'd feel bad if I forced you guys to do anything different from your regular routine. Besides, I have some work of my own that I need to do."

"It's not a big deal, Charlene, Stu-san and I can do this later."

"Hmm...is that true Stuart?" Charlene asked.

"Hey!" Kane pouted.

Her eyes dropped to his wonderful mouth and feeling those wicked urges driving her to want to do something reckless she turned her attention fully on Stuart.

"Stuart?" she repeated.

"Unfortunately no, if we don't get this done now it will become hectic trying to get it taken care of between three scheduled back-to-back interviews, a press conference about your visit, a banquet in your honor and a midnight sound check."

The room seemed to suddenly crackle with tense silence as the bodyguard finished listing Kane's hectic schedule. All the laughter died from Kane's face as he let out a long, audible curse in very clear boarding school English.

"Charlene, I can explain." Kane began.

She held up a finger and cocked her head to one side. "Whoa, wait a minute. Did I hear him correctly? Is there going to be a *press conference* in regards to *my* visit to Japan?"

Stuart shook his head and gave Kane a hard look, leaning towards him he whispered, "*Baka-janai?*"

Kane scowled at him. "I know it was stupid. *Bokutachi-dake-ni.*"

"Kane..." Stuart gave him a long look. "This isn't professional."

"*Onegai-shimasu*, Stu-san!"

"Yes, please Stuart, give us a moment alone. Kane has some explaining to do." She was so hurt and angry she couldn't keep the tremors from her voice.

How could he have tricked her this way? They had spent all this time talking and sharing their feelings over the past month. Was he so sure that he could sucker her into falling for him that he went ahead and booked a press conference to announce he had the part? Had all this been a game to him? Had the producers already given Kane a contract and he was just trying to make nice? My God, how could Abe do this to her? Surely, her manager didn't know the truth all along.

For a big man Stuart rose fluidly from the sofa. His tall figure turned and, ducking his head he stepped through the doorway and pushed the door closed behind him with a resounding click.

"Charlene, I realize hearing the news this way greatly upsets you," Kane said, moving to stand in front of her chair. He slid the rolling table that held the laptop aside and dropped to his knees, he covered her hand with his. "Trust me, it's not what you're thinking."

She coolly withdrew her hand. Charlene rubbed her forehead with her fingertips and pushed her braids behind her ears. Anything to keep her hands busy so she wouldn't slap his handsome face.

"I should have never agreed to come here. I thought after all we've talked about and the fact that you said you understood my feelings, it would be okay. And now…"

Her throat contracted and her eyes glazed over. Damned emotions, she couldn't afford to be weak in front of him now. "Why?"

Charlene felt wetness trickling down her cheeks and wiped them away with the back of her hand.

"Charlene," he whispered, and laid the palm of one hand along her cheek, caressing away another tear with the coarse padding of his thumb. "I had no choice. I am a public figure and there isn't much that I can do in Japan without it becoming public knowledge."

A quiver ran through her, and she wanted to put some distance between them but she couldn't move away from his touch. His hand felt good upon her face.

"Why didn't you discuss this with me before I came?"

"Because I was afraid you wouldn't come."

"Does doing this movie really mean that much to you, Kane?"

"Not as much as it did in the beginning. The reason I didn't tell you beforehand are for purely selfish reasons. I wanted to spend the next two weeks with you. *Kimi-no-koto zembu shiritai*."

"I wanted to know more about you too. Still…"

"Charlene, after our talks and emails, I felt close to you. I've never met anyone I could speak with so freely. You've never told me what you thought I wanted to hear nor do you treat me like a kid. All I could do was count the days before I could see you in person."

"Kane, I don't know what to say or what to believe." Charlene said quietly.

"Okay, to show you how serious I am that this entire thing is about you and only you, I will announce at the news conference that even though you have made a trip here to convince me otherwise." He took her hand in his, this time she didn't remove her hand. "I have decided to turn down the role of Blu due to the fact that when my contract is up with Takusa Entertainment in two months, I will be taking some much needed time off to pursue other interests."

Kane said the words with a finality Charlene could not ignore. He was serious.

"Kane..." she swallowed against the tightening in her throat. "Would you really give up your dream so easily? You know, in spite of our earlier agreement, the producers have every right to go over my head and sign you for *Blu's Diary*."

"So they told me."

Her eyes lowered in disappointment. She knew they were just pacifying her. They already had made the decision to hire Kane no matter what point she was trying to make by this visit, yet Kane was offering her an opportunity to be in control again, but at what cost to him?

"Kane, if you turn this opportunity down, it could ruin any hopes of them making another offer."

"That's the point of doing this in front of the media, Charlene. It will set things right and the backers will know I won't do this part without your approval.

"I don't know." Her brow puckered in concern.

"How about this? I will even put another offer on the table."

"Which is?"

"More than doing this film I aspire to create music with you. If I can't do the vocals for *Blu's Diary* soundtrack then I want to join you in Los Angeles in two months when my contract with Takusa ends and have you co-write my next CD. If you are more comfortable with this offer, than please by all means, publicly turn me down for the part of Blu."

"And what if I think you are perfect to play the lead in *Blu's Diary*?"

"Then I will be obligated to extend my contract until the end of the filming, but I would gladly do so for you. I want you to be happy." Kane lifted his eyes to stare into hers once more.

Charlene's pulse jumped. The perception of her knowing Kane longer than she did was overwhelming and somewhat frightening. What was happening to her? Was he weaving some kind of magic spell with those beautiful eyes of his or had she finally sailed off the deep end without wings?

"Kane, I...I don't know what to say. Why does my being happy matter to you? You don't really know me." Charlene reasoned. "This is your future we're talking about."

"I feel as if I've known you all my life." His dark, earnest eyes sought hers. One corner of his mouth pulled into a slight smile. "And I hope it to be our future."

"Huh?" Her eyebrows lifted in surprise that he voiced what she had been thinking. "Kane? What are you saying?"

"You don't get it yet, do you?"

"What is it I don't get?" She eyed him suspiciously, wondering if she should be frightened, even though she didn't feel any fear at all considering she was 30,000 feet in the air with a practical stranger hinting at only GOD knows what.

"This entire opportunity arose, because it our destiny to meet. Now it's left up to us."

J-Pop Love Song

"I read a lot of things about you, but being crazy wasn't one of them," she smiled smoothly, betraying nothing of her annoyance.

"Are you telling me you don't feel this connection between us?"

"I think I feel that way because, I've watched you in dramas and I've seen you in music videos and in interviews. It isn't unusual to *feel* you *know* an entertainer—"

"Charlie-chan, you're making excuses because you can feel this is different." Kane looked at her, his mouth curved, wry.

"What did you call me?" If a black woman's face could pale, she must be three-shades whiter now.

"*Charlie-chan*," he repeated. "What is it? Don't you like it? It just feels right saying it," he said thoughtfully. "Are you all right? You look as if you seen a ghost."

"That's exactly what I feel like." Charlene felt a chill. "Only Jason called me Charlie-chan as opposed to Charlene or Charlie, like my family and friends. I was Charlie-chan and he was Juno-kun." Her voice broke off into a whisper.

"If it makes you uncomfortable I won't call you that again."

Her tempered flared. "What kind of game are you playing? Do you think by emulating my dead husband, that I would suddenly see you as Blu? Is that what all the phone calls and emails were for before my visit? Did you just want to find out what motivated me to create Blu's character so you could hustle me?"

Kane shook his head and his lips quirked in a half-grin. "See, I knew if I was completely honest with you about my feelings that you might react this way."

"Kane, you're really pushing it," she warned. "Turn around and take me back home!"

"That is not possible, because we wouldn't have enough fuel to return to Los Angeles right now." Kane pointed out. "Charlene, do you really think that I could do such a thing? What are you listening to, your head's logic or what your natural feelings are telling you?"

"I think you're…"

"I know. *Crazy* or so you've already said," he supplied. "Look, Charlene, the one thing I don't want you to feel is frightened by me. If you honestly believe that I would use someone you loved dearly as a means to manipulate you then I will book a return flight for you once we stop to refuel."

Charlene bit her lip, frowning. She wasn't sure what to believe. Without a doubt, she was feeling frightened, not so much by him as she was by what she was feeling inside for him. Those eerie feelings of *déjà vu* whenever they were on the phone or certain words he would use in his emails and even earlier, the way they laughed and finished each other's words during breakfast. All of it had been real; no amount of acting could have prepared him to be so in harmony with her.

Then there were the dreams she had of him almost every night since his first phone call at the office to consider. The power of her thoughts of him, the awareness that she had been with him in cherished ways that she couldn't possibly know—everything had to have a rational explanation. Didn't it?

"I've put a lot on the line by telling you how I feel," Kane said in deep, husky tones. "Charlene, please don't make me regret this. If you believe that my feelings for you are motivated by self-interest, then all you have to do is tell the entire world that I didn't get the part."

"Then what?"

He shrugged his shoulders. "Then when I come to you at the end of my contractual obligations, free to take my life in another direction, hopefully with you; you will believe me when I say I want to get to know you better because I like you."

Charlene looked at him, accepting that no matter how crazy their connection seemed she wanted to know him better and she was attracted to him in ways she hadn't felt for anyone since her husband died.

"I must be as recklessly foolish as you are, to even consider that I could be falling for a kid," she shook her head giving in.

Relief shined in Kane's eyes and dimples appeared as he smiled suggestively at her. "So what are we going to do at the press conference tomorrow? Will I be working on your film and we keep it strictly professional or will you listen to your heart and free me to focus on what is happening between us?"

Her face grew somber. She watched him, his dark eyes happy, hopeful. Slowly she said, "I know what I want to do, but I have no idea on what I *should* do. I guess you'll have to wait until the press conference."

Chapter Five

CHARLENE HAD ENJOYED THE past sixteen hours resting and thinking after she'd checked into her hotel suite at the Transnational Tokyo Hotel. Kane and Stuart went onward to his scheduled appointments. Now with this being the day of the press conference to take place later that evening along with a cocktail party. She was still undecided about what she should do.

She was to meet Kane, Stuart and his manager, Mr. Takusa, downstairs outside the Charlton Meeting Hall where the press conference would take place and if she knew Kane, he would want an explanation before the event started and she definitely couldn't tell him she was still undecided.

Abe had safely arrived on an overnight flight from his business meeting in New York and was going to sleep up until two hours before she was scheduled to appear downstairs. She definitely needed to make sure they had enough time to go over what relevant data she was able to discuss about *Blu's Diary* and what she wasn't. Abe was the best at cock-blocking the journalists' unprofessional questions. At least he would be by her side to run interference if anything came up about Jason.

She really did hate these things and if you add in the pressure that Kane has placed upon her, the reality that she was back in this city and this particular hotel after all these years it was almost more than one woman could handle.

Why did Kane have to lay all of this on her now? Didn't he see how ridiculous it would be for them to be anything other than business associates? Even if he wasn't involved with her film, the simple truth of them seeing each other would affect his career and her movie deal. The backers would think she got emotionally involved with Kane on purpose.

"Damn, what do I do?"

Charlene was nervous about what was to come. How were Kane's fans going to feel about his decision to temporarily leave Japan to do an all English CD in America? What if he couldn't recover from this decision? Would he blame her for it? Hate her for it?

God, she didn't even want to think about the backlash from the public if they found out he was dating an African-American woman older than him. That had scandal written all over it. Still, selfishly she was delighted that her growing feelings for him weren't one-sided. She was as curious to explore what was developing between them as he was.

She would be lying to say she wasn't concerned about their age difference. It weighed heavy on her mind, but men had gloried in the youth of their partner, why should it be different for women? Especially women of her generation when men were already dating someone else, married, gay, in jail, or strung out on drugs; causing the pickings to be slimmed to none. It was a new day and she cared a lot about Kane, so why shouldn't she date him?

Walking over to the window, Charlene looked out into the Tokyo sky, glowing with the familiar background sun on the skyline and the beginning of twinkling lights coming from the buildings below. She gazed at the imposing concrete jungle finding some windows were dark, some alight, with the party of individuals working diligently inside.

She forgot how beautiful this city could be, the last time she was here was the most horrible time in her entire life and during that time she couldn't get away from here fast enough. Was Abe right, had time enabled people to dismiss the past, could this truly be her chance to begin again in the country she spent her rebellious youth?

Charlene closed her eyes for a minute and swallowed deeply. The monsters of her past were as vivid as if it just happened yesterday. The flashing lights, the screams and crying were so loud and all the flowing blood. Sudden queasiness caused her to stagger away from the window sinking onto the nearest cushioned seat.

"Please, I don't want to think about *you* now," she whispered to the emptiness of the room. Tears stung her eyes. She had loved him so completely in spite of the darkness that consumed him. The months she had spent here in Japan with Jason during his first concert tour since he'd left years prior to live with her in America were unbelievably beautiful memories to be treasured. Or so she thought.

Why after all they had been through together he didn't turn to her when he was in need. Charlene paused. Maybe, he did and she just was too busy with her own selfish needs to notice his. Until that one night when the life she lived ceased to exist, he got her and everyone else in the Japan's attention that night and for months afterwards.

Charlene had sworn she would never come back here. Yet, here she was in the same city, in the same hotel. Her teeth gritted together to duly prevent a sob from escaping. She would not shed any more tears for him; he took the easy way out and left her to deal with the fallout, so her sorrow was paid in full. She had to forget him, put the whole travesty behind her as if it never happened.

Easier stated than done, for as sure as she was sitting here in this same hotel someone will remember who she used to be. No matter how many years had passed or how much weight she had added, or how much she had aged, or the simple detail of reverting back to her maiden name, it probably wouldn't be enough to keep her past buried while she was in Tokyo.

The resounding knock at her suite door caused her to jump. It was too early for it to be Kane, and no one else knew she was here besides Abe who would be arriving tomorrow. Maybe it was a message from the front desk. Charlene made her way to the door and came up on her tiptoes to look through the security peeper in the door.

A light frown marred her features, the Asian gentleman at her door looked familiar, but she wasn't sure from where she knew him. She placed the chain on the door and cracked it open.

"*Konnichi-wa*." He inclined her head and she returned the courtesy. "My name is Keiko Takusa, of Takusa's Entertainment, Kane's manager."

Recognition alighted Charlene's face and she smiled. "Yes, of course. One moment." She pushed the door shut and released the chain. Reopening the door, she smiled up at him and stepped back. "Please, come in, Mr. Takusa. It's nice to finally get to meet you. My manager, Abe Goda has spoken highly of you and your agency."

"Thank you," he inclined his head once more before stepping into the suite and closing the door behind him. He removed his street shoes in the entranceway and slipped his feet into the supplied slippers before following Charlene inside to the sitting area and waited for her to sit first before he accepted her proffered seat.

"Mr. Takusa, I just had some tea brought up, would you care to join me," she offered out of politeness, but she had a sense this wasn't a social call to welcome her to Japan.

"Thank you, I must decline your hospitality. I have an appointment before the press conference and cannot stay long. So shall we get to the point of my visit?"

"Please do." Charlene moistened her lips nervously.

"Seeing you in person, you appear younger than your given age. Also, you are quite lovely, Alfred-san."

"Thank you."

"I now understand Kane's behavior and this is what brings me here," he said somberly "I assume you know what I'm speaking of."

"I suppose Kane spoke to you about allowing his contract with you to expire and relocate to Los Angeles to try something new." Charlene supplied calmly.

"Kane is still a young man; however in this business he is too far past his youth to try and reinvent himself," Takusa spoke plainly. "Do you mind if I smoke?" He reached inside his expensive navy colored suit jacket pocket.

"Yes, as a matter-of-fact, I do mind, besides it's a non-smoking room." She was quick to point out. "Look, Mr. Takusa, I don't know why you are here discussing this with me. Kane has obviously been thinking about this for some time and it really has nothing to do with me."

"It has *everything* to do with you Alfred-san. Meeting you has been a goal Kane's been personally pursuing since he developed this strange attachment to you when he was sixteen." Takusa told her. "Oh, I see you're surprised. So, he failed to mention this most important piece of information."

Charlene was stunned. Kane had said he had reached a creative lull and needed her to write songs for him more than he needed the lead in the film. However, he never mentioned some teenage crush. What was going on? Why would he have felt the need to hide such a thing?

"Why are you telling me this, Mr. Takusa?" She asked, recovering quickly. "It is no secret that my songs have been sung by many young Western and Asian artists over the years, including some who work for you. It's not uncommon for someone his age to develop a crush on the artist or the writer of the songs."

"It is when it's lasted this long and he has been waiting for an opportunity such as this one to become available."

"Aren't you the one who set up a meeting with my producers for Kane to be considered for the lead in the film?" Charlene lifted the cup of the now tepid tea and sipped to soothe her suddenly dry throat.

Takusa leaned forward in the chair, his hands clasped together in front of him while resting his elbows upon his knees. He looked her in the eye and said, "I admit that the part of Blu is a great opportunity for any of my young stars, not to mention the music you have written is quite brilliant. I can already picture one number one after another. This is going to be big."

"So what are you saying?" Her eyes widened in question.

"I'm saying that *yes*, I did contact a producer who is a friend of mine to throw my agency in for consideration. However, I never specified Kane to be up for this roll in your film. You see, Alfred-san, I consider you a threat to all the *particular* care I've invested in Kane and his future."

"How do you perceive me as a threat?" Her lashes fluttered in confusion. She placed the delicate china down with a clink and folded her hands together in her lap to ease the unsteadiness that vibrated through her body. "My only issue with Kane is that I don't know if he has what it takes to play such an imperfect character. However, he thinks he can do it and frankly it would be an excellent career move. Not only is the film set to premiere here, it is to do so worldwide when it's released. Why would you impede his success if you've worked as hard as you say?"

"Kane is more than just another client, he is more like my son. I have two daughters one sixteen and one twenty-two. I have been grooming him for more than singing and acting."

Charlene knew exactly where this conversation was going and for some reason she felt a sickness churning in her stomach. It wasn't unusual for a son to take on the responsibilities of his biological father, to marry into another family, accept their name and take on the business and nurturing of another family.

"I made sure that Kane had the required educational background to take my place someday. It has already been arranged. Kane will marry my eldest daughter, Arisa, and take my name."

"How does Kane feel about this? I mean, why would he contact me and go through all this trouble if he is already obligated to you and your daughter?"

"I was hoping *you* could tell me." He stated with a lift of dark bushy eyebrows.

"Me?"

"Tell me, has Kane hinted at anything that has been inappropriate."

Charlene cocked a brow. "Such as?"

"Such as asking to see you on a more personal level, Ms. Alfred." His voice hardened and his clipped English more stilted.

She could see the vein in his temple throbbing as his lips thinned. Finally, his true feelings were showing. He wasn't as calm about having this conversation with her as he appeared in the beginning. Charlene somehow found some comfort in the knowledge that she wasn't the only one uncomfortable in this room.

"You don't have to answer that, I can tell by the look on your face that Kane has made his intentions clear and I must tell you I am disappointed that he would betray me this way." He ground the words out between his teeth. "And with someone like you of all people. I see now that I've been too complacent on Yuza-chan."

Charlene reeled as if she'd been slapped. Her eyes narrowed. "How dare you speak to me like that! You...you act as if something shameful has happened between Kane and I, which it hasn't by the way, but if it did that's really none of your affair." His contemptuous snort sparked her anger further.

"Haven't you? Why else would you have come to Tokyo personally instead of allowing Mr. Goda to handle your affairs here as always? I would have thought this was the *last* place you would want to ever come to again, Ms. Alfred, or should I say, Mrs. Jason James!"

Charlene tensed. It had been a long time since she was called by her married name; the first time was right after her wedding and Jason said it over a glass of champagne.

So, is this why Takusa came to her room before the press conference? He wanted to remind her that he knew the reason she escaped Japan and returned to the States eight years ago.

As Charlene took in the aging man sitting across from her, his thin frame flawlessly dressed in a suit tailored perfectly to his shoulders and his silver hair clipped neatly against the back of his neck and swept off his wide brow. Even though he seemed to have a kind face, it no longer appeared so now.

No matter how kind Keiko Takusa seemed in the beginning, it was obvious he had been anticipating the possibility of this moment for some time and was already manipulating the outcome of whatever decisions Kane was trying to make without him. Charlene had a feeling there wasn't much Kane could do without Mr. Takusa finding out.

"I haven't been hiding from my past because I have nothing to be ashamed of, even though the media painted a horrific picture of what took place here. I went back to my maiden name because I wanted to achieve success on my own merits instead of riding the coattails of my dead rock star husband."

"Being married to you nearly destroyed Jason's career," Takusa said coldly.

"So, I would ruin the career of the man I help made successful. That's an asinine statement and I expected better from you, Takusa-san. From the time we met in high school, *I* was the one who wrote the songs for Jason and his band and later when he went solo."

"I'm not denying your talent, Alfred-san. However, you don't possess enough clout to make the public overlook the fact that an adored public figured is married. It's already a hard sell. Now, having him to marry outside his culture and abandon the country that made him successful is asking too much. It would destroy his career completely. Is this what you want?"

Charlene remained quiet as she took in what he was saying. As much as she didn't want to hear it, he was right. Hadn't she learned anything from her experience with Jason? What the hell had gotten into her lately? She wasn't thinking rationally; was she once more trying to find and relive the happiness she once knew before everything went so wrong? As if Takusa could read her thoughts he leapt on the uncertainty that showed on her face.

"Did you realize *you* were the reason your late husband couldn't find commercial backing here in Japan when he tried to stage a comeback? That is, until I helped him by calling in favors to a few financial directors I was working for at that time. It was *I* who had convinced them that if they handled it properly, he would be forgiven."

Charlene was stunned speechless. All those years Jason had lied to her. He always led her to believe that he didn't go back to Japan is because he was too busy, when in truth they hadn't wanted him back because he was married to her. "Why..."

"I see." Takusa folded one hand over the other in front of him. "Your expression tells me you didn't know that Jason was blackballed when he chose to drop his local band and go solo in America, just to be with you. His fans felt betrayed, as if he abandoned all that he was. It was because of *your* influence that I decided to start my own entertainment group and assure that our future talents were safe from people like you." He looked at her, his mouth crooked, wry. "For some reason, you are here again in the same situation, but this time, you've chosen the wrong young man. *Kane* is mine, Alfred-san. I created him and you aren't going to take him from me or my family."

His tone and his unfounded accusation was like a splash of bitterly cold water against Charlene's face. She didn't care what he said, she never asked Jason to give up what he had to be with her. She had done everything she could to support his career from a long distance. When he had arrived in the States to propose, his decision was already made. She wouldn't take blame for loving a man she loved since they were teenagers. She also wouldn't take the blame for any decisions Kane made. She was sick and tired of all the guilt trips.

"Mr. Takusa, what Kane does is *his* business. I'm not some witch walking around Tokyo weaving magic amongst its men," she pointed out wryly. "Neither was I born yesterday. This little social visit isn't about Kane's best interests, but yours!"

He didn't try to deny it. "Of course it's about my interest, Alfred-san. Do you know how much is riding on Kane's continued success, not just for me but for the investors, fans, and yes even my daughter's future happiness?"

Charlene wasn't one who easily backed down; she'd spent too many years coping with stubborn and controlling old men like him. She wasn't about to roll over and submit now. "I'll refrain from calling hotel security and having you removed from my suite, only because I know you are worried...and because it wouldn't look good for you in the media." She grinned coldly as Takusa regarded her with a cautious respect. "They would assume some shady dealing between us and ask a lot of questions you wouldn't want me to answer. And I'm not the only threat to you Mr. Takusa. Everyone knows Kane has only two months left on his long term contract that ends once he turns twenty-five. Until recently, you've felt secure that he would do your bidding without question. You've even assured it by offering up your own daughter, haven't you? After all, if guilt isn't working, what better way than a contract of marriage?"

"You are in no position to speak to me about underhanded business ventures, Ms. Alfred. Do you believe by seducing Kane you will be able to take his career into your own hands and write most of his songs, like you did for your husband?"

J-Pop Love Song

"There isn't anything underhanded about what I'm doing here. Also, my husband *benefited* from my talents. The fact that his last CD is still amongst the Billboard top 100 attests to that, and all the choices were his own. I never forced any of his decisions, nor did I ask him to marry me." Charlene retorted. "You are really a piece of work, Mr. Takusa. You come into my room, accuse me of just about everything but murder, insult my ethnicity and I'm just supposed to smile and say *domo*? Kane is the one who invited *me* here! I was against him playing the part of Blu, but for totally different reasons." She waved her hands about in frustration before balling them into fist in her lap to keep them still.

"I only agreed to this meeting with Kane because I needed to come here to Japan to scout locations with Abe. I assure you once it's concluded I'll be leaving and Abe will be taking care of the rest, including any necessary contracts and the like, except for cutting the soundtrack, of course."

"Does Kane realize your interest is only professional? Have you made this very clear with him? The reason I ask, is because I know him better than anyone and from the conversation I just had with him, he believes the developing feelings he has for you are mutual."

Charlene's eyes grew wide, her mouth dropped open. She knew of his intentions but she thought he could possibly be just a younger man flirting with an older woman and wasn't sure how seriously to take his offer. That was, until now. He had already discussed his is interest in her with Takusa? Surly Kane wasn't being that reckless; she hadn't even given him an answer.

"Alfred-san, Kane has never shown much interest in girls his own age. He's always been odd like that." Takusa stated as if that explained everything. "I tell you this because I don't want you to think you are his first, nor will you be his last. After he gets what he wants he will cast you aside like all the others."

"The others?" She asked coldly. "Oh you mean the women from the hostess club you take him to, to relieve his urges. How do you expect him to have a normal relationship in that type of a situation?"

Takusa laughed and shook his head. "Is that what he's told you? Then I see he's already laying the groundwork to get you into his bed. I admit one such as you, would be a rare conquest for him indeed."

"What are you saying?"

"I'm saying that Kane has a thing for conquering the hearts of older women, maybe it has to do with his mother dying and leaving him at such an early age."

Charlene hadn't been expecting that. She wondered what else Kane had left out in order to paint himself in a better light. Maybe, Takusa was the one lying otherwise why would he be here with threats and warnings if Kane was playing games?

"So do you make a habit out of paying his potential conquest a call to warn them or do I warrant special attention because you're afraid it could jeopardize his viable chances of acting in my film?" Her eyes narrowed suspiciously on his thin face.

"*So ka*, I see, you are as shrewd as I thought you were." He chuckled. "This is actually the first visit I felt I had to make, Alfred-san," he openly admitted. "Honestly, it has nothing to do with this film, I've already been assured Kane has the part. It would just be better publicity if you were on board with the rest of us."

"If you aren't worried about the movie, then why am I privy to your special one-on-one attention?"

"Because you are Kane's fantasy come to life. He's been waiting for this day to come for years."

"That's silly," and Charlene rolled her eyes. "If you are implying he has been infatuated with me before we even spoke, well…"

"I'm not implying anything, Alfred-san, I'm saying that for years I have known that Kane's has this crazy obsession with *you*," he said bluntly. "He's probably one of your biggest fans. Did he not tell you this?"

"Yes, but you're mistaken that he's has this crazy notion in his head about hooking up with me for years. He was just a kid when Jason died." She just shook her head, wishing all of it, including the old man would just go away. "Why? What would be the reason? He's has this crazy crush and he just wants to have sex with me? Is that what all this drama is about?"

"I'm not mistaken and I'm hoping for both of our sake that is all it is. If it is, then you having sex with him should stop this foolishness, shouldn't it?"

"Is that why you're here? You're actually asking me to *fuck* Kane?"

"*Yareyare*, geeze!" Takusa sighed. "You needn't be so crass."

"Sorry," Charlene smiled poisonously, "Blame it on the company. I don't know, but this seems to be turning into a pretty *ridiculous* situation to me!"

"Alfred-san, what I'm proceeding to tell you is going to seem even more foolish, but I strongly believe you should know what is truly going on here. If you still feel as if I'm trying to deceive you in some way, after I finished, then we aren't any worse off than we were before I arrived, are we?"

"I'm not sure about that, Mr. Takusa, but I will listen to what you have to say." Her voice was cold and exact.

"I hadn't realized the extinct of Kane's obsession with you, Alfred-san, until I accidentally opened his online journal while using his laptop. What I read disturbed me deeply." The pause was dramatic and Takusa took a deep breath before continuing, "Since he started keeping this diary when he was sixteen, he has been infatuated with you. It's the *why*, that you may find interesting." Takusa arched an inquiring shaggy brow. "I can see the skepticism on your face, so I brought you this." He pulled the USB flash drive from his inside jacket pocket. "It's all on here." He picked up her hand and placed it on her palm. "You can read it for yourself."

"Why should I believe any of this, Takusa-san? You could have typed this up yourself," Charlene accused. "You said you're willing to do anything to keep Kane safe and happy, even if what you're doing may eventually destroy him, so tell me why would he not have tried to contact me long before if he was as obsessed as you claim he is? We just started communicating a month ago!" She moved over to the window where she was standing earlier, her back to him.

"Again, I do not blame you for not trusting me," Takusa said, trying a conciliatory tone that Charlene wasn't fooled by for even a minute. The old man was ruthless. "And I know this all sounds crazy. The reason he never contacted you before was the contract stipulations he has with me. Now I fear he is about to ruin all that we both have worked hard for because he is free to pursue you.

As far as that being fake, then please, sign on your own computer and I will take you to his online journal. His sign-on name is *Juno-kun*, password...*Charlie-chan*.

Charlene gasped and turned to look at him a feeling of alarm welled up inside her. How did he know? "Where...where did he come up with that name and password?"

"You should already know the answer to that, Alfred-san. How would Kane know the pet names you and Jason had for each other since meeting in school?" Takusa stood and walked over to stand in front of her. "Can I ask you a very personal question? Have you've ever lost a child?"

Charlene froze and suddenly she couldn't breathe. When she finally managed to speak, it was to yell at him. "Get out! *Hottoite-kure-yo!*"

"Forgive me, but I can't leave until I've told you everything I know and we have reached some understanding as to what has to be done to rectify this situation. Kane's future depends on what happens here tonight." Takusa stated firmly.

"How...how could you possibly know to ask me such a thing?"

"I didn't know, Alfred-san." He sighed heavily. "Yet Kane knows the exact date of your miscarriage. I assume this was not public knowledge? Still as I read it I would have sworn he had been there, with you during this critical moment, even though this wasn't a viable likelihood. He was just a child at the time."

"Oh God, I...I'm going to be sick." Charlene swooned. Thankfully the strength of Takusa's arms was around her before she hit the carpet. Easily he guided her to the chair he had occupied upon his arrival.

He left her for a moment, returning with a glass and bottled water. Pouring her a glass, she reached with trembling hands and accepted with a mumbled word of thanks.

"Is that better?"

She nodded, but still there was numbness all over her body. No one knew about her miscarriage but Jason, and he was dead. She'd become pregnant during her senior year of high school and before she could tell her parents or do anything about it, she began to bleed and heavily clot. The doctor had explained that she had lost the baby, and that it wasn't an uncommon occurrence, especially in first pregnancies. They never spoke of it again and proceeded to be more careful afterwards to make sure she didn't get pregnant again until they were ready.

Tears welled up in Charlene's eyes. "I swear no one knew. To this day my parents still don't know."

"Could someone have leaked it out at the doctor's office?"

"Why would they? We were just kids with big dreams when that happened. I'm telling you, no one knew and when we did become successful, nobody could trace the incident to me. I used Jason's real father's last name, *Juno*. Since he was orphaned, no one knew what his father's surname was. It's not even listed on his birth certificate. The only thing Jason told me was about his mother getting pregnant by a wealthy married man and that he abandoned her when she told him."

"Ah, *so ka*," A frown wrinkled his brow. "If that is so then I can only believe the conclusion Kane has come to in regards to his attachment to you."

"Which is?" she asked before taking a sip from the glass of water at her lips. "What are you not telling me Mr. Takusa?"

Takusa shook his head and the lines of concern in his brow deepened as he continued to scowl. "This is the part that might really disturb you. In our culture as you know, such things are alleged by those who are believers and I suppose Kane is one of those people."

"What are you trying to say, exactly?" Her face showed her confusion. The more he tried to explain the more baffled she was becoming. If she were smart, she would book a return flight out of here within the hour and not look back.

"Kane believes that when Jason James died, his essence, memories and emotions for you, possessed him through his dreams. He believes that through him your deceased husband is trying to make peace with you for all that had happened."

"I grew up here, Mr. Takusa, and have heard of such things but I've never known any documented proof or met anyone who've experienced such a thing," she said with the little calmness she had left.

"Alfred-san, I can only tell you what Kane believes. He believes that if he does what your husband wants, he will he no longer be haunted by Jamess-san's restless spirit."

"And what is it that Jason supposedly wants?"

"Your complete happiness and unfortunately for me, Kane believes he's the one chosen to make you happy."

"This is so not happening." She laughed hysterically, not giving a damn what Takusa thought of her now. The entire normal world had gone stark raving bat shit and she was right in the thick of it. "I mean, we read about this stuff, right, and secretly watch it on television. Hell, I might have even thought about writing some crazy shit like this in one of my stories, but it's not real!"

"Now, you see my position." Takusa pleaded. "Only you can set Kane free from this foolishness."

"And how do you suppose I do that?" She balked, shrugging. "How can I even say anything without revealing we've invaded his personal thoughts?"

"We can't, that is why you have to take a different approach," Takusa said.

"What exactly are you asking me to do, Mr. Takusa?"

"Sleep with him so that he may finally get this curiosity of you out of his head and then break his heart, Alfred-san." He took her by the arms, looking down at her with intense brown eyes. "I realize I'm asking much of you considering I have no right to ask anything at all. However, I don't know what else to do. He's refusing to marry into my family and take the place I have held for him as my heir. They are supposed to marry once Yuza-chan his thirtieth birthday. Kane would be the first of many *talento's* to be allowed to take a wife and remain under contract in my agency. It is necessary if he is to be my heir."

"Will being your heir and married to your daughter make him happy?"

"I believe it could as long as he knew there was no possibility that you would ever consider being more then casual with him."

Charlene gave him a hard look.

"This is nothing personal against you, Alfred-san. You are a highly successful and talented woman and I'm sure you would be perfect but for someone else, maybe someone closer to your own age…and your own culture."

Charlene's nerves were frayed to the breaking point and she had no idea how much more she could take. She met Takusa's gaze with an even harder stare. "Besides whoring myself out, what else would you suggest I do to keep him away from me? You may not be familiar with the saying, 'once you go black, you never go back'. If he's also playing Blu, he's going to be seeing a lot of me."

"That is an unavoidable consequence, but I need Kane to do this film. It is the only way I can legally extend his contract through at least the completion of this film as long as he signs your production contract before his twenty-fifth birthday. The sooner the better." He dropped his hands to his sides. "That is why during the press conference tonight, you will announce that Kane has been chosen for the lead role."

She sighed. "Fine. I suspect you already know Kane wants me to ask him to take the role in order to publicly turn me down. He hopes that we can start dating once his contract with you expires."

"Actually I did not, but you can't let that happen. You must make sure he does take the contract offer, Alfred-san."

"Therefore breaking his heart," she murmured. "I suppose I could get Abe to help me with this, but I already told Kane that Abe and I are just friends, so I don't know if he'd believe we were all of a sudden dating."

"Goda-san wouldn't work because if Kane sees you are with another Asian man he will assume there is still hope. Yet, if he supposes you're falling for someone of say, your own cultural background, he would feel inadequate to compete." Takusa told her. "Let's say someone like Stu-san? He is more your age and I'm sure you will find you have more in common with him. He's as knowledgeable about Japan and its language as you are."

"He also seems to be the only best friend Kane has. Why would Stu agree to do this?"

"He already has, because like me he believes that Kane is more suited for my daughter."

"He actually said that?"

"Well, it doesn't hurt that he is also attracted to you."

"You've really been thinking about this for awhile haven't you?" Charlene couldn't keep the sarcasm from her voice. "I find it amazing the depths people will sink when they think they're doing the right thing for someone else."

Takusa actually looked hurt. "You can say about me what you will, but I'm here because I love Kane as I would a flesh and blood son. If anything he has been the son I never had, and like any good parent, I'm not beyond doing whatever is necessary for his future happiness and welfare."

"Mr. Takusa, I created Blu from all that is Jason. I genuinely thought if I wrote this partially fictional story utilizing all my personal pain, it would purge my heart. Instead it has forced me to miss Jason even more lately. I don't know, why but the truth is, in this past month just emailing and speaking with Kane has made me feel happier then I have been in a long time."

"Alfred-san—"

"What if this bond Kane and I have is real? I don't know if it's for the crazy reason he thinks it is, but I do know there is *something* between us. So if I readily agree to your plans and without thinking things through—I could be giving up on a second chance at having the love of a lifetime."

Even if such a thing was possible, could she consider Kane's feelings for her genuine or would she always wonder if Kane truly thought he was being influenced by her dead husband's nightly visits.

"A chance at love with Kane, or a second chance to be with the husband that you still have feelings for, and whose death you still feel guilty over?" Takusa asked in a calm forceful voice. "Let's say all of this is really happening. Do you believe feeding in to Kane's delusions is a healthy way to help him separate dreams from reality?"

No matter what Kane's reasoning for interjecting himself into her life, Charlene realized he didn't deserve to wake up one day and find he was married to a woman he didn't sincerely love. Nor did he deserve to lose everything he'd been working towards since his childhood if he really did love her.

Maybe Takusa was right, Kane just needed a good dose of reality. If she and Takusa didn't agree on anything else, they both agreed that the only way to make Kane move on was to show him there was no way he could make her happy. Charlene was sure once Takusa's daughter nursed his broken heart, nature and time would take care of the rest. Even as she stood there convincing herself her heart felt as if it was breaking.

"Mr. Takusa, I'll do as you ask but I need you to do something for me." She swallowed hard and squared her shoulders. "After I make the announcement, Kane will be locked into this contract for the long haul. I want him to start preparing for this role as soon as possible. It's going to take a lot out of him emotionally and the one thing I notice is he averages an eighteen hour day."

"As long as Kane is busy it means he's still popular and the more in demand he is, the more he can ask for."

"You mean the more *you* can ask for," she saw he was about to protest and she waved off his response. "Look, I want you to cancel all his future engagements. If he's going to do this intense part, then his singing silly pop songs isn't going to help. I want Kane to spend time somewhere where he can relax…somewhere away from the media and his fans. Maybe if he can get the chance to rest, he can banish these nightmares he having concerning James."

"Well, that will be diff…"

"I don't care." Charlene cut in briskly. "If you desire this to happen, then work with me. I also need you to be supportive and understanding when I hurt him. He will need you and your family if he's never had his heart broken before."

"There is no way that I can just stop his engagements for no reason. Even Kane will be suspicious if he all of sudden has free time on his hands."

For the first time in the moments since Takusa's visit, Charlene felt a little more in control. "Trust me I can and will keep Kane busy. I can have Abe add the stipulation of his exclusivity from the time he signs the contract until the completion of this production."

"Kane is very much in demand, Alfred-san," he said, not liking the new turn of events.

"Kane is no longer just your concern, Mr. Takusa. Now he has become mine, Abe's and my producers' until I turn him back over to you. I want him out of the

J-Pop Love Song

limelight. I want people to wonder what happened to him and then have him make a comeback with a more mature look and sound."

"You mean you want to change the figure I've worked thirteen years to build!"

"Excuse me, you meant to say the thirteen years that *Kane* worked to build. I don't see you doing two performances a day in two different cities, or signing autographs for hours, or fourteen hours on a music video set."

"You have no say in how I manage Kane's career. I admit I need your help, but I will not stand by and let you completely take over."

Charlene was amazed at how calm she felt negotiating Kane's future. She had done the same many times for Jason while they were together. She knew the games of this industry well and she also knew that she had Takusa by the balls, finally. If he chose to make her an enemy she would use her influence over Kane to persuade him to walk away from Takusa at the end of his two months.

"Takusa-san, I refuse to do as you ask unless I know that when all this is said and done, Kane will have more control over his own career and future." She moved and stepped in front of him to halt his pacing. "Now, you can lose him for good, because if we don't contract him for this film his intentions is to leave you at the end of his contract. If you do as I ask, then you and your daughter will have the duration of the film to convince him that he would be happier here in Tokyo with you."

Takusa's head and shoulders appeared to bow under the weight of personal defeat. Charlene knew she had him and it would be her gift towards making sure Kane would be happy. "I'm beginning to think I may have made a grave error in underestimating, Alfred-san."

"You're not the first man to have made such a stupid mistake," she told him bluntly. "I suppose you will just have to trust me. Do we have a deal?"

With reluctant admiration Takusa smiled and took her proffered hand in a confirming shake. "Under other circumstances, I might have considered you a worthy wife for my son, Alfred-san." Takusa conceded with a thin smile of admiration. "Never have I met a more clever woman. I think under our guidance Kane could be a international success in your country and mine."

"*Arigato*, Mr. Takusa, but I've already been a good wife to someone and look where that got me." Charlene released Takusa's hand. "I'm telling you now, if I see for one instant that you're undermining anything that I do to assure I get the best performance out of Kane, I'll make sure you never see him again after the film is completed."

"I don't like threats young woman." Takusa's eyes narrowed on her face.

"So now you know how I feel."

"I don't like doing business with someone I don't know, but Kane has left me no other recourse. What I'm wondering is if this fails, what will *you* do to assure that Kane ends up with my daughter, Alfred-san?"

"It may take some time, but I promise no matter what happens between Kane and I during the filming of *Blu's Diary*, I'll make sure he wants nothing to do with me and he'll be yours again," Charlene declared.

Walking to the suite door she yanked it open and said to Takusa, "Now, get the hell out of here. Oh yes, and never show up at my door without calling first."

With a huff he slipped his feet into his shoes by the door and sauntered out. Charlene slammed the door, leaned back against the wooden frame and slid down on her haunches holding her head in her hands. She allowed the tears to flow freely.

Chapter Six

KANE SAT WAITING ON THE platform half listening to the final words his publicist were speaking with regards to the upcoming press conference. They were just minutes away from beginning when the doors were pushed opened to allow the invited guests and media were admitted. Yet, all he could do was think about Charlene. Why was she running late?

He was exhausted. In the few hours he managed to sleep through he woke up ever hour on the hour with this burning need to see her or call her. This was the first time his desire for Charlene hadn't been brought on by the dreams, but from his realism.

To say he was happy to finally have her here in Tokyo with him was putting it mildly. He was anxious and extremely excited to know what was coming next. He felt his heart racing just from thinking about their future together. Maybe now Jason James could rest in peace now that he had brought them together or at least Kane hoped so. He no longer wanted his overall emotions to be about her dead husband's feelings. The more he communicated with her, laughed with her, and shared his hopes for the future with her, the more he realized *HE* wanted Charlie. Still, how was he going to tell her about the dreams without her thinking he was crazy or an obsessed fan.

Kane released a long sigh. He must have stared at the private entranceway that he had come through at least fifty times in the past fifteen minutes waiting for her appearance. *Damn,* he should have gone to her hotel suite even though she asked him not to. Besides when would he have had the chance?

In the past twenty-two hours since he saw her last, his every hour was filled with wardrobe fittings, dress rehearsal for the *Global Warming Benefit Concert,* and a last minute photo shoot in which he had no clue for what this time.

Kane was beginning to wonder if Takusa-san was deliberately keeping him away from Charlene. Why? Did he suspect something? How could he? He hadn't told Takusa he was still having the dreams, not since he was sent away to study in England. Still, if he suspected he still was infatuated with Charlene Alfred, why would he be the one to set up Kane's audition for the role of Blue's Diary? Was this all some sort of test set up by Takusa? He had more questions than answers, but after tonight's announcement when he turn down Charlene's offer and informed the public that he would be leaving Takusa Management group in two months, all would know where he stood.

A glimmer of panic went through him as he remembered the quick call he had managed to steal after getting a minute alone in the toilet. He had called to check on Charlene. The call had been brief, not because he wasn't prepared; he already had his excuses ready for his shadow crew that followed him everywhere. He would have feigned stomach issues and camped out in the toilet stall all night just to have some time to speak with Charlene. To surprise it wasn't necessary. She actually seemed impatient to get him *off* the phone. When he tried to address the press conference, she danced around the subject, not really confirming anything.

He couldn't shake the overall perception something was wrong. From his dreams he knew the intonation of her voice when, she was happy, angry, horny, sexually satisfied and sad. He heard the huskiness of her tone over the phone, she had been crying. Why? Was it because she was in this same hotel? He hoped by being here she could begin to heal, to realized even thought it was the same city and the same place she had lived with her husband, life has moved on and it was time for her to do the same.

Kane closed his eyes for a moment and rolled his tense shoulders beneath the dark gray wool-silk jacket. His hands fidgeted at the seemingly too tight baby-pink satin tie only to have his hands slapped away by his displeased personal stylist who proceeded to repair the damage done by his fingers. Kane returned the favor soon after the incident by bushing aside the stylist hands from applying last minute touch-ups to the already fashionably feathered hairdo. The spiked bangs nearly blocking one eye's view completely was driving him crazy, but he was in "star" mode and when you're voted the JPOP Star with the best hair for the sixth year in a row by the fans, you suffer in silent appreciation, and be contented that they care at all.

The stylist dabbed at the bead of moisture over his top lip with a sheet of rice paper. "*Kuso*! Shit, give me break! I can't breath, with you hovering over me. Go and find something to do," he snapped. His hand reached up to wash over his face and halted at the terrified look on the stylist face. In agitation Kane realized if he touched his face it would set off another ten minutes of touching up for the cameras.

It was occasions such as this when even the benefits of being in this industry wasn't worth it. He had been doing this so long he didn't remember what it was like to be a normal guy that could walk through *Shinjuku Station* without being mobbed.

Then just as quickly as he would forget, he would also remember. If he were just another "salary-man" on the streets of Tokyo, he most likely would have never realized Charlie existed. Kane often wondered if Jason James had chose him as a catalyst because he too knew what it felt like to be imprisoned by his own face.

Even though he had become accustomed to the dreams and accepted the silky thread of fate that bound him to Charlene Alfred, it still unnerved him that he knew her intimately through this otherworldly means.

Kane had been sixteen when the dreams started. He would wake up with sweat and semen stained sheets after bouts of heated sex with a black woman that seemed familiar, yet, she wasn't. That was the beginning and one he didn't mind at all, until she moaned another guy's name—*Juno-kun...Juno-kun*. It was *his* erotic dreams, yet another guy's name. He wrote it off believing it had something to do with something, he saw in a movie, read or ate. When the dreams became more vivid and persistent, he thought he was going mad and he became frightened by the possibility.

The only way for him to keep his sleeping dreams and his days from meshing into one was to purge everything in his online journal. Next, came the research. Reading everything he could get his hands on about the paranormal and the meaning of dreams. When he couldn't take the load of keeping it all to himself he may the mistake by asking Takusa-san a hypothetical question, which his answer had been to pull him from the dance troupe he was with at the time and send him to an English boarding school to complete his education and get some "much needed" rest.

After that, Kane chose to take a more unconventional method to find answers. An Irish soothsayer in England gave him guidance. From that point on Kane kept the dreams personal and started paying attention instead. Each morning upon rising, he would right everything he could remember on a notepad he kept by his desk. It didn't take long before he had two names Jason James and Charlene Alfred James. From that moment own, the information came easy for all he had to do is key in the name and the Internet did the rest.

Even though he was resolved to accept his fate after so many years, he didn't know how he was going to tell her the entire story. What would he say to her? "Charlene I had an ulterior motive in asking you to come to Japan. I'm somehow connected to your dead husband and he wants me to make you happy again." *Yeah right!*

Kane swallowed deeply placing the rose tinted shades onto the bridge of his nose and pushed them into place, clearing his throat. The time has come where he and the woman that has haunted his dreams for almost nine years could finally be together and not only did it scared the hell out of him, it also thrilled him with a happiness he had never felt before. None of his awards, money, or success felt as satisfying as the thought of joining Charlene in Los Angeles in two months.

It was at that moment he spotted the object of his thoughts walking in with Stu-san at her side from a different entrance than the one he'd been watching. Obviously, she had been here all along but housed in one of the smaller meeting rooms that were adjacent to the Hall. He was disappointed she hadn't considered seeking him out before the conference. He would have like to have passed the time he'd been wallowing deeply in his thoughts, speaking with her instead of worrying about her whereabouts.

Kane couldn't take his eyes off her. She was lovely from her neatly braided chignon down to her black leather pointed toed pumps. Dressed in an elegant powder blue sculpted collar jacket with front tapered lines over a black pencil skirt, he thought the sophisticate business assemble complimented the loveliness of her dark brown skin. It also didn't escape his attention that he wasn't the only appreciating Charlie's beauty. Stu-san hadn't taken his eyes off of her since they walked into the room.

His squared jaw tightened as the two stopped in the midst of walking. Stuart leaned in to whisper something in her ear and she laughed. Kane immediately jumped to his feet his expression turning sullen. *What the hell was going on?* he wondered.

"Glad to see you are here and raring to proceed." A familiar hand smacked down on top of Kane's shoulder and squeezed. He turned his quiet brooding gaze on the older man.

"Takusa-san," he spoke softly. With a little effort, he reined in his errant emotions and sat back down. "Of course, where else would I be?"

"*O-genki-desu-ka?* You seem tense."

"*Genki-dayo*, I'm fine. I just want to get this over with." His eyes narrowed to slits from behind his tinted shades. "Shouldn't you tell Stu-san he need to make one last sweep to make sure no one is trying to get in without proper invitations or credentials?"

"I asked Stuart-san to personally see to Alfred-san's welfare and assure none of the media would harass her," Takusa grunted. His piercing gaze staring at the two as he continued.

"Charlie-san is probably not accustomed to having someone on her heels like this, Takusa-san. She is a very independent woman." Kane commented. "I'll go and call him off."

"You will do no such thing." Takusa spoke abruptly. "Do not make a scene by being overly familiar with the woman! Kane, must I continue to remind you of how unprofessional it is to commonly refer to her in such an intimate manner? Continue to use *Alfred-san* or *Ms. Alfred*, she is, after all, your senior and I don't want you accidentally calling her anything else in front of the press."

"I'm not an idiot, Takusa-san. Nor, do you need to treat me like a child." Kane could see his exact tone sparked his mentor's anger, but he no longer cared. There was a lot Takusa did that he didn't care about these days, having Stuart to watch over Charlene without asking him first was one of them. "What about recalling Stu-san?"

The other man gave him an exacting stare. "As far as Stuart-san is concerned, he needs no further instructions from you, he does as I tell him."

"Alfred-san isn't Stu-san's to watch over," he mumbled, his tone coolly disapproving.

"As far as I can tell, he doesn't appear to find his current duties distasteful." Takusa said with a feigned smile. "They have much in common, don't you suppose?"

"Takusa-san, just because they both were born in America and they both are of the same culture, doesn't mean they have much in common."

"Or it could mean everything."

"Are you deliberately being insensitive this evening?" Kane asked.

"Tell me, Kane, why are you against Alfred-san and Stuart-san being attracted to one another." His voice was heavy with sarcasm. "What business is it of yours?"

Takusa's eyes turned on him and narrowed in on his face. Kane avoided returning the older man's stare. He was allowing his emotions to get the better of him. He had to calm down and get his emotions in check before he blew everything.

"Its just Alfred-san is here only temporary, so why should Stu-san start something that can't lead anywhere?"

"True," Takusa shrugged his shoulders. "However, that still is none of our business."

J-Pop Love Song

"It is to me," Kane blurted out. Stammering, "Stu-san is...is not only my bodyguard, he's my good friend. I would hate for him to return to the states and force me to find someone as trustworthy," he lied.

"Indeed, are you sure that is all?"

Kane stared at the man before him. He tried to relax but he held his stare. "All that I want to say for now."

"Are you still having those dreams, Kane? The ones you mentioned once, before you went away to school?" Takusa mouth pulled into a thin lip smile. "You would tell me if you were still having...problems...wouldn't you, Son?"

"Takusa-san, I—"

"Ah...another time. I see just the person I've been wanting to speak with," Takusa interrupted. "I'll return before we start. I see Ms. Alfred's manager, Goda-san, has arrived. I must speak with him."

Kane released a sigh; he was about to tell Takusa he planned on leaving the management group.

"Kane, stick to your rehearsed responses if you are asked a question that we didn't discuss I will intervene. *Mada?* Are you ready"

"*Itsumo*. Always." Kane answered watching Takusa's back as he made his way down the opposite side of the platform with a smile and hand outstretched in polite welcome to Goda-san.

Kane stood as Charlene came on the stage. He captured her eyes with his before his lids slipped downward as he stared pointedly at Stuart's hand holding her elbow as they walked up the stairs.

"You're late." With a deliberately casual movement, he strolled closer. "Everyone is starting to take their seats. I'd hoped to speak with you *alone* before we began."

"I'm not late." Charlene stated coolly. "I made it here before you did. I was waiting in the other room, even though I have no idea as to why I'm having to explain this to you."

"Charlene-chan," his voice softened. "Can I talk with you for a moment?" He moved forward once more and came up short as Stuart stepped between them with a companionable smile, placing a more acceptable space between them.

"This is not the time or place Kane-kun." Stuart voiced standing with his hands crossed before him. "Smile for the cameras, you two." No sooner had he spoken before flashes of camera bulbs started to go off from all directions.

As if the flashes had set off a chain reaction, Kane, the celebrity, proceeded to do what he did best. A wide and charming smile replaced his early sulking face as he turned and stood with shoulders back and arms respectively hanging at his sides to pose for pictures with Charlene.

She obviously remembered the social graciousness of Japan as she stood with hands folded into one another over her feminine core, and smiled graciously. Kane felt an overwhelming since of adoration and pride to be standing by her side. It enabled him to fantasize of what their ordinary life could be like, working together, being seen as a power couple to the world. He would be able to follow his urges and bend down and whisper something in her ear. Place his hand on the small of her back intimately and introduce her proudly to his friends and working crew. He wondered if she was capable of picturing the same dream, or was she too much of a realist to believe they could beat the odds against them. This was one of the many things he wished to discuss with her.

As the requests for them to turn this way and that commenced, his insincere smile became genuine. He was relieved when the announcement to be seated sounded over the intercom. Kane bowed politely and mouth a thank you towards the media before turning towards Charlene, sweeping his hand subtly to indicate she should walk ahead of him and take her seat. For a brief moment he thought he saw something in her eyes. Was that a familiar recognition on her part? It was as if she already knew his secrets. Had she somehow feel the bond he had with James's restless spirit?

He began to say something to her and Stu-san moved forward to hold out Charlene's chair for her. "Charlene, there is no reason to worry, you'll do well." Stuart said as he held out her chair and smiled down at her before taking his protective stance a few steps behind their chairs.

Kane couldn't believe the beautiful smile she graced on Stu-san as she softly whispered her thanks. Kane simmered. When she turned her dark gaze on him as he stared at her heatedly, he was grateful that his shades shielded the agitation showing in his eyes from others, but she was close enough to see it. To his amazement she appeared completely unaffected as she dismissed him entirely. She looked straight ahead out at the honored guest, her long eyelashes lowered demurely, and she smiled prettily as the cameras ate up her subtle dark beauty. His frustration continued to mount.

It wasn't lost on him that Stu-san used her given name freely, as if they were old friends or lovers. Kane was seething and it took everything in him to get through the next hour of questions after questions. If Charlene was nervous as Stu-san implied, then she was better at acting than he was, for she gave no evidence of discomfort. Her command of the Japanese language was excellent with just enough flaws followed by embarrassed apologies that she became endearing into the hearts of all in attendance. Including him.

During the first thirty minutes, he felt like a prized monkey there for show. He didn't even have to speak. Just an occasional nod and smile seemed to keep everyone contented. Today, Charlene Alfred was definitely the star of the show. Silent pride swelled his heart as he watched and listened. He wanted to grin like and idiot, but he maintained his dark and brooding leading man persona.

The one matter Kane was curious about was, why she was upset at him? Of course, springing his desire to move to the United States and get to know her better had seemed, a bit rash, but she had no way of knowing he's had nine years to accept that they would have a future together. He was a decent guy, had a great career and from what she said his physical appearance wasn't too bad. He had to grin at the memory of her indirectly complimenting his ass. He liked her ass too.

"Kane-san! We see you have a big grin on your face. Is there something you know about the outcome of today's press conference that we don't know?"

Kane felt Takusa elbow him in the rib causing him to snap out of his musings. Abashed he listened intently as the reporter repeated the question to him.

"*Wakaru-wake nai-yo*, there's no way I have of knowing if I have the part or not until Alfred-san and her manager, Goda-san, makes the announcement." He sighed and his hands spread open in a gesture of appeasement. "I'm just happy to have been invited," Kane finished lightheartedly.

"*Kore mite*, Kane-san!" Someone yelled and Kane did as asked, turned, posed, and smiled as the person took his picture.

"*Kakko tsukenna-yo!*" Another yelled and the hall erupted in laughter.

Kane laughed graciously. "I'm not trying to be cool, trust me, I'm anxious to find out what direction my future will be taking. I hope it is the path that I have been dreaming of most of my life."

Kane eased a side-glance at Charlene who was sitting quietly with a Mona Lisa smile on her glorious mouth, her eyes resting demurely on the microphone and stand on the table in front of her.

Why shouldn't she be calm? He thought grimly. She was holding all the power in her hands or at least the control of his contentment.

"*Suminasen*, excuse me, please hold any further questions until after the announcement has been made." Abe Goda said into the microphone in front of him before leaning over to whisper something in Charlene's ear. He pulled back, looking at her for a long pause before turning his attention back to the audience. "We are ready to make the announcement."

Something about Abe Goda's protectiveness of Charlene caused added nervousness to build inside Kane. It was bad enough she barely spared him a glance. She hardly said two words to him. He leaned towards her and felt Takusa tight grip on his forearm and refrained from making a public spectacle of himself in front of hundreds of gossip hungry reporters with their eager little cameras, posed to take any given photo that would imply they were more then business acquaintances. It wouldn't do to cause Charlene any public embarrassment.

Charlie-san, just two more months and I'll be a free man. He thought to himself. He felt optimistic that after all the pomp and circumstance came to an end she would allow him to come up to her room to discuss their future.

Most of all he need her to listen as he explained about his dreams involving her and her deceased husband; then again, how could he expect her in a matter of minutes to trust what took him years to believe. Kane forced himself to keep his eyes straight ahead as she leaned over to speak into the mic.

"*Komban-wa*. Good evening." Charlene spoke into the microphone pushing it back a little as her voice echoed loudly through the hall. "Let me start by saying, *osewani narimashita*, thank you for your kindness. For those of you who don't know me, I'm Charlene Alfred. Dozo *yoroshiku*, please regard me kindly."

The occupants of the gathering applauded and Charlene smiled demurely bowing her head left, center, and right in thanks to all those who stood before her. Kane grinned with foolish pride at how well Charlene handled the genteel and respective customs of his homeland. From her elegant and respectful style of dressing to her sitting respectfully with knees closed and hands folded sedately in her lap. She did it so well he had no clue as to what she might be thinking at this moment. Therefore, he waited for her next words with anxious anticipation just like the rest of her captivated audience.

"*Arigato gozaimasu*." Her lips parted in a natural wide smile. The first full smile Kane had seen since she sat down beside him. "I'll be here along with my manager, Mr. Abe Goda, whom most of you are familiar with, working with the Film Commission for on-location shooting of *Blu's Diary* and I couldn't be happier that the beautiful city of Tokyo will host the premier of my film once it's completed."

Kane lifted his hands and applauded along with everyone else but he was finding it more difficult to sit still. He was excited and somewhat fearful of how the crowd would react when Charlene announced that he wouldn't be playing the role of Blu and his declaration that after his long-term contract was up with Takusa Entertainment in two months he was going on a hiatus.

"First I will announce the other professionals that have been signed to act in the film, Alfred-san or I will be glad to answer your questions. So please refrain from asking until the full list has been announced." Abe broadcasted.

Respective rumblings went around the room as Abe called out names of some well-known and not so known American and Japanese actors. Kane glanced over at Takusa who had a satisfied grin on his face. He hated disappointing his *sensei*, teacher, but there was just no way around it. He knew there were plans in the making for his future in the organization and in becoming Takusa's heir, but it wasn't enough for Kane. He had to follow his own heart and his own dreams and if he tried to explain once again to Takusa-san that Charlene was a part of his future, he knew once again Takusa would ignore his feelings.

"This brings us to the last name on the list." Abe paused.

Kane gave him all of his attention. Here it was, now all hell was going to break loose.

"On the behalf of Alfred-san and Sato Productions, I would like to offer this contract to Kane-san for the starring role in *Blu's Diary*."

The hall erupted in congratulations and roaring applause.

For a minute Kane was dumbstruck. He couldn't believe his ears. What Abe said kept echoing in his head, making no sense at all. He stared at Charlene, his brown eyes wide in question and hurt, and she stared back fixedly, not showing him any sign that she had made a mistake. Did she do this because her producers were pressing her to accept him? Yet, it couldn't be; they had already worked around that obstacle. Was she not interested in him at all? Had he been imagining the chemistry between them based on his on his own desires?

"Charlie-chan?" He leaned towards her and whispered. "What have you done? Why?"

"Kane." Takusa warned placing his hand on his shoulder and he shrugged it away uncaring of what anyone thought of him. He wanted an answer.

"Kane, don't." Charlene pleaded her eyes seemed unusually bright. "You said it was my decision and I think no one would play the part of Blu better than you. Please don't let me down."

He watched in numb silence as she plastered a smile on her face and slid the contract in front of him and offered him an ink pen. He couldn't deny her, but he did expect an explanation after this nightmare had happened. If she had wanted him to be in her film, why hadn't she returned his phone calls and let him know before hand her decision?

Kane accepted the pen and glared at Takusa as he assured him it was a substantial and sound contract, as if he gave a damn. He scrawled his signature on the line and felt a misery so deep it was a physical pain. Within moments, years of well thought out planning to get to this point where he and the object of

J-Pop Love Song

his desire occupied the same space and he was once again bound to the terms of his contract until the production of Blu's Diary comes to an end.

He settled back in his chair and proceeded to perform the role of a lifetime as a ridiculously happy Japanese pop star while catering to the reporters' non-stop questions.

♪

Charlene never thought she would be in Japan in the middle of another press conference feeling as miserable as she did in the conference following her husband's suicide. Yet, here she was again, and this time she was responsible for making someone else as miserable as she was.

Even though Kane wore tinted glasses, she was close enough to him to see the pain she caused him by putting him on the spot. Now more than ever she felt as if she should have met with him before the meeting and explained, but listening to Abe, she realized if she had done so she would have allowed Kane to talk her out of what she knew was best for him.

"Are you going to be all right? You look kind of green." Abe commented as he leaned towards her and whispered his words close to her ear.

"I don't know how much longer I can do this," she replied in a hushed whisper.

"Most of the questions are being addressed to Kane." He patted her hand. "It should be over soon."

"That doesn't make me feel better. Did you see his face when you announced his name? I don't want him subjected to going through this any longer than necessary. Just do what you can to wrap this up and make sure I get to speak with Kane alone before we change and go to the cocktail party."

"As you wish." Abe sighed and they returned their attention to the next question asked.

"Kane-san, your career is about to take a massive turn away from the pop music genre. How do you feel about performing a different style of songs as written by Alfred-san?"

Kane lean forward and voiced into the microphone. "I have had the opportunity to go through the songs just in case I had the opportunity to play this very complicated character. To my surprise, I actually like the places Alfred-san took me vocally. I was capable of discovering qualities of debt in my performance that I did not expect."

"Over here, Kane-san!" Kane turned towards the voice. "You've been actively involved in music and drama since you were twelve years old, now starring in a film that will be distributed world wide debuting you in the United States, you are assured to be more busy." The female reporter stated. "Does this give you any time to pursue a romantic life?"

Kane gave a half grin and jokingly said, "Romantic life? What's that?"

Laughter.

"In all honesty, living this life is like a double edge sword. You are in a position to attract all these beautiful women, yet you don't have time to enjoy any of them. How just is that?" He winked behind his glasses, shrugged his shoulders and held his hand wide and once again, the crowd chuckled.

Charlene doesn't think she had ever witnessed any thing so impressive. He really was good at hiding his feelings. In spite of the similarities at first, the more time she spent in Kane's presences the more she realized he was nothing like Jason, who wore his emotions on his sleeve for the world to see. There would have been no way her explosive husband could have been able to maintain a cheerful demeanor in the midst of all these questions.

For the first time Charlene didn't feel as if she was looking at a young man younger than her but, a grown man wiser than his years and she also realized that she may have made the biggest mistake of her life.

"Alfred-san, has there been anyone in your life since your husband the late Japanese rock singer James-kun died unexpectedly?" Someone yelled out and a hush swept over the room.

Charlene had expected her past to come up eventually, but she hadn't expected them to be so blunt in the questioning. She drew a long harsh breath. "I…"

"Forgive me for interrupting, but Ms. Alfred's personal life has no bearings on this evening's announcement, nor such a painful reminder during such a joyous occasion." Abe piped in to her relief.

"I completely agree," Takusa second. "If there is no more questions to the matter at hand we will bring this evening to a close. I am delighted all of you could be here to witness this momentous occasion in Kane's career. This concludes the press conference. *Arigato gozaimasu!*"

Everyone on the panel bowed and thanked the press as Stuart and the house security led them off stage into a more private cluster of rooms.

Charlene turned to find herself alone with Kane. Obviously, Abe had done as she asked and afforded her some lone time with him.

"Are you all right Charlie-chan?" he asked softly removing the glasses and allowing her full view to his eyes now lightly lined with kohl to bring out their deep sleepy beauty even more. She couldn't take her eyes off him, no longer was he Kane-kun, the young man on the plane with her. He was *Kane* the superstar in the posters and photographs.

Yet, the eyes glaring at her was not the come hither stare she come to know and love in his publicity shots. This live and breathing man was very pissed and openly disappointed in her.

"Yes," she managed to say, licking dry lips. "I should have been better prepared to answer questions about Jason, but it's already been a long day."

"I couldn't agree more," Kane said coldly. "I believe you owe me some type of explanation. Why did you wait until the press conference to spring this on me? Why didn't you return any of my calls? What if I had made a complete ass out of myself out there!"

"You handled everything perfectly," she said.

"That's not the point, Charlene." He ran a hand through his hair and rubbed the back of his neck. "For a moment, before I saw the pleading in your eyes, I almost begged you in front of the entire world not to do this of me. Do you know what you've done to us?"

Charlene put some space between them she had to. His nearness radiated a vitality that drew her like a magnet. Her heart pounded eager and erratic as a summer storm. His steady gaze bore into her in silent expectation.

J-Pop Love Song

"Kane, I explained how important this film is to me. Getting it done and getting it done well, is my utmost concern. I don't have time to explore something more personal between us and I don't want to risk the possibility of you not playing the lead in my film just because we woke up one day and realized what a big mistake we made." She spread her hands wide, hoping he would believe her.

"What if I told you I was willing to take that chance and give up all that I have to spend the rest of my life making you happy."

The force of his admission took her off guard and the smoldering flame she saw in his eyes drove away all thoughts of what she was going to say.

"Kane..."

"*Kisu shite-mo ii?* May I kiss you?" He closed the space between them.

"I wish you wouldn't," she protested as his hand encircled her waist and rested in the small of her back.

His other calloused hand took her face and cradled it gently as his cheek moved against hers. She could feel the warmth of his body through her clothes. A breathless gasp escaped her mouth as his chest brushed against her sensitive nipples. He pressed closer against her. She couldn't take her eyes off his mouth as he drew her closer.

"Charlie-chan, I gave you what you wanted this evening and now it is time for you to give me something I've been wanting."

As her lips parted with objections, Kane caught her words into his mouth as his lips covered hers. His kiss was slow, thoughtful, and searching. She closed her eyes and kissed him back, trembling violently, but her logical mind wouldn't let her give in to the emotions he brought forth from a place she had thought died with her husband.

His timid start gave way to open boldness as his hand smoothed downward from her waste to the curve of her bottom he cupped her and held her against his erection. He left no room for doubt as to how much he desired her.

Crazy, she thought. Being with him like this is crazy. Kane fingers slid caressingly over her breast, his thumb flickering over the budding hardness of her nipple through her top. She couldn't breathe.

"Charlene, Charlene," he whispered his mouth sliding down her throat. His hand was moving up beneath her skirt caressing her thighs covered in silky nylons. She moaned, eyes rolling heavenward, the pleasure of being touched this way after so long was almost painful.

This was insane, she thought; when I know he's so young and to foolishly reckless to realize what could happen to both of their careers if someone where to walk in and catch them. It's simple madness! Why don't I stop him?

Because she never wanted anything as much as she wanted Kane at this moment. What if the truth of her future happiness was with Kane and she was giving up on her last chance to find passion, and happiness? However, if she didn't stop him from kissing her right now then it was only for one insane reason. There could only be one reason a reasonable, aging woman, would lose all sensibilities in the arms of a twenty-four year old man.

For one insane moment she wanted their fate to be decided for them. All it would take was one forward reporter armed with a camera in hand walking in on them at this moment. Why was she allowing him to hold her this way? Because she was falling in love with him.

She felt an overpowering shock as the realization. No! It wasn't possible, she reasoned through her sexually feverish mind. She vowed that after Jason died there would never be another love for her and there hadn't been. What made Kane different from the older and more experienced men that had attempted to kiss her on the occasional blind date?

Before Kane came into her life, Charlene had no dreams of finding love again. Now, that the possibility exists she felt a dangerous urge to allow herself to be swept up in his youthful recklessness.

"I want you, Charlie-chan, please tell me what I can do to make you want me too," Kane pleaded, his voice deep with need, yet when he wasn't kissing her she could think logically. He was asking her what to do, because he was too young and experienced to know exactly what was best. That is why she had to be logical one. The adult in this situation and encourage him to forget this foolishness and work hard towards his future.

"Kane," she pushed at his chest and he eased back but didn't release her as he looked at her with questioning eyes. "When was the last time you had sex?"

"Huh?"

"This is what this is all about, right? It's been awhile since you had any intimacy. Or maybe you're just interested in knowing what's it's like to be with a black woman?"

"Charlene, that's not it at all."

His face flushed, beaded with sweat and straining with strained passion was the most beautiful thing she had seen in awhile. She reached up and stroked the wealth of dark hair back from his temples.

"Kane, I know about your dreams. That you believe that my dead husband has been hunting your dreams and need you to make me happy." Charlene spoke softly almost motherly in her understanding. He released her.

"Takusa, told you," Kane said flatly. "You must think I truly am crazy." His mouth twisted wryly.

"No, actually I don't. Sometimes I dream of Jason and I wake up and I swear I can smell his scent on my hands, but I know it was a dream. I suppose for you, you grew up watching his music videos and interviews that they continue to sell and play on the anniversary of his death. It stands to reason—"

"Don't you see there is no reasoning?" Kane walked across the small lounge and dropped down into a chair his wrist resting on his spread knees as he leaned forward with in deep thought. "There is no reasoning the truth, Charlene."

"Kane..." She moved to stand before him and he looked up her.

"Don't...don't do that," he interrupted, his voice giving her pause in the way she was handling the situation.

She swallowed deeply. "Do what?"

"Treat me like a child, because you aren't adult enough to face what is really going on between us and take it to the next level."

Taken aback Charlene eyes widened. "I don't know what you mean."

"You know exactly what I mean. Out there in front of the entire world, you could have listened to your heart and respected my decision. Instead you did

J-Pop Love Song

what you thought was best without consulting me." His voice was calm, and his gaze steady. "Tell me Charlene when you made this decision were you truly thinking what was best for me, or was it all about what is best for you?"

"I don't know what you mean." She defended her actions. "I've never made it a secret of how important making this film is to me, but I was also thinking about you. Don't you think you've given up too much of your life to chunk it all away on the theory that you are the only man that could make me happy?" Charlene crossed her arms across her chest and looked at him shaking her head. "Trust me, you aren't."

"So are you saying that for that brief moment in my arms that you weren't thinking what it could be like to stay in my arms forever? Did it not cross your mind once that all of this mess you created today could be solved if only someone walked in and caught us together?"

Charlene's face reddened with guilt. Maybe he was a psychic; maybe that is why Jason was reaching out to him in his dreams. Oh hell, what was she thinking? This entire situation was too surreal to believe and at any moment, she would wake up and find out her entire life had been some long ridiculous dream.

Kane stood and she stepped back. "I'm right aren't I?"

"I don't know what you're talking about."

"*Honto-no-kotti itte.*" His movements were easy and graceful as he stalked her until her back was pressing firmly against the wall. He placed his palms flat on the wall boxing her escape.

"I am being honest." She panted. "What are you doing?"

"Do you know how beautiful you are, even when you're lying?"

A feeling of panic swept through her, she didn't know if she could deny him this time if he were to kiss her again.

His gaze traveled over her face and searched her eyes. "I can see it in your eyes that you want me just as bad as I want you, Charlie-san."

"Don't be foolish. It's just sexual. I don't know about you, but it's been awhile for me. You could be anybody." She said spitefully.

He didn't even flinch. "*Sawatte.*"

Her eyebrows arched a fraction. "Huh?"

What had gotten into him? He was actually smiling.

"You know you want to," his voice was husky and to damned sexy for his own good.

This wasn't going as she planned. He was getting to her instead of her pushing him away. "I don't want to touch you."

"*Sugoku suki.*"

"You're not crazy about me, you're just crazy." She swallowed tightly as his nose brushed against her nose.

"Prove to me that this is purely sexual and I will give up on believing there can be a future for us."

"Huh?"

"Tonight, after the cocktail party, I will come to you. Give me this one night and I promise from tomorrow on it will be business and I will work my ass off to give you an award winning performance."

"And if I say, no?"

"I will have to go to the press and tell them I pulled out of the project because you seduced me, the poor innocent, Kane."

"You wouldn't dare," she balked.

"Try me," He cocked a brow.

"Look, you already have the part you no longer have to act as Blu. This is something he would do to get his way." She chuckled and rolled her eyes.

His expression didn't change. "Think what you will Charlie-chan. Tonight, at midnight I will be at your door and if you don't let me in, then I will take advantage of all the leftover reporters here in this hotel and call my own little press conference."

Her expression became blank. "You're serious, aren't you?"

"I have nothing to lose, I had planned on walking away from this in the first place in two months time, I just hoped it would be with you," he reminded her needlessly.

"This is blackmail." Her breasts rose and fell under her labored breathing.

"*S-dana!* That's right!" His eyes roamed over her face and her breast. "Besides if you are so sure we are both just horny, then what are you afraid of?"

"I'm not afraid. I know there is no way it's can be anything else."

"We'll see." He pushed himself off the wall and shoved his hands in his pocket.

"If I do this I don't ever want to have this discussing with you again, do you understand? If you come to my room tonight and we have sex, I will never be able to look at you the same. You will do your business dealings with the director and Abe. Is that what you want?"

"You know it's not," his chiseled chin lifted stubbornly. "But either way I'm going to lose you. At least this way, I will get to know if the real thing is as good as my dreams."

"I can't believe I bought into that public persona of you being a sweet and nice guy," Charlene sneered.

She wanted to take back her words when she saw the genuine hurt in his eyes. The muscle in his jaw worked profusely and his Adam's-apple bobbed as he swallowed back his emotions.

"I had hoped you of all people would look past this mask I am forced to wear and see, I'm just a man, like any other. If you can't see that, then maybe tonight will prove us both wrong."

He turned on his heel and opened the door sauntering out of the room brushing past Abe who seemed to be personally assuring their privacy along with Stuart who gave her a long unsmiling look before falling in behind Kane and disappearing from her site as they turned a corner.

Abe came in. "Is everything okay?"

She looked up at her friend and shook her head. She allowed herself to let go. Her face crumpled into tears and she welcomed the familiar gentle comfort of Abe arms. Thank God he always there when she needed him she didn't know how she would function without him.

"It'll be okay, Charlie," he assured her.

"No," she shook her head against his chest. "It won't, because I think I've fallen in love with him."

In her grief, she failed to see the disappointment on Abe's face.

Chapter Seven

"You look absolutely delicious."

Charlene winked at Abe as he stood in her hotel room door in a black single button suit with satin lapels, white shirt and a black satin tie.

"I'm nothing compared to you," he complimented taking her by the hand and twirling her around.

"Courtesy of Ms. Nicole Miller. Isn't a walking work of art?" Charlene released his hand and did a stylish catwalk across the room. The teal multicolored silk-charmeuse gown with its asymmetrical hemline flowed elegantly with each movement. The color perfectly complimented the brown tones of her skin. "I love her stuff; it allows my skin to breathe."

"I can see that." Abe lifted a dark eyebrow in shock. "Are you sure the back isn't cut—"

"Oh, I'm sure that it's low enough," she interrupted. "With the straps crisscrossing in the back like this it makes it's still proper, though my backside is my best feature." A slight frown creased her brow as she turned to face him again, sighing.

"It may be a bit much for Japan, Charlie."

She placed her hands on her hips. "I'm *not* Japanese, I'm American. Aren't I expected to be a little over the top? Not to mention the free publicity won't hurt. If they talk about the dress they talk about *me*, and if they talk about me they will talk about *Blu's Diary*."

Abe chuckled shaking his head. "I suppose."

"Come on, what's with the face?" Charlene smiled at Abe and picked up the silver handbag that matched the strappy sandals with their three-inch heel. "Hey, it's my last night of having fun before we have to get down to business isn't it?"

"Are you sure you're alright?" Abe asked, his tone becoming serious. "I know the signs. You're overly animated and it's usually because you're trying to pretend like you're okay. When that happens you get reckless." He moved in closer. "I can get you out of this evening if you wish."

"Why? So I can sit up here in the room wondering if I've made the biggest mistake of my life?"

"It wasn't a mistake. You have too much to risk at this point in your career. So does Kane. He is very young Charlie, and has lived most of his life in a bubble. Would he be faithful to you once he's free to make his own decisions?"

"Abe..."

"You know I'm not saying anything to you that you haven't already asked yourself." Abe took her hands in his. "Trust me, don't beat yourself up over this. You made the best decision for the both of you even if Kane can't appreciate what you've done for him yet. Someday he will understand."

Charlene's lashes lowered as she remembered Kane's threat to come to her room at midnight. Would he really take the risk and do such a thing? If he did, how was she going to handle the situation? If she turned him away, what would he do? She didn't need a scandal before the filming started or the investors would pull the plug. If she were honest, she didn't really want to turn him away.

She really should come clean with Abe but this was personal and she didn't want to hurt Kane anymore than she already had. This was something she had to work out for herself and if she had to give Kane the one night he asked for, then it was best if they remained the only two who knew about it.

"Charlene? Did you hear what I said?"

It took a moment before she realized Abe was still speaking to her. Charlene didn't ask him to repeat his words because she didn't want to hear them. She wasn't in the mood to discuss Kane with Abe or listen to any more advice on what was best for her. Without a word she grabbed the faux fur wrap off the couch.

"Charlie..."

"Look, I appreciate your concern for me, but I don't think Kane will understand someday. Hell, how could he when I don't even understand what's going on between us. I haven't been interested in a man for nine years and now that I am, it's the same old shit." She shook her head in frustration. "Here I am reliving my old life. The only difference now is instead of my being told I can't love this man because of our cultural differences, I'm being told it won't work because I'm too old for him, he's my employee, and we're risking everything."

"I know it unfair, but it's the truth," Abe reasoned.

She nodded with a grim smile. "Yeah, it is. Still, it's *my* decision to make and I'm trying to make the right one, but I don't have to be happy about it. Now, come on, we better go downstairs." She released a deep chuckle, needing to lighten the mood and changed the subject. "I'm already being daring by wearing this dress; I don't need to be late too."

"After you." They made their way to the elevator. The brief ride was quiet and the doors opened allowing them to step out.

Charlene and Abe were about three feet from the elevator, when he was intercepted by an enthusiastic business acquaintance. She looked ahead to see Kane was waiting for her in the designated entrance of the private dining room where the celebratory event was occurring.

He wore black leather pants with a matching black leather dinner jacket over a white shirt and a white satin necktie and he looked devastatingly handsome. Charlene tried to quash the sudden racing of her pulses. Her mounting passionate feelings for him were becoming almost painful.

"*Konbanwa,* Charlie-chan." His deep brown eyes appraised her thoroughly before coming to rest on her face. "*Kirei-dayo,* you look beautiful." The warmth of his smiled echoed in his voice.

"Good evening. Thank you, you're not looking to shabby yourself," she said

J-Pop Love Song

returning his infectious smile. He walked slowly by her side, stopping when she stopped. "Maybe you should go in first. I will wait here for Abe."

"I don't think so." The words were clipped and told her clearly that he didn't wish to debate the matter. "I'll be your escort for tonight. It has been decided. Mmm, *li kaori*, you smell sweet."

"Stop sniffing at me." She whispered with a grin on her lips as they paused and took a requested photo. He had the nerve to wink at her momentarily turning his back towards the reporter pretending to straighten his tie.

When they were alone once more she asked, "Who asked you to escort me?"

"Sniff you?"

Charlene rolled her eyes and counted to ten backwards. "No, escort me tonight."

"I suggested it to your publicist and she agreed. Believing it would be great press, of course. Two cultures showing the world how they can get along in business."

"Well, it's strange that *my* publicist didn't fill me in, because I would have objected. It may appear inappropriate, especially after the tabloids put a spin on any pictures that are taken without our permission." Charlene protested. "A press conference is one thing, but this is completely different. This is a social setting."

Mildly he murmured, "Mmm, I can't tell since you are currently being antisocial to me."

Flushed, she laughed, relaxing. "Sorry, it's been a long day."

"Besides, no one would believe a well accomplished African American woman such as yourself, would want me for anything other then business of course." His sarcasm was evident. "They will assume you're tolerating me for the sake of your film."

"They would be right," she mumbled, a mischievous glint flickered in her eyes.

A smile curved his lip, but he said nothing. He grasped her by the elbow and escorted her to the table with seating for a party of eight. She saw the name cards and indeed Kane was on one side and Abe on the other. She decided this was going to be an interesting evening. Charlene was suspicious and wondered if Kane switched the name card to suit his own needs.

Most of all, where was Stuart? How could she continue flirting with him if he wasn't around? Is that why Kane wanted to spend *this night* with her? Had he realized everyone would be too busy to notice how he was spending his time?

"Have you been thinking about what we spoke of earlier?" He asked holding her chair out while she sat down shrugging off her wrap. Kane passed it to an attendant and ordered drinks for them before taking his seat beside her.

Charlene stared at him.

"*Nani?* What, is it?"

"How…how did you know I drink grape *Chu-hi* served cold in a tall frosted glass?"

"I just knew. I read it somewhere, maybe." He shrugged. "Something else we seem to have in common, I take my alcohol light too; accept for an occasional beer with the band of course. My preference is for the white peach *Chu-hi*, I find the grape too sweet for my taste."

"Oh really," she giggled. "This coming from the guy that ate *all* the marshmallow cereal."

Kane chuckled. "That's different. I have the milk and cereal to ease the impact of the marshmallows so it's a perfect balance. I take it you like *Chu-his'* because of the sweetness?"

"No, I don't like the taste of alcohol, but I always found myself in these type of situations with Jason hounding me to stop being a prude and drink up. He said I was being insincere saying, "*Kampai!* Cheers!" with a glass of sparkling water." She grinned at the memory."

"What about sake?"

"Are you kidding? Rice wine knocks me right on my ass," she laughed.

"Yeah," Kane agreed, laughing with her. "*Watashi mo*, me too."

"I finally found something that I was willing to meet Jason halfway with. Since *Chu-his* is similar to a wine cooler, I could sip, get a little buzz and fit in with his crowd of friends." Charlene couldn't dismiss how much she was enjoying the simple conversation about things so normal. It was as comfortable as their first all-night phone conversation and when they first met in person. For the moment, she allowed herself to forget everything that has happened since they stepped off the plane.

Charlene lifted her eyes to find Kane watching her intently.

"Charlie-chan, I don't want you to feel that you have to do the accepted thing just to please my friends. If you have true friends they don't have to approve but they will accept you because you're my choice." He stated.

Her mouth twisted wryly. "This coming from a man who is practically *blackmailing* me into having sex with him."

"That's different." He shrugged. "*Boku-wa kimi-no kareshi*, I'm yours, so you should want to please me."

Charlene ignored how good his words mad her feel. "You are the worst, to do this just to get sex out me!"

"Honestly, I can't believe you took me seriously." Kane sighed and leaned in closer. "I said it because I wanted to hurt you, like you hurt me. I've never and will never, have to use blackmail for sex."

"So you weren't going to come to my room tonight?" she asked skeptically wondering what was he up to now.

"Yes, I was going to show up at your door tonight." He paused and corrected the statement. "That hasn't changed, but we don't have to have sex."

"Why?" She squealed bringing her voice down a notch when she received a curious glance from the party one table over. "If you don't want to have sex with me, why are you still coming to my room?"

"Is that disappointment I hear?" He gave her a devastated grin and her heartbeat increased. *Yes*, she was disappointed, but she was happy that he wasn't shiftless enough to follow through on his threat.

"Don't be silly," she rebuked.

"I can be silly," Kane acknowledged. "I can also be childish, spoiled, and lovable. I am aware that you're American and Black, and that you're old enough to be my young mother, and anything else you might throw at me. Still, noting you say can change the fact that I'm crazy about you." His voice had deepened, his head nearly touched hers and his slanted drooping lids, half-veiled his eyes.

She felt the intensity of his concentration on her, sensed the tension in his lean body. The hair on the back of her neck stood on end from the sexual charge she felt coursing between them. She knew with one part of her mind that she should get up and place as much space between them as possible. She couldn't move.

"Charlie-chan, I was hoping to spend the night making you see how impossible it is to try and push me away. I am a part of you and you are a part of me, if you would accept that fact, everything would go so much smoother for us."

"Kane—"

"You, don't have to say anything. I've waited this long for you. I can continue to wait, until you're ready to accept the truth," he interrupted.

Charlene tensed, remembering what Takusa had said. She had yet to read his online journal for herself because she felt it was such an invasion on his privacy. She's already going to make him hate, her she didn't want to add that to her growing list of offenses. "There is no reason for you to wait. I do think you are best for the part of Blu but my happiness is not your concern. Do you understand what I'm saying? I'm freeing you from any obligation you may be feeling towards me."

She sat unflinching as his eyes silently searched her face.

"You've been speaking with Takusa-san, haven't you?" He finally said.

"Kane."

"What did he tell you?"

"We can't discuss this here," she spoke softly.

He leaned back in his chair. His clenched hands rested against his flat stomach. She noted the muscles in his jaw seized as he clenched down on his back teeth. "I won't give you a hard time as far as the film is concern, but if you readily agree with *him*, then there is nothing more for us to discuss."

Charlene's eyes grew wide with surprise. She didn't know whether to be relieved or disappointed that he was giving in so easily. "Just like that? Yet you would still do the movie."

"Of course, I'm a professional first and also I want this to go well for you because I know it's important to you. As far as how I personally feel, what can I do if you've already made up your mind about me? How can I expect you to fall in love with me when you can't even trust what you are feeling?" He lifted an eyebrow.

"Kane—" She swallowed back the urge to cry.

"Shhh, as you've said, this isn't the time or place and I see Takusa-san is coming this way." She felt his calloused hand reach for hers' under the table and held it. He had the beautiful long fingers of a musician; they felt wonderfully familiar and reassuring.

"Charlie-chan, if my feelings do matter to you, I have a place where we can go to tonight and seriously, we don't have to make love; I just want to be with you before things start to get crazy." He grinned mischievously. "No pun intended."

She responded with a stunned look. Why didn't she just tell him the truth?

She didn't think he was crazy and he hadn't misread her feelings, she *was* beginning to care about him…very much. Still, doesn't this let her off the hook? He was offering to do his best playing Blu regardless of what she decided to do about tonight.

"Don't look so serious, beautiful." He winked and grinned. "We can pick this up later tonight, when we're alone. I want to tell you everything in my own words. Takusa-san had no right bringing his suspicions to you."

"I…I…"

Charlene halted her words and tugged her hand from his, as Mr. Takusa appeared handsomely dressed with an equally smartly dressed Asian woman by his side. Introductions were made as others took their places around the table. Other members including a few producers of *Blu's Diary* filled the remaining seating including Abe who came up short. His face remained detached, but she could tell he was annoyed. When he sat beside her and leaned towards her and softly mumbled that the seating arrangements had been rearranged, she realized why.

She turned to look at Kane with accusing eyes and a muscle quivered in his jaw as he battled to keep from laughing. He really was childish, she thought. He was also more handsome than the first time she met him, in the person. She didn't know if she should strangle him or kiss him. Biting down on her back teeth to keep from smiling at him, like an idiot, she turned her attention to Abe.

In between the polite pointless conversations they waited for the meal to commence over shrimp cocktails. Charlene seized the opportunity to appreciate her surroundings after Abe was pulled into conversing with a beautiful Asian model sitting next to him. Another seating arrangement she probably could thank Kane for.

Takusa had changed seats with his wife upon sitting, and she was placed next to Kane. Her constant gracious chatter kept his rapt attention off of her. In any case she had free time on her hands in between nibbles of shrimp to sit quietly and take in her elegant surroundings.

In the gold, white, and red cultured dining room, yards of material billowed from shimmering crystal and gold chandeliers adorning the ceiling. There invited, round dining tables set up for intimates groups to balance out the thirteen hundred guests. Charlene had no idea as to why most of them were invited except for being close partners of the investors. She noted a few familiar faces of celebrities she had worked with at the television studio during her last stay in Tokyo, but their successful careers had blossomed just like her own. Looking at them in their elegant attire, she could no longer picture them getting blitzed on warmed cups of sake until sun up like they did in the early days with Jason and his motley crew.

Dinner was served consisting of the most superior ingredients of the season, prepared with the time-honored masterpieces of expert artisan chefs. All items were arranged stylishly on dishes and plates of colorful porcelain, ceramics, and the like, each with its own contour to display the portions to perfection. The First courses consisted of sushi and sashimi, followed by lemon grass clear soup with dumplings, salmon with black sesame seed crust, then the main course of grain fed beef with a mushroom teriyaki cream sauce.

J-Pop Love Song

By the time the next dish of prawn and vegetable tempura arrived, Charlene was thankful she chose to wear the loose fitting dress that left room for a full stomach. She was even more thankful for the break before the chef surprised them with an especially made sweet concoction from the in-house French pastry chef.

She leaned over to listen to Kane as her attention was stolen away by his beautiful laugh. She observed him lifting Mrs. Tanaka's hand to his lip in a fond kiss. She seemed to be a likeable, calm and polite woman and seemed to get along very well with Kane. He was very respectful and playfully attentive as if she was a mother figure to him. Most likely, with him being with Mr. Takusa since he was a young boy and losing his mother at an early age, she probably *was* the only motherly influence Kane had in his life.

Charlene wondered how polite would Mrs. Takusa continue to be with her if she knew that she was a possible threat to her daughter marrying Kane. She imagined Takusa was either keeping her in the dark about the situation or had already told her he'd handled her. The one thing Takusa didn't know about Charlene, was she didn't like being treated like a child. Speaking of children, she wondered where was the Kane's future "fiancée" this evening.

Maybe Takusa hadn't wanted to start the rumors yet by pairing his prize moneymaker with a date and blow the "available" image he had built around Kane's persona. Then again, it was in his newly signed contract that he maintained the appearance. She personally thought it was a stupid stipulation to put on anyone, but she had seen many films flop because of the personal love life of celebrities involved.

It was difficult for her to not return the tenderness of Kane's stare when he chanced to look at her, his meaningful, intimate gaze made her nervous yet invigorated that a man still found her attractive, it had been so long since she's felt like a woman. Had any of the others noticed the way their eyes met and held, the way his voice changed every time he spoke to her and the breathlessness in hers as she answered his questions? She prayed they hadn't. It was a relief knowing that they couldn't see that under the table he continuously moved his knee against hers, and every so often his fingers would graze lightly over her thigh.

Each contact of his flesh against hers, no matter how fleeting made her have a never-ending feeling of anticipation as she waited for his next touch. It was almost unbearable. She wished she didn't feel this way, because she had so many conflicting emotions, and she hadn't decided yet what to do about these growing feelings she had for him. It didn't help that he was so straight forth about his feelings. That was and unexpected flaw in his character.

"Charlie?"

She licked her lips and like a guilty child she looked at an inquiring Abe. "Did you say something?"

"I said you looked a bit flushed, are you okay or is jet lag setting in?"

She gave him a reassuring grin, "Yeah, that must be what it is. It's been a busy and exciting few days."

"Just give me the word and I'll cover for you if you wish to leave early."

She nodded in appreciation. After fixing his gaze upon her face for another moment he seemed to be pacified by the excuse and his attention returned to the fashion model at his side.

Immediately her mind went back to the object of her thoughts. Unlike the Japanese men she had come in contact with over the years, Kan was very forthcoming in with his emotions.

Charlene hadn't even had a chance to adjust to her own feelings and there he was confessing his own. It was another reminder of his impetuous youth and lack of experience. Kane had yet to learn, that things such as this should be taken at a slower pace and that there were many roadblocks to such a relationship. It didn't matter what country they were in, and older woman with a younger male was considered taboo.

It just couldn't work between them, even if they weren't public figures. She definitely wanted a baby within the first year of marrying and he probably wanted to wait a few more years. As it is she would be in her sixties when her first child graduated from high school. That thought made her chance another look at Kane. He would still be in the prime of his life. Charlene released a deep sigh. Kane was right, she over-think things when she should just go with the flow. Why was she thinking about it in the first place? Hadn't she already made her decision?

Dessert ended and after-dinner drinks were served before the "open bar" announcement was made. The music ensemble proceeded to play. Some guest made their way to the dance floor while others networked amongst the tables, the remaining few moved out on the veranda for a smoke. Charlene wasn't completely sure what to do; she really wasn't in the right temperament for business discussion or grinning nicely, while speaking only when spoken too. Maybe, this would be a good time to make her escape.

"Alfred-san, will you dance with me?"

Charlene's nerves bristled. She should have known Kane was going to ask her to dance, and he did so before she could make a run for it. There was also no way to turn him down seeing how he asked in view of those still at the table. If she was to turn him down it might give the wrong notion as to why and come morning media tongues would be wagging that there was already creative discord brewing. Then the rumors would start. Charlene decided the less intrigued into their personal lives the more the media would concentrate on the merits of the drama.

She smiled and stood while Kane held the chair for her. He permitted her to lead the way to the dance floor. She was surprised when he took her in his arms like a professional ballroom dancer and led her around the floor.

"Close your mouth," Kane grinned.

"You are a wonderful lead," she laughed up at him. "Lessons, or is this just something else you're good at?"

"I'm good at it...after lessons," he chuckled. "I guess you missed the movie where I played a prince?" He lifted a question brow.

"No, I saw it," she admitted. "I just don't remember seeing you dance like this in it."

"That's because if you blinked you missed the entire thirty second scene. I had to take three months of lessons to shoot that scene and for the sake of time accept for those brief seconds the rest ended up as bonus footage on the DVD release." He shook his head.

"Ah, maybe I need to watch it again. I'll check out the extras this time," she teased.

"Don't bother, you have the real thing at your disposal anytime you want me, Charlie-chan. All you have to do is say the word and I'll be your prince."

Charlene's eyes twinkled with mirth. "Do you ever stop?"

"Do you really want me to?" He asked coolly. His eyes watched her steadily as she felt his hand burning hot against the nakedness of her exposed back. As if he was thinking the same thing she was he said, "I love the feel of your soft skin against my hand," he commented as if he read her thoughts.

"You shouldn't speak to me like this," she warned ignoring the delight she felt at his words.

"*Nanji-goro kaeru-no?* What time are you leaving?"

"*Kimentenai.* I haven't decided."

"*Tsumanne!*" He rolled his eyes in frustration.

"How can you be bored with all this excitement? Great things are about to happen for the both of us." She looked at him from beneath fringed lashes.

"You're joking, right? These things are not for us; they are just another reason for a team of suits, discussing more business and get drunk at the same time. They don't care what the artist think." He mouth twisted wryly. "So, how about I go first, because you're after all the honored guest and you will be required to make the necessary rounds before you can escape for the evening. When you leave here, go up to your room, throw on some jeans and comfortable shoes and I'll take you to a great all-night spot where we can really dance."

"You must be joking," she nearly stepped on his expensive shoe, but with unexpected smoothness he twirled her to where it looked like an intentional move instead of a near stumble. "What about Mr. Takusa and Abe?"

"Stu-san will cover for us," Kane stated.

"I wouldn't count on it." Charlene murmured knowing the arrangement Takusa was supposed to set up with Stuart.

Kane's eyes narrowed as if he was searching for something in her face. She adverted her gazed to look over his shoulder. She gasped as he whirled her once and then again causing her abdomen to press into his semi-hardness leaving her breathless and giggling up at him like a silly schoolgirl. She felt as if she was on a ride in an amusement park. Were her feet even touching the ground when he did that?

"That's better, I like it when you're looking at me." He chastised with a boyish smile. "Don't react to what I'm about to say because Takusa and your watch dog manager Goda-san are watching us, but I know the deal Takusa-san made with Stu-san."

Charlene gawked at him in silent disbelief. Once more it was his graceful reflexes that saved them from another possible dance floor fiasco. "H...how?"

"Stu-san told me after the press conference," he explained.

"So is this the real reason you withdrew from following up on your threat of sex or sabotage?" Her growing agitation caused her to become tense in his arms. She had to staunch the urge to walk off the floor and leaving him standing there alone. Kane must have sensed her dark thoughts for his hold tightened on her fingers and waist.

"The one fact my manager keeps purposely forgetting, Charlie-chan, is Stusan works for me, not him. Also, he can't be bought; he's more than an employee. He's become my best friend over the years. He knows me better than anyone."

"Well that explains why I haven't been able to properly seduce Stuart." She shot him a scornful look. "For your information, I haven't said I would be with you, what if I'm interested in getting to know Stuart better? What right do you have to interfere?"

"I can't believe that you would even listen to Takusa-san, Charlie-chan." Kane looked at her with accusing eyes and asked, "Tell me why? Why would you willingly agree to be my managers, flunky? Did he promise you something or did he say something about me that give you pause about giving give me an opportunity to date you?"

"The song is about to end," she sidestepped his question.

"*Yameta*, forget it! I'll stand here and hold you in the middle of all these people until the next song starts if you don't tell me why you allowed Takusa-san to do your thinking for you?"

Charlene felt panic rising in her chest and she wanted to childishly stump her food in frustration. "Because he made a lot of sense. I have too much to lose and so do you and for what! Some foolishness that my dead husband has been coming to you in your dreams since you were a boy and Jason has told you we're destined for each other." She hissed in a low voice so only he could hear. "Do you know how insane that is?"

"So, it comes down to that." He rolled his eyes heavenward. "I can't believe the son-of-a-bitch told you. It's none of his business. I was going to tell you—."

"As you should have from the beginning!" She replaced her frown with a fake smile on her lips when she glimpsed Abe watching them from the sidelines of the dance floor, the model still glue to his hips. Just like Stuart was to Kane, Abe was to her, and she couldn't hide much from him. Her friend wouldn't think twice about coming out to rescue her from Kane's arms and the last thing she wanted was a scene.

A little too late she saw Kane look over to where Abe was standing. His arm tightened around her waist nearly bringing her full flushed against every hard plain of his body. "I see the way *he* looks at you and I don't like it. Are you still sticking to the story that Goda-san isn't your lover?" Kane asked unexpectedly.

The fact that this man was only twenty-five amazed her; he was like an oldsoul in his shrewdness. He never seemed to miss a thing. "I've only been with one man Kane, my husband."

The song stopped, neither of them noticed.

"Really?" Kane's voice raised an octave and she thought she was going to be blinded by smugness of his white smile. "That pleases me."

"Why should it please you? It's none of your business," she countered.

How he managed to shrug his shoulders and not miss a step amazed her.

"Because it's as it should be," was all he said.

They came to an abrupt halt, Charlene swayed on her feet Kane released her so quickly, grinning sheepishly he placed at least an arms length between them

J-Pop Love Song

as rumblings of voices, laughter, and applause brought them both to their senses.

"Thank you, for the dance," she said as she saw Abe making his way across the floor towards them.

"Stu-san will be up to get you in about two hours and he will bring you to where I'll be waiting." Kane stated with a polite bow, a smile plastered on his lips, his dark eyes alight with anger she hadn't ever seen coming from him before. "It will be as if you have a midnight tryst with Stuart, that should really please Takusa-san, and you do want to please him, don't you?"

"Fuck you." She said through a clenched teeth smile, her jaws aching from the effort.

"You will."

"How can you be so sure?" Her smile slipped, she wasn't as good at this pretending as he was.

"You mean besides the fact that a part of you wants to be with me? Still, if that isn't a good enough reason then I'm sure you're pissed enough to try once again to convince me that what I feel for you isn't real." He paused and clucked his tongue at her before adding, "Oops, your beautiful smile is slipping. Be careful, your merciless guard dog and mine are throwing daggers at my back, I can feel it." He winked with a saucy wiggling of his dark eyebrows.

"Kane don't wait for me," she grounded out with a beautiful toothy smile. "This game is over. I won't be there."

"*Kimi-no-koto maji-nanda*. I *am* serious about you, even if you insist on playing childish games with me. I will play along and I'll be waiting, and if you don't come tome, I will come to you."

"*Nande?* How come? Why are you doing this to me?"

"Besides the obvious?" He snorted bitterly. "I'm interested in seeing what your *plan-B* is, now that you're *A-plan* to use my best friend, Stuart, has failed."

"I'm sorry I hurt you, but don't do this Kane," her bottom lip trembled. "It's only going to make matters worse, if we have this night together."

"Giving up is not a viable option, Alfred-san." He stared at her. The music started up once more, and others filing past them bumped against them to move onto the dance floor. She observed his hands clenching into fists by his sides as he took one step forward as if to take her in his arms again. Charlene tensed, because if he touched her, she would shatter into pieces right here, be damned to anyone watching or taking photographs.

To her relief and disappointment he shoved his hands into the front pockets of the leather pants he wore and turned on his heels, lightly barely into a surly Abe in passing. Abe was there to rescues her, in his usual protective way, but this time he was too late. She was already down for the count.

Chapter Eight

CHARLENE FELT LIKE A GIDDY teenager sneaking out of the window of her parents' house as she followed Stuart into a private service elevator leading to the parking garage.

"Stuart, I want to apologize for assuming you would go along with Takusa's scheme. Tonight when someone younger reminded me of how juvenile I was by trying to manipulate someone's feelings, I felt like an idiot. Something I haven't felt in a long time." She chuckled, shaking her head. "I shouldn't have used you like that. I'm sorry."

Charlene was conscious of Stuart's scrutiny. She waited for his anger, but was pleasantly relieved when his wide mouth spread into a smile.

"Don't beat yourself up over it. Kane is not like most kids his age. It's why it was easy for me to forget and become his friend regardless of our age difference. I've never felt like the older and wiser one hangin' around him." Stuart grinned. "I seriously doubt Kane ever knew what it felt like to just be a kid. From an early age he had to watch over his mother who suffered from depression. When she died, he didn't really know what to do with himself." Charlene felt her heart ache go out even further for the singer.

"The only time I've seen Kane completely at ease and genuinely happy was the other day with you on the jet. During that same flight he was actually jealous of me. At the press conference he looked like he wanted to kick my ass. I think he sincerely cares for you."

Charlene fidgeted, shoving her fingers in her back jean pockets to still them. "I realize there is a lot to Kane I don't know. There is also more going on here then meets the eye between him and his manager, and I've walked right into the middle of it. Still, it's no excuse for the role I've played in this so far; you've been cool with me and very forgiving. Thank you."

"No problem." Stuart assured her. "Trust me, I know Mr. Takusa can run a convincing game of guilt on people, he's been doing it to Kane for as long as I can remember. Before Kane and I became friends, he had nobody he could just kick it with, and definitely no one who would be his ally against Takusa." The bodyguard steepled his fingers in thought. "I let Takusa believe I'm his spy, but it's Kane's back that I watch over. I'm always on the side of the underdog and Kane's the underdog in this situation."

Charlene smiled. For some reason it made her feel better, knowing Kane had a true friend. "I'm glad my first instincts about you weren't wrong."

J-Pop Love Song

"Likewise." Stuart said then added, "I must say this stunt tonight is also another first for him and it's risky, because Takusa usually has someone on his ass at all times. Hey, who am I to stop romance."

She was surprised when Stuart winked at her. "Is that what you believe is going on here?" she asked in a raised voice before sheepishly confessing, "I admit I do have a purpose for agreeing to meet Kane tonight, but I'm afraid it's not as romantic as you may think. I was hoping after tonight Kane would disperse of this fantasy…"

"I understand your need to fool yourself, because it's a surreal situation." Stuart sympathized. "Still, this isn't some childish "fantasy", Charlie. These episodes are very real to him, and since I'm around him all the time, it's a reality I've had to face also."

"So, you know about his dreams?"

"How can I not know about them? It's been a nightmare for me too." Stuart released a deep sigh. "Kane's dreams aren't always happy memories of times he's spent with you, times I might add *aren't even his own*. Sometimes they're horrible, causing him to hurt himself or worse."

He paused as if giving her time to take in his words. She was stunned. *Oh, Kane.* Why was Jason doing this to him? He chose to die, so why did he believe he had the right to torture someone else into living the life he so cowardly gave up on?

"Oh, I can tell by the look on your face that if Kane or Takusa told you anything, they've chosen to leave out the entire truth. Well, the facts aren't mine for the tellin', but there are some things you deserve to know, especially if you plan on spending any nights alone with Kane."

"I don't—."

Stuart lifted his hands palm side up to halt any excuse she was about to give him. "Hey, none my of my business. You're both grown and I'm not here to judge."

Charlene understood and was grateful for Stuart's apparent blessing. "You said sometimes the dreams cause Kane to hurt himself?"

"You know how your husband died…"

"I don't like to think about it, but yes, of course." Charlene answered quietly. "I was there…afterwards, that is. I had to identify the body, at least what was left of it to be identified."

"Then you must know the horror of what Kane has to re-live in those dreams. It starts with him crying in his sleep and then cries out your name, waking up just short of hitting the ground after leaping from the hotel roof. It's why he suffers from insomnia. He loves dreaming of you, but he never knows when it's going to be a nightmare instead. He won't take pills because he's scared that he will become addicted, due to his dabbling in drugs when he was hanging out with the wrong crowd as a kid."

"This whole thing is getting stranger by the minute." She released a bitter chuckle and dipped her head. "And to think I didn't want him for this role because I thought he was some rich pampered kid who had no clue about what Blu had to do to survive."

"That's what everyone is supposed to think because it keeps them from finding his skeletons. Takusa's spent a lot of time and money convincing the public that there is nothing else to find, that Kane was born into a elite family of business entrepreneurs. The truth is, the rift with his father caused him to have a life as hard as any kid wandering homeless on the streets of Tokyo."

"Why are Kane and his father on the outs?"

Stuart shook his head. "No one knows, not even me. Kane won't talk about it."

"I bet that bastard Takusa knows."

"Probably, which is why he's gone to such lengths to cover it up. As for Kane, what I wanted you to know is, in spite of his protest against taking sleeping pills, sometimes when he's wired and going non-stop for days surviving on a couple hours of sleep here or there, I *have* to slip him meds for his own good. During the times he's out, he'll sleep for days and be perfectly fine, then the vicious cycle starts all over again."

Charlene heard the frustration and concern in Stuart's voice. She also understood the protectiveness he felt for Kane. It was enough to make anyone want to take care of him, including her. There had to be a way to free him of Jason's ghost.

How the hell did one handle a situation such as this? If there were truly a course of action to keep Jason from haunting him, wouldn't Takusa and Stuart have determined one by now?

Maybe they had, and she was it. Regardless, the only way to get to the bottom of everything was to start at the beginning. She needed to figure out just why Jason had chosen *Kane*. Charlene shrugged off her thoughts as she realized Stuart was speaking to her.

"As you can see the pace Kane keeps is insane and I heard about what you did, asking that he remain focused on this project only." He smiled and reached out to squeeze her shoulder. "Already you're helping him."

"Stuart, I *want* to help him." She drew in a sharp breath. "I know you say his feelings for me are real, but can I really believe they're true when he's being influenced by a dead man who just so happens to have been my husband? It sounds so crazy, but I have to assume it's the truth and go from there."

"If my Grand-mai was alive, I would have had an answer along time ago, but no one else in my family took up the old ways and well..."

"Still, there has to be someone here that could—."

"No way," Stuart interrupted vehemently. "Kane can't risk people finding out about it. You've lived here most of your life, so you know how they feel about mental illness and that is exactly what they will call it, especially if they find out his mother was a suicide." Leaning his weight against his parked car, Charlene listened quietly to Stuart's narrative, taking in as much about Kane's life as she could. "Being from a family where a mother kills herself is a curse on a kid. A so called "good" family wouldn't accept him as a son-in-law, because of the view that any family member who takes their own life may pass that mental defect to their children."

"Yeah, I know." Charlene's mouth formed a grim line. "I swear I wore the mark of Jason's suicide on my forehead for years the way people avoided me, especially when it came to doing business. It was like I pushed him off the

J-Pop Love Song

building myself. If it hadn't been for Abe Goda, I don't know if I could have ever started over again."

"Goda seems to be a good friend to you." Stuart said.

"The best. I'll always be grateful to him for going against some of the powers that be in Japan. It's allowed me the opportunity to spread my creative wings here and I know it shouldn't be important to me, but it is because I grew up in this country and it's a part of me as much as America is. Just because you aren't of pure Japanese blood, they don't seem to understand how you could love their country as much as they do." Charlene clasped her hands together in front of her. Deep in thought she looked at Stuart and asked bluntly, "I ruined everything for Kane, haven't I?"

"He was counting on being able to leave this situation in two months. Being in control of his future is important to him as is exploring his growing feelings for you."

"Feelings he's having because of Jason."

"Charlene, I'm sure there are *some influences* at work because of the dreams, but if you want my personal assessment—"

"I do."

"The try this on for size. I honestly believe Kane does care for you, and it has *nothing* to do with Jason. He'll probably kill me for telling you this, but he was like an excited thirteen year old getting his first love note from the cute girl at school." Stuart chuckled looking at her. "When he turned on his laptop and saw that he had an email from you every night, no matter what he was in the middle of he wanted to do nothing else but call you…"

"He can be so reckless." Charlene grinned at Stuart. "There was this one time he called between clothing changes during one of his shows. He was changing and trying to speak at the same time." She laughed quietly. "He was talking so fast in Japanese, I said yes to whatever he was asking just to get him off the phone before he pissed off his fans."

"Did you ever find out what you were saying, "yes" to?" Stuart asked.

"Sure I did, after my phone rang at four in the morning." She rolled her eyes. "I apparently agreed to him calling me at any time, day or night. After that it became a pattern with us talking until one of us or both fell asleep. Oddly enough I began to rely on those calls." Charlene blushed having admitted that.

"So, are you still willing to write Kane's feelings for you off as something completely supernatural?" Stuart lifted an inquiring eyebrow.

Charlene was the first to look away, fully understanding the question, but she wasn't sure of her answer. True, blaming it on a ghost would cause her problems go away, and she wouldn't have to deal with her own feelings.

"I hear what you're saying, and I swear if I didn't know about the dreams then I could believe his feelings for me are real, but I just don't know," she replied honestly. "It's bad enough I allowed Takusa to screw with my mind to get me to do what he wanted."

"He's had more years of practice, so don't blame yourself." Stuart touched her shoulder and smiled warmly. "Just watch your back around him. He doesn't have your best interests at heart, trust me."

"I wished you had warned me earlier. Now I'm feeling responsible for

Kane's current state. I feel I need to make this up to him but I just don't know how to go about it, and if I give in it could ruin both are careers." She met Stuart's eyes and asked, "You have any suggestions?"

"How about you take it one day at a time, starting with getting through tonight. You know when it comes to you, Kane is determined to have his way, and I can't blame him. The more I get to know about you, the more there is to like. I admit at first I had my doubts, considering that you had agreed to conspire with Takusa. I figured your personal greed was enough motivation."

"And now?"

"Now, my instincts are telling me you're the real thing and if Kane is to break the hold Takusa has over him and his career, you're the one to help him do it."

His statement didn't surprise Charlene; Kane probably was thinking the same thing. The question was could she help Kane in some way or would she cause him more grief?

She leaned her hip against the car next to Stuart's tall form and crossed her arms over her breast against the night's chill. "Tell me more about these "night terrors" you mentioned."

Stuart nodded. "They were pretty bad in the beginning. I even had to accompany him to that school in England, to ensure his safety, of course. We never knew when he would sleepwalk his way up to the rooftop of whatever building we were in. I used to have to sleep in one bed and him in the other with our ankles tied together so I would know when he got out of the bed."

"My God," she breathed. "It's that serious?"

"The only good thing about being away from Takusa's watchful eye was that we found someone who was able to help him find out what was happening to him through hypnotherapy. That's when we found out Kane was being haunted by Jason James."

"Couldn't we go back to this person and find out why he chose Kane? I would like both of them to find some form of peace."

"I don't know it that would work or not. My Louisiana Bayou Grand-mother would tell me about these "keys", one that opens the door to the other side and one that closes it. I don't know how the door opened for your husband to reach out to Kane, but I believe *you* are the key to closing it."

"The first question that we need a resolution for, is why Kane? I suppose once we solve that riddle everything else may fall into its proper place. I figured if it was just about me and my happiness, why would he select such a younger man that I may not have granted the time of the day if it hadn't been for the circumstances. Wouldn't Abe have been the best choice?" Charlene reasoned. "He's already a significant part of my life and in my age range."

"I never thought about it that way." Stuart pursed his lips in deep thought. "That would make more sense."

"For some reason, Jason brought me and Kane together because there could be someone associated with Kane that we were meant to discover. So far there is you and Takusa-san." Her eyes grew dark. "Maybe we all have a significant roll to play in this mystery.

"Jason could have also chose Kane because he was trying to get you back to Tokyo, whereas Abe was in America with you." Stuart deduced.

J-Pop Love Song

"That returns us to nowhere fast." Charlene rolled her eyes and cursed. "What do you know about Kane's father turning him over to Takusa at such an early age?"

"When he took over Kane's rearing, and trust me the kid needed it, at the time." Stuart shook his head with a grim expression. "I had been a bouncer and played in a local band at the time when I heard Takusa Entertainment Group was reviewing personal security to watch out for this thirteen year old kid. Obviously, the direction Kane was taking would have only landed him in the *Yakuza* or dead," he explained.

"*Yakuza?*" Her voice became shrilled. "The Japanese Mafia? Why?" Charlene grasped and tugged unconsciously at Stuart's old military jacket sleeve. "I got the impression Kane came from a wealthy and influential family."

"He does, but he's bitter about his mother's death and for reasons I don't know why, blames his father for it. The day of her funeral, he ran away from home the first time. The first few times his father would have him brought back, but nothing helped. Kane started hanging with the wrong crowd, doing all kinds of reckless shit."

Charlene saw Stuart hesitate as if he was deciding exactly what else to tell her. She realized as he continued telling her about Kane's life, he'd left out exactly what *reckless shit* Kane had done. She truly admired his loyalty to his friend, it said much about his character as a man.

"Kane just didn't care about anything anymore. He survived out of playing a guitar on the streets and in the subway for change. Takusa considered Kane too talented to go out like that, and he knew his family. So he paid a formal visit to his father and had Kane signed over to his care, of course Kane's father had no problem doing so."

"What kind of man would just give his kid away like that?"

"Never met him and don't care to." Stuart moistened his bottom lip, adding, "Takusa is a shrewd bastard but the man is the best at what he does, and for that I admire him. He gave up working for the talent agency he belonged to, and somehow came up with the cash flow to open his on business."

"He probably blackmailed someone," Charlene said snidely.

"Probably." Stuart chuckled. "Still you have to give him credit, he knows a good thing when he sees it. Kane became successful, more investors got on board and Takusa is now a leader in the entertainment industry with over two hundred entertainers on his payroll, however Kane has always been Takusa's personal pet project, and he's grooming him to some day own the empire he's built."

"Stuff he built off of Kane's back." Charlene murmured.

"Basically."

"I don't know why Takusa-san sees me as a threat, because I didn't come to Japan with the intent of stealing Kane away from him." Charlene replied crossing her arms over her breast.

"Hmm...let me see, Charlene," Stuart grinned down at her, his bright white smile illuminated in the soft lighting of the parking garage. "I suppose, the fact that Kane respects your opinion, and is most probable in love with you; that in itself is something for him to worry about. On top of that, you're the widow of a well-loved Japanese rock musician who continues to this day to hold all the copyrights to his music. You're a shrewd known player in the American music business, with a kick-ass Japanese manager-slash-attorney to back you up."

He nodded his head in approval and forged ahead singing her praises. "You're a sistha with nice enough portfolios to play at being a music mogul if you wished it, and talented enough to write songs in two languages that would be hits in both Japan and the United States. Hell yeah, I would say you could be imposing to someone who's had to do some shady business to get where he's at."

For some reason hearing Stuart sum her life up in a nutshell even impressed the hell out of her. He was right; Takusa should be worried, especially now that she was developing heartfelt feelings for Kane. Was she truly prepared to play against the big boys again? It has been awhile since she had to bother. Her life as a romance writer and composer was a private one. If she were to get involved with Kane she would be giving up the last of her solitude, for in order for both their careers to be successful she was going to have to put her ass on the line. Was she willing to go that far, even for him?

"Stuart, I think I should contract you on my publicity staff," she made light of her accomplishments. She did have much to be thankful for, and lived more then comfortably. So, why was she trying to hold on to her money and career with both hands? Without love in her life it didn't seem to mean as much to her as it did written on paper for others who cared about such things. She had been so driven by grief and loneliness that she never worked non-stop for wealth, but it came with her determination to work until she could forget the past. With all that God had blessed her with in this life she should be happy, but she wasn't.

Stuart released a long and noisy grunt before she noticed him staring intently at her face. He gave her a knowing smile. "Charlene, you're a woman a man can be proud having in his life, don't let Takusa, or anyone else make you feel because of your age you're not good enough for Kane. If you want him, go for it, and damn all else to hell, but just watch your back. You have always been the one hitch in Takusa's plans since Kane's first admitted wet dream about you," he finished teasingly.

Charlene looked away she could feel her face, ears, and neck burning. "Stop." She laughingly socked him in his muscular leather clad shoulder; he probably didn't feel a thing. "Stuart, I there so many things I want to ask you about Kane, but I suppose it is getting late and you probably have something else you could be doing," she reminded, knowing Kane was probably thinking she wasn't coming. Why was she worried about disappointing him, for all he knew, she wasn't coming.

"Charlene, I'm getting paid very well by the hour, so don't worry about me." He winked at her. "I know what Kane is hoping to accomplish tonight, but before you make a decision I want you to go in knowing as much as possible. It's only right that you have all the facts."

"I agree. Maybe if I knew more, I wouldn't be so back and forth on what I should do. Of course Kane deserves an honest explanation as to why I felt the need to go along with Takusa's plans, but most of all we need to come to some understanding before tonight is out. I don't know when we will have another opportunity such as this one." She tucked stray braids behind her ear in a nervous movement. "I can't continue doing business under this kind of pressure; it seems everywhere I turn I'm receiving one ultimatum or another. It makes me do irrational things, like listening to Takusa-san."

"Kane knows this party is in your honor and that there is a chance you would be very late. He's determined to wait, so don't worry. This has been the best opportunity to fill you in about Kane. That way, you can make up your own mind."

"I appreciate any support you can offer me, Stu." She reached out and briefly squeezed his hand.

A pause lingered between them as two young and pretty Asian women walked by, openly admiring Stuart. Stuart seemed oblivious to the come-hither stares as he gave her his full attention.

"Charlene, Kane doesn't have a personal life. He's constantly in the entertainer mode. I don't even know if he knows who he really is without out all the media frenzy. Since you've come into his life, he's been a different person...happier and actually trying to focus on writing music again," Stu told her, a thoughtful frown etching his forehead. "I have to admit Takusa was right about one thing, if he could bring you two together you probably could help Kane get his muse back. The one thing he hadn't anticipated are the genuine feelings Kane has for you. He figured once he saw you in person and saw that you weren't a young woman..." he trailed off obviously uncomfortable relaying what Takusa had thought about her.

Charlene could well imagine what that ass thought. She smiled at him hoping to ease his discomfort so that he would feel free to continue being as honest as he has been from the beginning.

"Well I'm sure he saw your arrival at the airport on the news, but I guarantee you the only reason he showed up on your doorstep was to make sure your looks weren't all makeup and mirrors. I would like to have been a fly on the wall when he got a real good look at you, sweetheart." Stuart released a husky laugh. "I bet you a million dollars he didn't decide to play on your sympathy until he saw that Kane didn't find your age a turn-off."

"Takusa wanted me to believe that Kane was willing to do anything for the part of Blu, but you're telling me that he could have prevented Kane and me from ever meeting if he thought there would be problems. So he used his influence with the Japanese investors so that I *would* come here, spend time with Kane, and then somehow break his heart so that he would hate me for the rest of his life and turn more to Takusa." The deviousness of Takusa made her shake in frustration. "And I almost fell for it."

"You nailed it on the head." Stuart stated. "Even though the big announcement has been made, it wouldn't surprise me that once Takusa realizes his plans completely failed, he'll have the same investors to withdraw the offer. They have up to ninety days to do so from what I understand."

Charlene dropped her hands by her side. "Would he really be that ruthless? This is a huge opportunity for Kane, even he should be smart enough to realize that."

"He'll do that and more if it means keeping you two away from each other." Stuart's face was hard. "Kane is his prized possession."

"But wouldn't that free Kane up from Takusa if the producers drop him?"

Stuart shook his head. "Takusa always has a backup plan so it's smart to have one of your own when dealing with him. Kane signed those contracts at the conference. Even if the movie deal fails for some reason or the other, Kane will still be legally obligated to Takusa Management Group for another two years."

"What if he breaks the contract?"

"Kane will forfeit seventy-five percent of his gross for the next two years no matter who he chooses to work for. Also, an additional forty percent of his current holdings, which is twenty percent for each year while in default of the contract. If for some reason Kane doesn't marry one of Takusa's daughters, he will have to sign back over the current fifteen shares of stock he has in Takusa Management."

"What in the hell kind of lawyer did he have, to get him such a bad fuckin' deal?" she asked angrily.

"Takusa's lawyers," Stuart voiced in disgust. "Of course."

She laughed bitterly. "That damned old bastard has it all wrapped up in a pretty bow, and I helped him. I asked Kane to sign the agreements."

"Yup."

"You should have warned me," she accused, the burden of what she had done weighing heavily on her heart.

"Yeah, I would have if I had known the facts, but I didn't until I read the damn thing until today."

"Did Kane know what he was signing?" she asked softly.

"He wouldn't acknowledge it, but I imagine he knows Takusa well enough to have suspected he would pull the same thing on him, he's done numerous times before to other artists that have tried to break out on their own. Of course, he hit up Kane harder than most."

Frantically, Charlene searched her thoughts for some kind of way of rectifying her mistake. "I'll speak to Takusa-san and tell him that I will leave here, have no further contact with Kane if he will release him from his current contract."

"I can't let you do that. Kane *needs you*, Charlene, besides, this entire farce Takusa had in getting you two together has been to keep that kid under his thumb for two more years or make him pay out of the ass. He's not about to have a soft heart now. As far as you're concerned, he thinks he's already knocked out two birds with one stone. If he doesn't contact the investors to take back the offer, Kane must appear available to his fans and romantically uninvolved for the duration of filming. He assumes your contract will limit you from being reckless by hooking up with Kane."

"He shouldn't make assumptions on how much this project means to me," she said bitterly.

"It means everything to you, doesn't it?" Stuart asked bluntly.

Did it? She wondered. Just yesterday, it was everything to her, but now she wasn't sure it was worth the misery of another person. Especially a sweet and too trusting person like Kane.

Deciding not to answer his question she said instead, "I'm the last thing Kane needs. Look how I've already unwittingly altered the course of his life. The best thing is to distance myself by returning home as soon as possible."

J-Pop Love Song

"Charlene…"

"It's getting chilly, can we finish this in the car?" She interrupted.

He unlocked the door of the sleek black automobile and held the door open for her. She slid in and the door closed. Charlene's mind was whirling in turmoil of all that she had learned so far. She wondered if it would be best to digest this information before gathering more. Then again, what if she didn't have another opportunity to speak with Stuart. She needed to know as much as she could in order to stay ahead of Takusa.

In the car Stuart turned toward Charlene, a scowl on his face. "If you let that old man have his way and send you running home with your tail between your legs, then everything stops right here with me." Stuart gritted out.

She remained silent, surprised by his sudden angry. She was just speaking the truth. Kane could come out ahead in the end career wise. "Stuart—"

"Tell me now, Charlene, are you one of those women that need to be in control of every aspect of your life and those around you? So when you hit a bit of hard times you run to the hills and leave chaos behind to work itself out?" Stuart asked sarcastically. "I would have thought you were a fighter, considering your old man." Stuart cut her a side-glance before staring straight ahead, his hands tightening on the steering wheel.

Charlene halted. "What the hell is that suppose to mean?"

Stuart sighed. "About seventeen years ago I had the chance to do a six city gig with your man, Jason James, as a stand-in for his original drummer." Stuart confessed.

"You knew Jason?" Her eyes widened in surprise, her shaking hands slid the seatbelt into place and the click sounded loud in the current tense silence of the car.

"It was before he went to the States and married you. I knew that you were writing his music back then. I also knew you were high school sweethearts." He showed a half grin. "He talked about you all the time. How smart you were, how talented and strong you were, you were the love of his life, he would say. Look, I know Jason may have screwed around on you during the duration of your relationship, but I hope you know he loved only you."

Charlene's eyes blurred for a moment and her lips compressed into a strait line as she bit back the tears and nodded. "I knew, that's why I put up with it and a lot more then I would have with anyone else. He was everything too me, my first love."

"After he relocated to the states I reenlisted and had a good run playing for the military band, serving my country and doing what I loved to do wasn't a bad trade. That was until I crushed my left hand in a training drill and received and honorary discharge. I couldn't play anymore, but I love the business, so I became a bodyguard. I remembered the first time I heard Kane refer to the woman in his dreams as *Charlie-chan*, I new the kid's dreams were real, because I remember Jason called you that all the time. I asked Kane if he had ever met Jason James. I know he was a kid, but they both he was starting out in the business doing backup dancing for other groups at the time. So it was possible, but he hadn't. Slowly all this crazy stuff started to unfold. Kane was able to tell me some shit that only J.J. could have known. Jason and I were the only ones at that shanty in

Taiwan, we—"

He caught himself, cleared his throat and knowing Jason, she could only imagine what he wasn't saying.

"Anyway, it freaked the hell out of me, but that was when I came a believer. I can't explain it, but in some weird unexplained way we all are connected by Jason." Stuart released a long breath. "It's as if I was meant to watch over Kane because I was the only one that could confirm that he wasn't lying about his dreams, and Kane was meant to someday meet you and you were meant to return to Japan."

"You're telling me this, why?"

"Because I don't know what part Takusa is suppose to play in all of this and I don't know why J. J. wanted you here to be with Kane. But I do know you have to stick around until we can figure it our. You owe Kane that much."

"I *do not* want to dance this dance again," she said more to herself than to Stuart, but he heard her.

"What dance?"

"After Jason, I swore I would never get serious about another musician. No offense, but you guys make the worse damned relationships."

"None taken," Stuart smiled staring straight ahead as he clicked his seatbelt and started up the engine. "I admit it, some of us may not be faithful, but we are loyal as hell when we choose to send our paycheck to that one woman. As long as you got the money coming, you know you man is still loyal and being with you is the one place he calls home, when he's on the road."

She smiled at his statement. "Do you have that one woman?"

"Yeah," He winked. "My momma."

"Why is it that instead of my attracting a good Momma's boy like you, I attract two men that both lost their mother's at an early age and have abandonment issues?" She shook her head.

"I don't know if I can do this again with Kane," she cursed quietly. "Do you know, if you search the Internet, you probably would find only a couple of pictures with Jason and I together. *I wasn't good for his image,*" she mimicked sarcastically. "One of the deadly sins of Japanese pop culture is the fact that this icon was just another somebody's husband. He stepped in his pants one leg at a time, you know? His agent referred to me as a *walking and talking, fucking career suicide*. However, they never said no to the music I was writing for him and recorded on tape, so he could learn them, because Jason couldn't read sheet music and he played only what he heard." Charlene laughed bitterly.

"That's rough."

"That's fucked!" she said angrily. "I wasn't some groupie. Even when I legally became his wife and his business partner, I didn't get the respect I deserved. What I hated about Jason most was he never stood up for me. He never said anything with they fed the rumor that we were getting a divorce, any other lie they made up about why he remained with me. Every day I wondered if that would be the day, Jason would be a man and fight for our love so that we could be together in and out of public."

A tear slid down her cheek and she wiped it away with the back of her hand. She wasn't crying because the memory was a sad one, she was crying because

J-Pop Love Song

after all these years, she was still hurt and angry that he had disappointed her. Not even writing *Blu's Diary* didn't seem to be enough to purge this anger. If it weren't enough, when would it ever be?

"If you don't mind my asking, what happened the night J. J. died?" Stuart inquired.

If she hadn't been enclosed in the darkness of the car with only the flashing overhead lights glaring by as they drove past, Charlene didn't know if she could have told him.

"The night Jason died we got into a big argument, or I should say *another argument*, he had been acting weird for weeks and he swore he wasn't back into the drugs, so I had no idea what was going on with him. I had just got my first television project at the station I worked for, mine alone to write and produced."

She smiled sadly at the bittersweet memory. "For once, it wasn't about him and his career, it was about me. Unlike the many times, he won awards and I was told not to be there, I wanted *him* by my side to celebrate with my coworkers and me. He told me he had a meeting and he couldn't make it. He went downstairs to the hotel lounge and got drunk, came back and tried to seduce me into staying at the hotel suite with him. It pissed me off, that he didn't have a meeting. Jason just didn't want to go with me."

"Are you saying what I think you're saying?" Stuart asked, keeping his eyes on the rode.

"I started wondering how many of the other gigs and ceremonies in his honor that I had missed had been because of Jason and not his managers? For the first time it dawned on me that he was ashamed to be seen with me in public. I felt like I would die, it broke my heart so."

"With Kane being interested in you, do you feel that some day you might find yourself in the same position, hiding from the public, keeping secrets, and telling lies?"

"Look at me," she cried. "I'm on my way to see Kane in secret," she frowned looking out of the car window as the night scenery sped by. "After what you and I have already talked about tonight, you think it's going to be different? I swore when I'm ready to love again it would be different."

He released a long sigh before saying, "I'm sorry Charlene. I had no right to lay a guilt trip on you about Kane."

"I would have understood if Kane hadn't signed those contracts. I just couldn't be the one to tell him not to do it because that was the sign he was looking for that I wanted us to be together and I don't, Stuart." she explained.

"Charlene, you really believe that or are you trying to sale yourself a bill of bullshit? I don't usually say much, about anything, but I see a lot, and what I see is some major chemistry between you and Kane."

"But—"

"Look, this is the last thing I will say about your business." He cut her off. "Just ask your self this question and be honest. If Kane wasn't Kane, but some Joe on the block who was the same age as you are and not in the music business would you be interested?"

She decided the question didn't warrant an answer but an inner reflection of her own to consider. What is the answer? She was in conflict from doing what was best for her emotional survival and doing what her heart told her she wanted to do. Maybe that was the problem, it had been so long since she'd been with anyone sexually and even though Kane hadn't said, it probably has been awhile for him too. Maybe once they got past the physical desire that kept things tense between them, the curiosity of each other would be gone. Would they be able to move ahead and work together if she slept with him this one night and purge him from her system?

Stuart wheeled the vehicle into a deserted office center parking lot, Charlene easily made out Kane as the headlights shined on his lone darkly clad figure. He had changed into casual attire consisting of a black bomber jacket, faded jeans cut and raveled at the knees, a plain black t-shirt tucked neatly in the low-riding waistline, finished off with a silver buckled belt and silver pointed toed boots sparkled in the oncoming headlights. As usual her body and heart reacted instantly, and she felt breathless.

Stuart cut the lights and he eased to where Kane was leaning against an impressive motorcycle, his booted feet crossed at the ankle, she continued admiring him as he pushed himself off the seat and leisurely came towards the car at it halted.

Her door opened and a beaming Kane gazed at her. "*Aitakatta*, I was lonely without you. Do you have your dancing shoes on?"

"About that—" she began.

"Awe," Kane interrupted. "Please, don't tell me I waited out here this long just for you to tell me you're not going to hang with me."

"No…but, do you mind if we go somewhere quiet. I rather we spend this time alone," Charlene stated.

Kane squatted inside the open car door reaching out to caress her hair behind her ear. His fingertips grazed her cheek and ear. She could feel the sexual magnetism that made him so self-confident. She saw the heart-rending tenderness of his gaze, her heart turned over in response, moisture pooled between her thighs, and her body ached for his touch.

She noted Kane glance at Stuart with a questioning gaze. Stuart shrugged his broad shoulders, his face neutral and void of any clue of the serious conversation they had on the way here.

"Do you want to take the car and I take your bike home?" Stuart asked.

"This is Charlene's night, so whatever she wants," Kane conceded.

"Well we can't talk on a motorcycle, but I'm okay with it as long as we can go somewhere private where we can." She said leaving the choice to Kane.

He took her hand and held it as she unfolded herself out of the automobile. "We will ride the bike. Stuart—"

"Here" Stuart called out. "Take the keys, you probably left you set on your car key ring."

"If we use your place, where will you be?" Kane lifted his eyebrows in question.

"A phone call away." Stuart ginned. "Call me when you're ready to go back to the hotel, Charlene. Kane, make sure you don't answer my home phone. If Mr. Takusa calls to check up on you, I prefer that he call me on my cell. You are the worst liar, so I don't want you to speak to him at all."

"What will you tell him?" Kane asked.

"You celebrated too much over and passed out drunk. "You're in the guest room and not to worry, no cameras were around while I was carrying your ass inside." Stuart laughingly said. "That'll be all he wants to hear anyway."

"I will be calling you in about a couple of hours," Charlene piped in.

"We'll see you in the morning as planned," Kane said in a calm, expressionless voice and slammed the car door leading her away from the car.

Charlene halted and turned back toward the car. "Make that one hour!" She lifted a forefinger in emphasis. "You're being a bit high-handed aren't you?" She turned her hard gaze on Kane.

"You say that as if it's the first time and don't count on returning to the hotel tonight," Kane murmured. "You're mine now." He closed the car door and stalked towards her intertwining her fingers with his, he tugged her towards the motorbike.

"What's that suppose to mean?" she asked, her voice growing shrilled.

"Give me this." He took her purse and stuffed it into the black studded saddlebag across the back of the bike.

Instead of telling her to move aside, Kane brushed his hard lean body against hers, reaching over to the other side of the saddlebag to remove a black all-weathered jacket.

"Here, put this on and use this helmet."

She sighed and jerked on the black wind-jacket, mumbling under her breath and if he cared about what she had to say, he wasn't letting on. He straddled the bike. Charlene zipped up the jacket and stood there wondering how she was going to hoist her 5'5" bottom-heavy frame over the back of the bike with him sitting on it, without embarrassing herself completely.

Kane noted her hesitation. "Need help, *chibi?*" He grinned at her. "Here, you can use my foot and grab my shoulders to hoist yourself over."

"First, don't call me *shorty*," Charlene balked. "No way am I going to put my foot on top of yours. I'm too heavy for that, I'd break your foot."

"Don't be silly," Kane chuckled. "I'm sturdier than I look and I can bench press more than you. Come on"

"Nope," she protested. "How about you get off and I'll straddle the lowest point of the motorcycle and scoot back on the seat?"

Kane shook his head and with a purposeful look on his face, he kicked back down the stand and slid off the bike. Before Charlene could voice another objection, he had his hands on her waist and hoisted her onto the seat. The helmet she was to use clattered on the ground and she cried out clutching his shoulders to keep her balance. Her jean-covered knees fell wide to accommodate his lean hips as he stood still between her legs.

Suddenly her whole being pulsated with waiting; his longing gaze bore into her eyes and she saw the heated passion burning in their dark debts. Something intense flared through their entrancement. There was a tingling in the pit of her stomach she couldn't remember the last time her feminine core throbbed with desire.

Charlene didn't question what she was about to do she just went with her feelings. Her legs came up and wrapped about his hips, she locked her ankles in the small of his back leaning forward until she was pressing her breast against his chest. Charlene wrapped her arms around his neck enjoying the feel of his breath, warm and moist against her face. Her heart raced. There was no turning back now.

She was kissing him with long denied desires. She had her eyes shut, breathing in his scent. His hand moved with precision between them to the snap at the top of her jeans. She felt it give way and moaned against his mouth.

He tasted wonderful. One kiss wasn't enough. Excited to get closer her fingers buried deep in the luxury of his hair, as he became the aggressor of the kiss and plundered her mouth.

Somewhere in her crazed passion filled brain and ringing ears, Charlene heard the passing sound of a motor and the blaring of a horn it wasn't close, but close enough to bring her to her senses. It was bad enough she wanted him so badly she felt sick with yearning, she was also stupid enough to want him to take here right here in the open where anyone could pass by, including someone with a camera phone that had no clue of the goldmine they would have scored with this picture.

It didn't matter if it was dark; it wasn't dark enough to be fucking on top of a motorcycle in the parking lot of an office complex. What if there was a cleaning crew in the building looking down on them right now?

She broke the kiss and halted his hand easing down her zipper. "No, no, no," she kept saying. "Kane, stop, we can't do this here." She heard Kane curse softly as he broke away, panting as hard as she was. Only he seemed unable to draw in a deep breath until he started to speak.

"*Suminasen,* I'm sorry, Charlie-chan, but please tell me we can keep kissing somewhere else. I want you so bad I feel as if my heart is going to explode, amongst other things." He groaned in frustration his jaw clinched tightly.

"I don't know what you're doing to me Kane; I used to have some common sense until I met you. Now all I can do is think about how much I want to be with you." She reached down and refastened her pants. "What's wrong with me?"

"Charlie-chan, let me do the thinking for a change." Kane said his frustration making him sound angry. "I'm clear about what I want."

"Kane…"

"*Aishiteru!*" he swore. "I want you. I want to wake up beside you and I want to stand on the stage at Budokkan singing love songs with everyone in the world knowing those words are meant for only you."

"Kane, don't say things like that. You—"

Don't tell me what I can and cannot do." He pulled back putting space between them, running fingers through his hair, looking for something to do with his hands besides grab Charlene and kiss her until she couldn't breathe. "I may be younger than you, but stop treating me like a child. Okay, I get it, you don't know if you can reciprocate my feelings, but after that kiss I know you at least find me sexually attractive. If that's all you have to give to me for now, I'll take it."

If that is all I have to give you, *period,* will it be enough?" She couldn't take her eyes off his face. The look in his eyes as he moved closer nearly broke her resolve.

I'll accept things for now, but don't think I'm not going to change your mind." His passionate self-assurance made her want to believe everything he said.

♪

"God, you're driving me crazy," she growled and chuckled at the same time. Tears welled up in her eyes. Lovingly she cupped his ears and tilted his head down until his forehead rested against hers, his sweet breath blowing hot against her face. "Don't allow me to break you heart, Kane."

"Do you want to break my heart?"

"No," she sighed. "But loving and trusting another man after Jason scares the hell out of me. I'm too old to go through changes and I definitely swore off musicians for the rest of my life."

He grinned ruefully. "It scares the hell out of me too. I've never been in love before; you're the only woman I've wanted more then my music. I always thought if we could get the chance to know each other, what brought us together and our age difference wouldn't matter."

Now that you've met me do you still believe that?"

"*Hai,* yes, especially now that I've come to know you love marshmallow cereal as much as I do," he teased lifting his head to place a kiss to her brow. He rested his chin on top of her had while she buried her face against the side of his neck and breathe in the essence of his masculine scent.

"Charlie-chan, we both need time because of our circumstances and I know learning about my dreams is adding confusion to whether you can believe me when I tell you how I feel, but those are *my* feelings." She felt bereft as he pulled back dropping his hands to his side. "At least let's enjoy tonight as if we were in love. Let me see if it feels as wonderful as I've imagined it."

Quietly Charlene closed her eyes, listening to her inner voices. What did she want? *Him,* they shouted and they weren't budging. With her mind made up Charlene opened her eyes and eased around on the seat until she straddled the bike. Clearing the tightness in her throat, she stole a look at Kane and saw his back towards her. Something powerful in his stance, something Takusa probably didn't know exist made her realize she'd made the right decision. Kane wasn't giving up. Kane-sama, if we don't get going, we won't have enough time to enjoy what's left of this night…together." Her voice was husky, teasing. "You don't leave a girl waiting."

He turned to face her, a seductive smile on the face that fueled a thousand adolescent girl fantasies.

She accepted the helmet he retrieved from the ground and slipped it on, but not before he stole her breath with another kiss.

Without another word between them, he mounted the bike and she slipped her arms securely around his slender waist, and locked her fingers together across his hard abdomen. Charlene leaned her breast against his back and pressed her face into his leather-clad shoulder. Tonight she would follow Kane into heaven or hell depending on which dream came to claim him, but this time she would be his dream catcher.

She wouldn't allow Jason James to destroy another life.

Chapter Nine

CHARLENE FELT EMOTIONALLY AND physically exhausted as she dropped down on the overstuffed floor pillows close to a couple of a small low tea tables. She did a quick once over of the apartment Stuart allowed them to borrow upon entering. She did notice it was quaint and sparse in all but the necessities as if he really didn't care about making it into a home. It was also very clean, and she assumed he had a cleaning service since, like Kane, he must spend a lot of time on the road. She wondered what was Kane's place was like? Would she ever get the chance to see it or did Takusa have claim on that too? She really was beginning to hate that old man.

She looked up at the object of her thoughts as he quietly padded on socked feet across the tatami matted floor. Upon their arrival, they left their shoes in the tiled *genkan*, entryway, turning the toe of their shoes to face the door, as was customary for those who were visiting.

"I made us some warmed tea." Kane offered and handed her the cup in which she nestled between her cold fingers. The ride on the bike in the night air had left her body warm but her fingers chilled. "Stu-san only comes here on his days off," Kane said, confirming her thoughts. "It's not stocked with anything perishable but there is plenty of prepackage ramen noodles if you get hungry." There was something very intimate about walking around in socks and sharing a beverage while lounging on the floor. She knew the custom was done to protect the delicate mats since they were often used as bedding. This was one of many things about being in Japan with the juxtaposition of the old, genteel ways and new customs that made her feel as if she'd never left.

"*Arigato*, there is no way I can eat anymore tonight." She smiled and patted her stomach. "This is a nice place, but pretty small for a big guy like Stuart."

"He spends more time at my place than he does here. It's more convenient with my crazy schedule, but the room's not much bigger." Kane chuckled. "I guess after being in the military and traveling by tour bus all those years, cramped spaces aren't that hard on him."

"So Takusa doesn't mind Stuart living with you?"

"Takusa-san thinks Stuart's spying on me for him, so no, he doesn't mind." Kane's conspiratorial gleam was infectious. "The apartment complex is owned by Takusa-san's corporation. It's kind of like a dormitory. All the male artists under his management group live in one apartment unit and the female artists live in the other."

"So he treats all of his entertainers like he treats you?"

Kane sat with graceful ease on the pillows beside her without even spilling his tea, and easily crossing his long legs in front of him. "Being the first and one of the oldest, he expects more from me, but he is strict on all of us. Our reputations, as well as our careers, are dependent upon keeping up the wholesome and positive image of good role models."

He took another deep swig of tea.

"So, no Britneys or Lindsays huh? In theory it makes sense, but it seems a bit extreme to me," Charlene said, imagining all the young starlets in America having to live under those rules. "But what happens once you reach the age of consent?"

"I believe there is a certain responsibility we owe to the fans." Kane continued thoughtfully. "We as entertainers have a lot of power and when we do stupid things like underage drinking or getting into altercations in public, the fans see that and think you condone it." He ran an idle hand through his hair, something Charlene noticed he did often when in thought. "I have to be honest and say that it's hard to not just want to be a normal guy and raise a little hell every now and then, but it's a fair trade considering that I get the live the dream of millions."

"You never cease to amaze me," Charlene murmured and sipped her tea to hide the stupid grin that somehow emerged on her face. She was even more surprised when she blurted out, "Your pedestal is getting pretty high in my book too."

"And as much as I would like you to adore and drool all over me, literally," Kane winked as she mock-threatened to toss her tea in his direction. "I'm just a man with the same hopes for love and happiness as any other man."

"I never really thought about success that way," Charlene stated thoughtfully. "I never occurred to me how many of my books or songs affected others. It's always been about the need to purge myself of all these emotions that can be overwhelming at times." Her eyes caught his. "Looking at our lives in comparison, I feel as if I've become very selfish in my drive to succeed and have forgotten how much I love doing what I do. Like you, I'm living the dreams of millions with my words."

"Think about the impact Jason James' death had on his fans? How many of them emulated him by committing suicide?" Kane's voice was bitter, and with good reason. "He never once stopped to think about his fans…or you."

Charlene shivered at the memory and swallowed more tea enjoying the warmth of Kane's closeness. "I have spent every day of my life since then trying *not* to think about it," she replied, idly toying with a braid. Kane's habit was beginning to rub off on her. "What I *do* think about, is how sad our society really is when we have turn to celebrities for validation. Kids should see that the real heroes are their hardworking parents who make it possible for them to buy those CD's, movie and concert tickets."

"I agree, but I can also understand if they don't." Kane said softly. "Not everyone has a parent or parents that are heroes. I loved my mother but she was weak and I wished to be *nothing* like my father."

"Would you prefer to be more like Takusa? I mean, aren't you being groomed to marry into his family and take over his empire? Isn't he trying to mold you into what he is, a manipulative bastard who only cares about the bottom line and not human emotions?"

Kane slammed the empty cup on the floor beside him causing Charlene to jump back startled more by the force of the movement than from the noise. She was thankful for the soft matting or it might have shattered to pieces from the impact.

"I see that Takusa has told you *his* mapped-out version of my future." He said between clenched teeth. "Since we are talking about my manager's tendency for manipulation, why don't you tell me what buttons of yours did he push?" Charlene reeled back guiltily in the force of Kane's anger. "Or maybe you agree with him. Do you think marrying Takusa's daughter is what's best for me and my future?"

With a calmness she somehow mustered, Charlene stretched and placed her cup on the low table beside the pillows and squeezed her hands together in her lap. She took a long indrawn breath. "You have a perfect right to be angry, but see this from my side. When Takusa first told me about your dreams, I just thought it was infatuation. I agreed with the plan because it seemed the best way to keep you from being hurt if you realized I didn't return your feelings."

"However, Charlene, I think you do." Kane's eyes never wavered though his voice was soft.

"Why would you say that?" Her brow puckered in a frown.

"Because I think the truth is, you are afraid. You are afraid of your feelings for me and you're afraid to love again."

"You have no right—"

He forged ahead in spite of the warning glare she gave him. He was a very brave man.

"I believe it is why you haven't bothered to remarry after losing your husband, and why you pretend to not notice Abe Goda-san is in love with you," he queried with a lifted eyebrow as if to push his point.

Charlene blushed like a foolish kid caught in a lie. How in the hell did Kane manage to understand her as well as he did? Was she that transparent, or was he getting all of his insights from beyond the grave? If Jason had a hand in making Kane so intuitive about her she'd resurrect the bastard and then kill him all over again. This put her at a disadvantage.

The worst part was that in spite of everything, Kane was breaking down her resistance little by little.

She bent her head to hide the smile that came to her lips. This entire situation was crazy. Yet, he had a point; she had managed to keep herself busy all these years so she wouldn't have to deal with all those painful emotions. Apparently her peaceful days were over.

"I see you're trying to come up with an answer that will throw me off, but I got your number Charlie-chan, so move on to the second question. Do you think Takusa's daughter could make me happier then you could?"

Damn. It must be an entirely new game in the Japanese dating world these days, because he wasn't holding anything back. "K...Kane, have you ever realized how blunt you are?"

"Have you realized how you ask questions when you don't want to answer them?" He was being difficult but all she could think about was kissing him.

She rolled her eyes at him and said, "Honestly, I believe your marrying Takusa's daughter would be a good move if you're looking to become both successful and powerful in the Japanese music industry."

"*Sokka*, I see," Kane muttered. "Thank you for that *generic* answer. Now, tell me what you *really* think."

Charlene went ballistic. "I *think* you can't be kissing me like a lover one moment and then asking me about another woman the next!"

Uncomfortable silence lingered between them and Charlene forged ahead to cover her vulnerability.

"Look Kane, why do you care how I feel? Only you know what will be best for your future and Mr. Takusa is offering the chance of a lifetime. However, you aren't some witless boy looking for a break in life. You're multi-talented enough to have an excellent future regardless of whom you choose to spend the rest of your life with." Releasing a shaky sigh she added, "I have confidence in you to make the best decisions for your own happiness."

He reached out and intertwined his fingers with hers. "I like who I am when I'm with you, Charlie-chan. Your certainty in me makes me feel as if I can do anything. I just wish you would let me do the same for you."

The deep appreciation in his voice warmed her heart. She looked up from where his lighter hand intertwined with her darker one into eyes so lovingly expressive her pulse raced, her breathing became constricted, and only when it became painful, she realized she was holding her breath. She freed it in a long sigh. The movement of his thumb in the palm of her hand was just a whisper of a caress, yet she could feel it as if he was stoking her between her thighs. As if both zones on her body held some connection between them. So much so, she actually had to bite down on the inside of her bottom lip to keep from moaning.

"Please don't," he begged.

"Don't what?" She asked in confusion.

"Don't pull away from me."

"Did I?"

"You were about to."

"How—"

"My skin is so sensitive against your skin, I could physically feel the slightest movement of your hand in mine. Your survival instinct is to put as much distance between you and me as possible, even though your eyes are telling me running away is the last thing you really want to do. And kisses don't lie."

That very survival instinct was telling her she was crazy to let this go any further, that he was younger than she, and that he was haunted by the specter of her dead husband. None of it mattered; Kane was very much a man, and his deep brown eyes told her he was aware that she was very much a woman, and they were here alone. She knew that he also knew that if he touched her, she would respond to him even if it went against everything her logical brain was telling her she shouldn't do.

"Kane, I don't love you," she blurted out, wondering if that was said for his sake or a mere reminder to herself to not lose her reasoning over one night alone in his company.

"So you keep saying. Now tell me, if that is true, what do you have to lose by allowing me to love you?" He challenged, leaning in closer.

Everything, her mind screamed but her heart said *nothing* because secretly she wanted him to love her, desire her, and put his claim on her. It was this thought that made her and accept Kane's gentle kiss. He smelled so clean and masculine, his breath of minted tea. She wanted to get as close as possible and never let go. She went willingly as he tugged her by the hand until she was lying across his lap. He put his arms around her. His face so close to hers she could see two tiny endearing moles beneath his left eye.

"How can any one man be so beautiful," she whispered pushing the lock of hair back off his brow with her fingers, but it fell again like a hair waterfall. He nuzzled against her hand like a eager puppy.

"Don't be silly, men can't be beautiful," he told her. "You, on the other hand…"

"But you are," she insisted. "There's this unusual innocence in your face that you don't usually see in men your age. I don't know whether to make love to you or cuddle you against my breast and sing you a lullaby."

"Make love to me," he growled, licking his lips. "And you'll find out that I left my boyhood far behind."

She put one hand on either side of his face and lifted her head to touch his lips with hers. She smiled against his mouth as he released a contented sigh of relief, blowing hot air through his nose against her face. Obviously he had feared she would choose to sing to him instead. How could she not kiss him? She wanted him and there was nothing nurturing about her yearnings.

♪

The deepening passion of her kiss was everything Kane could have expected and more. He felt her hands tugging his t-shirt out of the back of his pants and nearly whimpered aloud as her soft fingertips made contact with his heated skin.

He couldn't believe that after all these years of dreaming about her, she was here in his arms wanting him as much as he did her. Yes, she did say she didn't love him, but he was sure she wouldn't be here with him if she didn't feel something. He just hoped that within time, she would realize they were destined to be together.

Things would have been so much easier if Jason James had imposed himself in her dreams too, then she would have been prepared to receive him. Then again, maybe not, because it nearly drove him crazy until he learned to accept the inevitable.

Besides, Charlene was a woman worth fighting for and worth keeping. If it meant going up against his mentor, he would be prepared to do so. But she had to give him something to hold on to. He needed some sign that she was in this for the long haul.

"*Kimi-no-koto zembu shiritai,*" He wanted to know everything about her.

"Shhh, for now, *kisu shite*, kiss me." She laid a warm finger on his lips. "We can talk more later."

"Did I say that aloud?"

She grinned and nuzzled his nose with hers. "Yup," she answered, and he took advantage of her parted lips.

His hands pulled her blouse out of the waist of her jeans, and she sat up and allowed him to pull it over her head. He waited while she did the same with his t-shirt.

Together they positioned the floor cushions comfortably. He held out his hand to her, without hesitation, she placed hers in his, and he guided her until they both were lying down.

Kane explored her face, her neck, her ears, slowly with his lips and mouth. He could feel the intense warmth of her body against his, the soft fleshiness of her thighs against his muscular legs.

His obvious need molded itself into the apex of her legs. He prayed that she wouldn't pick now to develop a conscience and stop him because he didn't know if he could at this point. He only hoped that with his excitement he didn't embarrass himself completely and release before they even got their clothes off. He willed himself to think about something else so that he could slow down the anxious pace his needy libido had set for him.

He released the top snap of her jeans remembering where they stopped earlier. He hesitated only a moment before easing down her zipper releasing a silent prayer of thanksgiving.

"You're shaking," He lifted his head to gaze down at her.

"That's not me, it's you." She lifted her bottom to slide off her pants and kick them aside.

Kane's mouth dropped as he took in her beautiful curvy brown body encased in a pair of the sexiest black lace underwear he'd ever seen. His mouth went dry. Reaching out to touch the slight roundness of her tummy, he saw his hand was trembling. Charlene was right.

"Let me help you out of these." Charlene's throaty voice snapped him out of his reverence of looking at her partially naked flesh. Kane fell back against the cushioned softness lifting his head to watch her fingers deftly undo his belt buckle. There was something very sexy about her slender well-groomed pink polished fingers releasing the buttons of his black jeans. He lifted his hips allowing her to ease them down, and over his feet. Haphazardly she tossed over her shoulders. The head of his erection jutted forth, the hard outline obvious beneath the white briefs. He felt his face growing flushed.

Kane gasped, nearly coming up off the floor as her nails grazed against his cock, a wet spot appeared above its sphere head. He looked up to see if she noticed and she smiled at him playfully, her eyes shimmering bright with mischief. He found her more exquisite and for this moment in time, she was all his, and he wouldn't trade all the success and money in the world for her. Now if he could only keep her. No, he couldn't worry about that now, he just needed to enjoy what she was willing to share with him.

"I can't believe how much you're trembling." Charlene commented kissing his chest. "Are you sure you've done this before?"

"I'm sure. I've just never made love to someone I care about," he confessed truthfully. His dark head fell back with a moan as he felt her hot wet tongue and mouth teasing and suckling his nipples.

She released his small hard nipple with a moist "pop" and murmured, "Mmm, then it's sort of like your first time. I like the thought of being your first."

Was that happiness he heard in her voice? Was she really glad to be here with him? He ran a hand through her loose braids and tugged lightly. She lifted her head to look at him.

She looked at him. "What?" she asked. "You want to stop?"

"God, no," he groaned.

She cocked her head to the side in question, and he didn't speak quickly enough because she asked, "Would you prefer to take the lead? Do you want to touch me?"

"Yes!" He gulped. "I mean, I do…I will…" Kane cursed softly as he stumbled out his words. "What I trying to say is I wanted to look into your eyes, so I could see if you were happy to be here…with me."

Charlene chuckled and rested her chin under her hand on his tight as. "Don't I look happy? That is behind this glazed expression of horniness?"

Kane laughed and relaxed. He realized if they could be intimate and laughing like this, he should be able to tell her what was on his mind. "Charlie-chan, are you here because you want me as much as I want you or is this what one would call "pity sex"?" he asked honestly, knowing he risked throwing ice water on the situation.

It was important to him that Charlene was here tonight for all the tight reasons, not because she feared he may walk away from her movie, or because she assumed one night would make him not want her anymore. *She was wrong; he knew afterwards he would desire her even more, because she would no longer be a dream image.*

"You're looking into my eyes, Kane, what are they telling you?" she asked, her voice barely a husky whisper.

"That you love me more than life, and you plan on marrying me in the future," he grinned his dark eyebrows lifted, joking, *not really*.

"Ouch!" He cried out when she pinched one of his sensitive nipples, he also felt a new rush of heat straight to his penis causing it to move against his stomach. "*Ikkene*, shit!"

"Mmm, even though your mouth don't know when to shut up, I see, I have your body's undivided attention." Charlene winked with a sexy laugh and licked the red spot she pinched. That only made his body react once more, and he was impressed by his own endowments. He'd never known himself to be so big. Maybe he just never looked at it from this angle before, either way, Kane had much to be proud of.

His eyes went back to her face as she continued, "Let me get serious for a moment, or we could waste the entire night on talk. Kane, I'm not a foolish schoolgirl who has no clue about what she's doing or why she's doing it. Seriously, I won't lie to you, I've wanted to make love to you from the first moment I saw you, and it's been awhile since I've had thoughts like that about anyone." She released a loud sigh. "Did I imagine it was a viable possibility? No, because young guys like you, are mere fantasies for someone my age, who finds that even men my age, don't want someone my age, they want, someone younger."

"Abe Goda-san, wants you," he pouted.

She gave him a beautifully disarming smile. He merely stared, tongue-tied on surprise as he waited to hear more of her raw and honest confession.

"Get this strait once and for all, Abe wants me because he's comfortable being around me, like and old shoe. Abe has loved only one woman his entire life, a girl he grew up with, and she was forced to marry someone else to protect her father's company. He was relieved to get the opportunity to relocate to the States with me and start anew." She shook her head. "We talked about marriage once, just because it would be convenient for us both to live our lives the way we wanted and stop all the rumored speculations about us. We love each other and what you see in his eyes is protectiveness because he's had to be. You should have seen me after Jason's death and the scandal, I was a mess and I depended on him for everything. I was too frightened to leave the house for two years."

"I had no idea."

"Of course not, no one did, not even my family. Abe covered for me and I released my first novel, which was *Blu's Diary* during that time, so my family never suspected when they would have to come to my house for Thanksgiving or Christmas dinner it was because I couldn't step out the door without having panic attacks."

"How did you get over it?"

"Abe pissed me off." She laughed.

"Huh?"

"He had the nerve to go off on my ass one day, I don't even remember what it was about," Charlene shook her head and shrugged. "All I know is he ended up calling me a "black bitch" and for some reason that day it went all over me like, wild fire. Next thing I know I was flailing about, all up in his chest, with fists, crying and cursing like a woman possessed. When I came to my senses we were standing out on the back terrace of my home. He had stood there and took my beating, not once did he try to stop me or defend himself. I fell upon my knees, depleted and the sweetest sense of peace swept through me, it was like nothing I ever felt."

"Goda-san had done it intentionally." Kane surmised. Having a new respect for the older man he thought was his competition for Charlene's affection.

She nodded, a half smile on her lips. "I hadn't realized until then how much I hated Jason for being a fucking coward, leaving me to clean up his mess, alone." She looked deeply into his eyes. "So, baby, I wouldn't be here tonight with you if I didn't want you and only you." She openly admitted and it warmed his heart.

"Charlene," Kane murmured. His mouth softly moved upward in a foolish grin.

"Admittedly, I feel some guilt about letting you down at the press conference, but in all fairness, I had no idea what you were up against with Takusa. I wished you had felt you could confide everything to me from the beginning, but I can understand in your situation, you've haven't had many people you can trust." She came further up his body; her breasts pressed against his chest and her lips barely a breath away. "So, yes, for now I'm happy."

Kane lifted his arms and wrapped them about her; his fingers easily released the hooks on her bra. "*Mo ichido itte kureru?* Say it again?"

"Kane, you make me happy," she repeated and said, "If anyone is to be on the receiving end of "pity sex", it's me. It's been a long...long...long..."

She trailed off in a giggle when his hands reached down and cupped the full roundness of her buttocks with both hands and squeezed. He had wanted to give into this need since she walked in front of him up the airplane stairs.

In return she did a little punishing of her own. Charlene pushed her hips into him causing her mons to grind against his erection. They both moaned in unison.

Kane breached the space between them and caressed her lips with his tongue; he nipped at her full bottom lip, Charlene, returned the favor by sucking on his. He tried to go slow at first, to control the incessant beating of arousal strumming through his body. He drew back and panted for breath, if he didn't think about something else for a moment he was going to embarrass himself just like it was his first time. What was wrong with him? He didn't want her to think he was totally oblivious to how to please a woman.

"*Sugoku suki*, I'm so crazy about you, Charlene. You do realize, this is going to be more then sex for me for me, don't you?"

"Yes, I do, so don't tell me, show me," she moaned cupping his face with both hands guiding his lips back to hers. He sighed against her open mouth.

She sighed back.

Heatedly, heatedly, she increased the urgency of the kiss, moving her lips over his with an expertise he found impressive and his penis jumped once...twice...and he knew he was getting close to losing his dignity. Instead he shed his pride and told her exactly what had been on his mind for sometime. Kane realized too late maybe he ought to have waited until after they made love.

"Charlene," he croaked hoarsely. "Please, promise me this won't be the last time we're together. Allow me the opportunity to show you that it's me who loves you, and not some dream phantom manipulating my will."

Her lips went immediately pliant at the side of his throat, and he sighed regretfully as she rolled off of him, with a loud frustrated groan, onto her back beside him.

"Kane, I know you want me to say that there will be more nights like this one, but I can't promise you anymore than what I can give you, at this moment, I'm sorry." She closed her eyes and he could see her biting at the inside of her bottom lip.

He noticed it was something she did when she was frustrated. At the moment it was a feeling he understood well, but he could slowly feel his breathing returning to normal. He really should have masturbated and gained some long needed release before being with her, because his desire for her was more than he anticipated. With these new emotions, he felt as if he was all over the place. She probably thought him too young to be with her, after his behavior tonight. *Dumb..dumb..dumb...*

"I understand, I'm sorry for pushing." He reached out and intertwined her fingers with his and brought the back of her hand to his lips. "*Gomen nasai*, pardon me, for ruining the moment."

"It's not ruined, just delayed, *again*," she reassured him and her lips puckered as she blew out a long sigh. He felt relieved. The heat of her desire for him continued to shine brightly in her smoldering eyes as she turned her head opening her eyes to look at him, and he returned her stare.

"You're not upset?" He asked her.

"Of course not. Tonight was not just about us coming together sexually. I also came here to reach a mutual ground that will be comfortable for the both of us. It's going to make things difficult for us when we start to work together in the studio, if we don't come to some form of understanding. Baby, as a musician, you've already experience what tension and stress can do to you creatively." She paused before adding.

He couldn't argue with that, they did need to put everything out in the open to be considered, and so far he had, at least most of it. There was still something about his past he wanted to tell her, but not yet. He'd already said too much, if he continued down his current path, no matter how understanding she was being he knew she would be ready to bolt out of here in a heartbeat. He had to be patient and respect the fact that she needed more time to accept the changes he would bring to her life.

"Kane, let's start with what your expectations are after tonight." Charlene stated breaking the silence.

Kane released a long-winded breath. He really had blown the mood. What was he asking or expecting of her? Did he want her to give him some insincere promise she had no intentions of keeping? Why was he in such a hurry? He knew why. Now that he had her in his life he was scared some other man, more mature, and more in tune with her lifestyle, someone she could proudly walk on their arm in public and not place her entire career in Japan over it. She needed a man that came with fewer complications.

Could he truly ask her to put her personal life on hold and give him the chance to catch up, and become a man independent of Takusa? He would be older in two years, but hell, she would be older too, so it would always be there between them. There was no catching up when it came to age, so him being too young was something that she had to accept and love him regardless. Could she?

"Come on Kane, I'm laying here half naked with all my flaws hanging out and so are you, though you are perfect, and I hate you for it..."

He laughed amazed that she could still maintain her humor even in this quiet moment of awkwardness. It was one of the many reasons he loved her.

"I told you about the few women I've had sex with were paid to be with me." Kane reminded quietly. "It's not very flattering to admit such a thing, but I learned a lot about the actual act. Yet, no one told me how much more intense it would be when you were with someone you deeply cared for. Charlene, it scares me to death that I won't please you."

Charlene came up on her elbow and looked down at him. "*Boy*, is that what has you so worried?" She smiled tenderly and his heart melted more. "I see you do have much more to learn about women."

He smiled sheepishly and looked away bracing himself for what was to come. Maybe she would remain the night, or maybe she would change her mind after he foolishly just reminded her once again of the differences by his lack of experience in these matters.

"Kane, you had me wanting you so bad just moments ago, I thought I was going to turn into a foolish woman, and start begging," Charlene confessed with a roll of her eyes and a shake of her head. "Everything about you pleases me, the more I get to know you the more foolish my thinking becomes. While we were kissing, I pretended that I had the right to kiss you like this, and how it would be if the world outside this door would disappear, so that I could listen to my heart."

Kane surprised by her confession, couldn't hide the elation he was feeling. He reached out for her and she staid him off.

"But..."

He felt as if his world collapsed with the use of one word. He had no desire to hear her finish the statement. He just wanted to revel in the happiness of believing she wasn't about to rain on his parade.

"I understand. You don't have to explain anymore. Let's just enjoy being together, right now." He grabbed her and rolled with her laughing as she ended up beneath him. She held on to her unhooked bra with one hand. He braced himself above her on his hands.

"Kane!" Charlene cried out giggling. "Let me finish."

"I know what you're going to say, Charlie-chan." He looked her in the eyes. "I know this is where you're going to turn into the beautiful voice of reasoning you do so well. It's okay, I understand why this may be—"

"Will be," she interrupted.

He rolled his eyes, a habit he was picking up from her, and sighed. "Will be," *NOT*! "Our first and last time together like this," he quickly added, "As long as we're working together."

"Good." Charlene caught his hand and held it against her chest and he could feel her the steady flutter of her heart beating. "I take it your ready to stop wasting anymore of this one and only night together talking. Are you ready to make this a night neither one of us will never forget?"

"It already has been a *day* that I will treasure, Charlie-chan, starting with our dance. I just hope now that I'm obligated for a few more years you will wait for me," he whispered against her mouth, his hand easing the straps of her bra off her shoulders and finished removing the obstacle between him and a piece of heaven. "If you do fall in love again, let it be me, don't automatically brush me aside in your mind because you think I'm too young. Don't let our high-profile careers get in the way of your feelings. We both can afford to go anywhere, maybe Europe if not the States. Somewhere where you can be comfortable to love me not just like this but in the open where I can proudly show you off to the world."

"Oh, Kane, please stop, you're killing me," Charlene groaned and place her fingertips over his lips. She looked at him, long, endearing and loving? For a moment he could swear he saw more than she was willing to confess too. Was she already in love with him? *Damn!* Why couldn't he be more experienced in these things? Maybe he was wishful thinking and should listen to what she was saying.

He realized for his sake, Charlene made it very clear they weren't in a relationship. So if this wasn't a relationship, and it wasn't pity sex, what the hell was going on here between the two of them? If she was in love with him, why was she keeping it from him when they were alone? Didn't she realize how much

J-Pop Love Song

it would mean to him to know for sure? Why couldn't she just say the words, once, and for his sake give him the hope he greatly needed to help him through the months ahead.

Instead of asking all the questions that ran rampant in his head, he released a long exasperating breath and said, "Charlie-chan, I wonder if I'm as dense as you're making me feel, or if you're sending me mixed signals." His voice broke with huskiness.

"You're saying 'no' every time I try to speak of the future. Then when I think I have come to some conclusion about your feelings, and respect your wishes, I look into your eyes, and I see how you respond to my touch, and when you touch me I feel as if…if…you love me! *Chikusho*, damn it, Charlene, which of you is with me right now? The one that gives me hope or the one that takes it away?"

"I'm so sorry. I don't mean to mislead you, but I'm confused. I do want to follow my heart and open myself up to you, but I just can't do it, not now. Too many people are depending on the conclusion and success of this project." He could tell from the desperation in her voice she needed him to understand. "I must see this through, I made a contractual commitment, and I gave friends my word…"

"Charlene-san—" He stopped short in dismay when she lifted her eyes, the pain flickering there emphasized her state of distress over the tough choices she was being forced to make. He ached with an inner pain and heaviness centered in his chest.

"Kane," she licked her lips nervously. "Let's pretend that we are in love, and that we do have a future, that there is no difference in our age or cultures. Let there be no one wishing to keep us apart, and that we are two normal people with normal lives. Please, give me this one insane moment. Make me forget the heartbreaks of the past. Most of all make me forget all that awaits us beyond these walls."

Her voice echoed his longings. He could see the unshed tears in her eyes, and finally he understood. Yes, she had obligations just like he did, but he also knew they could still make it work, as long as they were in it together. Yet, the one thing strong and independent Charlene Alfred, who had the world at her feet wasn't saying was, she was afraid to love again.

With the perceptiveness of one beyond his years, Kane gave in to her pleas and her needs for it made him happy to do so. He would do anything to protect her heart, body and soul from anyone ever hurting or disappointing her again. Jason James had been a selfish *baka*, idiot. He had no idea what precious gift he had been given. The bastard deserved to find no peace in the afterlife.

At that moment Kane forgot to be nervous, or uncertain. He knew what he wanted and as long as he held fast to his dreams, Charlene would have no choice but to give in to what she knew in her heart to be the truth. He slid to the side, keeping her trapped in place by one heavy long leg. He finished removing her black-lace bra and threw it over his shoulder not caring where it landed.

Kane's eyes feasted on her exquisite breasts; they weren't overly large, nor were they adolescent or augmented perky. He didn't care; everything about her was beautiful to him. He cupped one breast in the palm of his hands and strummed her nipple with his thumb, back and forth. Dark aureoles and huge upturned nipples extended towards his awaiting mouth. He tasted the nipple closest to his parted lips. Charlene moaned softly, he heard it as an encouragement to continue.

Her fingers buried deeply into his hair. He kissed, licked and sucked her breast and nipple. She arched against his mouth as their legs intertwined. Eagerly he moved to the other breast. A smile curved his lips as she cried out and tugged his hair. Kane made a mental note that her left breast was much more sensitive than the right.

"*Charlene, zutto issho-ni itai, I want to stay this way with you forever.*" In his heart he said the words he knew he wouldn't say aloud. For now he would let her have her way until she was ready to accept their destiny and shout it to the world.

Chapter Ten

AFTER MUCH PLAYFUL LAUGHTER, they managed to get what was left of their clothing off, tossing the various items haphazardly across the room. Charlene felt silly at the sight of Kane's white boxer-briefs landing on the lamp.

She returned his kisses in between chuckles and tore her lips away from his to say in a husky voice, "Kane, I really think you need to get your underwear off the lamp."

"They'll keep."

"What if they start to burn? Do we really want to set off the fire alarm and sprinklers in Stuart's home?"

Kane softly cursed and rolled up on his feet.

Charlene took full advantage of the view. Even naked as the day he was born, Kane was rock star gorgeous from head to toe. Not just handsome, he was beautiful even if he didn't find the word appropriate for a man; it was the truth, from his perfectly cleft square chin to his soulful almond shaped dark eyes. He had a straight nose, gloriously shaped lips, and sexy long black eye lashes.

Mercy, Mercy, he was fine. Kane was a powerfully built man with lean muscles. His legs and thighs, showed the long developed definition of a runner. His black hair was a bit long on the top, but it suited him adding to his boyish appeal. He didn't have a lot of ass, but it was enough to fill out a pair of jeans and make a sista turn around to watch him walk away.

Accept at this moment, *she* was watching him walk towards her and what he was packing made him the second Japanese male she slept with, dispel the "small penis" myth. Charlene thought his cock was more than a mouthful. So much so, she was willing to mouth test the theory to find out exactly how much of his generous length she could take in before gagging.

She allowed herself to become lost in Kane's kisses; he was no longer teasing and playful in his love-play, he was damn serious, and she could feel the difference down to her curling toes. Kane put a knee between her legs and nudged her open, allowing his erection to tease at the moistness between her legs, but he wasn't even trying to insert it inside her even though she was lifting her hips against him.

Instead he held her hands over her head and he was kissing her.

His kiss was so good and so long, she felt her juices seeping from her pussy and didn't need any more foreplay; she was more then ready to have his long hot cock inside her. She called his name in frustration, tearing her mouth form his.

"Kane," she moaned. "Don't make me wait."

"I've waited a long time for this, Charlie-chan." His hot breath blew against her face. "Relax and allow me to love you, my way."

She groaned, wondering if she was going to make it before she gave into the urge to flip him over onto his ass, impale herself and fuck him senseless. As if he sensed her desperation, he deepened the erotic rolling of his tongue against hers and shifted until his knee was pressing against her vagina. Understanding what he was doing Charlene started to bump and grind against his hard knee earnestly. It didn't take long. Her nails bit into his hands, her body went still beneath him and she opened her mouth to cry out her first release.

Charlene felt her body ease somewhat, the orgasm took the edge off and now she could lay back and enjoy his wonderful ministrations. She was learning something new about Kane; he did everything thoroughly, and in his own good time. She melted under his mouth as he tasted every part of her heated flesh. It had been a long time since she felt thoroughly loved by a man and she wanted to know what Kane would feel like buried deep inside. But for now she reveled in his arousing sexual scent, the caresses from his beautiful musicians hands, his grunts, moan and sighs she would remember always.

Kane's erection pressed against her stomach and she lifted her hips up to meet him while one hand kneaded her breast and tweaked her tender nipples. He used his other hand to palm and squeeze one fleshy cheek of her bottom. He tore his mouth away from hers, surveying her with dark smoldering eyes, a foolish dimpled grin on his face.

"I know that look, don't you dare stop again," Charlene warned pinching his forearm.

He pinched her butt in return and smoothed the place with his palm. "I know that look and I thought women appreciate long foreplay."

"Yeah, sometimes, but I feel as if we have been *fore-playing* since your first phone call over a month ago." She gave him a saucy wink. "God, it's hot in here."

"Yeah it is, but I don't want to move to open a window." He hissed in a deep breath and let it out slowly. "Charlie-chan, I love the feel of your wet pussy rubbing against my penis." He closed his eyes and threw back his head.

"Mmm, dirty talk with an accent is so sexy." She slowed her pace so he could get the full abrasive feel of her pubic hair against his baby smooth cock. She gasped and her thigh quivered as his penis rocked against her sensitive clitoris. She moaned and bit down on her bottom lip.

His long lashes flew up and he looked her in the eyes. "Do you think you can come again, this way?"

"Ah...mmm...yes. I can feel it...fuck...it's close," she managed and had to fight to keep her eyes from rolling in the back of her head as his back bowed deep. Kane made sure she was getting the full length of his shaft to rub her hooded clit against.

"Come for me, Charlene, come on baby. I want all my attention focused on your face this time." He urged. She found his boldness turned her own even more. "*Mo ichido so-shite*, do that again."

"Oh, Kane...*shit*..." She moaned her hips moving in frenzy as she felt herself peaking.

"*Motto haiku*, faster sweetheart, that's it. Come...for me baby...let me see you," he urged. "*Yokatta?* Do you like that?"

Charlene felt her movements become extremely slippery as she felt the blossoming sensation heralding another orgasm. A flush of heat spread over her breast, up her chest, neck, and over her ears, before the sound of rushing waves drowned out her moans. She wanted to keep her eyes open and watch his face as he watched her, but she couldn't. As her orgasm slammed into her, she cried out; involuntarily her eyes rolled and lashes closed.

Before she stopped floating, Charlene felt her ass leaving the cushioned softness. Her eyes fluttered open and with an orgasmic glazed vision she watch Kane position her legs over his shoulders and bury his face between her legs.

Her clitoris was so tender she cried out in pleasure pain. "Kane...I don't know if you can do...ah...do...fuck it!" She sighed and her fingers gripped the pillow held on for dear life as he teased the hypersensitive nubbin.

He added a finger, then another as the muscles of her vagina grabbed at his fingers greedily. His tongue made loud licking, lapping sounds. Her thighs tightened around his neck and she felt his fingers slide from her body as he relieved the pressure of her legs from around him and eased them back to the ground. But he didn't stop, he just palmed her full ass in his hands and used his shoulders to open her wider to him.

Kane licked and sucked on her labia in the ultimate kiss, nibbled on the flesh of her inner thighs. She knew she would have several love bites on her inner thigh come morning, but she didn't care. Just the thought of being able to see and feel his mark on her long after made her pussy weep. She could feel him chasing her love juices before they reached her dark pucker. Charlene came again, screaming his name.

She felt Kane leave her for a moment, and she rested limp with legs splayed, totally useless to help him roll on the condom. But before she could miss him he was back between her legs. He braced himself up on his arms and she slid her hand up his slippery, sweat covered back as he pressed at her opening while reaching between them to position his penis where it needed to go and easily it slip into her wetness. He went deep. Her legs trembled, and her nails raked down his back.

In her mind she knew she was where she belonged and she wanted to remain with Kane forever, but they only had this time, this moment. Her wet passage squeezed him with strong vaginal muscles and he gasped and grunted into the side of her neck where he buried his face.

Charlene's muscles milked him and she marveled at how perfect he felt buried inside her. His hips began to rock against her, creating a wonderful gliding sensation. Withdrawing all but the head, she fought to keep him from leaving her and it became a battle of sexual domination. She spread her legs wider drawing her knees up towards her breast and cupped his small tight bottom guiding the rhythm of his strokes. Her nails dug in and he hissed but didn't stop moving.

She gazed up at him in wonder, sweat rolled off his face onto her sheen covered face, drops more from the tips of his hair dangling over her face as he looked down between them to see his blushed colored cock pounding into her. It was an erotic vision indeed.

Tears fell out of the corner of Charlene's eyes. She was so in love with him.

"Ch...Charlene, am I hurting you?"

What could she say? *No, but my heart his breaking to pieces. I can't let you go now that I found you.* As much as she wished she had the strength to ask him to give everything up for her, she wouldn't. He would just hate her later once the newness of their love wore off and the sex became predictable. It was hard to imagine them ever tiring of one another, but it could. It happened with Jason—he loved her until the day he died, but it hadn't been enough to keep him from seeking his pleasure elsewhere.

"Don't stop," she said aloud. "Just love me."

"I do...I do..."

Kane continued to do as she asked. She buried her damp face against the side of his neck as she pulled the full weight of his body on top of her. The muskiness of their lovemaking was a perfume to their senses and skin against skin was their love song. Charlene's third orgasm rocked her. Kane's grip became so tight she could barely breathe. His body racked in spasms. She caught his outcry in her mouth. He trembled and rocked against her while she covered his passion-filled face with kisses holding him to her as if she was afraid to allow even the smallest amount of space between them.

A few moments passed, he raised his head and whispered, "I wasn't saying it in the intensity of the moment, Charlie-chan, I love you so much, I can't imagine this being our first and last time. It just can't be." There was a deep sadness in his eyes.

She bit her bottom lip and buried her hands in his damp hair pressing his face into her heated skin, so he couldn't see the regret. She desperately wanted to reassure him, but reality was waiting for them. Her cell phone was off and so was his. There was no telling how many messages were waiting to quickly remind them of the outside world.

She continued to hold him. Her legs felt cramped and achy from her position. His breathing slowed, and he became heavy as he went limp in sleep. She didn't care; she didn't want to let him go, not yet. Charlene held him and didn't dare make a move. Instead she silently prayed for the world around them to disappear.

♪

It was two hours before dawn when Charlene awakened to the sound of Kane's light snoring. Regardless of only getting a few hours sleep and the sweet dull ache between her legs she grinned and stretched like a satisfied kitten. Her movements sent a whiff of stale musky sex to her nostrils reminding her that she needed to get a shower and call Stuart to take her back to the hotel.

Charlene's face flushed. How was she going to face Stuart? He would know what they had done, considering she didn't call him within the hour as she said she would. Well, even if she had to keep this a guarded secret from the rest of the world, it was nice that they have at least one person they both could be honest and forthcoming with about the extent of their relationship.

She turned and looked at Kane, a night's growth of a beard shadowed his face and made him appear older. His face was so smooth and flawless he she wouldn't have thought he would have to shave but every few days. Even his chest was a baby smooth and void of hair except for the fine line running from the below his navel to the thick black patch nestled around a thankfully, limp, penis. As well it should be. The boy was insatiable, greedy even, and she hurt all over. Charlene loved the feeling of being thoroughly fucked. She put her hand over her mouth to stifle a silly giggle.

She felt like a teenager again. Kane had put her ass in positions that she'd only seen pictures of, but his enthusiasm made her daring enough to try. He must have had some book of sexual positions. Some she was down with while a few she told him were out of the question. There was nothing like the blossoming eagerness of youth. *Sigh.*

Charlene bit her bottom lip to stifle a groan as aching pain shot through her legs and arms. She managed to crawl halfway before managing to stand and creep quietly into the bathroom, pushing the door closed behind her. She turned on the shower and ran her fingers underneath the showerhead waiting for it to heat up. Sitting on the toilet to relieve her bladder, she noticed the empty box of condoms and packaging. Noting it was a box of six she giggled and put the box back in the trash reliving each time they made use of a new condom in her memory. *Sigh.*

"Sorry Stuart, I believe Kane is going to owe you a new box of condoms, my friend. Bless you for having them handy or we would have been shit out of luck, with Kane's "one" in his wallet." She giggled again and rolled her eyes at her silliness.

She found a towel on the back of the bathroom door, but no washcloth. She decided she would have to make do with her hands. Rolling her head from side to side, she tested the soreness in her shoulders and stepped under the shower. Not seeing soap, or body wash she poured vanilla scented shampoo in her palm and made use of it spreading it over her body.

Using her hands, she went to work washing. She noticed the bruises and beard-burns from their love-play and shook her head closing her eyes…remembering so clearly, she could still smell his scent. She smiled.

"I hope that smile is because you're thinking about me." She jumped, startled and opened her eyes to find the object of her growing obsession peeking at her from the open corner of the shower curtain. "Is there enough room in there for me? I got a washcloth."

"That's the ticket you need to get in here." She came up on tiptoes, kissed him on the mouth and took the cloth from his hand. She turned her face up to the spray of water, and he stepped in behind her taking the cloth from her hand, wetting and soaping it up with shampoo from the opened bottle.

"Let me." He murmured hotly against the shell of her ear.

She braced her hands against the wall and nearly purred from the long even strokes he made across her back with the cloth. "That feels wonderful," she sighed.

"You feel wonderful." He kissed a trail up the side of her neck. "Being inside you was incredible. I already miss the feeling of you're hot liquid pussy snuggled around me," He whispered against her ear. "I'm sorry for the bruises, but seeing my mark on you makes me feel as if you belong to me."

She moaned. "What are you doing, trying to do get me horny again?"

"Is it working?"

"I don't know. Why don't you check and see for yourself."

He reached down between them and inserted a finger from behind. She gasped and tensed for a moment. "Sweetheart, are you too tender for me to take you again?"

Yes, she should have said, but even though she ached, she hurt more from the thought of never being able to share intimate moments like this one with him again. Only when he made love to her she could forget. "*Daijobu,* it's okay...ah, don't stop. I love your hands, you have such wonderful fingers."

"That is the advantage to playing musical instruments. It keeps the fingers pliable." He inserted two more fingers and she moved back against his hand. As he got her worked up she felt his finger drop away leaving her momentarily empty and reaching behind her she grasped his cock and guided him to her opening. He hesitated for a moment, but the eagerness of her body assured him once again, she wasn't that sore and proceeded to impale herself on his erection.

A long hiss of protest escaped Kane. She loved the sounds of guttural sex and wet skin pounding against wet skin. She pushed and withdrew as he braced his legs wide enough to let her ride. His arms holding the both of them in place by bracing his palms against the small stall walls, they went at it until the water turned cold and hit them surprising them into a startling orgasm at the same time. Charlene reached blindly to slap off the streaming water as Kane's fingers bit into her hips holding her in place as he jerked and finished his release.

"Damn, now we need to shower again." They giggled and kissed.

"Not in here you won't. I know Stuart's shower, it takes about two hours for it to heat up again." He looked at her apologetically.

"No way!" She laughed in between his kisses. "I got to get back to the hotel before Abe picks me up for our breakfast meeting. We start scouting locations today."

Kane moved away. He became quiet; wrapping a towel he must have gotten from the same place he retrieved the washcloth, around his hips. He handed her the towel she draped over the sink area and shared the one he used to towel dry his hair.

As if she wasn't standing in the bathroom Kane parted the towel and pissed in the toilet. She shook her head, for some reason seeing him so comfortable felt more intimate then making love. Charlene turned her back to him, tucked the towel she dried with around at her breast and used the other to dabble at her wet braids.

She heard the toilet flush and stepped aside as he washed his hands in the sink, their gazes locking and each smiling at one another in the bathroom mirror. He cut off the water and dried his hands on the towel around his naked lean hips.

Then he leaned against the sink and stared at her. She couldn't read his face for he appeared to be very calm and void of all thoughts.

Charlene halted and looked at him...waiting.

"What?" He asked his brow lifted a fraction.

"I got to pee and wash up in the sink before I put my clothes back on. I really don't look forward to wearing the same underwear but that can't be helped until

I get back to the hotel."

"Can I watch?" He wiggled his eyebrows.

"Uh, no." She giggled feeling her ears grow warm.

He lingered in the doorway.

"What is it?" She asked.

He shrugged. "I'm scared to let you out of my sight. You can't imagine what my mind went through when I woke up and found you gone. Something tells me, when I walk out of this bathroom and close the door, it's over, and I don't want it to be."

"Kane..." She didn't say it aloud, but she felt the same way. Still, she must make him see reason. "We had an understanding. I have no regrets about what happened between us, and I will never forget it, but it is, what it is. One night between consenting *adults*."

His shoulders drooped as he released a long sigh. He nodded.

"If Stuart has some coffee somewhere in there, I sure would love some and anything that is edible, I'm starving!" She came up on her tiptoes and pressed her lips to his. He wrapped his arms around her and held on desperately. She almost broke down in his arms.

With exaggerated happiness, she pushed him out the door, "Go...go...go! Coffee, if not, strong black tea will do, *onegai-shimasu*, please!" She managed to close the door and lock it. Charlene leaned her head against it taking in deep gulps of breath she shriveled a little inside at the sadness she gleamed in his eyes before she shut him out. Terrible regrets assailed her; not for making love to him, or unwittingly giving her heart to him forever, but for the public lives they led.

No one would understand and Kane was too young to lose everything now. She remembered how his face lit up when he talked about fan loyalty and proper behavior. Didn't he realized that my Japanese society him being with her like this would be seen as improper behavior. Could he really be asked to give up his homeland for the sake of love? No, he would just resent her in the years ahead. She was doing the right thing.

Charlene blasted the sink water hoping it drowned out her sobs. The permanent feeling of loss made her knees weakened and she fell to the bathroom floor. She didn't think anything would hurt as much as loosing her husband, until now. Knowing the man you loved was alive and loved her in return, yet she couldn't be with him, was a living hell. She hadn't anticipated letting it all go would hurt this much. Rocking back and forth, she wept.

Charlene would have been flabbergasted if she knew that Kane was on his knees outside the bathroom door listening to her sobbing, while sharing her distress and shedding tears of his own. What were they going to do, now?

Chapter Eleven

IT HAD BEEN TWO MONTHS SINCE that night Kane spent the happiest time of his life and a month, since they started filming. He rarely got to see Charlene on the set, but when he did, such as days like this on, it took everything in him to keep from rushing over to her and taking her in his arms.

Especially when she was looking so healthy and beautiful, he was happy to see her well, but he was pissed that she didn't seem to be missing him half as much as he missed her. He was angry and frustrated beyond reason, trying everything to forget the one night they shared. He tried running an extra mile, and he even tried sex with someone else, by making appointment with his now ex-regular mistress.

Kane realized afterwards, sex with another woman could not erase his body's memories of sex with the woman he loved. She didn't have Charlene's smell, brown skin, or fleshiness that filled and overflowed in his hands. He paid her and left with nothing to show for it but this empty ache in his chest.

Damn her, he silently cursed her. She's ruined him for anyone else, yet she didn't want him either. What was he supposed to do? Did she really think he could just walk away, without regrets? Broodingly, he stared at her. Charlene wore a black silk suit that ended mid-calf over a pristine white silk blouse, black medium-high-heeled pumps and diamonds with pearl, studded earrings. There his love stood; beautiful, flawless and as usual, in her serene "all business" face.

He assumed she wasn't staying for the full shoot or she would have been dressed more casual. It also didn't pass Kane's attention that she seemed to be extra chummy with that manager, Abe Goda-san, these days. Had she decided to use him to help her forget what they shared? Angrily, he wondered how was that working for her? Maybe he had been a naive fool to believe that her making love to him had been extraordinarily special. What if it was always that way for her? If she didn't regret their situation as mush as he did, why did she cry? Maybe it was tears of regret over what they done, and not the fact that they couldn't be together. All these questions were driving him crazy.

Damn her, for not excepting his calls, unless it was business. He desperately needed to speak with her. *Hell,* they were at least friends before they became lovers. Well, in all fairness they were friends before he signed the contract, so being lovers probably didn't have anything to do with her keeping things professional. She warned him before hand, he just hoped them becoming

J-Pop Love Song

intimate would bring them closer not push them apart.

His birthday was in two days, he wondered if she would show up for his twenty-fifth birthday bash. It was the least; she could do, considering he gave up his freedom to do this film for her. In two days, he would have been walking away from Takusa and his hold on him. Instead, Takusa was taking full advantage of the extra time to woo him into the family fold and for some asinine reason, his daughter; Arisa had joined in the mission. Why, he wondered? It was no secret she was in love with a guy she met while away at school.

As if thinking about her brought her to the film set, Arisa came walking towards him with a tide kerchief in her hands. She had a lovely smile on her face. Kane took in her petite slender frame in the finest Paris fashion that money could buy. She has skin of porcelain, high cheekbones, short nose and full lips; her black hair was razor edge and hung long to the small of her back. Any man would be proud to have her standing by his side.

Any man but him, he practically grew up with Arisa-kun and he always thought of her and her and Sakura-kun as his sisters. No one had been more surprised, than he, when he found out about the marriage arrangement his father had made with Takusa-san about his future.

"Kane-kun, I was told you were back here. I made a *bento* lunch for us." Arisa said in their native tongue, standing before him, unknowingly blocking his view of Charlene. He shifted to the other side in the director styled chair with his name on the back.

"I'm really busy today Arisa-kun, you should have called first." Kane stated a little more briskly then he intended.

"I did call and your assistant said you were having lunch on the set today due to time constraints and I was welcome to stop by." She smiled sweetly; her voice was just as delicate as her features. "Whom are you staring at?" She asked turning on her heels to look behind her, her face didn't change as she said, "So, is that the Black-American woman, that has been in the news lately. She looks a lot younger then I expected, seeing how she is a woman in her forties."

"Early forties. You make it sound ancient," Kane grunted, not really thinking anything she stated required a polite input. What was it about people and ages?

"I was surprised when I found out she had been married to Jason James-san. Looking at her I would not have thought they would have been a good match." Her upper lip curved in distaste as she surveyed Kane's face, he seemed too interested in the woman for her comfort. "I wonder what kind of Japanese man would take a black woman as his wife? Quite daring don't you think?"

"Did you say something?" Kane asked, turning his hard stare on Arisa after feeling her steady gaze on him.

"I was saying isn't it strange to be working on a film that Alfred-san is the writer for?" She had his full attention now.

"Why would you say that?" He asked his eyes narrowing on her face, and he swallowed the discomfort building in his throat.

"Your dreams. When we were younger, I remember you saying that you had dreams of Jason James and he happened to be her husband. I suppose this explains the dreams. It was a sign that you were fated to star in this film."

Kane relaxed and smiled at Arisa. "I suppose you're right. It's been so long ago, I had forgotten about that," he lied smoothly. "So, what are we having for lunch today?" He asked thinking to change the subject to safer grounds.

"Your favorites," Arisa winked at him "Is there somewhere I can spread it out for us to have a picnic."

"Why don't you two use my trailer office, I'm about to leave for the evening." A familiar throaty voice said. Kane immediately tense as he looked up from Arisa to Charlene coming up behind her, apparently privy to the end of their conversation.

"*Konnichi-wa*, Alfred-san, it is such a pleasure to meet you." Arisa beamed switching to fluent English, she handed Kane the lunch box and held out her hand to Charlene who took it in a shake. "I am, Arisa Takusa."

He looked at the two women's clasped hands one so notably different from the other.

Charlene grew still for a moment before she returned the younger woman's smile, saying, "It's nice to finally meet you Arisa Takusa-san, I have heard wonderful things about you from your father, he is very proud of you. Congratulations, are in order it seems."

"Charlie-chan—" Kane interrupted thinking she was referring to the engagement that wasn't going to happen if he could help it.

"I heard you graduated with honors from your medical school." Charlene supplied, glancing at Kane. He flushed, feeling foolish under her reprimanding stare.

Arisa gave Kane a curious look. He cursed inwardly realizing slip, by calling Charlene by a name that spoke of an intimate friendship. Being the ever-gracious Arisa, she bowed her head with thanks and a dimpled smile at Charlene. "I'm just happy to have a break before I start my internship."

"Well, I didn't mean to interrupt, but I heard you say you were looking for a location to have lunch." Charlene stated. "As I mentioned, my office is available, and there is a table and some chairs in there and you can eat in peace."

He could tell Charlene was tense. Kane wondered if she felt the least bit jealous of him being with Arisa? He saw jealous every time he saw her with Abe, even though she explained the friendship.

"That won't—"

"Thank you very much, Alfred-san, we would be happy to accept your offer." Arisa interrupted Kane. "Perhaps you would care to join us. I made extra *sushi*. I also have *onigiri* rice balls stuffed with grill salmon, and fresh fruit for desert."

Kane frowned in concern as he saw Charlene place a finger over her mouth and swallow deeply he could have sworn she was turning a putrid shade of green as Arisa was calling off the foods she had fixed for lunch. Her other hand was on her stomach. Was she sick?

"Arisa-kun, enough. Alfred-san, is my boss and a very busy woman, I'm sure she had much to do." Kane jumped in and almost smiled as he saw relief washed over Charlene's face. He turned and called for Stu-san who was never to far out of reach.

"I'm sorry, I do go on so." Arisa smiled contritely. "I should have known you are a very busy woman."

"No, it was very kind of you to ask and maybe another time, but I do have an appointment I must leave for shortly. Thank you, it was a pleasure to meet you, Takusa-san." Charlene said politely. "You truly are a lovely, young woman."

"Please, call me Arisa."

"Alright, Arisa, only if you call be Charlene or Charlie, is fine."

Arisa giggled prettily behind her hand over her mouth. "I think Charlene is better than Charlie. I hope we can become fast friends, since you work closely with my father and my intended, Kane-kun. I'm sure we will see each other often."

"I'm sure." Charlene said softly.

"Stu-san, can you show Arisa a place to set up for lunch." Kane cleared his throat, shifting from foot to foot, handing the bento box to Stuart, who nodded and grinned knowingly.

Kane gave him a hard glare.

"Oh, Stu-san I put extra smoked sardines in your rice balls. I know how you love them," Arisa exclaimed in her usual happy manner.

It seemed a little too joyful, since Charlene walked up, or so Kane thought. Surly, she wasn't jealous, that wasn't possible. Regardless, he was relieved to get the women separated. It didn't need Arisa feeling Charlene in on his negative antics as a rambunctious youth.

"Oh yes, Charlene-san, I do hope you will be staying in Japan after the film has completed. Yuza-san and I would love for you to put in an appearance at out wedding."

"Stuart," Kane sighed. "Please…"

"Are you trying to starve me to death, Arisa-san? Come and let me take you somewhere so you can feed me."

Kane heard Arisa girlish giggle and cringed closing his eyes for a moment, yet feeling Charlene's stare on him. He opened his eyes and his heart leaped into the back of his throat. She was beautiful, but up close like this, he could see she had dark rings beneath her eyes.

"How have you been, Charlie-chan?"

"I've been a bit under the weather lately, but otherwise I feel good," she smiled a closed lip smile. "How about you? I've been looking at the daily's and you're doing a wonderful job."

"Thank you. What do you mean you've been under the weather? Have you seen a doctor?"

"Kane, don't worry about it, I have an appointment today with a doctor I used some years ago, she's an old acquaintance of my mother's and had no problems fitting me in." He saw how she continuously looked over his shoulder, at her watch, or at her shoes, avoided his eyes.

"Is this how it's going to be from now on when we find ourselves face to face?" He asked briskly.

"Well, I won't be attending your wedding, that's for sure." She said coldly and he flinched.

"Charlene, there is not going to be a wedding."

"Oh, so this poor girl, is walking around making plans and no one has bother to tell her the truth?"

"Charlene…" He reached out to touch her hand and she took a step back looking at her feet again.

"I see, I'm not even allowed to touch you in any way." His voice hardened with frustration.

"Kane, you know why and you have to stop staring at me like that," she stated.

"Like what? Like a man that adores look at the woman he loves."

Charlene looked around. "Don't do this, not now...not here."

"Tell me, when? When can I see you? I miss our talks. You won't answer my calls or emails," he hissed in hushed whispers, hating this cloak and dagger stuff.

"Next week, we have studio time together to work on the soundtrack. We can talk then. But until that time, you have to stop trying to contact me, I can't take anymore," she confessed.

He saw the tears in her eyes and felt his heart breaking. He wanted to put his arms around her and comfort her. Kiss her until she was breathless. Hell, kiss her until he was breathless. He missed her so much it was physically painful. There was no way she could truly expect him to be happy pretending like he wasn't in love with her.

"I don't mean to harass you. Yet, it's not fair of you cutting me completely out of your life. I knew we couldn't be lovers but you didn't say we couldn't remain friends or I..." Kane saw her sway on her feet and quickly wrapped his arm around her shoulders.

"What's going on, here? Charlie, are you alright?" Abe brushed Kane's hands from her shoulders and held Charlene against him. If he wasn't so concerned for Charlie-chan, or he let Goda-san have it once and for all.

Charlene touched her temple, "I'm fine. Abe, it's time for my appointment do you think you can drive me. I think it must have been something I ate."

"Charlie-chan—"

"I believe I see your fiancée waving at you, Kane-san. Don't you think you better see to her? I will take care of Charlie, like I always have." Abe interrupted.

Kane stepped forward.

"Kane, please don't cause a scene, for my sake." Charlene intervened between the two men.

Kane grudgingly conceded saying, "Call me and tell me what the doctor said."

"This truly is none of your business and it's inappropriate behavior towards your employer." Abe said to Kane. "Don't mistake her kindness, for anymore then it is."

"Abe, stop please, I'm going to be late." Charlene pleaded her eyes locked with his for a brief moment.

Abe escorted Charlene away. He envied and resented the older man's rights to touch her publicly and show his care for her so openly.

Kane seethed in silence. Hearing Arisa call his name once again only worsened his ire. He took a deep breath, plastered on his best smile, and joined her for lunch. Thoughts of Charlene's sickly pallor weighed heavy on his heart and mind. What good was he if he couldn't even be there for her when she was sick?

♫

J-Pop Love Song

"Charlene-san, did you hear what I said?"

"I heard you Dr. Hiroshi, I'm just not believing what I'm hearing." Charlene said in numb disbelief. "There must be some mistake."

"No mistake, I ran the analysis twice. You're about six to eight weeks along."

"Has to be first and last time I made love to anyone...but how...I mean..."

Dr. Hiroshi chuckled. "I know what you mean. It happens, and you said yourself you haven't had a need for birth control for years."

"Still...we were safe! He wore a condom every time, I'm sure of it."

"Did one break or come off?"

Charlene was shaking her head as she asked. "I mean no one can be a hundred percent sure, about anything during heated moments like that. If it had, I'm sure K...*he*, would have said something."

The doctor patted her hand and smiled with her round kind face. "I'm sorry dear but there is only one way you got pregnant, unless you were artificially inseminated and we know that wasn't the case. So somewhere in there, the condom must've not been utilized."

A knowing look came to Charlene's face. It hit her, the one time; she made love to Kane without protection. Heat spread across her face, neck, and shoulders in memory. In the shower, it was the only time, she didn't even think about protection, nor had she gave a damn about the consequences at that moment. She remembered he smelled good, looked good, tasted good and felt even better. Mixing in her emotional state, it made her careless and stupid.

She had even noticed the empty box of condoms in the bathroom garbage. She also remembered Kane's moment of hesitation before entering her; he realized they had no protection. Why hadn't he said something? Well, in all fairness, she grabbed him and guided his penis inside. *Damn*, she cursed under her breath. She had thought it felt different, more intense and desperate, because she thought it would be their last time, but actually because it was different. They had created a new life.

"I know that this wasn't planned and you're at a terribly busy time in your life. So I feel I must tell you if you plan on having this baby..."

"Oh there is no doubts, or anything to think about, I'm keeping my baby." Charlene said quickly and explained. "You were there Dr. Hiroshi. You know what I went through for those years Jason and I were together. I thought it was my fault for not wanting that first child while I was in high school. I mean I was devastated after I lost it but in some ways I was relieved. I couldn't tell my parents and when I miscarried I never had to tell them."

"So when Jason and I finally married. We wanted another baby very much. That's when mom introduce me to you, and you know, I had a difficult time conceiving and each time I did, it ended in a miscarriage, I felt cursed. I just couldn't try anymore. Then Jason died." She twisted her hands together in her lap. "This may be my last chance, because of my age my chances were even worse of being able to conceive naturally, but I have! It's a blessing, and I will do *anything* I have to, to have this baby."

Dr. Hiroshi grinned with understanding. She reached out and squeezed her hands, her touch was oddly mothering and comforting. It made Charlene desperate to see her own mother and this news helped to finalize her decision to return to the States.

"Charlene-san, even though everything seems to be progressing as a healthy pregnancy, there is still things to consider. I don't need to tell you being over forty, in a high stressed career, and adding in your history of miscarriages, you need to put you and your baby's health above all else. In your current situation can you do this?"

"I will have to find a way, won't I?" Charlene smiled from ear to ear. She knew she should be upset or at the very least scared to death. Only she didn't feel anything but happiness. She was going to have a child, a baby conceived out of love. The baby she always wanted. In the next two years she had aimed to ask Abe to father a child for her, by then she would have had more time; but, this way was so much better, and she would make time. Now, she would always have a part of Kane with her, for always.

"From the look on your face, you undoubtedly care very much about this man who fathered the baby. I take it, he will be supportive through this process."

Charlene's smile faded, her head dropped, and a protective hand stole to her stomach. "I do love the father, and he loves me, but I'm afraid it is impossible for him to be a part of my or the baby's life."

"*Sokka*, I see."

"Dr. Hiroshi, how much longer do you suppose I can work before I would need to take a break?"

"Well, the first trimester is important and your blood pressure is a bit elevated. I recommend you take a medical holiday and retire somewhere where you can focus on yourself and the pregnancy. I recommend as much bed-rest as possible, Charlene-san."

"I see." Charlene looked down at her hands folded in her lap. "If I don't, you're saying I could lose this child, also."

Grimly she said, "I'm afraid there is always the chance, even by doing as I ask. I'm sorry, but you want to give yourself the best odds imaginable."

Charlene nodded. "I know as long as I stay here in Tokyo, I'll want to be hands on with the film; plus, this is a matter which I don't wish to be all over the tabloids. I don't think I can handle the press hounding me about my personal life trying to find out who the father is. I remember all to well what it was like after Jason's death."

"I can only imagine what that must have been like for you. I also understand your need to get away. I have several discreet private spas I can recommend—"

"Ohm, if it's okay to fly during this time, Dr. Hiroshi—" Charlene interrupted. "I was thinking of going to spend some time with my parents."

"Wonderful, your mother will be delighted. Last time I spoke to her she was missing you very much." The Doctor smiled at her. "I don't foresee a problem, just make it sooner, then later. If possible you may want to take a private flight so you can keep your feet elevated, and the airport is so hectic these days, you're definitely going to feel added stress going through the airline process."

"Oh, isn't it horrible," Charlene laughed. "A private airplane out shouldn't be a problem, I will have Abe check into it."

Dr. Hiroshi scribbled out a prescription and handed it to her. "This is for your pre-natal vitamins. There is also one for folic acid supplements. You need to get started today. I will want to see you back here in two week, so don't plan on leaving until after I give you the final go ahead."

A frown flitted across Charlene's face. "Are you saying there's a chance I may not be able to travel?"

"We will see. I just want to make sure after being on the regimented diet, if your blood pressure has stabilized. Also, once you're a little further along, I recommend an amniocentesis to check on the developing of the fetus."

"What will you be looking for?" Her eyes grew wide with concern.

"Don't worry, it's routine. We check for Down syndrome or birth defects. Also we need to keep an eye out for preeclampsia, hypothyroidism or gestational diabetes."

"I'm sorry, what is *pre-e-clamp-sia?*" Charlene questioned, unafraid to ask the important questions. She wanted to make sure nothing went wrong.

"High blood pressure caused by your pregnancy," she explained. "The nurse will have a packet with all this information and more on all of the risk. Also a copy of the special diet I want you to start, that will aid in helping with your blood pressure, not to mention you're a tad overweight."

"I've always been a tad overweight," Charlene murmured. "Thank you so much, Dr. Hiroshi."

"Alfred-san, I truly can't stress enough, that for the first twenty weeks of your pregnancy, your chances for miscarriage is at it's highest. If there is any vaginal bleeding, a brownish discharge and or cramps in lower back, pelvic or abdomen—please admit yourself in the emergency room. Also, pay close attention, to any decrease in breast tenderness or nausea; these too are signs of potential trouble. If you know what to look for, you stand a better chance at taking preventive measures to save the child."

They stood.

"Thank you so much. Doctor, I can't stress how imperative it is that my pregnancy remains a private matter…that includes mi mom for now."

"That goes without saying, Alfred-san. I would never divulge a patient's information." She assured her. "I'm here if you have any questions or concerns."

She thanked the doctor once again and went out into the waiting room where a concerned Abe sat impatiently tapping his feet on the floor. He came to his feet immediately.

"Well?" he asked coming to her side straight away. "You're working too hard, aren't you?"

"I'm fine." She smiled up at him. "How about we discuss this in the car," she suggested.

Stoically he nodded carefully placing a protective hand on the small of her back, he held the door open for her.

In the car, they set in silence, until Abe released a frustrated sigh and pulled off the road into a hotel parking lot. He cut the engine and stared at her. "I keep waiting for you to tell me something, and now, I'm going crazy with concern. With that said, Charlie, I'm not moving this car until you let me know what the hell is wrong with you?"

She didn't know how else to say it, except to say it straight. Besides, she needed to rely on him now more then ever.

"I'm two months pregnant," she blurted out.

Abe washed a hand over his face. "What? How...I mean, who? Shit, Charlie, I didn't even know you've been seeing anyone...that way."

"Does it matter?"

"Hell yeah, it matters!" Abe shouted. What am I going to tell the investors? You think they're only hard on the actors? You know how things work around here. When a woman becomes pregnant even as a salary worker, she is expected to retire for the duration of the pregnancy. Some are never allowed to return to their positions. As far as an unmarried female public figure...you are still unmarried aren't you, Charlie? Or is that something else you've been leaving me in the dark about?"

"Abe, come on," she scowled. "You know didn't run off and to something as stupid as to marry and leave a paper trail."

Being privy to every aspect of her life, Charlene could understand his being upset that she had been secretive about her feelings for Kane. She knew he would calm down eventually and be more acceptable to everything else she had to say.

"Charlie, how could you be so damned careless and in these days and times? What if it was something worse then a pregnancy? It's not too late for the worse, such as *HIV*...fuck, Charlie; do I even know the guy? Shit, how are we going to keep the media from getting wind of this?"

"Are you finished?" She lifted her brows at him in question. " Because if you are I need, Abe, my best friend, not Goda-san, my business manager for this conversation. Is that okay?"

Abe released a long breath and smiled a sad closed lipped smile. He took her hand in his. "You are going to drive me crazy." He shook his head at her. "Okay, professional Abe has left the car. Still, Charlie, you know I can handle transactions a lot better then I can, women issues."

"I know this, that's why you're still unattached." She grinned hoping to lighten the mood. From his grim expression, it wasn't working.

"What are you going to do?" Abe asked.

"Have it of course."

"That goes without saying," he waved a hand. "I *know* you've always wanted a kid. I just wish you had waited until after the project, as we discussed before." His broad brow puckered in a frown.

"So do I. It wasn't as if I went out there looking to make *this* happen. It was a one time thing," she spread her hands wide. "If anyone knows about "one time" sex romps, it's you."

"Yeah, I do, but that's not you, Charlie." Abe pointed out. "You're not a one-night stand woman. You're a keeper and any man worth his grain of salt, would know this and choose not to sleep with you, because it would be too easy to fall in love with you.

Charlene blushed and squeezed his hand. "You're completely bias, you know."

"Well, if you going to play these games, you have to always play it safe. You obviously didn't, and that worries me more then the fact that you're pregnant. You do understand why I would feel this way don't you?"

"Yes, but I assure you, he wasn't a random stranger I picked up at a club, I care for him and I trust him. Besides, the doctor did a HIV swab test to the inside of my mouth, it was negative, and the blood work will confirm it. I knew it would be, but it was standard along with the pregnancy test before they do a Pap smear test."

"What did the doctor say? Is it okay for you to have this baby? It's not going to affect your health is it?" he asked.

"It could, because of my age, of course. So far, everything is progressing normal and that was before I knew."

"You had no idea?"

"For your information, we did use protection all but the one time, I didn't think about it, and I assumed the missed periods were due to added stress or hell, early menopause." She tugged her hand from his and fooled with the hem of her skirt. "That's why I went to the doctor, I didn't know what was wrong with me. I haven't been sleeping well lately, so for the first month I chalked it up to fatigue."

"Charlie, why didn't you tell me you hadn't been sleeping? I could have taken over some of your appointments." Abe offered.

"I know, but you were already doing the bulk of the work, and I needed the distraction. The good thing is, now that I know what is wrong with me, I can make sure I take better care of myself," she assured him instinctively placing a hand over her stomach.

"Charlie, you can't have the baby here in Japan, the reporters will eat you alive, they will start pulling commercial support for the film and then investors will want to bail."

"I know from experience, how this works, Abe." Charlene smiled at him. "I've already decided to go visit my parents. I don't want them hearing this from anyone but me."

Abe grabbed her hand again she knew it was to keep her from nervously plucking at her skirt. "You know Charlene there is one way you can stay here and have the baby."

"Oh boy, this is serious, you called me Charlene"," she giggled nervously. She knew what was coming next; it wouldn't be Abe, if he weren't always trying to "fix" things.

"Marry me. Let me be a father to your baby, that is, unless the natural father wants to be involved." Abe said his voice as businesslike as usual. "I could take care of you and the child."

"He would, but it's not possible." She shook her head sadly. Placing her free palm against her friend's cheek she graciously smiled and looked into his eyes. "You are such an extraordinary man. You deserve a woman that can love you and give you children of your own. I'm fortunate enough to have you in my corner and I'm not going to take advantage of our friendship. Besides, I don't—"

"You don't love me that way," he finished with a sigh. Pulling away from her the touch of her hand on his face, she allowed it to drop to her side. "So the fact that I love you doesn't make a damned difference, does it?"

The sincerity was apparent in his voice. Her heart went out to him, but he wasn't Kane, and she knew she could never love anyone else as deeply.

"I know you love me Abe, but you're not *in love* with me or you would have sealed the deal years ago. Yes, I had considering settling for a marriage that was like a business transaction, but I can't raise this child in that kind of marriage. This baby was a gift given to me by a man who has truly shown me what mutual love is. I never had that with Jason, I always loved and thought about his welfare more then he mine."

"Still, Charlie, if he can't be there for you..."

"Abe, I finally realize, what my mother has been trying to tell me for years. When it's real, you can't settle for anything less, then *everything* you deserve." Charlene declared. "So, if I can't have the same type of married happiness as like my parents, than I don't want it at all."

"Oh boy, wait until your parents hear about this." Abe shook his head.

"They will be shocked and then happy, it will be their first grandchild, and they are getting up in the years." She assured him.

"Yes, and they will ask you the same question I want to ask?"

"Which is?"

"Who is the father and why can't he do the right thing by marrying you if you're so "in love"?"

"If I thought telling you would make you feel better about the situation, I would, but I know it won't." Charlene crossed her arms over her breasts and winced at the sensitivity of her nipples.

"I won't push," he assured her. "I need to know when you want to leave, I think it's best that we hire a private plane. It would be less likely to be a leak about your sudden departure. We can do without the media frenzy. I will also have your publicists send out a press release after you've left to explain you had a family emergency and had to cut your trip short."

"In about three weeks I should be ready. I have a follow-up appointment for few more routine tests with the Doctor. I also need to personally oversee the soundtrack vocals with Kane, you can send me the final drafts of the ones we've laid so far." She rattled off the mental list in her head. "The remaining tracks, I suppose I can do a studio demo and send them for him to hear how I want it done. If it isn't good enough—well, we will cross that bridge when we come to it."

"Speaking of Kane—"

"Were we speaking *of* Kane? I thought we were discussing business?"

"Isn't *HE* business?" Abe asked bluntly. "I'm curious as to what was going on between you two earlier, on the film set? Is he still coming on to you?"

Charlene looked out the car window at nothing in particular; she just couldn't look at Abe in the eyes and lie to him. "Creative differences, but we will work it out at the studio."

"If he's giving you a hard time, let me know and I will handle him once and for all," Abe mumbled. He restarted the car and looked before easing into traffic.

"Why do you dislike Kane so?"

Abe shrugged. "I don't dislike him. It's just he's always looking at you in a disrespectful manner. He also touching you every chance he gets, as if he has a right to do so. He's just a kid on your film, if he has problems he should go through his manager and he will come to me."

Charlene chuckled. "Watch it Abe Goda, if I didn't know you better, I would think you were acting like a jealous lover."

"You are laughing at my feelings?" Abe glanced at her before turning his attention back to the road. "I'm not joking. I really would marry you in a heartbeat if you would have me, Charlie. We would be good together."

"We are good together. As business partners." Her voice softened. "You're trying to avoid getting your heart broken again. That's the only reason you're willing to settle for me."

"You needn't bring that up." Abe said, a silken thread of warning in his voice.

"I'm not. I'm just making a point. You don't look at me as a woman that you can't live without. You just know with me, you aren't risking anything." She touched his leg and squeezed. "You're my best friend. I trust you with my life, but not with my heart."

"If you trust me so much, why would you just lie to me about Kane."

Her eyes widened in surprise as she stared at him.

"Don't look at me like that? You believe you're the only one that's been paying attention in this crazy relationship we have? You don't lie well, Charlie. Tell me, are you going to tell Kane's, he's about to be a father, or do you plan on running away from it all?"

She was too startled by his statement to offer any objection. Why should she it was the truth. "How long have you known?"

"I didn't, until now. I was throwing out the net to see who I would catch." Abe answered, heatedly." I figured it had to be Stuart or Kane. I didn't want to believe you had been with that kid. What the hell are you thinking? I should have know by the long looks, when the two of you thought no one was paying attention."

A flicker of apprehension coursed through her. "My God, if you've noticed, how many others have noticed!"

"Calm down, Charlie. Your getting upset can't be good for the baby," Abe said is voice calming in that deep soothing way of his. "I noticed because I've never seen you watch any man the way you watch him, its as if you're memorizing his every movement. As far as others noticing, what if they did, Kane is a pop star and handsome as hell, you would seem more suspect if you didn't stare."

Immediately she felt better. She didn't have to lie to her friend anymore. It was such a relief to be able to talk freely of her feelings for Kane to someone. Stuart has been too busy to talk for long and she couldn't tell Kane she missed him, it would just make things harder on him. "He really is *too gorgeous* for his own good," she longingly giggled.

"So it seems." Abe made his point by glancing down at her stomach.

"I wish I could say it was just his good looks that I was attracted to, that would be so much easier to get over, but its everything about him." She felt a warm glow flow through her just thinking about how he made her feel.

"You are truly in love, aren't you?"

"Foolishly."

"This is not a win situation, Charlie, you could get hurt." He said in a dull and troubled voice.

"I'm already hurting," she admitted. "The morning after making love to Kane, I wanted to shout it to the world how good it felt to be in love. If it were just my career to consider I would risk it. We could make a go of it in the States,

It won't be any worse than the way I was treated and perceived after marrying Jason, but I can't destroy Kane like that. He's too young and this is his home, his people. He's about to hit the peak of his career. I have no right to take that from him, just because I love him."

"Shouldn't that be his decision to make? I know if I were in Kane's shoes and it was the woman I loved, I would go through hell to be by her side."

"Like you were willing to do for—"

"Don't even say her name." Abe said between clenched teeth. "Like you are doing for Kane now, *SHE* made all the decisions in our relationship. I loved her enough to leave the choice up to her." He shook his head. "Hoping...no, *praying* she would choose me, over her family. She didn't. End of story."

"Abe..."

"You should tell Kane he is going to be a father, Charlie. It's only right," he reasoned.

She shook her head, tears burning in her eyes. Now she had a reason for her crazy emotional state. "It would complicate his life more than it is already. He's had enough hardships and I don't want to become one of them. He needs to move on, love someone is age, and be happy."

"What about your happiness?"

She smiled looking at her hand resting protectively on her stomach. "I will carry a piece of him under my heart and every time I look at him or her, I will always be grateful for this gift he has unknowingly given me. That is enough happiness for me."

"What you're saying is, you love him enough to let him go, just like that. He gets the fun and has none of the responsibilities," Abe balked.

"No, it's not like that. Kane would have come with me to the Doctor's office if I had let him. You saw how concerned he was. That wasn't acting." She quickly defended him and added, "He even offered to give up everything to prove his sincerity, but I couldn't allow him be so reckless. How could I live happily without wondering when he would start to resent me for it?"

"Charlie, I still think if this kid is as in love with you as you say, then he would want to know you're carrying his child. He will want to make the choice to be a part of it's life or not!" Abe argued. "You aren't doing Kane any favors by leaving him out of the loop. Eventually, the truth always comes out, and when it does he will resent you for the precious time he's lost with his baby."

"Then, so be it, Abe!" She responded sharply, abandoning all pretenses that she was happy with her decision when she was miserable.

She very much wanted Kane to be a part of their baby's life! Hell, she wanted him to be a part of her life. This wasn't some sudden emotional decision she'd made out of the blue, she'd been thinking of nothing else since he declared his feelings for her. Still, baby or not, she'd already made her choice to live her life without Kane.

"Abe, letting go of the person you love, isn't easy for anyone, in spite of what you might think, due to your own circumstances. In this situation I'm the older and wiser one, right? I'm suppose to make the tough decisions for the both of us."

"That's crazy talk," Abe snorted guiding the vehicle into the parking garage of the hotel. "Kane will be twenty-five in what, a couple of days? I don't know about you, but at twenty-five, I was quite capable of making grown-up decisions."

"Must we continue to talk about this? I've already made up my mind." Charlene argued releasing a long agitated sigh.

Abe steered the car in the assigned space and moved the gear into park.

Looking at Charlene with a grim frown he said, "I hope for your sake, Charlie, that your mind *is* made up."

"Why you saying it like that?" She scowled at him.

"Well, you're about to get your chance to convince the father of your baby, that you are just swell, without him."

Charlene looked over to where Abe was staring. To her dismay standing by the elevators of the parking garage, stood a brooding Kane with hands shoved in his jean pockets, leaning against the wall...waiting.

She rested her head against the headrest of the vehicle. "You think he would notice if we backed out and made a run for it?"

"Notice? Hell, I think he might even jump on that motorcycle next to him and give chase," Abe grinned.

"Hey, what's that smile about, I thought you didn't like him." Charlene pointed out. "I would think you would be trying to help me to get as far away from him as possible," she fussed.

"That was before I realized the feelings are mutual. I thought the youngster was harassing you because of a conversation we had not so long ago," he teased. "Now, I'm beginning to think you were doing some flirting of your own."

She groaned. "You suppose to be nice to pregnant women."

"Don't look at me that way, Charlie? I'm not the one in the middle of a "baby momma" drama episode. It's all on you, my friend." He winked. "So get out and handle your business."

"You aren't coming?" She demanded, more than asked.

"Nope."

"How will it look with Kane and I being seen, going into my hotel, together?" She squeaked, reaching for straws.

"Let's see. You're his boss, you're black, and you're much older. First, they will assume it's all business, because it's implausible that you could be anything else to a guy that looks like him. No rudeness intended, but you know how these things are. Yet, if this little scene becomes a constant scenario, then it's obvious that there is "something" going on, and the rumors will start. After that, the reporters will bring up all the old dirt on you and Kane separately. Of course, eventually, they will search for new dirt about you two being *together,* and if they can't find anything they will make it up with all kinds of pretty pictures."

Charlene lips spread into a quirky half smile. "You got it all figured out."

"It's what I do," he reminded her. "I watch your butt. Seeing how you didn't need my help to sneak off and sleep with the guy, you don't need my help to convince him that you don't really love him."

"Ass," she spat.

"You, love my ass."

"I do." She grinned and opened the car door. "Now do me a favor and save my stupid ass in say, fifteen minutes."

"Whatever you say," he said sarcastically and started the car. "I'll call you later."

"Abe," she hissed. "Do you think he suspects something? Come on don't do this to me. I need you to bully him like you usually do and make him leave."

"*If*, I had done it to you, you wouldn't be in this mess. Now close my door, like a good girl and start cleaning up your own mess." Abe arched his eyebrows until she slammed the car door. He had the nerve to wink at her!

As soon as she walked around to the front of the car Kane caught her gaze and she felt a fluttering of hummingbird wings in her stomach, she wished it was the baby, but she knew it was her nerves. Avoid telling him how much she loved him was one thing, but lying outright, was another and Abe was right, she wasn't a good liar. Still, this is what's best for Kane, isn't it? Would he be happy knowing he was going to be a father or would that be the one thing that would push him away, forever?

Maybe telling him would be exactly what she needed to scare him into thinking logically about this situation. A lot of men run away from such responsibility. No, something tells her Kane wasn't one of those men. Jason could be a selfish ass, and he even he wanted to take responsibility for his baby. It's not in their cultural makeup to run from their responsibilities, especially when it comes to creating another life. Not to say there aren't some exceptions to every racial makeup, but she knew in her heart Kane would be very traditional when it came to the woman he love and the mother of his child.

"We need to talk." Kane marched up to her and took her hand, pulling her along to and on the elevator. Thank goodness, they were the only two on it, especially after hearing the discerning words that came out of his mouth next.

"What did the Doctor say, Charlie-chan? Are you pregnant?"

Her mouth dropped open. The elevator door closed.

Chapter Twelve

As soon as the elevator stopped on her floor and the exit opened, Charlene rushed out of the elevator with Kane on her heels. She slid in the key card and threw opened the hotel door, tossing her purse on the table by the door. The door slammed behind her, and she jumped.

"Answer my question, Charlene." He demanded.

She removed her jacket and placed it across a chair. "Why would you ask me such a thing, you know we were careful?"

"Then look into my eyes and tell me it's not true," he challenged.

She lifted her head and looked into him eyes. "I asked you, why do you assume I might be pregnant?"

Kane looked away and mumbled, "For starters, we were out of condoms that last time, in the shower."

Charlene's eyes narrowed and her lips tightened.

Kane paced.

"Then, you did realize before you entered me you didn't have protection." She walked over to the service mini-fridge and pulled out a bottle of water. Offering him one, he declined, mumbling something about needing something stronger, she pretended not to hear, but silently she agreed.

"*Chigau-yo!* That is so wrong!" He bellowed. "Are you actually trying to accuse me of intentionally trying to get you pregnant? Because, I believe you were there too, and if I remember correctly *you* grabbed me. Charlene, you can't tell me you couldn't feel the difference because I sure in the hell did. It was the first time I ever had sex without a condom, and I swear it was the best fucking feel—"

"Kane!" Charlene could feel the heat spreading across her face. "Okay, I get it, and I'm not accusing you of anything. It's you accusing me of being pregnant, remember?"

"How am I supposed to know about such things? It's not like I ever got anyone pregnant before." He cleared his throat. "I assumed you didn't mind and maybe you couldn't get pregnant after one quick unprotected time."

Charlene gave him a hard look. "You call that *quick?*"

It was his turn to blush. "Err, I mean, it was quickest…you know…*time*…we did *it* that night." He shrugged and splayed his hands. "You grabbed hold of me, and so I assumed it would be okay since being under the spray of the water it should wash most of it away…" His voice trailed off. "Right?"

"Oh God," Charlene moaned aloud. She rolled and closed her eyes; she was not ready to have this conversation yet. She chuckled and bit her bottom lip to keep from laughing outright. *Wash it away? If that were only true, women would be fucking freely in the shower instead of paying for birth control that could wreak havoc on their bodies after long-term use. What was she going to do with this man?* Love him until the day she died.

"The other reason I considered you might be pregnant by your reaction to Arisa spouting off what was in the bento box for lunch, you proved that dark skinned people can turn green." He lifted a brow at her as if waiting for her to say something, when she didn't he forged ahead. "That brings me back to my question. Are you pregnant with my child or not?"

Charlene remained quiet, guilt weighed heavily in her chest. She took a deep swig of the water from the bottle and placed the bottle on top of the mini-frig, before saying, "Maybe, it was the thought of the two of you together and married is what made me ill. She was a lot prettier, than I expected, not to mention very young."

"So you're saying you were jealous?" An easy grin came to his handsome face, and he came to stand in front of her. "You don't have to be jealous. I've missed only you."

She smiled. Familiar warmth spread through her body. "I've missed you, too."

"Then tell me the truth, Charlie-chan, are you pregnant with my baby?" He asked again.

Her smile faded, and she placed some space between them, moving to stand in her adopted comfort spot in front of the hotel room window, gazing out over Tokyo. "Kane, why do you keep asking me that?" she asked softly.

"Because, Charlie-chan, I noticed no matter how many times I ask the question, you avoid an answer. Like now." He sighed and came up behind her placing his hands over the natural swell of her abdomen as if he was trying to sense for himself if it was true or not. "How hard is it to tell me 'no' if it's not true and if it is true, I deserve to know if I'm going to be a father," he reasoned.

Silence grew and the room became stifling with tension. Her head felt as if would burst as she tried to think of something to say, anything to say, but the truth.

"Please, leave." She closed her eyes, having to lie was eating her up inside. In the end it would be the best thing for Kane. She didn't want to be one of those pathetic women that made a man feel trapped by using the pregnancy. She already told him it was over. "I just had an upset stomach."

He stiffened as if she had struck him and hissed in her ear. "Why are you lying?" He released her and moved away. "I never thought you to be a liar, Charlene."

"How do you know if I'm lying?"

"Because I spent over eight hours admiring, tasting, and touching every part of your body. To me your stomach feels a little firmer. Pressing against the back of you, from behind, your ass felt a little fuller, than it did when I took you from the rear."

"Kane..."

J-Pop Love Song

"Nani? What? You need more proof? Charlie-chan, you have two moles on your left inner thigh, another one under your right breast, and another under your left butt cheek. You also have a map shaped birthmark on your lower abdomen. On your right hand next to your little finger there's a faded scar. Need I go further?"

Charlene's mouth dropped wide in stunned disbelief. "N...no." She spoke in an unfamiliar shaky voice becoming annoyed at the transparency of her feelings, more so, when she started to cry. "I'm sorry." She turned to face him.

"*Ite-na!*" His lips puckered in a boyish pout and a scowl marred his features. Kane stared at her with accusing eyes. "Why are you deliberately trying to hurt me, is it such a crime to fall in love with you? How can I believe others will understand my feelings for you when you don't?"

"Please, let me explain," she begged.

"*You*, of all people, keeping the fact of something like this from me hurts more, than anything my father or Takusa has ever done to me." Tears choked his voice and he bent over at the waist bracing his hands on his thighs. "Fuck! I can't breathe."

"Kane..." Charlene cried out in concern moving towards him. He held up a finger. She stopped in her tracks wringing her hands together.

"Don't...touch...me," he warned. "Not, right now. I'm so angry there is no telling what I might do. I can't believe it, you weren't going to tell me about the baby." He accused in genuine disbelief. "*Kuso!* Shit! *Kuso!*"

"We'd already decided to not continue," she replied in a low, tormented voice. She felt a wretchedness of guilt she'd never known before. "I...I thought it would be best if you didn't know. It would make it easier for you to let me go—"

"Best for who, Charlene...*you*? Also, *you* were the one that decided we couldn't move forward together. Are you really that self-centered? Does everything always have to be about *you*?"

She saw his dark eyes water with unshed tears. A smothering sob escaped him as he stood, a hand rubbing his chest as he looked her in the eyes and continued, "Not once, have you taken in consideration what I want." He wheezed.

"Please...calm down, so you can catch your breath, Kane. You're experiencing a panic anxiety attack," she gulped hard, hot tears slipping down her cheeks. "I want to make you understand—"

"*Nani?* Understand what?" He asked brushing away tears. "How can anyone understand a woman that keeps such a thing to herself? How could you even consider it, knowing the relationship I have with my own father? Don't you know how important it is to me, to be everything to my baby, that my father wasn't for me?"

"I know, I'm sorry!" She covered her mouth with her hands to keep from weeping aloud. She was feeling completely helpless. Longing to touch him, needing to explain and hoping for his forgiveness.

She waited while he close his eyes and took in deep breaths, once his breathing seemed to return to normal, she chanced telling him the truth.

"I never meant to hurt you. I...I love you." She admitted. "I do. I didn't want to, but I do, and because I love you, I genuinely thought it best to let you go because...because..." she hiccupped. "I didn't want to do *exactly this*, to you!

Can't you see? I couldn't bear the thought of you giving up everything for me? I couldn't live with the guilt of ruining your life, knowing you would hate me in the future."

He walked slowly towards her his hands pressed together in front of him as if he was praying. "Damn you, Charlene. I can't believe you would choose now to tell me you *love me*. Do you know how I've longed to hear you say those three brief words to me? Fuck! Tell me how is it possible to love someone and yet, lie to their face about something as important as this?"

Defeated, Charlene felt her eyes flutter close and her knees grew weak. She started to sink in misery. Before she hit the ground Kane had quickly gathered her in his arms in a bear hug. He held her limp body snugly and they both went down on their knees on the floor.

In her abject state of mind, it finally hit Charlene full force. Nothing she had done up to this moment had been for Kane's sake. She was protecting herself. She didn't want to be hurt again, so she made all the decision that would protect her heart and not once had she really considered his.

"Baby, I'm so sorry. You're right, I've been thinking only of how I felt." How desperately she needed him. Charlene clung to him while burying her wet face against his pale blue sweater. "Don't hate me Kane," she wept. "Please."

"Shhh," he whispered into her hair. "This can't be good for our baby."

"I admit it. I've pushed you away. Now, look at me. I've stooped so low as to start lying to you. All because, loving you frightens me," she hiccupped. "Losing Jason hurt so much, but losing you *would* kill me, I know it!"

"*Shimpai shinai-de*, don't worry," he crooned. "It's wasn't your ability to love that ended up hurting you Charlie-chan, it was the man you chose to give your love to. I can see it on your face, you're wondering, if you are making the same mistake with me."

Her eyelids drooped downward; she didn't want him to see how close he was to the fact.

"Bay-bee, come on, let me see those beautiful brown eyes," he affectionately crooked a finger beneath her chin and tilted her face towards his. "It's okay, that you feel this way, as long as you are willing to drop the illusion and admit the undisputed fact."

"The facts?"

"Yes, you have spent the years buying into the hype that was the legend James-san. Now open your eyes and accept the truth of your life with this man. He was unworthy of the unconditional care you gave him, and he never loved you as much as you loved him."

"Kane—"

"No, Charlene, you've been sheltering this man's image for years. You don't have to do that anymore, he's been dead long enough he's become a legend in his own right and not off your devotion."

"I know you're right, it's just I've been doing it for so long..."

"Well now you have me, the baby and your dreams to focus on, and if we are to work, you can't continue blaming me for Jason's deceptions," he stated. "I can't live with you waiting for me to hurt you."

"Kane, I don't want to, but I haven't been with anyone but Jason. What if it's subconsciously embedded, and I don't know how to stop it?" she asked frantically. She genuinely believed she had faced every aspect of the broken pieces of her life that her husband had left with his suicide, until now. Considering she never thought she'd fall in love again, she never anticipated handling this situation.

"Maybe it would help once you learn more about me. Charlene, it's true, there are some similarities between Jason and me, but not as much as you may think. There is a plausible reasoning for the dreams." She noticed that he seemed to be in some form of inner turmoil.

"Bay-bee, I can't remember if I told you this...*demo*, but, when I was in England, I found someone who specialized in dreams and such. When the night terrors started, and I came close to jumping off a roof, I was desperate to do something. During hypnotherapy I learned something that only I and Stu-san knows, and I made him swear to keep it to himself."

"Can...can you tell me?" she asked, still uncertain as to where Kane was going with this confession.

"With you, I don't want any secrets between us, and I hope I can trust you to keep my confidences."

"I know after what I just pulled about the baby, you may feel wary about trusting me again, but I promise you, no more lies between us, Kane." She spoke with quiet, but desperate, firmness.

"The therapy allowed me to remember that Takusa purposely fed me information on Jason James, since his death."

"I don't understand, for what purpose?"

"Who knows," he shrugged. "Maybe good business practices. Think about it, your husband had an obsessively large fan base, and it continues to grow more so even after his death."

"True, I have the yearly residual checks to prove it." Charlene added. "So Takusa, realized that if he continued to groom you in Jason's image, but a more "pop version", of course, then people will see the similarities and—"

"I would be an entertainment force to be reckoned with as the years go by," he finished.

"You got to admire the old bastard, he plans ahead," Charlene said with resentful admiration.

"Yes, and he rarely leaves anything to chance. That's why he has to stay at least one step ahead at all times. It's been hard as hell keeping the fact that I know what he did to me from him."

"Ohm, about that Kane. I never read it myself because I couldn't invade your privacy that way, but I believe there is something you should know." Charlene looked away, feeling ashamed that she hadn't told him before now.

"*Nani?* What is it? Read what?"

"Takusa somehow, got into your laptop and read the dream journal you kept. He printed up a copy and gave it to me the first night I was here. He wanted to prove to me that you had some crazy obsession about Jason and thought yourself in love with me."

His face lit-up with a sudden understanding he grinned a closed lip smile. "*Sokka,* I see. Now, I understand why you were so willing to side with Takusa instead of speaking to me about it first. Those entries were pretty wild. I'm sorry, I suppose what happened at the Press Conference is my fault."

"What?" Her brows tilted as she looked at him with uncertainty. "Why are you taking the blame for that and I assumed that you would be livid after finding out Takusa was snooping and reading what you thought was your private thoughts."

"*Yosh*. I did it on purpose" To her surprise he threw back his head and laughed.

She didn't. She was completely confused.

"You see, I knew he would find a way to hack into my computer, or he would have never would have given me one as a gift. Of course it was, so he could spy on me, so I created that diary especially for his benefit. Trust me, he never got any further then I allowed him to. I have several security programs on my computer that kept the important stuff hidden from him."

Charlene grinned in understanding. She definitely found his ability to outsmart Takusa sexy as hell, and she also felt proud, proud and lucky to have him in love with her.

"It was the only way. If I hadn't fed him some form of bull he would have never thought I needed that time to "rest" and attend school in England. I was determined to get as far away from him as he would allow me to go, and find out what was wrong with me."

"I'm so thankful, I carried that secret with me, not sure if I should say anything because I didn't know if it was true or not, but it worried me because I wasn't sure if you truly loved me because of the dreams and if so..."

He tugged her into his arms, spreading his legs out in front of him and settled her between them to hold her from behind. His chin rested against her temple. "Yet, knowing I may be a nut you managed to fall in love with me anyway, and trusted me enough to give me your body. That means a lot to me."

"I couldn't help myself, you're so fine," she teased, well a little because it was true.

"Well, I'll have to use that fineness to keep wooing you everyday of your life." He pressed a kiss to the side of her brow.

"I look forward to it." She smiled, thinking about it. "Kane, you said through your therapy you remember what Takusa did to you. What did he do to make you start having these dreams and nightmares of Jason?"

"Before I could go searching for help, I had to face some truths, that I didn't want to face. Such as Takusa wasn't the father I always wished for and he didn't truly have my best interest at heart."

She heard his voice, full of sadness and disappointment. "I bet it was difficult for you to understand what was going on at that age. There you were a child, with yet another adult letting you down."

"It wasn't just hard it was damn near impossible for me to reason. Takusa came into my life and gave me hope. I probably would still be his biggest supporter if it hadn't been for Stu-san seeing what I couldn't. He said he seen it done over and over again in the military. I was lucky he knew the signs. He took me under his wing, and became the big brother I sorely needed."

"I can see that, he still watches over you, and he very loyal to your friendship.

He refused to take me to you, unless my intentions were pure. At this moment, I can honestly say they weren't, considering I was more confuse afterwards, that is, about everything except the fact that I had fallen in love with you," she confided.

"I'm was just happy you came. You gave me hope." She leaned her head back and accepted the sweet taste of his mouth pressed against hers. Charlene moaned when he broke the kiss, but she realized that Kane had more he wanted to say to her and eager to know everything about him, she listened.

"Charlene, day and night, for years, Takusa forced-fed me footage of your husband's performances," he admitted to her. "I would sleep with headset music of his voice blaring in my ears and he also had me reading countless biographies written about this man and any other materials he could find, be it facts or rumors in regards to his life."

"That man, is a piece of work," she whispered more to herself, not sure if she wanted to hear anymore.

"I wanted to tell you all of this from the beginning, but—"

"How could you, when the very first time you trusted me to be there for you, at the press conference, I let you down?" she said firmly.

She noticed he didn't agree or disagree; it wasn't necessary, they both knew she made a grave mistake by not discussing it with him. The thing they had to do now was move forward from here on.

"With Takusa bombarding me with film footage of Jason's performances and feeding his music in my room every night while I slept along with biographical reading tapes of his life; it stands to reason that I would *feel* as if your husband had come back to haunt and possess my waking thoughts."

"Sick son-of-a-bitch, something really needs to be done about, or even two years from now he will still be on our heels. After hearing all of this, I know he's not going to give up on controlling your life Kane. He's invested years into this and probably feels you owe him." Charlene reasoned.

"He has no one to blame but himself. If he had let things be, I would have done anything he asked, because I longed to have a substantial fatherly influence in my life. Except his little plan backfired, not only did I learn about Jason, I learned everything about you, because the man couldn't be mentioned with out you. You wrote his songs."

Lightly he fingered a braid.

"During those times when I was awake and listened to Jason's music and lyrics, I could feel the love, heartache, loneliness, and need that were all yours. You have your own style, like *Prince*, it doesn't matter who is singing it; you know he wrote it. Charlie-chan, every song you wrote during that time sounded like a personal cry out to your husband to wake up, and realize how blessed he was. Through your music, I fell in love with you and even though I knew I was too young, I wanted to take care of you and give you all the things he didn't."

She wasn't sure what she should say so she didn't say anything, she just allowed him to speak.

"I couldn't do anything for you, because I had nothing that was my own." His hands spread wide as if he was beseeching her to understand, "The only thing I had to offer was the fact that I'm a better man than Jason James ever thought to be." He declared in a clear and forceful voice.

She looked up, offering him a smile and a saucy wink. "Yes, you are."

He smiled suggestively, his arms brushed against her tender breast and a thrill of pleasure moistened between her legs.

"The one thing that you and Stuart knows now, that Takusa doesn't, is he only thinks he has the upper hand in my life because I allowed him to."

"Why do you continue to agree to this craziness for so long? Was it because of your original contract? Do you fear what he can do to your career?" she questioned.

"I admit, I love what I do and I'm damned good at it, but the only reason I agreed to continue allowing Takusa to run my career and life is because he had the means to make success happen sooner and also through him I could someday meet you in person."

"Why didn't you email me through my fan website, I personally answer all my emails, not always in a timely manner, but I do answer them"

"Say what? Do what? How would you have responded if some strange Japanese teen male, or young adult emailed you this story and then confessed his love for you? *Jodan daro*, you must be joking. You probably would have gave it to Goda-san to handle and he would have put me on a stalker watch list."

She chuckled. "You're right, I probably would have."

I had it all planned out. Once I turned twenty-five everything changes. All I had to do is keep up the pretense until then. Afterwards, I could come to you as a man worthy of your attention and hopefully love."

"Kane, I don't need anything, just you," she assured him.

He shook his head, a light scowl on his face. "*Yareyare*, geeze! There is no way I could proudly step up to a woman as beautiful and successful as you are, and expect you to take me on looks alone. If I had, the moment family and friends put their two cents in about our relationship, you would start doubting my intentions. You would begin to wonder about my motives, thinking I could possibly be using you like Jason did."

"Kane, that's not true. I…"

"No, bay-bee, the *truth* is you wouldn't had any security in loving a man that has nothing of his own to bring to the relationship."

His voice was uncompromising, yet oddly gentle while his eyes were sharp and assessing on her face. There was no reason to continue denying what he was saying. She smiled back, realizing that he was probably right. Eventually she *would* have wondered why a man so dropped dead gorgeous, *young*, and talented would risk so much to be with her, unless he saw a bigger payoff. It happens.

She knew from her previous marriage all it would take is one moment of doubt to instantly bring on an onslaught of other ones. Such as was he lying about his feelings? Was he cheating? Did he pretend to be with someone younger and prettier in order to make love to her? Did he wish he had married a woman of his own culture? The questions and the stress that came with this type of relationship could be endless and she for one had no desire to have another relationship scenario like that one.

Removing his hands from under hers he pushed the hair off his face, she moved to withdraw her touch from his knees and quickly he reached out and caught her hands in his bringing with it the warmth of personal contact. She laced his fingers with her own, their palms kissed.

"Charlie-chan, there is something that I want to tell you, that *no one* knows, not even Stuart," he began.

His expressive face changed and became almost somber. She started to worry about what he was going to say next.

"Bay-bee what is it? You can tell me anything." She encouraged him to continue when he seemed to dally.

"My mother left me enough funds, that once I turn twenty-five, I can do whatever I want, or do nothing at all. It's in a private trust that was set up by her father in case she found marriage to a man she didn't love, completely unbearable. The only reason I can guess she didn't want to use it to save herself, was because if she left him, he would have been allowed to keep me, and that would give him the right to banish her from ever seeing me again."

"Because there is no joint custody in Japan," she surmised.

"Yes." He agreed. "I suspect she felt trapped by it all, and that's why she killed herself instead."

"Baby," Charlene brought one of his hands up to her cheek and rubbed her face against the back of it. "I'm so sorry about you losing your mother in such a way, that had to be horrible."

"It was," his voice grew husky. The Adam's apple in his throat bobbed with strained emotions. "I found her, hanging in the closet of her bedroom when I got in from school."

She tugged his arms about her tighter as she felt a chill creep through her at the imagine horror of finding her mother that way. No, she couldn't even imagine such a scene.

"Charlene if only she had took the money and ran. At least when I was older own, I could have found her." He face twisted with despair. "Taking her life the way she did left me no choices at all. I never felt so helpless in my entire life. Still, I understood why she felt the need to do it, that heartless bastard, would bring other women into our home. She would have to sleep in her own room, while they slept in her bed. The last of his lovers, he is married too now. While that bitch lived in our home pretending to be his wife, my mother practically became no better than a servant." She winced as his hands tightened in hers, immediately he eased his hold.

Charlene looked at him with loving eyes as he stared sadly at their clasped hands. She could see the pain of loss was still deep. He looked down at her with tearful eyes and their stare met and held.

"I was admitted to a mental hospital and when I was finally allowed to go home, I couldn't get out of there fast enough. I ran away and lived in a smart box along the banks of the river for a few months."

"Smart box?"

"Yeah, it's a makeshift home you make by using cardboard or preferably, wood or bamboo and make a box, then you cover it in a blue fabric sheet to try to give you a little relief from the elements."

"Oh, yeah I remember seeing those when I lived here, I'm shameful to say I never paid much attention to them as I was chauffeured from appointment to appointment. To think I probably passed your temporary home and never even knew it. I have more time to give back for the blessings I have now, and I admit it has made me a better person." She dropped her eyes. "What did you do about food?"

"I played my guitar and sang on the streets to make enough to eat off of. Was it hard? Yes. But I wouldn't have changed a thing. I grew up quickly and I learned how to take care of myself with any means necessary. The only thing is unlike all the other kids and elderly I came in contact with, I knew if I could survive until I was twenty-five, I would be okay. As fate would have it, Takusa swept in and took me under his wing, so that stint didn't last long at all."

"Your just a couple of days away from you inheritance," she pointed out.

"Yes, and I already have my mothers lawyer who his very discreet and trustworthy, he's getting a large enough commission from the inheritance to assure it. Due to wise investments and money marketing accounts, it has grown to a ridiculously substantial amount. I've already have order plans to build income based housing to help the homeless in our community." He said proudly.

"If you don't mind, can that be a project we can work on together? Abe is very good at setting up things like this. He can assure that majority of the money is placed into the project and not abused for greasing palms and pockets." she said kicking into serious mode.

His smiled deepened in to laughter and he hugged her rocking her back and forth.

"*Atarimar-dayo!* Of course, but only after you bring our child safely into the world. So, I would be willing to work with Abe, as long as you stay out of it. Speaking of pregnancy, we need to discuss your doctor visit."

"We will," she answered. "But I'm enjoying hearing all of this about you. I feel as if my entire life has been an open book for anyone to look up and read about, but I didn't realize how much I still had to learn about you."

"Charlie, as of now, our relationship is no longer just in your hands. No more making decisions for the both of us and no more using our careers as an excuse to keep running from me." He kissed her brow. "Yourself and the baby are all that you should be thinking of. It will also be the driving force that will help me working out my obligations to your production company and figuring out what to do about keeping Takusa from interfering. No matter what, I refuse to put my personal happiness on hold any longer, do you understand?"

Quietly she nodded.

"Now that you know I have backup finance, you don't have to worry about what will happen to me, if I were to tell Takusa to shove it." He said with bravado.

"Yes, that will leave you with money, but it's your career you love. You've worked hard, built a name and you have fans that depend on you." Charlene finally asked the question that needed to be asked, "Are you sure this is something you won't come to resent *me* for later?"

"Hey, what is this?" He tilted his head in puzzlement, "Aren't you the one who told me I was talented enough to make it anywhere? Didn't you say I could do anything I wanted to do?" He pressed his mouth to hers and murmured, "*Zutto kimi-o omotteru*, I will always love you, Charlie-chan, never doubt that.

J-Pop Love Song

Now, as far as starting from zero again, it isn't a bad thing. I mean, if I can't find work I might have to be a "house dad" or worse, your "toy boy" for awhile," he teased.

"Yeah…you think so?" She nodded and grinned. "I believe that is "boy toy," Charlene managed before accepting the intrusion of his tongue in a sweet tender kiss.

Charlene hated to disappoint others that trusted her, but she couldn't think about that anymore, she had a life growing inside her, and a man that trusted her to return his love unconditionally. She was over forty and time was growing shorter. She deserved happiness this happiness.

She couldn't wait to be able to see Kane's smile everyday. The past couple of months he'd been working hard for her movie and doing everything asked of him without complaint, but she could tell he wasn't truly happy. She knew she had a lot to do with the change and she would do what she had to, to show him he could trust her again with his heart. She would take better care of it this time.

She looked up into Kane's eyes as he pulled his head back to gaze at her. "I can see that brain of your working and I guess I need to finish saying what I have to say before you get started trying to run the show again." He winked.

She blushed. He knew her well.

"Charlene, we will keep are private lives as quiet as we can be, but that doesn't include hiding our love from our friends, and your family. We shouldn't have to. Those who love us will only try to help us build the strongest fortress possible to raise our family in. Those that don't, probably never will and we should accept it and move on, together," he pointed out bluntly. "It's not like I'm the only Japanese entertainer to fall in love or to have the woman he love to become pregnant before marriage."

"Yeah, but you may be the only Japanese one to fall in love with a black American woman, nearly sixteen years older then you."

He grinned sheepishly. "True." He chuckled. "Well, so what, it's not like *you're* not use to controversy."

She lovingly nipped at his chin.

"The one thing I know I'm going to do is let Takusa-san know that you are my future. He can represent me or sue me; I don't care anymore. If he keeps pushing I will disappear and if we can still make the film if you wish it without the investors that choose to bail out on the project. I will reimburse them their loss and we can start fresh. I can't guarantee it will be shown here, but we have to think positive, right?"

"Kane, your birthday party is the day after tomorrow. All the arrangements have been made. Can't you wait to tell Takusa afterwards, at least."

"If I wait, Charlene, Takusa is going to use my party as a platform to announce my engagement to Arisa and make the world think her baby is mine. I can't allow that to happen."

"Arisa is pregnant too?" Charlene shrieked trying to pull away from him. "What the hell?"

"Stop struggling, it's not mine, silly. I've never slept with Arisa. She's been trying to tell Takusa for weeks she was in love with a guy she met at medical school. When she got up the nerve to tell him she was pregnant, he came to me and asked for my help. He won't listen to anyone. Arisa doesn't love me. She is as much a pawn for Takusa-san greed as I have been all these years. The sad part is she isn't trying to fight it anymore, it seems."

"Regardless, Takusa has no right to make such an announcement. He can't, because the investors contract—"

"Has a loophole, and he found it." He interrupted. "Trust me, a pregnant girlfriend is a loophole. Because not marrying her, would be worse publicity, than the pregnancy."

"Yeah, unless the girl is also your boss, and everything else we already mentioned," she quirked an arched eyebrow at him. "Will she have the baby if you don't marry her?"

A crestfallen look came over his face. "Charlene, I didn't asked this before because I, well I just couldn't bare to think that you would even consider it, but..."

"What?"

"Because this was unplanned, did you consider getting rid of my baby?"

"*NO!*" She answered without hesitation. "God, no, I didn't even think of it as an option. With or without you, this bay is mine. I'm not a young woman, anymore, and this may be it for me. Besides, even though it wasn't planned, it's a part of you, why would I want to get rid of it?"

He hugged her releasing a relieved sigh. "I'm so thankful to hear you say that. I can't tell you what to do with your body, but I want to have this child with you." He leaned back, looking into her eyes and added, "*You* are giving me everything I've always wanted Charlie-chan, a family of my own and I'm ready for this next phase of my life."

"I love you, so much." She felt drunk with the joy of being able to say it aloud.

Kane smiled that dimpled smile that warmed her to her toes and gave hope to the hopeless.

"When I came here Charlie-chan, all I know is I was scared something was really wrong with you and if it was serious I had no say. I wouldn't even be allowed to see you in the hospital, if your family or Abe Goda- san were to deny me entrance. So pregnant or not, I came here with a purpose in mind and I wasn't leaving until I got my way."

"You can ask me anything."

"I'm happy to hear you say that."

Her eyes grew wide as he came to his feet pulling her up with him. He dropped to one knee before her. "What...what are you doing?"

"What I should have done the moment your ass wiggled at me as we were going up the steps to enter the plane," he said taking her hand in his. "I should have made my intentions known."

"Kane, don't. You don't—"

"Charlene, I've been miserable these past couple of months. I haven't been able to function nor have I forgotten the one night you trusted me completely and made love with me. When I heard you crying in the bathroom the morning afterwards—"

"You heard—"

J-Pop Love Song

"*SÙ-dana!* Don't interrupt me. I've rehearsed this a thousand times in my head waiting in that fucking parking garage." He frowned at her and she smiled. "You're no longer a vision that hunts my dream, but a love that hunts my soul, and without you breathing next to me, I feel as if I can't breathe at all."

"Oh damn," she sniffled placing her free hand over her mouth. In a muffled voice she said, "That sounds like a wonderful line for a song,"

"Charlie-chan, stop interrupting me. I have something important to say, Charlene Alfred-san..."

"I'm not the one interrupting, you saying all this sweet stuff, what is a girl suppose to do?"

He put a finger to her lips. "Are you going to let me finish this? My knee is going numb."

She snorted on a tearful giggled and nodded. "Can you hurry this up, I'm dying to kiss you."

"I could be at this all night," he grumbled. Then a foolish grin came to his mouth and he added, "I want to do more than kiss you."

"Kane!" She laughed shifting from foot to foot all of sudden feeling a deep need to pee. "Either ask, or let me go and pee first."

"You're sure you're older then me?" He shook his head.

"Okay, that's it—"

"*Kekkon shite-kureru!* Will you marry me?" He yelled it out over her voice, more like an exclamation then a question.

She looked at him a big foolish grin on her face. "Can I speak now?"

"As if you ever stopped speaking. I know...I know, you talk a lot when you're nervous." He laughingly squeezed her hands. "You're killing me, Charlie-chan, give me an answer."

"*Kisu shite*. Kiss me first."

"No lips on lips until I hear what I want to hear." Kane stated holding her at arm length.

"Of course it's a, YES, crazy boy!" Charlene squealed and threw herself against him, knocking him onto his back and straddling his waist. She sprayed his handsome face with kisses. Never had she been so scared of losing something in her entire life, as she had the moment she realized how much she could and had hurt him. He was her heart, her soul, her everything, and living another day of life without him in it was never, ever going to be an option she would consider again.

Kane relished waking up next to Charlene spooned against his side, her thick dark brown leg thrown over his thighs and her hand left arm rested under her head and her right hand resting on his abdomen. He remembered how her hand stroked him with loving tenderness and his cock hardened.

Should he awaken her? Of course, he should. Kane ran feather light touches along her thigh causing her to murmur sleep filled protests shifting from her side to her back. With a lascivious grin, he took his nose and hair stroking across her chest, her breast already growing fuller from his child beating beneath her heart, over her stomach where his babe nurtured from her exquisite body.

He kissed his child by pressing his lips against the small gentle swell of her lower belly. He couldn't tell she was even pregnant; he couldn't wait to see her grow lovelier with the fullness of his child inside her. He couldn't believe it, this time last year before his birthday he was busy flitting from concert stage to concert stage, he couldn't even slow down to have a proper birthday. They wheeled a birthday cake on a cart on the stage he was performing on and he blew out his candles in a concert hall of 1800 of intimate strangers.

Silently he had wished for this woman to realize he existed, for he had no idea how he would ever be able to meet her without divine intervention. Even with his recognition and success in Asia, he couldn't get easy access to someone like Charlene without a personal invite. At this moment when all his silent prayers were coming true, instead of relaxing in his happiness, he was scared to death that something would go wrong. He closed his eyes and said another silent prayer.

A gentle smile came to Kane's lips as he felt fingers burying in his hair. She lightly tugged and he lifted his head to see her lazy sleepy grin. Foolishly, his heart did a summersault, and he could feel himself falling in love all over again. She was the one, the only one for him and there was nothing to fear. There was no way he would get this close to ultimate happiness and lose it. He was determined to fight for their happiness, his freedom and most of all his new family.

"What are you doing down there?" she asked.

He lifted and eyebrow in question.

"What?"

"*Sekushii-dane*, you're so damned sexy," he kissed her stomach. "And, if you must know, I'm having a man to man talk with my son."

"What if he, is a she?" she asked.

"Well, I guess I told *her* all our secrets so now she's knows what to watch out for from all the play-yas." He winked.

"You're being silly," Charlene chuckled.

"No, I'm being deprived." He grinned. "I'm hungry for something, *sweet*."

"Mmm, something with sugar sounds wonderful. Why don't you call room service and order us something?" She suggested. The menu is under the phone."

"*Me?*" He asked sarcastically, quirking a thick dark eyebrow. "What am I suppose to tell them, I'm here in Alfred-san's hotel room at 1:00 am having a business meeting? Because you know we will be reading about it in the morning paper, with a snapshot from a cell phone of me opening the door. Even if I'm dressed it will be seen as suspicious with it just being the two of us."

Fully awakened she cursed softly. "Damn," she apologized sheepishly. "How could I have forgotten that we aren't like everyone else? That is why I took up writing books, I could remain private in my success, but on thing led to another and the next thing I know I'm in the thick of being a public figure once more. I don't know how we're going to pull this off until the end of the filming."

"Don't start to worry, honey, love always prevail." Kane assured her, realizing how cliché that sounded, but he could always hope it was a true statement since someone made it up.

Charlene shook her head, "If you weren't a song writer, I would swear you were the corniest man I've ever met." She giggled ruffling his hair and added. "I know in our business where we sell love, dreams, and hope to others—yours through music and acting, and mine with music and writing, it's hard to be realistic about anything."

"I hear what you're saying, but *my dreams* have been very real for me, Charlie-chan. So have you and I hope you see me as something real and substantial in your life, because I hear to stay."

She looked away.

"Charlene, *kocci mite*, I need you to look at me." Their eyes met and held. "I am a corny guy, trust me, my fans would be mortified that I'm not as cool as I pretend to be in public. What you have is the real me, not Kane the persona, but Yuza Kaneishi." He explained. "When I come home to you, I'm going to be a husband and a father and you're going to love, support, and yell at me and the kids." He grinned foolishly.

She returned his smile and continued to massage his scalp with her adoring fingers.

"I'm just an average computer geek trying to make a decent living, love my woman, and make myself a *real* family."

"I can't see you as a computer geek."

"Well, you haven't had the chance to actually see me in my personal environment, not I you in yours. This is a hotel, where dreams and fantasies of relationships can begin, but it's not who we are. We don't always have room service at out fingertips, and there is personal things lying around speaks for who we are and our personalities. I love to play computer games, and I have a bunch of them with a kick ass high-tech system of three computer screens. When I'm not working I wear prefer to wear my glasses." He announced with a solid nod.

"You wear glasses?"

"Yes, I do. I also fart in my sleep sometimes, or so Stuart says, but he may have been yanking my chain because I can't remember doing it." He laughed with her. "I have night terrors sometimes when I have insomnia and sleep walk, I've been able to control it better, when we get up in the mornings, you will see I put my pants on one leg at a time."

"Oh my God!" Charlene cried and covered her face. "You aren't perfect?" Charlene murmured. Her voice smothered by her fingers. "Oh no, I won't be Charlene Kane, but Charlene Kaneishi? How can I be the wife of a game playing Japanese computer *otaku?* My reputation will be ruined."

"Charlie-chan, I know, *Suminasen*, forgive me, I should have said all this before we slept together, but I was afraid you be disappointed in me," Kane spoke softly.

He saw her peep at him from behind her hands before dropping them to her sides and a look of disbelief came to her face.

"Kane, are you serious? Do you think any of this would make a difference to how I feel about you? My love doesn't come easy, but when it comes, it's forever. I know there is much for us to learn about each other, but look at how much we already know. I look forward to spending every day of my life learning more about you. I don't want us laying out our perfections and imperfections waiting for approval. I want to live our lives making tiny discoveries every day and deal with it together."

"You mean that?" He asked, surprised. It had been so long since he could be more then "Kane" to someone else besides Stuart. It touched his heart.

"Of course I do," She assured him then with a serious look said. "That is until the day you fart on me in your sleep, then fella, it's over...forever."

He began to tickle her sides and she thrashed and they laughed together until she begged him to stop.

"Now, that you're finish confessing, lets say, I call for something food and desert. Something, cold and creamy." She made a move to sit up to reach for the bedside phone.

Kane eased her back down on the pillow with one hand on her chest. "Not yet, when I said I was hungry earlier, it wasn't just for food." He gave her a smoldering look. "I was just about to have desert on my own before you interrupted." He admonished wickedly.

"Oh really?" Up on her elbows she cocked her head to the side in question. "I thought you said you were talking to the baby?" She reminded.

"I was. I was apologizing for all the times I've already bumped his head with my penis, and the many times I plan on doing it again in the future."

"Oh my God!" Charlene's laughter rang out through the bedroom. He gloried in the sweet sound of her happiness. She lifted the pillow from his side of the bed and hit him.

"Hit me all you want, but I'm going to lick you until it hurts." Kane clamped his arms around her thighs and drew her to him until her thighs were over his shoulders and the essence of her moist pussy in his face. He inhaled her scent bumping her clitoris with the tip of his nose. "I love the way you smell, but it's the taste of you that drive me insane."

"Oh, Kane."

He held onto Charlene while she whimpered and rotated her hips to accommodate the tongue-lashing he gave her. He licked and suckled the two soft folds of skin until they were heavy and plump. He licked her opening and darted inside for a better taste. He had to pull at her legs to lessen the pressure from her thighs but he didn't let up on what he was doing, even when she painfully pulled at his hair.

Kane kissed and suckled leaving his passion marks on her inner thigh. He was so impassioned by her response he had the urge to suck the Japanese *Hanko* signature of his name on her inner thigh, like a dog pissing on his territory, he wanted to place his loving brand on her. But he wasn't so far gone that he wasn't aware that she would box his hears if he kept at it too long.

Instead, he settled for a few passionate bruising here and there and went back to her pleasure button lapping and sucking until she was literally fucking his face. She was as hungry to accept his loving, as he was to give it to her.

She painted and screamed his name over and over. Her fingers moved from his head to claw and twist at the bottom sheet of the bed. For the second time, he felt her thighs involuntarily began to shake and shudder. He eased up over her, his hand stroking her to ease her through the orgasm. He tenderly kissed her, their tongues dueling like dancing snakes as he shared the taste of her juices with her.

He rolled on to his back and brought her over with him, not breaking the kiss, she straddled his lap, reached behind her and guided his pulsing penis inside her. She broke the kiss and leaned back bracing her hands against his chest until he was buried to his balls and she began to ride.

"Fuck, you feel so good," he groaned his hands moving from her waist to play with her breast and she cussed.

"Be careful, they're tender," she reminded him.

"*Suminasen*, is this better?" He breathe heavily easing his anxiousness and played more gently before moving his fingers between them and pressed against her mons and clitoris like she liked it. He received a loud moan and a string of Japanese curse words he didn't know she was familiar with. He grinned and vibrated his forefinger with added pressure to the protruding swollen gland of her clitoris.

"Oh, shit...fuck...I can feel you," Kane grunted trusting, the muscles in his stomach rippling with effort.

Her pussy gripped him like rippling fingers on a flute. From his view on the bottom he could admire her body, it reminded him of the cello when he held it in his hands, hollows and curves in all the best places—small on the top, big on the bottom. His cock was the bow playing her bringing forth-erotic sounds of lovemaking from her lips. Charlene released a high-pitched squeal, he held her while her body rocked and shook with another forceful orgasm.

Kane was relieved, because he didn't think he could hold on any longer. He cupped her bottom forcing her forward. Her breast flattened into his chest and he could feel her sucking on the side of his neck. It drove him nuts, his upward trust grew and the bed mattress moved with each rapid trust. His entire body went tense and he buried his hands in her braid, holding her face against his sweat soaked skin. He jerked groaned and cursed once more as one...two...painful spasms rippled through him as he shot his sperm inside her. A hot tear rolled down the side of his face the release was so intense.

The laid there his penis still inside her, their skin practically stuck together from the mingled sweat and allowed their breathing to ease back to normal. He kissed her, slapped and rubbed her bottom. "I didn't hurt you did I?"

"No, but I don't know if I will ever be able to walk again," she moaned and lifted her head brushing back the braids out of her face.

"Well, I raring to go, but this time I'm starving for real, my stomach that is."

'I can feel your stomach grumbling, but thought it was mine. "I will call and place an order."

He hissed as she lifted herself off of him and moved onto the mattress. His penis felt as tender as she indicated her breast was, but he needed to get up. He rolled out of bed and did a full body stretch. More for her benefit because she seemed to be enjoying the view. He looked down at himself, his entire body was flushed all over and his penis was shiny and slick from a mixture of him and her. He lifted the towel from the floor beside the bed where they dropped it after showering earlier and wrapped it around his hips.

"Hey, so what's up with that, you got me whipped so I don't get no cuddling?" She came up on her knees crawling to the end of the bed. Placing her hands on his hips she asked, "Where are you going? I figured we could shower together after we eat, and then get some much needed sleep."

He couldn't resist touching her once more, even if it was to make sure she was real. He cupped the back of her head and kissed her.

"I love you. Thank you for allowing me to be a part of your life," he said.

"You're welcome," she returned his kiss before smiling up at him. "What do you want to eat?"

"Anything is fine with me, for now, I got to get to work!" He released her clapping his hands and rubbing his palms together in anticipation.

"Huh? You're going to work at this time of morning? What kind of work?"

"Musicians do their best working at night, you know this." He pressed his lips to her forehead in a kiss. "The good thing about loving such a talented woman, you know there is no stopping creative flow." He pressed his lips to her forehead.

She moaned and fell back on the bed rolling on to her side, she propped her head up on one elbow. "Where the hell do you get all this energy?"

"Charlie-chan!" Kane jumped on the bed. "You inspire me and I feel like shouting, "I love you" to the world, I can't do that, so I'm going to write a song for you and the world can hear it. It will be my way of shouting."

"So that is what you were doing," she laughed out. "You were tapping out the notes on my clitoris with your finger while we were making love!"

"You felt that?"

"I felt everything, it just hadn't occurred to me until now that is what you were doing, I thought you had learned a few tricks I had yet to discovered," she teased.

Seriously he said, "Oh Charlie-chan, the most perfect melody came to my head. I promise you, it embodies your essence, and I got to get it out of my head before I go crazy." He hopped off the bed and rushed out of the bedroom room. "Hey, you mind, if I use some of your sheet music paper," he yelled from the other room.

"Go ahead," she called out. He paused to just look at her for a moment.

He saw her shaking her head with a big grin before she fell back wearily against the stack of pillows, closing her eyes, a arm draped over her head. All he could think to himself, was she wasn't a dream, and she was here, with him. She loved him, not the ghost of Jason James.

"There's some already on the piano!" She yelled.

"Yeah, I see it!" He yelled back, tearing his gaze away. "Hey, got to love these fancy hotel suites, we could hide out in here for years, making love, writing music, making love again." He laughingly called out, grabbing two bottles of water from the mini-frig and downing one before he went to the door and asked, "Want some water?"

"I'll get one in a minute I need to make myself a little fresh and presentable for room service. You can play but no singing aloud Kane. Work on the melody and you can do the rest later. Once you open that mouth of yours with that beautiful voice I will have ears pressed to the door."

"Yes, bay–bee." He winked.

"Kane, sweetheart, one more thing. About your statement of staying in here for years." She scrunched her nose up. "I'm not having this baby in this hotel room, with only you in attendance, so don't even think about it."

He nodded and laughed quietly as he made his way to the white baby grand in the corner of the suite close to the sweeping windows and the alighted night view of the Tokyo Tower.

He sat down and played the first chord and for the first time since he was a boy and his mother was alive, he felt he belonged somewhere. He knew as long as Charlene laid waiting for him, no matter where he was he had a home to come back to. If it took everything he had, he would do a better job at protecting Charlene and their baby, and then he had at watching over his mother.

By morning, lying naked in bed, Charlene's *room* phone rang. She refused to answer it. Kane's *cell* phone rang and he couldn't move to answer it. Her cell phone range and she was too busy to answer it. By the time the loud knocking sounded on the suite door, they both were too exhausted to answer it.

When they finally came up for air, she retrieved her messages, one of them being a threat from Abe.

"*Charlie, you either call me or I swear I will get the hotel desk clerk to open the damned door, and all the media will know about you and lover boy!*"

Charlene called immediately. Kane grudgingly did the same at her request, calling Stu-san to cover for him. Everyone else would have to wait. Emotionally and physically exhausted, they slept.

Chapter Thirteen

Takusa-san Estates

"Is he still there? He isn't returning my calls." Takusa bellowed. "*Sokka*, I see, well don't you dare leave until Kane does. I knew I couldn't rely on his personal watchdog Stuart-san. The black bastard's been covering for him once again. Keep me updated and don't let Kane out of your sight!"

Takusa slammed down the phone and cursed.

Charlene Alfred had played him for a fool. He should have known better than to believe she would actually stick to the program. She was seducing Kane, and pulling him in deeper. What was she up to? Now he understood why Kane had turned him down flat, about helping him with Arisa's situation by marrying her sooner than planned. He even offered him added stock in his business, and still, he wasn't interested. Now he knew why, he was sleeping with that American woman. Everything was quickly slipping from his fingers, and he had to get in control of the situation. "*Chichi?* Did you wish to see me?"

Takusa looked up at his eldest daughter as she timidly entered the office. "Did you have lunch with Kane yesterday as I told you to do?" He started in on her immediately, barely able to tolerate looking at her face. She was another one, that was ruining his plans, and after all he's done for her over the years, grooming her to be an exceptional wife to Kane. *Whore, just like her mother*.

"Err…yes, but he seemed distracted," Arisa answered. "He didn't even finish lunch, he picked at it before rushing off back to work. He left me to clean up with Stu-san. When we went to find him, they said he left for the remainder of the day. He had told them he had and emergency, and to shoot around him."

"If Stuart was with you he probably wasn't aware Kane went off to secretly meet up with Alfred-san," he said gruffly and released a long sigh. "That stupid boy, is doing everything in his power to ruin what we've worked so hard to create."

"I met Alfred-san on the set, *Chichi*," Arisa said taking a seat across from her father. "She seemed very nice and…"

"Nice, you say?" Takusa snapped. "That "nice" woman is stealing your fiancé from right under your stupid nose."

"Kane's not my fiancé." She clasped her hands together in her lap. "He's like my brother. I can't love him that way. Don't ask me to start now. I genuinely believed I could do this for you, but I can't!"

J-Pop Love Song

"Arisa, I don't have time for your whining! I have invested time an energy into making you a well rounded young woman, and I will not see you married to some country doctor, you've dishonored yourself with." He cursed. "Do you understand me? Get Kane in your bed. It's not like you're a fucking virgin anymore."

"*Chichi*, how could you ask me to do such a thing?" Her eyes sparkled with unshed tears. "Kane loves Alfred-san, you should see his face when he looks at her, and she looks at him in the same manner. I won't be a part of breaking them apart."

"You know nothing! You think successful marriages can be built on love? It's a foolish emotion that serves no purpose," Takusa argued.

"Not true. I love Marcus O'Ryan and it means everything to us," she cried. "Do you hear me, it's over *Chichi!* I'm no longer under your thumb. I'm about to have a career of my own and Marcus is successful in his own private practice. We intend to work together. I don't need anything from you, but if you want to see your first grandchild you will accept my choices."

"You truly believe that I care about you or that baby you're carrying? Why should I? You don't even carry my blood in your veins!" Takusa said bitterly.

"What are you saying, *Chichi?*"

"Arisa, I'm saying you will do as I asked and in time Kane will see your child as his own, as I did with you."

A stunned expression alighted her pretty face as she stared at him in disbelief.

"No," protested softly. "That's not true. Why are you saying this?"

"You, are not my daughter Arisa" he said bluntly. "Your mother's father, paid me a large sum of money to marry your. Of course I knew he needed me and money wasn't enough for me to spend the rest of my life with a woman, spoiled and unable to fend for herself."

"Stop! I don't want to hear anymore."

"No, you need to hear this because I want you to realize how grateful you should be. Do you know the stigmata you would have carried as a child if your mother gave birth to you out of wedlock and by a married man that was employed by her father's company? His management business would have faltered from the bad publicity. Of course being his most loyal employee at the time he approached me with and offer."

"Please, don't do this."

"I knew I had him where I wanted him. He was desperate, and he needed me to help make it all go away. So, I made him an offer of my own. If he set me up in my own business with unlimited capital to get me off the ground, in addition to introducing me to the right connections in this field, we had a deal."

"If this is true, then that would mean you've lied to me all these years!" She yelled. "You've controlled and manipulated all my choices, and now you're telling me you aren't even my father? You are a heartless bastard."

"Heartless? Maybe, but being a bastard is all on you." His mouth twisted in grim smile. "Arisa, I've invested too much time into grooming you to be the perfect wife for Kane's persona. You will become the elite couple of Japan and on Kane's thirtieth birthday, I will retire him from the entertainment field, he will take on my family's name and take his position by my side, in my empire. By the time I finish, the Takusa name will be known worldwide. Extended branches of my management group will broaden to the Western capital. Arisa, I will not lose sight of my goals, nor will I lose my son to that Black American bitch!"

"I can't believe this." Shaking her head in disbelief, she came up on her feet. "I see, you can't give me your love, but Kane is not your blood, yet he seems to be everything to you. Is it because you wanted a son so badly you're willing to step on all of our feelings to get what you want?"

Ignoring her distress Takusa continued. "My reasons are none of your concern, Arisa. You will do as you're told or I'll make sure that man you're in love with can't ever practice again."

"He has no ties to Japan, except me and I'm leaving. So your threats can't reach him in Paris. Allow Kane to be happy and let me go!" She wept freely.

You're right, I have no influences in Paris, but I do have other connections that you will not want to force me to use. Tell me, how difficult is it for a surgeon to maintain his practice with damaged hands?

"You wouldn't dare," she gasped. "You would actually physically harm someone to achieve this crazy dream of yours?"

"You wouldn't understand why this is so important to me, Arisa. You've never lived without a roof over your head. You don't know what it feels like to be so hungry you resort to eating unimaginable things to survive and doing even worse to stay alive." Takusa fought the bitter bile that arose to the back of his throat and took a deep swig from the cup before him.

"Please," she sobbed. "I will go to mother, she will understand."

"You mother has everything she could possibly want. I give her the wealth she is accustomed to, prestigious standing in the community, and she is allowed the freedom to discreetly find her pleasures elsewhere. Do you think she would jeopardize her happiness for yours? Don't count on it."

"What about Sakura, she is your blood right? Why not let her marry Kane?"

"That is not possible," Takusa said abruptly. "Besides the fact she is sixteen and has been primed to be prima ballerina since she was five, she is represented by my company and already has a position waiting for her in Matsuyama's Ballet Company. I don't foresee her marrying and definitely not having any children for some years to come...if ever."

"So, only what's best for your daughter's career, while you destroy mine."

"I believe you've already done that by getting pregnant. Do you expect you will have time to be a fit mother and have a medical career at the same time? Yes, I know women do it all the time, but they don't do both well, one must suffer for the other. You must pick one lot in life and focus obsessively on it to achieve greatness."

"I can do it. Besides, I won't be alone!"

"Are you so dense you've forgotten my threat already?"

"I hate you!"

"So you've said. Now, don't you think you have something you need to be doing? I can't force you to do away with this child, but I can force Kane to marry you. At least I know for sure that you are fertile and my expectations are that after you have that child, you will get pregnant again, but this time with Kane's child. You might as well get started on my future heirs."

J-Pop Love Song

"First, I'm your whore, now I'm your breeding cattle," Arisa spattered bitterly.

Through cruel eyes he watched Arisa place a protective hand over her abdomen turning her back towards him. Dismally, she walked towards the door He took great pleasure seeing her proud slender shoulders stooped in despair. Women were the biggest commodities and burden for any man, but fortunate for him, he learned a long time ago to use them to his advantage before they had the common sense to use him first.

Now, if someone could teach that proud American bitch, Charlene Alfred-san, her submissive place in a man's world of business, his problems would be solved. What allure did she hold, that drew Japanese men to be so protective of her? There was Jason James-san, then Abe Goda-san, and now Kane, all risking everything to remain by her side.

Still, she was a well-prepared adversary. She had wealth and prestige in places he couldn't reach and if he were to put a halt to her project it would be a temporary fix, for she could still release it in other countries. *Damn!* What was her Achilles heel?

First he must make things clear with his daughter. "Before you leave Arisa, I want you aware that you will be contained to your room, your cell phone, phone, and computer confiscated until you remember your place in this family. When you do leave you will have a bodyguard with you." He released a long sigh. "I don't know why you've made things harder, than they had to be. You've always known what was expected of you; don't think I don't know that's why you got pregnant. You hoped to change your fate? Well, it didn't work. You will be at your best for Kane's birthday party, where I shall announce you engagement."

"I pray that I live to see the day you will know what it feels like to have everything you love dearly taken away from you. That is if you ever loved anything dearly besides your entertainment empire." Her palms were bleeding from the crescent moon shaped creases made from her fingernails as she balled her hands into fists. "I hope you pay for every life you've ruined."

"There are two things I love dearly and trust me, I will do what I must, to hold on to them." He vowed. "Now get the hell out. It disgusts me to look at you and think about the disgrace you've brought on my name." Takusa turned in his chair and looked at the future architectural design of Takusa Enterprise. He was so close to making it all a reality and nothing, and no one was going to stop him. Not Arisa, not Kane, and especially not Charlene Alfred-san.

Takusa flipped open his cell phone and pushed redial. "It's me again. Is Kane still in there? *Sokka*." Takusa felt a surge of anger rip through him. "I don't care what you have to do. Go up there and get his ass out, but be discreet. I don't want the local media getting wind of this. Bring Kane straight to me, do not stop for anything and I want you to do it, NOW!"

♪

Kane's hard stare narrowed suspiciously on Takusa-san's calm demeanor. Something was wrong and he'd have to be on his guard.

"It's obvious you are back to your old tricks of having me followed. Nevertheless, I thought you would be more upset than this."

He was on top of the world after leaving Charlene's suite, and he was ready to battle the old man tooth and nail for the woman he loved, but the look of weariness on his mentor's face left him conflicted. For the first time, he could see the frailties of age setting in and he wondered if he was well.

Takusa crossed his legs and took a sip of tea. "What can I do? You've always told me that you had feelings for Alfred-san because of your dreams. I had hoped that meeting her in person would have dispelled those feelings. I obviously was wrong; you obviously are in love with this woman and you've thrown all sense to the winds. Knowing what you both risk, only the foolish emotion of love can make people do stupid things."

"Don't be so cynical, Takusa-san. Love can also create wonderful things. I'm writing music again and now my dreams of succeeding means so much more to me. Even you can see the advantages of having someone as gifted like Charlene in our lives. If you would just accept this, all three of us will rule the music industry worldwide."

"As far as I am concerned, she has already proved her disloyalty to me through her influence of you. I don't trust her." Takusa pointed an accusing finger at Kane. "After years of you knowing your purpose in this world, suddenly you doubt and question me."

Kane shook his head. "That has nothing to do with Charlene and you know that. You've known for a long time that I am not happy being a pop star, that I want to write and perform *real* music."

Takusa would not concede the field. "How do you know she really loves you and she's not just trying to bring back her dead husband through you?"

"Don't be ridiculous," Kane shot back, surprised and angered by Takusa's venom. "The next thing you're going to claim is that she's looking to take over Takusa Enterprises."

"And you think it's impossible?" Takusa demanded. "The Americans are a shrewd and devious lot. Anything is possible with them. They do not understand loyalty the way we Japanese do."

"Listen to yourself. You know how crazy that sounds?" Kane had never heard such paranoia from a man who maintained order and calm no matter what. "You're speaking of Charlene as if she were *you*. She is happy with her life and her career. She was offered a chance to turn her book into a film, and she accepted it. It's more of a personal quest for her then some insane desire to conquer the world like you!"

"So you say." Takusa snorted.

"If anything, you should be thanking her." Kane continued. "Since getting to know Charlene, it's been like an awakening for me. It's only strengthened what I already felt all these years and the more I come to know her the deeper my love grows for her."

Takusa just waved a dismissive hand.

"Most of all, I *like* who I am when I'm with her. She doesn't care if I'm Kane the *talento*, talented musician and actor. Charlene loves me for *me*."

"*Sokka*, I see. *You're* now an expert on women?"

"No, but I am an expert when it comes to making Charlene happy and I plan on spending the rest of my life doing just that." Kane stated firmly. "I asked her to marry me and she accepted."

For the first time since they started the conversation, Kane saw a brief look of something other than the all-knowing smile Takusa worn since he entered his office. "We decided to do it privately and quietly. "We plan on doing it again in a more public fashion at a later date."

"I...I hope you haven't done anything that foolish already." Takusa commented.

"Of course not, I wish to talk to her family first, but after that we will make it official."

"You know even when you procure a license things like this has a way of going public, Kane. Once that happens you know what will come next? You will first lose you endorsements and then your unaired televised dramas will be pulled or a disclaimer added that the films were created before the mishap..."

"My marrying Charlene is not a mishap, Takusa-san." Kane said angrily, thinking how narrow-minded to penalize an entertainer for expressing natural human emotions. Why did his private matters be aired in public? He'd given years of him time, talent, blood and sweat to bring a little happiness to people he never knew, so why did it matter if he wanted a little happiness for himself?

"Gomen nasai, I'm sorry, I have to be the one to point this out to you, but you've been in this business long enough to know how things are. Even with all your success, some greater than you have tried to survive this sort of damage to their careers, and failed." Takusa pointed out. "Are you ready for the consequences of your action?"

"*Sensei*, Teacher," he leaned forward in his chair. "Have you listened to the music I recorded lately? That is because of Charlene. Can't you hear how I've evolved? It's better than anything I have ever done before."

"*Hai*, yes, I've seen your progress and I'm proud of you. It's been awhile since you called me Teacher, Yuza-kun." A reflective half smile came to the older man's lips.

"About as long as it's been since you referred to me as Yuza-kun." Kane smiled back at him.

"Seems like a long time ago." Takusa looked at him in the eyes. "You use to trust my word as law back then."

"When I was a boy you were someone I looked up to. I wanted to immolate you, but once you purposely made this image of "Kane", you allowed your reality to slip away from you. It's as if you no longer cared for the kid that made it all possible, but under the hairstyle, shades and designer clothing. It's still me." Kane ran a hand through his hair. "Did you think, that eventually I would forget my own dreams?"

"Kane, you are so much more then you give yourself credit for. Please, a few more years are all I'm asking of you. You're young still, so what's a few more years to you?"

"Everything. My time is now." Kane pleaded for understanding hoping he was getting through to his mentor. "I genuinely assumed when I trusted you with my future instead of some other already established entertainment group and I did everything you asked of me, it was because you knew what I wanted. You said that once I turned twenty-five, we could retire this character, and I would be allowed to do my style of music.

"Son—"

"I'm a rock musician at heart, *Sensei*, you've always known this, and I need to breakaway from this pop idol persona you've built around me. It was okay while I was a kid, but I'm a man now, and I can no longer write sweet nonsense music with saccharine lyrics. There is a lot I need to say in my music without you inhibiting my every movement."

"Didn't I allow you to do the Global Warming concert? Isn't that enough?"

"Not for me. Do you know when the last time I got to speak in public and it not be pre-scripted?" Kane got up from his seat and walked over to look at the array of awards he won over the years. He didn't even get the honor of putting them in his own place. No, everything about Kane belonged to Takusa.

"Is this conversation we're having about you wanting to change over to rock music genre or is it really about Alfred-san?"

"Both. We both know Kane can't be with Charlene, because everything will go crazy and all of three of us will lose. Yet, if you formally announced the retirement of Kane at my birthday party, then once I complete the film I can come back as Yuza, bigger better and stronger then ever. A new look, new music…"

"New management?" Takusa interrupted.

"Not if you're willing to grow with me." Kane stated and turned to look at the other man.

"If I was to agree to this, will you marry Arisa and take on my name?" Takusa asked.

"I am willing to take on your name, continue to learn the industry and put a hundred percent into the job. I will help to build a legacy for your daughters to pass down to their children. While supporting Charlene in her endeavors to produce a legacy for our children." Kane paused before making a point of staring Takusa straight in the eye and finished by saying, "But, no matter what Charlene will be my partner for life and by my side every step of the way."

"Then, I can't agree." Takusa's face-hardened. "Not now. Not ever." The answer was swift and final. "I have invested years in marketing and promoting you as *Kane*, but I will take all that you have and keep taking, before I allow you to marry that woman. I didn't want to say this, but if you push me I can make things difficult for Alfred-san getting her film completed here. Goda-san may find difficulties in obtaining a few of the licenses—"

"Do you really hate her so much that you'd sacrifice not only Takusa Entertainment's profits, but those of the investors you call friends?" Kane stepped away from the glass award case and strode towards Takusa with measured steps. It took all the self-control he possessed not to hit the man.

"That would only be the beginning."

Kane didn't care about himself, but he did care a great deal about Charlene's dream. He didn't want be the cause of it slipping away, but he didn't want to give her up either. As far as he was concerned, if it came to that, he'd sacrifice his own career.

Knowing her, she'd be angry with him for even considering such an action, all the while telling the investors the deal was off if it came to losing him.

He sincerely hoped it was the truth, because Takusa seemed more than

J-Pop Love Song

capable of doing whatever it took to get his way.

"You'd really rather have your name dragged through the mud than to meet me half way?"

Takusa's eyes were hardened glass. "That and more, Kane, believe me. Given time, I can rebuild my reputation. You don't have that luxury and neither does Alfred-san."

Kane couldn't believe what he was hearing. "Why?"

"My resentment is personal. I will not allow her to win this time."

"What the hell does *that* mean?"

The older man didn't answer. Instead he ordered, "Tell Alfred-san it is over and get her to return to the States. I don't care how you do it."

Kane said nothing, his mind struggling to accept the old man's ruthlessness. Takusa must have seen his silence as a signal and drove the knife in deeper.

Steepling his fingers, his smile was predatory. "Do you have any idea of what a desperate man will do in order to get what he wants?"

"*Yamero-yo!*" Kane spun around ready to do battle.

"I will *stop* when you forget all this foolishness and get back on track."

Kane's hands fell dejectedly at his sides. Takusa merely smiled, assured that he would be obeyed as always. The younger man wanted nothing more than to wrap his hands around his mentor's throat and squeeze.

Killing Takusa would make things worse, he thought, but Kane wasn't ready to give up. "What would you do if I just walked away from everything right now?"

Takusa shook his head. "Kane-san, this isn't that damned film; this is reality. If you are even considering leaving Japan with that woman, I will have you arrested for embezzlement of funds."

Kane exploded. "You could never prove that," he said with a bravado he didn't quite feel.

"I do not make idle threats without the power to back them up. Tell me, Kane, when did you actually *read* something I put in front of you to sign?"

"I read everything, Takusa-san." Kane replied, his tone deadly serious. "Remember, I learned that from *you*."

"Except at the press conference. You took Alfred-san at her word that everything was fine and you signed the two items before you. The one on top that she saw, but the second sheet was something I slipped in. My personal safety net, so to speak."

"*Nani?* What was it?"

"Oh, just something that incriminates you should the need ever arise." Takusa sat up straight in his executive chair, his dark eyes full of malice. "A signed confession that you have been skimming off the box receipts for some time to supplement some narcotic habit, or even a mistress." Takusa looked feral now. "I have a few club promoters in my employ who are willing to testify that you have been blackmailing them or you would abruptly cancel a show and they'd lose money."

Kane bluffed. "No one would believe that."

"With your signed confession, my witnesses, and your intimate association with Alfred-san, whom I will also implicate as your motivation, as well as your sudden desire to leave my company, the public will believe *everything*." Takusa stated smoothly. "Especially because Alfred-san is not Japanese. You know as well as I that many do not hold African-Americans in high esteem."

Kane felt sick as he blindly stumbled for the chair beside him and plopped down. Silence reigned. How could the man who sat across from him, the man who'd been like a father to him, be willing to destroy him? For years he'd believed that Takusa cared about his future. Now, he knew the truth. Takusa cared for no one but himself. He was ridiculously wealthy, had prestige and power and it was not enough.

His cell phone buzzed and with numb fingers he checked to see who was calling. It was Charlene, probably wondering how his meeting with Takusa-san was going. She had wanted to come with him, but thank God, he had insisted on doing this alone. Kane felt truly helpless and didn't know what to say to Charlene at this moment.

Kane ignored the call and let it go to voicemail.

When he could finally speak, he asked the same question from before. "*Nande?* Why?" He glared at Takusa with impotent hatred. "If you hate me so much then why did you choose me to marry Arisa and take over Takusa Entertainment? You know I don't love her, that I love Charlene."

Takusa's shoulders grew tense and he yelled "Do not mention that woman's name in my presence again! It is because of her that you have forgotten what you owe me, to your own kind."

"*Sokka,* I see."

"Kane, at the time I took you in I didn't know I wouldn't have a son of my own When your mother...died ...I thought if your father wasn't going to care for you, it was the least I could do out of the respect for your mother's memory."

"Kane, I made sure you had an education at the best schools. I also made sure you had a wonderful career in the entertainment industry, allowing you to make influential connections and to give you firsthand experience about the business. Now because of me, you have a flawless career up until now. I can see you achieving even greater stature than I have."

"I'm not you, Takusa-san. I don't need anymore than I have. I love what I do, but it doesn't make up my entire life. I'm contented with Charlene, please don't force me to give her up." His voice cracked with pain. "I don't want power and I don't want to live your dreams for you. I never did," he admitted sincerely.

"Think of the legacy the Takusa name shall have...your name...your legacy to pass on to the son that you and Arisa will have some day. All that we accomplished will go down in business history. I needed a son to do that and unfortunately not being able to produce any more children. You are the chosen one to carry the torch of my legacy."

"Everything I have done up until now has been for the sake of the Takusa legacy, but I draw the line when it comes to marrying Arisa, I don't love her, and she doesn't love me." Kane continued to reason.

Takusa chuckled and lit a cigarette. "Enough of this conversation. I have a meeting in about fifteen minutes, and I strongly believe you need to convince Alfred-san to return home. The separation should do you both some good. If after you and Arisa get married, and she gives me my first grandson, by you of course, then, if you still fancy the black woman make her your mistress. At her age she should be grateful you're interested at all."

"Go to hell!" Kane shot up. "You're a wretched old man and I don't know why I've never seen it before. I allowed you to control every aspect of my life since I was twelve years old because I respected you more then I respected my real father. Now I see the two of you are alike. You've never been the man I thought you were!"

"Until those fucking dreams started, Kane, you were happy with the thought of following in my footsteps." Takusa fired back. "If I tell you why Jason Jamessan chose to come to you instead of anyone else you will realized that woman never had anything to do with this!"

"What are you saying? What other reason could there be?"

Takusa took a deep drag on his cigarette and stubbed it out in the crystal ashtray on his desk. "I assumed you would come to your senses eventually and see how ridiculous it was to actually believe you were in love with a black woman sixteen years older than you. A woman you hadn't even met!"

"I *am* in love with her." Kane's patience was gone with the old man and it was time he accepted the facts whether he liked them or not. "Takusa-san, from the moment I first saw her, I knew she was mine, and I was meant to spend the remainder of my life with her. Charlene is *my happiness*. I need you to understand this. You can't ask me to give up the one thing, I ever asked for, in my entire life. Why are you doing this to me?"

"Arisa asked the same thing, but to you it's should be obvious. You are my son and my heir. That gives me the right to interfere." That should have explained everything as far as Takusa was concerned.

Kane looked at the other man. He had heard it all before, when Takusa felt his hold slipping, he would remind him of how grateful he should feel that he treated him like a blood. But it wasn't going to work this time. He wasn't his real son, and he no longer needed the unconditional care of a father. He was going to be a father. Be the type of father he'd never had.

A cold sweat marred Kane's brow. Suddenly, he felt as if he couldn't breathe. He tugged at his collar around his neck and murmured in a choked voice, "I got to get out of here."

Wallowing in anger and frustration he made his way across the room. Before he could open the door, Takusa called out to him. He closed his eyes and paused bracing his shoulders for whatever Takusa would say next. Whatever it was, he was sure he wasn't going to like it. His fingers tightened around the doorknob.

"Don't forget your birthday party tomorrow evening, Stuart-san will be waiting to take you to the stylist and wardrobe at 4:00 pm sharp. Don't get any ideas. You will follow the script."

"I will be there." Kane said grinding down on his back teeth. "If I convince Charlene to return to America, will you assure me that nothing will happen to her or her film project?"

Takusa chuckled. "Kane, you have my word. You continue to do as you're told, and I will make sure nothing happens to the woman. Trust me, women are resilient creatures. Alfred-san will see that you've moved on without her, once she returns to America, and your calls stop coming. Eventually, she will move on. Time heals all wounds, including yours."

Kane turned the knob, yanked opened the door and sauntered through the front office ignoring the stares of the many Takusa Entertainment employees as he made his way to the elevators. Tears burned in his eyes as he wondered what he was going to tell Charlene.

With proud erect shoulders he stepped inside. He yielded to the compulsive sobs that shook him and pounded a closed fist against the wall. He had lost.

♪

Charlene smiled a soft endearing closed lipped smile as she came out of her bedroom in a thick hotel bathrobe and bare feet to see Kane standing in a matching robe in her favorite spot by the window looking out at the Tokyo illuminated skyline.

A light frown marred her brow as she saw him rub and massage the back of his neck with his hand. She wondered about his restlessness all evening and hoped he would volunteer to share what had happened during his talk with Takusa but he had been quiet during dinner, after making love and during their bubble bath together.

Upon his arrival the intensity of his lovemaking upon his arrival frightened her for at first, because the moment she answered the door and the door closed. He was lifting her against him guiding her legs around his hips and his hot mouth hard pressed against hers. Before she knew it she was pressed between him and the wall with her sweatpants and underwear dangling from one ankle. He was full clothed and his hard cock stood at attention from the unbuckled, unzipped, jeans on his hips. He didn't even take time to remove her t-shirt before he was impaling her on him taking her against the wall as her ankles locked about his lean hips.

He was so inflamed; she actually had to remind him of his strength and her delicate state. Otherwise, there were no complaints, for her orgasm had been so intense she swooned against him and he panic and they both went to the ground. After worrying him, he became extremely tender and slow during their next coupling in the bath, so much so they both held each other and cried until his penis softened inside her and slipped out on its own accord.

Generally, at this point they would be resting against stacked pillows holding hands or facing each other and talked about any and everything that came to mind, but not today. It could only mean one thing, the meeting didn't go well; she wasn't surprised, yet obviously Kane had more faith in his guardian than she had.

Quietly she strolled across the room and came up behind him, Charlene put her arms around his waist, before she felt him place his warm hands over hers, rubbing smoothly back and forth against her skin. "I didn't startle you did I?"

"I saw your reflection in the window," his deep soothing voice answered.

She leaned into his strength. "Are you ready to talk about it?"

"Talk about what?"

She felt the tension in his back. "About what Takusa said to upset you?"

"I can't keep much hidden from you, can I?" He released a soft laugh and turned until he was holding her.

"Were you trying to?"

He dipped his head and kissed her until she was breathless.

Charlene broke the kiss as she felt him reaching for the tied sash at her waist. Grabbing his hands, she stilled them. "I know what you're doing and it's not going to work this time."

"What do you mean?" He asked with the most innocent face she ever seen on an adult male.

"Do you imagine that I don't notice that every time something happens that you don't wish to discuss you make love to me until I'm too tired to talk. Well, it's not going to work this time because we need to talk about this, sweetheart." She turned and led him by the hand over to sit on the sofa. "We are partners, you can't keep things from me, if we're going to make this work."

As they set facing each other, she waited patiently until he was ready to speak. A feeling of anxious tenseness swept through her as he continued to sit there looking at nothing in particular.

"I suppose you suspected by now, it didn't go well with Takusa-san." Kane voiced softly.

"I'm sorry it didn't go as well as you had hoped, but honestly, I'm not surprised at all. After not being in Tokyo more then a day, Takusa was at my door with a plan to keep us a part. I don't expect much has changed for him since then." Charlene tersely said.

"No it hasn't. If anything, he's gotten worse. He is blackmailing me with bogus embezzlement charges, saying that if I tried to leave, or back down when he announce the engagement to Arisa at my party, he will contact the authorities."

Charlene brow creased with worry, as she looked at him "Can he do it?"

"Yes, but I didn't do it I swear. He snuck in a letter of confession beneath your contract at the press conference, and I didn't read it."

She reached out and caressed his damp hair off his face. "Baby, that goes without saying. Besides, you didn't read the contracts because of me. I encouraged you."

He clasped her hand and kissed her palm before holding it between them. "We aren't going to place any blame on each other. This is all Takusa's devious doings."

"Okay, what are you leaving out?"

"Charlie-chan—"

"He threatened to do something to me didn't he?"

"It's a possibility and I couldn't bare it if anything happened to you and the baby."

"Oh God, you didn't tell him about the baby did you?" Her eyes widened with concern and she grasped at his hand frantically.

"No, of course not. I wanted too, but I made you a promise."

Relief stole over her face.

"More then ever, you have to return to the states while I figure out what to do. It's the only way I can assure you are safe." He cupped her face and she lifted her face to him to accept his kiss.

As he pulled back she lingered close and said, "Protecting our baby is my priority also, but I can't rest safely knowing that bastard has this kind of hold over you. The moment I leave here without you, I have a feeling, I will never see you again and it scares me to death."

"Bay-bee, I will be okay, and I will work hard to get the film done as quickly as possible," he assured her but she wasn't convinced.

"I'm sure you will and good for the film, but you will also be fucking married to Arisa by the time that is finished and I won't have it." She argued. "Don't you see the bastard is not going to give up? First he will demand the wedding and as soon as that girl has the baby she is carrying, that is if nothing happens to the baby, you never know with the way Takusa is thinking. But, he will want a grandchild, next. His demands and threats will never stop coming, unless we stop him."

"Charlie-chan, you are being stubborn about this. How can I take care of what is precious to me if you're going to fight me every step of the way." His voice went up in volume.

"Kane, the one advantage of being with an older woman, or at least *this* older woman is you don't have to bullshit around about your feelings, or the truth, in order to keep from hurting mine. I also need you to love me not take care of me like I'm helpless. I'm not without resources of my own and it hurts me as much to have you threatened as it does you when he threatened me," she explained.

"Okay, I see we going to have to decide who is wearing the pants in the family." He grumbled.

"Excuse me, but we both are. I have one leg in one side, and you have yours in the other. In this relationship, we are equals. Trust me there is no doubt when it comes to the bedroom, you are definitely wearing the hell out those pants, darlin'." She purred and went in for another kiss, this one lingering and needy. They both parted with a sigh. Forehead to forehead, they had to make some decisions. Together.

Charlene reached out and caressed his beautiful and sexy full bottom lip with the soft padding of her thumb. "We are up against a wall here, and I get out the big guns, I need to know if you believe Takusa-san was serious about his threats?" She laced her finger with his.

He frowned and looked her in the eyes. "I hate to say it, but I think he's desperate enough to do anything, Charlie-chan. Why do you ask?"

Charlene released a light laugh. "Because once I get this ball rolling there is not going to be any stopping it? If we were on my home turf, I could handle Takusa and his threats but I don't have that kind of clout in Japan. But I know someone who do and once I make that call, things are going to happen really fast."

"You're scaring me, Charlene, what are you talking about, putting a hit-man on Takusa or what?"

She giggled and slapped his arm playfully, "No boy, but by the time this person gets through with him if he won't cooperate and release you from everything, then he may wish we did send a hit-man instead."

"Now, I know I'm worried. Who you going to call the President of the United States?"

"Don't' even joke." She glared at Kane. "This is big and we need someone

J-Pop Love Song

with serious connections here in Japan."

"This sounds more dangerous than Takusa's threat, Charlie-chan." Kane scowled at her.

"It depends on you and how far you're willing to go against Takusa and his wishes." Charlene sighed. "Do you want to marry Arisa and go on without me and the baby or do you want us to stand ground for what we believe in?"

"If it keeps you and my baby safe. I'm willing to go as far as I have to." Kane assured her. "Go ahead, we have to do something and soon my birthday is tomorrow night."

She nodded and leaned to the side grabbing her cell phone off the table. She looked into Kane in the eyes. "Are you sure, there is absolutely no reasoning with this man, nothing you can say that will sway him?"

"I'm sure, I tried it all before I came. I assumed once, I had gotten to him, but then I realized he was just waiting to spring the blackmail threat on me." Kane answered. "Go ahead and make the call."

She placed her finger against his lips as she pushed a speed dial number and held the cell phone to her ear...waiting. "Hello, Daddy, I need your help."

Chapter Fourteen

KANE TURNED OVER ON HIS stomach and sighed, his eyes still closed as he continued to wallow in contentment from the best night of sharing a bed with Charlene. This was a habit he was greatly looking forward to and when he had to go on the road again he would sorely miss this feeling. He just prayed she would be joining him as much as possible in the future.

Thinking of Charlene and her loving late night surprise brought a sleepy grin to his mouth. The sexy minx had instantly brought his birthday in with a big orgasmic bang! At 12:28 am, the exact hour of his birth, she turned on a seduction by proceeding to give him a full body massage with warmed almond oil. The part he loved the most was when her lips and mouth came into play. She nipped, licked, and sucked every part of his body leaving his painful erection to be the last thing she touched. Never had he hurt and felt so good at the same time.

Once she put her hot wet mouth on his penis, she had him singing her praises in four languages. She had loved on his cock and balls with her mouth and fingers until his toes curled, and he was whimpering like some simple-minded girl. Never had he been so mortified as he was by his lightening ejaculation. Afterwards, he was so exhausted he couldn't return the favor and worse yet, for the first time, since they became intimate, he fell asleep first.

Still, he couldn't think of a better way to make up for it then some heavy morning loving. He could picture it now; unwrapping Charlene's luscious hot body from the bed sheet would be his first Birthday present of the day. "*Happy Birthday to me.*" Kane hummed to himself.

Kane paused before rolling over to wakeup Charlene. She was after all sleeping for two, and he probably should let her sleep on a little longer. Besides, he had to resolve the more serious issues clouding his mind. His ardor cooled somewhat, and he released a heavy frustrated sigh.

The crucial data he had read that William Alfred-san had faxed to them was surreal. Finally, he had Takusa-san where he wanted him and because of what he had learned, he didn't know if he could use the evidence against him.

Takusa's empire would crumble if he were to turn over all that he had acquired to the authorities, but many innocent investors would lose as well, including his wife and daughters. He sincerely hoped the threat of exposure would be enough to get Takusa-san to hand over the bogus confession letter and allowed him and Charlene to live happily without outside interference. In all honesty Kane didn't want to be the one to take him down and because of the circumstances that had come to light, he could ask Charlene to do so either.

Still he couldn't think about that, not now. There was only one important goal in this situation and that was being able to be with Charlene and to raise his child. Everything else was secondary. As of today he could afford to take care Charlie-chan in the manner into which she was accustomed. Between both of them they could afford to take risk and start over if necessary. They just had to learn to do it together. Just like this situation.

Kane had been amazed when Charlene allowed him to stay the night after what they read in those documents. She not only allowed him to stay another night with her, she also became an emotional rock for him. She went out of her way to shower him with comfort while giving him pleasures beyond his wildest dream, and not once did she demand anything in return.

The one thing he realized about Charlene was once she made up her mind, she was a strong force to reckon with. Yet, what he loved the most about being with her was her ability to see the best in him. Every day he was discovering something amazing about her. What an awesome feeling it was to be loved by a woman who was sure of her abilities and secure in her own body.

Kane turned over onto his back, his eyes still tightly closed, hesitant about facing what was ahead of him today or at least not the part where he would have to talk to Takusa once more.

Releasing a stifled yawn his long arms stretched above his head, the bones in his wrist and arms popping loudly as he stretched like a contented cat. He couldn't put it off any longer, he had to get up and face his day, and it was going to be a long one.

Wiping the sleep out of his eyes with the back of his knuckles, he released another yawn. His eyes fluttered opened and his eyebrows shot up in surprise. The onset of a smile tipped the corners of his mouth as he gazed up into a river of color. Counting, there were exactly twenty-five *Happy Birthday* balloons floating contained in the canopy of the four-post bed against the ceiling. *Charlene*.

Kane turned to kiss her awake and thank her properly until she was moaning his name, when he saw that her side of the bed was empty. A panicky feeling stole through him. Had she lain awake all night thinking about everything and decided to put as much distance between him and all this mess, he brought with him?

When Charlene had given him the telephone to speak to her father and tell him all that he knew about Takusa-san, the retired General was furious at him for placing his daughter in danger. Kane earnestly apologized and told her father the truth. He loved her, and wasn't going to give her up without a fight. Charlene was now *his* responsibility and he would be accompanying her to the United States to meet him and the family, at that time, he could do, whatever he wanted to him if he judged he wasn't honorable in his intentions. After that, he and William Alfred-san had an understanding.

With one phone call, Kane had answers to a lifetime of questions that plagued his entire youth. Since he didn't feel any different from knowing everything, he wondered if he had fully digested the relevant data yet. The only question that remained was why hadn't Takusa been honest with him from the beginning?

There still must be one missing piece that only Takusa had.

It didn't matter how hesitant Kane felt about using this information. If Takusa continued to threaten the woman he loved and his happiness, he couldn't let the information go to waste. Charlene's father had called in some big favors from some of Japan's most political and powerful elites to that had the ability to hack into Takusa's private files using only his computer address. They had to have some serious skills for they did it in less then six hours.

Now the questioned that racked his brain is, "Where in the hell is Charlene?" He murmured scratching his head glancing up at the balloons. "*Ikkene*, Oh shit! What if she decided to go to see Takusa on her own!" He murmured kicking off the expensive silk bedcovers to the floor in his haste before bolting naked from the bed, and running into the sitting area only to stopped short in surprise.

Both dressed in business attire and looking up at him with startled expressions, sat Charlene and Abe with the faxed papers scattered on the table before them.

Kane swallowed and dropped his hands to his crotch only partially succeeding at hiding his manly goods, more out of spontaneous alarm, then embarrassment over his nakedness.

Abe was the first to break the stunned silence.

"Young man, sporting your *natural suit*, for your *birthday* may seem humorous but I can guarantee you are infringing on the public lewdness clause in your contract." Abe said in his most official voice.

"There is no member of the public in here, but you Goda-san," Kane stated.

"Might I also add, your being in the hotel suite of the author of your current film, *em-bare-ass-ingly* naked, is definitely infringing on about four pages of warnings in the aforementioned contract."

Kane's eyes narrowed at Goda-san "cute" play of words.

"Abe, play nice, it's his birthday and he can walk around naked if he wants to." Charlene chastised her lawyer and he saw her steal a glance at his body. A spark of yearning flashed in her eyes before she looked away.

"Charlie," Abe pointedly turned his reprimanding stare on her. "I think you are trying to get caught. You're not happy unless you have me working over time covering your ass."

"You don't have to do that any more, Goda-san." Kane injected. "I watch over her *ass* just fine."

"Yeah, then why is she pregnant. You should have been careful!" Abe snapped.

"Look—" Kane's eyes narrowed and he stepped forward.

Charlene shook her head and grinned sheepishly. "Okay fellas, stay in your respective corners."

"You told me last night over the phone, *he* wasn't staying." Abe pointed out.

"Well, we got distracted and…"

"Save me from the details." He grimaced. "What if you had been in here meeting with someone else this morning and *he* came running in here like that?"

"*He*, got a name," Kane muttered, and rolled his eyes.

Abe ignored him.

"It wouldn't have happened." Charlene told Abe with an assuring smile.

"Besides you. I would have utilized the lounge for a breakfast meeting or one of the hotel conference rooms. So stop looking at excuses, to be a pain in the ass you love to watch out for."

"I can't believe it, now you're sounding like, my old Charlie." Abe grinned at her and winked. "Glad to have you back."

Charlene chuckled.

Kane bristled. She had the nerve to laugh. What did she think she was doing? Couldn't she see Goda-san was flirting with her and in front of him!

"She's *MY*, old...well, not old, like old..." Kane sputtered realizing he put his foot in his mouth too late. Charlie-chan, did I tell you how beautiful you look this morning?" Kane mumbled.

"Just this morning," Abe instigated.

"Every morning! Hey, you stop winking at her before I knock your eye out. I'm sure winking at your *boss* has to be inappropriate...somewhere." Kane halted realizing no one was listening to him.

"Charlene, what about this morning? You opened the door for me this morning in your bathrobe? What if there had been a photographer waiting outside that door to take a snap shot me walking into your suite, while you're undressed?" Abe asked Charlene.

Kane scowled.

"I was dressed and you know it. I just had the robe over my dress so I wouldn't get any makeup power on it." Her eyes narrowed on Abe. "I know what you're doing and you need to stop it."

"Damn, you've always been good at reading me." Abe laughed out.

"Of course, look how long we've been together." She playfully socked him in the shoulder. "Still, you keep me on my toes."

"*Anone*, excuse me," Kane, called out.

"Apparently, I m slipping, Charlie." Abe commented, pointedly looking at the barely visible roundness of her abdomen.

"Oh, that's a cheap shot," she laughed. "A good one, but cheap, none the less."

"*Anone! Mo sugu deru,* I'm going to have to leave soon, Charlene." Kane reminded her.

"Okay, baby." Charlene answered. "Abe, did you read this part right here? What do you think?"

Kane's scowl deepened as he noticed, she didn't even bother to look at him when she answered.

"I made some notes, look through it before I pick you up tonight. Also, Charlie, don't forget you have to be ready by 6:00 pm." Abe demanded. "Don't be a minute late, the traffic will be maddening."

"I'll be ready." Charlene lifted a brow at Abe. "Do you know that you tell me the exact same thing every time we go out, no matter what city we're in?"

"I do not!" Abe argued removing his glasses and placing them on the table.

Kane couldn't believe he was standing here naked; watching these two bickered like some old married couple! Silently he pouted.

Did they have any idea how many fans, would pay to see him naked like this? How many women would love to have him wake up in her hotel room? Yet, here he was envious at how much, they seemed to have in common. They were around to the same age and worked closely together. Hell, they even looked good together. He supposed what bothered him most was, Abe Goda could escort Charlene to his birthday party tonight. Jealousy at Charlene's easy rapport with Abe burned in his chest, and he felt the immediate need to lash out.

"Charlie-chan! I assumed by now you would have wished me a proper *Happy Birthday*, but I see that I'm just in your way. So I'll get out of your and Goda-san's way," he bellowed.

Charlene and Abe both turned to stare at him with open mouth stares. He couldn't believe they actually appeared to be surprised to find him still standing there.

He too wondered why he was still standing there like an idiot waiting for her crumbs of acknowledgement. No, he knew why. It was his *special day* and he wanted her to make a big deal about this being his big day! Yes, the balloons were sweet, but where was the kisses she gave him when they were alone? Did she not want to kiss him in front of Goda-san?

Yeah, his ego was feeling bruised and he was also feeling bratty. So much so, Kane childishly stomped his foot in frustration. His hands balled up in fists by his side as he interrupted, the two, "Charlie-chan, where is my morning kiss?"

"Hmm, looks like you have one child already," Abe snorted on a laugh and received a warning stare from Charlene, but Kane could see she wanted to laugh too.

Oh, he would make her pay later, he promised himself. He would kiss her and hold out penetrating her until she was begging for it.

"Oh baby, I'm sorry. I thought you went to throw something on, or went back to bed. Because if you had, when I finished up here I would have awakened your in my usual way," she crooned pushing herself up from the sofa.

She gave him a big saucy grin and closed the space between them throwing her body against his. He caught her. He couldn't help but grin at her she was so adorable.

"*Otanjou-bi omedetou gozaimasu*, have a wonderful birthday, my love!" She landed a serious wet kiss just below his lips.

Kane cupped her face and dipped his head to slant his parted mouth over hers properly and moan aloud as he felt her tongue dart between his lips. Keeping his eyes open to give Goda-san a cocky wink, over her shoulder. The older man laughed shaking his head, and crossing his arms over his chest.

His heart skipped a beat and he grinned like an idiot as she pulled back to stare up at him.

"*Domo arigato gozaimasu*, thank you very much, bay-bee," he thanked her, beaming. "Now, I feel much better."

"When you're pleased. I'm pleased," Charlene assured him, touching his unshaven face tenderly.

She seemed to be glowing with cheerfulness and that made him happy. What better present could he asked for? He had nothing to worry about after all. It was obvious in her face how much she loved him. His eyes burned from the overpowering sentiments that welled up in his chest.

"I love you, Charlie-chan." Kane murmured seriously before capturing her

J-Pop Love Song

mouth once more, this time savoring a slow merging of mouth against mouth.

She was open and accepting of his kiss. A throaty familiar moan came from her throat as she tightened her grip around his neck, stopping short of grinding herself against him.

Abe released a loud yawn.

Kane released a soft curse against her mouth. You would think the man would have the decency to quietly leave the suite.

Abe coughed, "Ahem," he interrupted. "I hate to interrupt this touching moment, however, you need to go and take a cold shower. Because, your anticipated *gift* from Charlene, is going to have to wait until we finish going over this faxes."

"Go over what? Basically, Takusa is in debt to the *Yakuza*, Japanese Mafia, for his latest rebuilding project. If his legit investors were to find out and pull their monies he wouldn't be able to pay the *Yakuza* the accumulated interest, therefore in order to stay alive he would need to sell off his empire, including my contract."

"I'm impress you are more then a face and talent," Abe grudgingly gave him a compliment.

Kane allowed Charlene to turn to face Abe, but he still wasn't ready to let go of her yet. He wrapped his arms about her waist and pulled her back against him. She also made a good shield against his current state of arousal.

"From what Charlie-chan tells me, Goda-san, you're a pretty good lawyer to have on my side. I want you to know I appreciate you doing this for me. I'm going to need all the help I can get if Takusa won't listen to reason. I don't look forward to belonging to the *Yakuza* for the next two years. I may need you to help me buy my contract back." Kane spoke seriously or as serious as a naked man with a hard-on could.

He knew he should go and get dressed, but he thought eventually Abe Goda-san would take a hint and offer to leave them alone and come back later. Yet, after seeing Abe was already back in business mode, he realized he wasn't getting any physical loving from Charlene this morning.

"Well, hopefully it won't come to that." Abe caressed his goatee thoughtfully as he spoke, "I must say Takusa seems to have gotten in over his head, but the concept of what he is trying to achieve is sheer genius and I wouldn't mind investing some of my own funds. That is, if he could pay this huge debt and keeps it legit from here on. I believe looking at this in long-term, Takusa-san will make a contributing impact on the Asian entertainment industry."

"Abe, I agree. Trust me, I rather have Takusa as a business ally, than an enemy. If we all worked towards the same goal we can unite different cultures through music and entertainment. The one deciding factor that has blended races and promote acceptance for centuries. With the threes of us helping Takusa see his dream through, with our connections we could make it bigger by marginally extending to the States and Europe." Charlene chimed in.

"That would be excellent, if we could convince him of how feasible it would be to all."

She shook her head, "Not, if he can't move pass his desire to do it all by himself, then he is going to fail. He's expanding faster than he's bringing in workable funds. He's threatened to take all that Kane has vested, but in truth, looking at his records, if Kane were to leave him, everyone will know he's has no movable capital."

Abe nodded. "It's probably why he's so desperate to keep Kane under contract. If you hadn't renew the contract he would have had to paid you all your earnings over the years, which is a substantial amount and he doesn't have it at the moment."

"I can't imagine what he would have done if he knew I was coming into my mother's inheritance left by her father." Kane stated.

"Are you sure he doesn't know?" Abe asked. "That is exactly what he needs to save him, and if you marry his daughter, he know you will feel beholden as family to open your resources to him.

"I know I'm not marry Arisa, that is out of the question." Kane released a long breath. "As far as his knowing about my money, who knows? Maybe. After seeing how quickly Charlene's father got a hold of this information, I don't believe anything on the computer is one hundred percent safe."

"Kane I have to ask, after reading this file, can you truly do what may be necessary to gain your freedom? I mean, I also see there is some unexpected information here in regards to you. What are you going to do, now that you know?" Abe cocked a brow in question.

"Are you deliberately trying to goad me again?"

"Not in particular, but I think it needs to be addressed." Abe retorted. "What about you Charlie? Does what you know now change anything?"

"Oh, I see, this isn't you trying to access the situation. You're trying to see if the news about me is bad enough to make Charlene change her mind about me!" Kane argued. "You want her for yourself. I see how well you two get along."

Abe sighed. "Don't be so childish, Kane. Trust me if Charlie and I felt that way about each other, you would never have gotten your foot in the door. This is about destroying a man's life and I need to know what are my limitations or if there are any, because once I start playing hardball, there will be no turning back."

"Yeah right," Kane muttered.

"Look Kid," Abe stood placing his hands on his hips. "Would it help you feel more secure about my friendship with Charlie, if I told you I was gay?"

Kane mouth dropped wide in surprise and he tucked Charlene closer to assure his parts were covered really well and heard her laughing. He didn't know what was so funny. "Yes, I would feel better. Are you gay?"

"No." Abe chuckled. "I just asked if it would help."

Kane made a move to choke the other man, and felt Charlene pressing all her weight against him.

"Abe, enough!" Charlene covered her face and shook her head. Her shoulders shook with laughter.

"*Kande*. Bite me." Kane said to both parties in the room.

"Okay, am I the only adult still in this room?" Charlene managed to say with a straight face. "Abe, we will let you know if we need you to handle the situation after I discuss it with my, future husband. If you could stay until my breakfast for two arrives I would appreciate it, and then you can go about your business…in your suite."

"Using me as camouflage for your tryst is getting old fast," Abe murmured.

"I'm the 'future husband' she was referring too, just in case you got confused again," Kane said with a cocky grin.

"Yuza Kaneishi, also known as, Kane. Go get showered and dressed, so that by the time breakfast arrives we can eat, because the mother of your child is starving." She stated. "Also, every time you show a sign of jealousy, it means you question my love for you."

She turned in his arms, and he looked into her eyes.

"Baby, do you question my love for you?" Charlene asked him, and he grinned. Was she serious?

As if Abe could read his thoughts he said. "For future reference, Kane-san, if she uses your full name, she's in serious mode." Abe offered.

Kane looked at him over her head, and his jealousy disappeared. He saw that he and Abe were on the same page. Kane finally accepted he had nothing to fear. It was Charlene's choice, and she chose him.

"I love you, and if you get rid of the tall man in the blue suit, I could show you just how much." Kane wiggled his eyebrows at her.

"Mmm...don't tempt me." She pouted prettily at him. "Baby, I really am hungry. The diet the doctor has me on doesn't allow me to snack on my junk food in between meals. So when it's time to eat, I want to eat."

"So you're telling me I'm not going to get *any* Birthday sex today, am I?"

"We will, say tonight after a certain party? You want to spend the night again?" She lifted a sexy arched eyebrow at him in question.

"How about we at least take a shower together?"

"Baby, we both have a full day ahead, and you have an early fitting. I'm already dressed for my first meeting. Then I have to go to my stylist. I believe I will wear my hair down tonight. You've never seen me without it braided, I will even brush it all over your naked body tonight, so you can feel how silky it is."

"*Sokka*, I see, you're going to make me simmer on a slow boil all day. Is this torture because I went to sleep on you last night?" He quickly stole a peck from her parted lips.

"If you hadn't I would be losing my touch." A serene smile came to her face as she said, "I can't wait until we are a real family and everyone will know I'm this happy because of you."

Kane looked at her and the double meaning of his gaze was very obvious. Something wonderful and intense flared between them. No words needed to be said. He just stood there and drank in the essence of her nearness.

He didn't care how the rest of the day went from that point on. His morning was complete, minus Abe Goda-san of course. Charlene confirmed that nothing had changed, they were going to be a family, no matter what, and to hear her say it aloud in front of someone that knew her well meant everything. For her, he could face Takusa-san and do what was necessary to keep her safe.

Grinning, Kane did a hip-hop boogie into the bedroom, naked ass shining, and all. "This is the best Birthday ever," he declared aloud.

"I can't believe it." Charlene shook her head. "I have the man, every woman in Asia wants to sleep with, naked in my hotel room, and I'm missing this great photo opportunity."

"Don't fret Charlie, something tells me, with this guy, you'll get several more opportunities." Abe mumbled and picked up his glasses replacing them on his nose, he focused his attention on the papers before him.

♪

While Kane made his call, Charlene placed everything that was on the service tray on the table. The meal consisted of a traditional Japanese breakfast of miso-soup made of soybean paste and *dashi*, soup stock. She placed white chunks of tofu in each of their bowl with seaweed and poured the soup on top garnish from green onions. She placed the bowls in the customary setting of the steamed rice on the left side and the soup on the right. Between them to share were a rolled omelet, *umeboshi*, sour plums, and grilled fish.

Charlene looked at Kane across the table as he closed his cell phone and held it against his head. His eyes were closed. She could see the conversation with Stuart hadn't gone well.

"What's going on?" She asked once they finished, and he still hadn't elaborated on his phone conversation.

Kane released a long breath and looked at her, a frown marred his forehead "Stu-san, is on his way to pick me up. Unfortunately, Takusa-san left late last night to go to Odawara. He said he would be back sometime today and told Stuart to keep an eye on me and make sure I make my appointments today."

"Why do you suppose, he went to the Kanagawa, Japan?" She questioned.

"I have no idea." Kane explained to her. "There's no way he could know his personal files were hacked into could he?"

"I'm sure Daddy got the best. He knows how important it is that we be do this without it leading back to us. So if Takusa suspects someone infiltrated his computer files, he wouldn't know where to begin he has so many enemies." Charlie sipped her green tea. "The bastard deserves to worry as much as he worried us." She bit her bottom lip willing herself to shut up once she saw the hurt in his dark eyes. "I'm sorry."

"I'm trying to process all of this Charlie-chan." Kane shrugged and laid the mobile phone on the table. "There is no need for you to apologize, baby-bee. You have every right to think the worse of him. Just because we know the reasoning behind his madness, doesn't mean he can be trusted." He put his hands together in front of him and said, "*Itadakimas!*" before picking up the chop sticks and pulling them apart. He lifted a large portion of sticky rice with the chopsticks and dipped it in his soup before shoving it into his mouth.

"Still, I wouldn't want anyone speaking about my father that way and I should give you the same respect, no matter how angry I am with him for wanting to keep up apart." Charlene asked spooning the broth from her soup into her mouth to test her unpredictable stomach. "What are you thinking?"

Kane shook his head. "I was wondering how Takusa-san could walk around in his daily life with all these fucking secrets? I think I more disappointed than anything. I went from one unstable family situation to another. I sometimes wonder if I'm going to ever get it right."

Charlene reached across the small table and touched the hand that wasn't

J-Pop Love Song

holding the chopsticks. "Baby, *we're* going to make it right, do hear me? I am fortunate to have a wonderful, supportive and loving family. Now you will have a mother again, a father, and a younger brother and sister. The twins will drive you crazy, trust me."

"I can't wait to have some form of normalcy in my life." His face lightened up with excitement as he asked, "Do your family do barbecues and have these big holidays with a loads of family, friends, and lots of children running wild all over the place? You know, like in the American Black films I've seen."

Charlene threw back her head and laughed. "You bet, I have more family then you can shake a stick at. Old friends come to town along with aunt, uncles, and so many cousins I lost count years ago. My parents live on a forty acre ranch in Texas. There is a guest house with four bedrooms and seven bedrooms in the main house. The first thing you must learn about my parents is they love to have visitors and entertain."

"Sounds wonderful. Tell me more." Kane encouraged as he ate his soup.

"Okay. Well, we have horses. Do you ride?"

"Yes, I learned while living in England." He answered in between bites. "I love horses."

"Then you and my mother, will get along fabulous. We also have this big wagon for hayrides during the Spring and Fall. My Father is a retired Cardiologist and my Mother, a retired Pediatrician, but they are still very active in doing charity work for the local hospitals. Every year they host the Holloween Hunted Cornfield and donate the proceeds to the hospital." She paused and took a bite of rice.

"Your Father sounded stern over the phone, but it's obvious how much he loves you." Kane smiled at her. "I look forward to meeting them both."

"I'm sure they will love you. They have been very supportive of my choices over the years. I don't foresee it changing now."

"Did they like Jason James?"

"Jason was not family oriented at all. I guess because he grew up in a Catholic orphanage. Because he was only half Japanese, he always had a problem association with the culture he was born in. His mother who was an American Caucasian abandon him. He didn't know nothing about his father accept he was a Japanese boy his mother when to school with. He really had no idea how to accommodate a family environment. He didn't understand that you had to give as much as you take."

"Did you love him, like you love me?"

Charlene was surprised by the question, but now that it lingered between them she had to address it.

"After finding a man like you I'm not sure I even knew what it felt like to love. I see how one-sided my life with Jason had been. I won't lie, I loved him as much as I could, but with Jason, I felt he needed me to care for him. He was just incapable of taking care of himself. So I believed that is what being in love meant and so I put all my dreams on hold to make his come true. It wasn't when I started pursuing my own dreams, that I realized how one-sided our marriage was," she confided. "Being loved by you Kane, has taught me that I can have what my parents have. I find you taking care of me instead of expecting me to take care of you. So that allows me to open myself to you and work at making this a equal partnership in love."

Kane dropped his head a serene smile on his lips. "*Shimpai shita,*" he sighed.

"You were worried? Why?"

"I guess because everything I read about you and Jason James, you seemed to be the ideal couple and then it all seemed to go wrong. I just don't' want that being us twenty years from now." Kane spoke honestly.

"Well," Charlene chuckled. "I don't' know about you, but seeing how I will be over sixty, I believe I will have my hands full keeping up with our twenty year old son or daughter."

He laughed and nodded. Charlene was grateful when the conversation turned back to more fonder memories then her life with Jason.

"You live in California, right?"

"Yes."

"Do you manage to get home to Texas to visit your parents often?"

"Usually, no matter what I'm doing I try to keep the time open so I can go home to help put up the scarecrows in the corn field for Halloween and remain there through Christmas. It was easier to do when I was just writing novels."

"You haven't been able to do that lately?" He asked picking up a piece of grill fish.

"An old friend contacted me about composing again for a soundtrack, just a couple of songs. After that, I realized how much I missed music. The only probably with composing is I have to be hands on with the vocalist and because of that, I've been able to make it home, but only for about three days each time. This was the first year I didn't think I would make it at all, because I had planned to remain in Japan, but with the pregnancy, it looks as if I will be there. Resting." She licked her tongue at him and wrinkled her nose. "I met this young man that happened to be very virile and hit the spot on the first shot."

"You bet, bay-bee." Kane bragged with a cocky smile. "I like how your face lights up when you speak about your family." Kane put down the empty bowl he was holding. "I can't tell you how much, I look forward to being a part of your world."

"Trust me baby, you are going to be begging me to get you out of there by the close of the first night of one of our holidays. It gets crazy." She picked up a pickled plumb and popped it in her mouth. Heaven.

As they ate in silence. Her heart ached for him. No child should be without the wonderful memories she's had over the years. Even her childhood in in Japan she had the full love and support of her parents. She didn't know what was worse Jason James never knowing the love of a family, or Kane having one that was disfunctional.

"When your mother was alive, didn't she celebrate holidays with you?" she asked.

"My mother made a big deal out of Christmas when I was younger, but the last couple of years before her death, she wasn't able to do that either. You can't imagine what depression can do to a family."

"No but I know what it can do to a marriage." Charlene said.

"Father, never missed a holiday." Kane grinned bitterly and continued, "With

J-Pop Love Song

his mistress and their child. I carried a lot of anger for him over the years and Takusa used that anger to his advantage. Now that I know why my father hated me." He closed his eyes for a brief moment. "I feel like such a fool."

"You shouldn't feel that way, you were a child and all the adults in this situation were wrong." She pointed out heatedly.

"Too late to change it now. It's something I must accept. It's not like more anger is going to change anything. Neither is wishing it wasn't true." Kane stated looking into her eyes. "What about you, Charlie-chan? Do you think less of me, now that you know?"

She took a bite of tofu, shaking her head. "Of course not, what kind of person would I be, if I did? I fell in love with you Kane, and I know that blood linage is a big deal to your culture, but I don't believe that it dictates the type of person you are." She grinned and playfully blew him a kiss. "I'm afraid you're stuck with me, so you might as well get use to it."

He reached across the table and intertwined his fingers with hers. His phone rang, and he dropped the chopsticks poised over his rice bowl instead of releasing her hand. Picking up the mobile phone, Kane flipped it open with his thumb. "*Nanni?* Any reporters hanging around? *Sokka*, I see. I'll be down, just do a walk through of the parking garage in case someone is hiding behind a car. It would be easy for them to pay security to allow them access. Call me back when you're ready to go." He closed the phone and clicked it in the holder at his waist.

"You haven't finished your breakfast," Charlene fretted.

Kane nodded. "Sorry bay-bee, I don't want to leave you, but there is much to do before tonight."

"I know." Her face clouded with sadness. "You have to do your thing, and I have to do mine. The only bad part is when we see each other tonight, we will be once again pretending to be polite business acquaintances. I hate this, especially on this momentous night for you." Tears misted in her brown eyes.

"Oh, Charlie-chan," he groaned. Standing up Kane came around the table and pulled her up from the chair. He looped his arms around her shoulders, holding her against him. She leaned her forehead against his shoulder, and he cradled her head.

"Kane, I don't know how much more of this, I can take, and it's just the beginning," she cried.

"*Chikusho!* Damn it! I don't want to leave you like this." Kane released her and cupped her face in his hands. He tilted her face up to look at him. "Don't cry, or I swear I won't be able to walk out that door."

"I can't help it. Hormones," she sniffled and forced a laugh, hoping to ease his distress somehow. Her left hand curved around the nape of his neck under his thick soft hair. With a sigh she accepted the coaxing of his lips bushing hers, parting them. He began kissing her with a hunger that stole her breath with its ferocity. Loud moaning and wet open-mouthed kisses flooded the hotel suite. Charlene felt herself easily being lifted. The sounds of dishes rattling as her buttocks hit the table.

She felt his hands trembling as they pulled her blouse from the waistband of her skirt. She tugged to release the belt from the big silver buckle. Her hands stopping as he moved to giving her nibbling kisses along the arch of her neck. A low keening sound came from the back of her throat as he pushed her blouse up and pulled a sensitive breast from her bra cup and took into his mouth and began to tug. She dug her nails into his back and cried out, "Ohhh God! That feels sooo good." She arched into his mouth. He released her in a loud wet pop, her eyes opened. "Nooo! Don't stop!"

"Fuck!" Kane swore. His handsome face twisted in frustration. He pulled the slender cell phone from the holster at his waist. "*Nanni!* What? Yes, it's a bad time, Stu-san. I know I told you to call me back. It's not funny. Give me five minutes. None of your business!" Charlene accepted his free hand as he helped her off the table.

With trembling fingers she straightened her dishevel clothing. Her body was throbbing for him to finish what he started.

"Sorry, bay-bee, I got to go," Kane's deep voice soothed her somewhat, but it wasn't enough to ease her restlessness.

"Kane, we need to make a decision about Takusa. What do you want me to tell Abe?

"Charlie-chan, I can't give Goda-san a response until I speak with Takusa-san once more. I owe him that much. He's *my Father*."

Charlene guffawed. "Kane, just because you're just finding out that Takusa is your biological father, doesn't mean he's all of a sudden a *decent* person. Have you already forgotten he wants to keep up a part? He's known all along you were his son and he's deliberately kept it hidden from you just so he could keep telling the world he saved from the mean streets!"

"Sweetheart," he touched the side of her face, and she looked up into his eyes. He sighed and dropped his hand to his side. "I can see you're upset with me."

She knew he didn't need the added stress, but he couldn't think she would be happy about giving Takusa another opportunity. "Kane, I don't feel right about this. For all we know your Father is out there somewhere, thinking he has the upper hand, and there is no telling what he might be planning at this very moment."

"I know better than anyone Takusa-san has his faults, Charlene, but there are still many questions that I need answers to. Also, if we take Takusa down, we take everything he built with him and lots of people depend on him for their livelihood. Tell me you understand why I must give him another chance."

Reluctantly, she nodded. "Just don't let him guilt you into getting what he wants, Kane."

He stole another kiss. "See you soon. Call me if you need me, but, please don't spend the next few hours worrying over this. No matter what I will be here tonight, with you."

With those final words he was gone. Charlene felt as if he took all of her happiness with him. She wouldn't be at ease until he was with her once more.

Chapter Fifteen

CHARLENE SAT QUIETLY IN THE back of the chauffeur driven Rolls Royce staring out the window, while Abe spoke on his mobile phone. She had exhausted herself worrying about the outcome of tonight festivities. It was nice to look at the view and not talk or think to much on if Kane got to Takusa or not. She had called a couple of times, but it went directly to his voice mail and she hadn't bothered to leave a message. He probably had to turn it off due to all the *Birthday Wishes* he probably was receiving. She knew if there had been any change, he would have called her.

As they took the route towards Ueno Park, she realized how much, she had missed the urban beauty of Tokyo at night. The lights of the temples and gardens illuminated the nightlife along with the concrete and glass blocks of buildings. It was like a giant sprawling amusement park. She made a mental note to make a special night trip outing to eat at one of the many small *yatai*, food stands, out in the open air.

"What are you thinking about?"

"At the moment?" Charlene grinned. "Food. I have a craving for *yakatori*, grilled chicken skewers, and *tonkotsu*,thin ramen noodles in pork bone soup."

"If you wish, we could stop, I wouldn't mind having some hot pot *oden*, vegetables, eggs and fish cakes stewed in broth. It sounds like a better plan than going to the "kid's" party." The pensive sound of Abe's voice caused her to force her eyes from the view to look at him.

"You're serious, aren't you?"

"I don't know. It's just something doesn't feel right and Takusa no where to be found before such a big event leaves me worried." Abe spoke honestly. "Come on, you can't tell me you're not a bit tense about this precarious situation. Not to mention it being the first time since Kane, and you have been in a huge public setting since becoming intimate. You two can barely keep your hands off each other in front of me, you genuinely suppose it's going to be any easier in a crowd of people?"

"We do what we must." Charlene stirred uneasily in the seat. She was uncomfortable with the fact that he'd spoken the blunt reality. It would be hard enough to look at Kane without all the love, she felt for him, outwardly showing on her face for the world to see. She could only hope he understands why it will be impossible for her to sit by him at dinner or have his arms around her on the dance floor.

Charlene took in a deep breath as they turned onto the Tokyo red light district of Shinjuku Kabuki-cho.

"We're almost at *Club Complex Code*, it's not to late to make a run for it." Abe's cool voice broke into her thoughts.

"Are you kidding? After spending four hours in my stylist chair getting my braids taken down and my hair done, *and* spending a small fortune on this black pleated Armani Collezioni 'Cady' jacket. Oh, and don't make me tell you how hard a time I had shopping for a pair of leather pants to fit over my newly big 'baby' butt in the city of Tokyo." Charlene said tersely and added with a slight smile of defiance. "I tell you someone better take notice and snap a picture."

Abe threw back his head and laugh. "Well I'm glad you're feeling better because we have arrived."

Charlene looked out the window and realized this wasn't a birthday party for Kane as much as it was a showcase for Takusa and his entire stable of entertainers. There as no way Kane could have this many friends and his bodyguard Stuart is the only one he's ever confided in.

There were people everywhere with three lines going through security. One for VIP's on a computerized guest list, another for the press, and one for the fans that had to wait and see if there was any room left. Security had to make sure it didn't go over the 1700 full capacity number.

She wondered if Kane or Takusa had arrived yet. Maybe they were together and that is why he hadn't had the chance to call her. If he was here he probably was already ready to crawl out of skin. He didn't mind performing in front of large crowds, but he wasn't the type to hang out in one. That was how he got his reputation as being cool and elusive, when actually he felt awkward being himself, and he didn't like to have to be in the "Kane" mode during his personal time. Well, from the looks of things, there wasn't anything personal about this party.

"Are you okay?" Abe leaned down and asked close to her ear. A hand on her arm looped around her shoulder and his other arm outstretched to keep anyone from bumping into her.

"For now, but ask me again later. I think this is going to be and early night for me, so don't get lost."

"No problem, whenever you ready let me know. All you have to do really is make a polite appearance, take a few pictures, to show your good wishes of Kane's birthday."

Abe paused as a photographer politely asked them for a picture. The man thanked them, and they pushed forward.

"Afterwards, we can stop to get something to eat and take it back to the hotel if you don't wish to stick around and get full off appetizers." Abe finished.

"Sounds good, but I will hang around as long as Kane needs me. He needs to see some familiar faces in this mess." Charlene sneered. "I'm going to make sure on his next birthday, it's family, intimate friends only, and a home cooked meal."

They moved slowly through the VIP line and thankful made it to the security check point. Abe gave them their names, and they gave them proof of their identification. The security guard checked it against the information on the computer screen. With a smile he returned the passports back to them and secured pink wristbands around their wrists.

Once again they stopped on a low platform place set up for the reporters to take pictures before entering, seeing how no cameras were allowed inside after the performances started. This time several flashes went off and their names were called asking them to turn this way and that. She envied Abe's tinted glasses and now knew why Kane wore shades at night to these things. The spot light and the camera flashes were almost blinding. Charlene felt sweat beading on her top lip from the heat of the lights and leaned into Abe as a wave of nausea hit her.

"Hey, are you sure you're going to be alright?"

"I just need to get inside, it's hot under these lights, and I would kill for a bottle of water." She murmured while continuing to smile for the cameras. She waved and bowed her head in thanks before Abe ushered her off the platform into the club. "Damn, this place is big enough to get lost in."

Abe nodded and said, "I've been here a couple of times while in town on business. It's actually the happening spot to be in. They have a main room several smaller rooms set up for more intimate gathering, individual karaoke rooms."

The farther inside they ventured, the more Charlene realized unless she sought Kane out, or he searched for her, there was no way they would have to worry about accidentally bumping into each other. There was a stage setup with instruments and microphones, but currently no band, just a few soundmen walking around rechecking equipment. Huge speakers were housed on each side of the stage. A large dance floor in front remained while the rest of the dance floor housed black cloth covered tables with intimate lighting with chairs around them.

A glass enclosed DJ booth towered above beside another entrance with two ceiling-high creative screens, currently showing music videos from Takusa Entertainment Group. Just as she suspected, this wasn't just a birthday party for Kane it was a way for Takusa to showcase all of his entertainers at Kane's expense.

Charlene shook her head in disgust crossing her arms over her breast.

"What is it?" Abe asked.

"It's a bit much don't you think?"

"I think Takusa-san is being the genius businessman that he is." Abe said. "It appears as if he has turned a private birthday party into a business expense." Abe chuckled. "Meaning, prefectural tax, right offs."

Charlene heard the grudging admiration in Abe's voice and she couldn't be angry about it. From a business perspective this was a great idea. Free media attention for his entire group of artists, and an opportunity for many important people in the industry to see them in live action. After this event Takusa Entertainment is sure to be buzzing with calls. He would get back every dollar he put into this and more. *What a generous man.* She thought sarcastically.

"Just steer me towards some bottled water," Charlene stated.

"I can do that, pretty lady." A deep voice sounded beside her ear on the side that Abe wasn't standing on. She smiled and turned to see Stuart.

"Hello stranger, you've been keeping a low profile these days." She accepted his friendly hug.

"Yeah, sorry, but Kane has been keeping me busy running interference." His dark eyes looked at her knowingly, and she felt her face growing hot up to her ears.

"Well, I want to thank you for being our guardian angel. Without you and Abe, we both would go crazy, keeping all of this to ourselves."

Stuart winked at her. "No worries, as long as I'm around, even if unseen. I got Kane and your backs."

"So tell me, how is our birthday boy holding up?" Her brow puckered in concern. "I've tried to call him but my calls have been going to voicemail."

"Yeah, it's been crazy. He probably turned his cell off during the setup and sound check, because it kept giving him feedback through the speakers. He probably forgot to turn it back on because it's been none stop since he got a late start this morning."

Charlene nodded. "I'm not complaining. I understand how crazy things can get in this business, especially on days like this. I was just wondering if he got to Takusa. Kane did fill you in on what we found out, didn't he?"

"Yeah, isn't that some *shit?*" Stuart shook his head. "How can a man treat his own blood like, he's merchandise? I can't believe Kane strongly thinks the man has any saving grace, but that's the type of man Kane is. He likes to believe there is good in everyone. The only one I've known him to persistently hate was the man he believed was his father, but now he's realizing he's been blaming the wrong person."

"I don't know about that, it was wrong of the man to blame a child for the sins of the mother. I feel it was cruel to stay in a marriage and make everyone around him miserable by flaunting another woman and later, a child in their faces! So, in my book that doesn't make him much better than Takusa. I think all of them should pay for lying to an innocent child all these years," Charlene said bitterly.

"I agree, but as far as I know, Takusa has yet to appear before anyone. Which worries me. It's not like him to not be in the forefront of these things, soaking up the glory." Stuart touched the small of her back and grinned, saying, "But this not why I come to look for you. I'm here to assure that you are escorted backstage to Kane's dressing room. There is plenty of bottled water and anything else you and the little one may desire. If not, it's my duty to make sure you get your heart's desire."

"Does that include me?" Abe piped in.

Stuart nodded. "Of course, all conspirators must stick together."

"Lead the way," Abe stated.

"Whoa, before you two go chauffeuring me off at Kane's bidding. What about what I want? I don't think it's wise for me to be seen in such a private place as his dressing room."

Abe and Stuart looked at each other over her head.

"Uh, you only feel that way because you're secretly *doing* the kid," Abe teased. "But actually it's not unusually for an entertainer to have an entourage full of people in his or her dressing room before a performance. I shouldn't have to tell you this, but think back to the days with Jason. Wasn't he always partying up until performance time?"

That blew her argument. Jason on partied the night before, the day of and the night afterwards. Still she couldn't see Kane. This was such a bad idea. Charlene felt a rush a panic. Once she saw Kane it would be all over, everyone would see how much, she loved him, and in her current hormonal state, she might even do something stupid like crying. Then Kane would feel the need to come to her aid and he was under enough stress. She couldn't believe these two idiots couldn't see this, wasn't a good idea.

Abe and Stuart grabbed her by an arm. "Come on, you guys! Do you two think this is a good idea or am I the only one that believes this is completely insane? Hey, Abe Goda-san, I'm your boss. Why are you listening to Kane? Now of all times!"

"I never realized she was so bossy. Think it's because of the baby?" Stuart asked Abe.

"Nope. You just don't know her, as well as I do. She's always like this," Abe answered.

Stunned Charlene looked between the two men. *What is going on here? When had they become so chummy?* Her frown deepened. If anyone was noticing her being carted through the nightclub they were letting on.

"Does Kane know about this side of her?" Stuart asked.

"Oh yeah." Abe nodded.

"I can't believe he stills want to marry her." Stuart shook his head as if he was baffled by the idea.

Abe lips puckered in thought before saying, "Now, that is probably because of the baby."

"Hello, I'm still here." She reminded. "You two are being so rude."

"You're one to talk." Stuart snorted.

Abe laughed.

Charlene simmered. *Wait until I see Kane, this stinks of him being up to no good.*

♪

"Did you look at the documents to make sure everything is in order? I don't want anyone to be able to dispute this marriage once it's done. No loopholes." Kane asked.

"Except for both of your signatures in front of your two witnesses. I assure you that Goda-san Abe has left nothing to chance. He is a good friend of the family, I know how important this is to you, Kane-san."

"I really appreciate you doing this for us here instead of your office, but timing is everything, in this matter. *Domo arigato gozaimasu*, thank you very much." Kane bowed.

"*Atarimae-dayo*, of course, Kaneishi-san. I'm honored to be a part of this occasion. It was also wonderful of you to allow my daughter to come to your birthday party. She will see me as being the *kakkoii*, coolest papa ever." The older man grinned and nodded his head.

"*Suge*, awesome. Well, it's the least, I could do for the daughter of an elite municipal government official." Kane stated. "When I called Stu-san this morning, after leaving my fiancée, for his help, I had no idea he could make things happen this quickly. I'm sure he's going to make me pay big time for this one."

The two men laughed and waited for the appearance of the unsuspecting bride.

♪

By the time they had reached the backstage room Charlene was spoiling for a fight. Stuart and Abe couldn't release her fast enough before she was charging inside Kane's dressing room completely prepared to tell him how reckless he was being and how insensitive he had been not to return her calls.

"Kane—" She halted and her mouth grew wide. "Wow! Look at all the flowers you got. How beautiful," she gasped in awe, twirling around to take it all in. "Oh my God, you have some great fans, I bet you didn't even notice the ones I sent with all of these around." Charlene murmured as she strolled about stopping to admire each vase. There were about thirty of them of every flower imaginable.

"You look beautiful." Kane came towards her and stopped just a step away reaching out to finger her long hair and let it trail through his fingers. "Don't think I forgot the birthday promise you made to me about this hair against my body."

In her mind as she stared at him, she found him to be the beautiful one. The man was something to look at when he wasn't in "Kane" mode, but when he was he was simply breathtakingly gorgeous. The way those sinfully tight dressed in black and red leather pants with laced up crotch and a billowing sleeves white silk shirt with double buttons finished off the attire. He looked like a historical hero from one of her romance novels. *Damn*, he was her hero, and she was the luckiest woman alive. Anger was such a silly wasteful emotion, she thought.

Charlene grinned from ear to ear. She suddenly forgot everything she was going to say to him, and rushed forward throwing herself against him and wrapping her arms around his small waist. "God help me, I've missed you all day." Her eyes misted, and she felt foolish. Nuzzling her face against his chest thankful for that expensively applied airbrushed makeup that didn't come off so easily on ones clothing because she needed to hear his strong heart beating beneath her ear, confirming he was indeed real, and he was hers.

"*Nani?* What is this, tears?" He cupped her face in his hands. "Show me," he urged against her mouth. "Kiss me, and let me see if you missed me half as much as I missed you."

Charlene tightened her hold about his waist and slid her tongue between his lip sharing with him a kiss that expressed all the loneliness, fear, and frustrations she felt at not being able to reach in throughout the day.

The two men behind them cleared their throats with exaggerated rudeness causing them to pulled apart and look at them. Both their faces stunned as if they forgot they weren't alone.

Charlene felt her face burning in embarrassment; she really was getting careless lately. The door of the dressing room was still opened; anyone could have been walking by. The sounds of her stomach rumbling seemed to echo in the sudden quietness of the room. She placed a hand over her stomach willing it to stop.

Kane, Abe, and Stuart looked at her in surprise and all broke out laughing at

J-Pop Love Song

the same time.

Charlene face scrunched up with a pretty pout. "I can't help it, I'm so hungry. I still haven't received any water yet." She shot accusing eyes at Stuart.

"Oh my poor bay-bee." Kane leaned down and kissed her temple. He grasped her by the shoulders and turned her towards a corner in the room.

She thought she just died and went to heaven. Her face lit up as she looked past Kane's looked over the table laden with a pan, full of bottled water, on ice. She disengaged herself from Kane's hands and hurried forward.

"Oh yes! This is what I'm talking about." She opened a bottle and picked up one of the glasses poured it full. Savoring the water as it glided down her parched throat. With a refreshed sigh, she spied something she hadn't had since reaching Japan.

"Fried chicken!" she cried out. "Do you know how long it's been since I had some fried chicken? She picked up a cloth napkin and a chicken leg and took a big bite."

She didn't care if the guys were laughing at her. They would never understand how good this tasted at this moment. For some reason all food seemed to taste so much better later, but this hit the spot in particular.

"I've never wanted to be chicken leg so badly," Kane moaned with a chuckle. His arms crossed over his chest. He seemed transfixed on her lips chewing.

"Excuse me, Charlie, I don't believe *fried* chicken is on the Doctor's list of things you can have," Abe was the first one to be logical in his speaking as usual.

"Hey, it's okay," she reasoned. "After all, it's a *birthday party*," Charlene managed to say in between bites. Her eyes rolling and closing as she released a contented sigh through her nose.

"Yeah but it's not *your birthday*." Abe laughed and shook his head.

She impolitely extended her middle finger at him and warmly received another round of laughter for her troubles. Let them laugh if they wanted to, she thought; but, it could get serious if they come between her and this piece of chicken.

"Oh, Kane you got to try this. Tell me where you got it from, and I will send them a 'thank you' card."

Abe snorted, "Don't believe that she just wants to know where she can go to get it all the time."

"You deliberately trying to get me to fire you?" Charlene retorted at him.

She lifted what was left of the chicken leg up to Kane's lips, and he brushed her hand aside choosing to taste it from her lips instead. When he broke the kiss he licked his lips.

"*Che, che*, damn, good chicken, as usual." He looked over at Stuart. "Thanks again for doing this for me. Well done, my friend, as always. As you can see, she loves it."

"Of course every one loves my fried chicken." Stuart grinned.

"Oh Stuart, marry me." Charlene crooned playfully.

"Hey!" Kane scowled nudging her with his hip.

"Just joking, baby." She lifted her face towards his to receive another kiss. Charlene discarded the bone in the nearby food waste bin. They had a bin for everything, recycling was a big deal in Tokyo. She wiped her mouth and fingers with the cloth napkin, but only soap and water would get rid of the smell on her hands. "You have a place that I can freshen up."

"Right here, but it's occupied at the moment. He should be out shortly." Kane stated.

Charlene came up short. "He? Is Takusa in there?"

"No, I haven't seen or heard from *him* all day."

"Then who—"

Before she could finish asking the bathroom door opened and Charlene stared at the short balding Asian man, she'd never met before stepping out.

"I apologize, for being so long. I had to call and check in with my wife to let her know our daughter is here with me." He turned his wide grin on Charlene and bowed in politeness saying, "*Konbanwa*, good evening. *Sokka*, I see, the bride has arrived. I suppose, we can get all the things officially settled, now."

Charlene blanched. "Excuse me?"

Kane slipped a hand around her waist and Charlene stiffened. He must be going out of his mind. Why did he tell this man they were engaged. She thought they agreed to keep it a guarded secret.

"Charlie-chan, this is Yaguchi-san, he is here to officially finalize our marriage papers. Stu-san and Goda-san will be our witnesses, so we can get married right now." Kane stated as if was the best idea he ever had. When she didn't say anything, he chimed, "No more waiting for something to go wrong! Isn't it a great idea?"

She felt a crazing fluttering in her stomach and her breathing became shallow as she her first instinct to panic took over. Charlene did the unexpected. She made a mad dash for the bathroom, slamming the door behind her.

Kane stood with wide eyes at the door, his hands on his hips.

"Well that went as well as expected," Abe commented.

Stuart chuckled.

Kane turned on Abe bellowing, "I believe you said this was a good idea."

"It is a good idea, but Charlie hates surprises, because she's a control fanatic. So, give her a moment. She'll be out in a minute or two." Abe dropped down in the nearest seat and plucked apple from a fruit basket beside the chair. The sound of his bite into the apple seemed loud in the silence of the room as the men waited.

Ten minutes passed.

"Okay, I'm going in," Kane said.

"I wouldn't do that if I was you," Abe, Stuart, and Yaguchi-san yelled at the same time.

Kane looked like he swallowed something sour. The older men in the room all chuckled.

"Give her the time she needs, Son," Yaguchi said. "Women, sometimes need to be alone to work things out in their own way. It's her wedding day after all, and this isn't the most romantic setting, women like to plan these things. Believe me, if you go charging in that room making demands, I can guarantee there will be no marriage taking place tonight."

"Stu-san, I love her. She might need me, or something could be wrong." Kane looked absolutely helpless and looked at his best friend. "I have to do something, if they were to call me before she gets out of there, I won't be able to just leave her. I got to know Charlie-chan is alright before I do anything else!"

"Let someone else start the show," Abe suggested.

"Can't." Stuart answered for Kane. "It's live."

"Your birthday party is being televised, live?" Abe shook his head. "That manager of yours is magnificent. Just by being in his presence, I learn something new every time, he knows how to make every opportunity count. Still, there is no way I could do something like this to Charlie. She would kick my ass and then fire me."

Charlene emerged from the washroom; she had heard everything being said through the door, especially Kane's distressful voice. "You're right about that." She said to Abe. "I hope you don't mind, but I made use of the vase of flowers in the bathroom."

Charlene had swept all of her hair to one side over her shoulder and used a hair clamp from her purse to attach a white peony flower above her right ear. In her hand she held a small bouquet of white wisteria and purple iris."

"Bay-bee, *yareyare*, geeze! Don't ever scare me like that again. I'm sorry I didn't mean to upset you. But, I spent all day with the help of Stu-san and Goda-san trying to get all the proper paperwork and such done. I figured since I didn't get to talk to Takusa-san, that if we were already married he couldn't come in here with Arisa and spring something like this one me. With us going on live tonight, I had no idea what to expect and once he got the chance to broadcast …"

"Kane, sweetheart, take a breath. It's okay. I'm okay, I admit I was a bit surprised, but I ran because the greasy cold chicken didn't settle too well on my stomach." She touched his face and smiled sheepishly. "Still, I don't regret one bite it was good going down. Thank you again, Stuart." She rubbed her stomach. "See, I've learned to be prepared for anything, especially lately, so I carry a traveling toothbrush kit in my purse for such occasions."

The men all laughed with relief.

"I guess we better make our relationship official." She kissed Kane once…and again. "It was an excellent idea, baby. I hope you don't mind that we do it again in a more formal way later." She wiped her lipstick off his mouth with her thumb. "My family will insist on it."

"As many times as you want, sweetheart, just don't scare me like that again." He pulled her against him in a bear hug, and she grunted but understood. She had felt the same desperation all day. It was good to hold him and be held.

Charlene and Kane made it official. There was nothing to say, just papers to sign by them and the witnesses. They received their copies in English and Japanese. Yaguchi-san placed his signed copies in his briefcase, and it was as official as an elaborate public affair.

Abe shook the official's hand and handed him a thick sealed envelope before opening the dressing room door and escorting the older man out of the room.

"Ten minutes Kane," Stuart grinned at the both of them with a big white toothy smile in his dark face. "Congratulations, I know you'll be happy. Just make sure there is enough sweetened marshmallow cereals in the house so you two will have nothing to argue over." He teased and closed the door leaving them alone.

"Konbanwa, Wife." Kane sat down and pulled her onto his lap.

"Good evening, Husband."

"I like that."

"Me too."

"I got something to give you." Kane said reaching into the inner pocket of his red and black leather jacket.

The feel of his leather-clad thighs against hers felt as wonderful as skin against skin. She squirmed in his lap, feeling a warm dampness between her legs. She'd wished they had time to finish what they had started on the table earlier that morning.

"Kane, you don't have to give me anything else. This is more then I could have wished for when I left my suite tonight. The flowers are beautiful...what? Why are you laughing?"

"The flowers really are gifts from co-workers, fans, people, I don't know, bay-bee. I can't take credit for the ambiance in the room. All I thought about was getting some of your favorite foods in here." He grinned at her sheepishly.

"It doesn't matter. You can get me in the bed quicker with a plate full of fried chicken, then you can a bouquet of flowers."

"Honto, really?" His brow raised in surprise. "You know Stuart had said that once about getting sex from some girls on a college campus for his chicken once. I thought he was joking."

"What!" Charlene mouth opened in suspended disbelief. "Well, that's not me. I was joking."

She felt Kane's entire body shaking as he laughed. "So was I, I heard it on a late night comedy show on an American Television broadcast."

She punched him in the shoulder. "I should have known Stuart wouldn't have told you some shit like that." Charlene laughed against his mouth. "What is that in your hand?"

"You don't think I would allow you to walk around without something that shows you are taken by me, do you?" Kane murmured opening the heart shaped porcelain jeweled box, which made a beautiful gift, alone.

Charlene, release a soft squeal of excitement. It was a beautiful ring set of a modestly large heart shaped diamond with alternate tiny diamonds and rubies encircling the band. The wedding band matched the band on the engagement ring.

"I hope you like it, I got yellow gold because I noticed its what you seem to own more of in your jewelry box. But, if you rather get platinum, or choose something else we can..."

"No, I love this and most men don't even notice the preference of gold and such women like to wear. I'm just flattered you noticed such a thing." Charlene held out her left hand. "Here put them on."

"Which goes first?" Kane brow puckered as held her hand.

"The wedding band, since we're married. It goes closest to the heart," she explained. The rings slid on easily, and she was amazed. "It's a perfect fit."

"Oh," Kane reached into his pocket and picked up her empty right hand and slid another ring on her finger. "I borrowed it. I didn't know how to ask without blowing the surprise, so I took one of your rings out of your jewelry box."

J-Pop Love Song

Charlene giggled and held up her left hand to the light. Her face grew serious, and she looked into him in the eyes. "You know Takusa-san is going to have a fit, when he finds out."

Kane shrugged. "I suppose, he should have been here to keep me out of trouble, then."

"Takusa not being the first here for a party this big that he is paying for seems a bit strange don't it?" Charlene, mouth twisted in thought before asking, "What about Arisa? Is she here?"

Kane released a long rush of air. "I'm supposing that is why Takusa isn't here yet. When I went home Arisa was gone. Packed up all her stuff and left a letter. Apparently, her mother helped her, after, she found out Takusa had told her the truth that she wasn't his father. He broke his promise to her, so she no longer felt a loyalty to him."

"You think Takusa went after her? After all he needed her to make his plans work, right?"

"I'm assuming that's a probability, otherwise I have no idea where he is or what's going on with him." Kane reached up and pulled her lips against his and murmured, "I don't care, now. We are together forever and as far as I'm concerned, I'm not hiding my love for you anymore, Charlie-chan. I believe the only way to keep you safe is to make it public."

He nibbled the corner of her mouth.

"Kane—" Charlene began to protest pulling back. She couldn't think when is mouth was touching her.

"No, Charlie-chan, no more excuses, or worrying about others." He interrupted her. "It's me and you; you know, the requirements for *the end* and *happy ever after*, like in one of your books. So get use to it. You and I won and everyone must accept it, including you."

"I want all of that too, but..."

"No "buts." *Kiite*, listen, bay-bee, just because I'm twenty-five don't mean I won't insist on wearing the pants in my family. I'm a man, so let me be one and protect what is mine, to the best of my abilities." He stated bluntly. "Your input matters to me, and if you see me steering us in the wrong direction that could hurt us as a couple, by all means tell me so, but you have to allow me some input and try to be the best husband to you, I can be. You know, women aren't the only ones who dreams about their future, marrying, and how their life is supposed to be."

Charlene's dark eyes softened into liquid pools of emotions as she looked in her young husband's eyes. The only experience she had with men had been gained while being with Jason, and he needed her for everything. Allowing someone else to share the authority would take some getting use too, but she was ready for a change. Nor could she ignore the unconditional love and sincerity on his face. She could see that he would work hard to help her make their home a happy one.

With a resigned sigh she said softly, "Yuza Kaneishi, you make me so proud to be your wife," she lovingly admitted.

A knock sounded on the door and Stuart stuck his head inside. "They're ready."

Ignoring Stuart, his arms tightened about her, and she leaned into him. "Trust me?" He asked.

"You know I do or I wouldn't be here married to you." She answered placing his strong beautiful hand on her stomach. "We both trust you."

As if he was about to go to war, they clung to each other as their lips meshed and their heartbeat synchronized as one.

"Kane, sorry Man, they need to touch you up before you go on stage and do a sound check on your headset." Stuart announced, this time a bit louder.

They giggled, and she stood. Kane took full advantage and cupped her full bottom in his hands as he came to his feet. "I like this, do you think you will keep it after the baby is born?"

"Stop, boy." She slapped playfully at his hands. "You need to get out there and do your thang. I have very expensive taste, you know."

"Have you decided where you want to set up houses yet?" he asked.

"I will be thinking about it and we can decided together."

Kane held his hand out to her. Charlene released a long contented breath of air. Linking her fingers with his, they walked out of the dressing room.

The newly married lovers were oblivious to the pair of dark eyes watching them exit from a distance in the blackness of the backstage area. After they turned the corner, he flipped open his phone and made a call.

Chapter Sixteen

AT THE EDGE OF THE STAGE, just out of sight, Kane kept his arm around Charlene's waist in a possessive grip. He was vaguely aware of the surprise, curiosity, questioning in the looks that the band, dancers, and other members of the Takusa Group gave them, but they didn't ask any questions.

The crowd were already worked up, chanting, "Kane! Kane! Kane!"

The band ran out on stage and took their places. Cheers. The lead guitarist stepped up to the microphone. "I can't hear you; I want you to get loud and show the birthday boy how much you love him…" A long pause and the band queued up his first song. "Ladies and gentleman…KANE!"

The audience erupted into madness. Kane kissed her mouth, "Time to go!" he muttered, and released her. The usual rush of adrenaline shot through him as he immediately fed off the energy of the inhabitants in the nightclub, the sound was deafening and he stood in the spotlight. He spread his arms wide and looked up to the sky, hands open, palm wide welcoming the calls, screams, and applause that embraced him.

"*Konbanwa!* Good evening!" he shouted into his microphone headset.

"*Konbanwa!* We love you Kane!" the audience roared back.

"I love you too!" Kane held up his hand to give the band a signal to bring the music down. "I want to thank all of you for coming out tonight to share my birthday with me."

Another round of cheers and applause came from the crowd.

"Before I and the rest of the Takusa Entertainment Group comes out to get this party started, I have something personally that I wish to share with all of you."

Kane grinned and paused as fans sung happy birthday to him.

"*Arigato!*" He bowed his dark head twice in appreciation. He stared over into the wings, but he could barely make out Charlene's shadow from the blinding front lights. He forged ahead, knowing no matter what she was by his side.

"Okay, thank you, but please allow me to say this and we can get the show started. I have done my best to give you the best performances and music possible during my career so far. I have been very disciplined in making my career first and foremost. I love what I do and I hope that you will continue to support me as I continue to work hard."

Another interruptions of cheers and applause sounded.

"I no longer want to take this wonderful journey alone and tonight, I was married."

A chorus of cheers went out along with more then a few collective gasps of shock. The band stop playing and a hush went over the room as if everyone finally realized he was being serious.

"I know this comes as a shock to everyone and I would have announced it at the end of the night but I figured some of you would be too drunk to believe me." Kane pointed to a few people in the audience. "Yeah, I'm talking about you, you, and yes most definitely, you!"

Laughter and applause rung out easing some of the tension in the room and Kane felt some of the fear that rushed his stomach as he said the last words, ease.

"I hope this doesn't change the way you look at me or how you feel when you listen to my music." His voice was thick with emotions. "Your loyalty and support mean the world to me. For those who can't wish me happiness, I can only say, *gomen-ne*, I'm sorry, *boku-no kimochi, wakatte*, please understand my feelings. *Li omoide-o arigato*, thanks for the beautiful memories. *Domo Arigato Gozaimasu!*" Kane bowed his hair draped forward. He stared at his knees fully humbling himself to any of his fans that felt slighted by the decisions he had made in his personal life.

Slowly the applause started and grew louder followed by cheers, and then deafening cheers and shouts sounded of people telling him to do his best.

Kane couldn't stop the emotions that welled up inside him and an overwhelming peace and satisfaction that this was the evidence he needed to know, his career would survive this regardless of what a few will do in protest. His fans only wanted his happiness. He gulped hard and arose to open his arms wide in his beginning stance, hot tears slipping down his cheeks.

"This will be the first song off my first English CD, I am working on, and I wrote this song for my wife, Charlene." The glowing lights dimmed as he cued up the song to the band, and finally he could see her beautiful face offstage, where he had left her standing earlier. Her face glistened with tears and his heart pounded. "I love you Charlie-chan!"

The audience wildly clapped, but all Kane cared about at that moment was Charlene blowing him a kiss. He reached out as if he caught it in his hand and put it to his mouth and sent her a wide smile.

By the time he finished the first song the audience had become putty in his hands; he felt them out there in the dark, alive and full of adoration. With exceptions to the feelings of love and sex with Charlene, there was no greater rush. In his usual fashion, Kane gave a memorable performance.

Charlene laughed, cried and felt glorious in those few minutes, while watching him. Kane had bravely gone out there on that stage, and in front of a live audience and a television camera, he told the world about their marriage and his love for her. The fallout that will come tomorrow will be outrageous, but she didn't care. She had never been so happy in her entire life.

She was high on love, and it was a glorious blessed feeling and when he looked over at her, their eyes met, she felt her entire body shudder with a need. She couldn't wait until they were alone tonight, their wedding night.

J-Pop Love Song

As the show progressed through, Charlene soaked up the essence of Kane the entertainer and realized while watching him live in his element, he was definitely a force to reckon with. She couldn't wait to discuss more about the English album he was working on, maybe he would allow her to collaborate with him on a few of the tracks.

She shook her head and chuckled silently. Was this all just some gloriously foolish dream? Was she going to wake up any minute now and all of this would be wishful thinking. Her eyes dropped to the glistening rings on her hand, and she realized, today was as real and solid as these wedding symbols of his love on her finger. She could relax now, everything would be well; it had to be.

Suddenly she was grabbed from behind. Charlene squirmed and tried to see who it was, but she was being held firmly around the waist with one big hand clamped over her mouth. A sickeningly sweet aroma seized her sense all she could reason was "Don't hurt my baby," before feeling a heaviness in her arms and legs. Her eyes darted back and forth in alarm, and she gagged against the smell that seemed to overwhelm her. The tight burning in her lungs became so unbearable she welcomed the darkness that besieged her.

It was a triumphant performance and Kane was flying high. He ran off stage with them chanting his name. Disappointment crossed his face when he noticed Charlene wasn't there waiting for. He could understand, after all she was pregnant, and she was tiring easy these days. The show went longer then he intended when they added two more songs due to the worked up crowd. Now they had another Takusa up and coming artist to feed off of.

Kane headed back to his dressing room, hoping that he would find his new bride napping, eating or just waiting for him. The thought that someone, who truly loved him, was waiting for him sent wonderful sweet emotions of comfort through him.

"Kane, did Charlie say where she was going?" Abe Goda asked as strolled towards him.

Kane toweled dry is sweat soaked hair with the draped towel around his neck. "When I went on stage I got the impression she was going to wait for me, but when I came off she wasn't there. Maybe she went back to the dressing room to get more chicken."

Kane grinned thinking about her savoring each bite as if it brought her closer to an orgasm with each chew. Nothing sexier than a woman who enjoys her food; he never understood the women who picked and shoved around the food on their plates and ate nothing.

Abe shook his head, "No, I just came by the dressing room on my way to the stage to see if she was with you."

"Have you checked with Stu-san? He's usually waiting for me offstage, and he's missing too. I told him to keep and eye on Charlene. Did you try her cell phone?"

"Going to voicemail." Abe frown deepened.

"Let's go back to the dressing room, and I'll shower and change. They are bound to come back there. We got the food and how long can my lady, go without food these days?"

Kane and Abe discussed the performance and his surprise announcement. The more the two men talked the more they realized that in spite of their age difference they had more in common then they thought. It didn't hurt that now Charlene was his wife he felt more secured about her being around men that were closer to her age.

Kane came out of the bathroom, showered and changed into blue jeans and a dark blue t-shirt. "Hey, did anyone check in?"

Abe shook his head, pacing the floor. His dark eyes intense as he looked at Kane and said, "Now, I'm beginning to worry."

"*Boku-mo*, me too. It's not like Stu-san to not check in like this; especially, if he has Charlene in his care, he would know I would want her by my side, especially tonight." Kane lifted up his cell phone and hit redial. Closing his phone he scowled. "I'm still getting voicemail and my gut is telling me something is wrong."

"I agree," Abe nodded.

Kane's eyes grew wide as he grabbed Abe by the arms. "You don't think there was a problem with the baby and Stuart too Charlie-chan to the hospital do you?"

"No way," Abe stated. "One of them would have called us by now."

Kane dropped his hands and his pounding heartbeat eased, but the nagging in his gut continued. "You're right."

Abe and Kane were started by the big bang as if someone had through something again the door. They both rushed forward to open the door. Something was jammed against it and it took them both pushing against it to shove it open.

"Stu-san!" Kane went down on his knees beside his friend. "Abe, go get a towel, there is also a first-aid kit in the bathroom in the cabinet under the sink." He ordered fingering the gash on the back of Stuart's head. The deep concern was etched on his youthful face.

With the aid of a conscious Stuart, they were able to get him in the dressing room on the sofa. It didn't take long before he and Abe was plying his with questions about Charlene.

"They took her," Stuart murmured.

"Who took her?" Kane bellowed, trying to remain calm, but it wasn't working.

"Two men in a black car. Looked like some of Takusa's henchmen."

"I swear, father or not, I will kill him!"

"Stand in line," Abe muttered.

"Is that how you got hurt, where you with her?"

"No," Stuart cleared his throat and thanked Abe for the bottle of water. "I got a call. They said they were security and wanted me to come to the parking garage because someone had been tampering around beneath the car. I went and checked it out and that is when someone tagged me in the back of my fuckin' head! Cowering sons-of-a-bitches! They couldn't even face me in a good fight."

"Charlene?"

"I don't' know, I left her watching your performance from the sideline. I was coming awake when I saw two men placing her in the car. She…looked to be unconscious…I don't know she wasn't moving!"

J-Pop Love Song

"Fuck! Fuck!" Kane paced. His first instincts were to panic, cry and completely lose all reason, but he realized that wouldn't get his wife back in his arms safely. The one thing he wouldn't accept is Takusa harming her. So there was no way she was dead. That was unacceptable. "Barely married three hours, and I've already failed to keep her safe."

"Don't be hard on yourself," Abe pat and squeezed his shoulder. "There is no way you could have seen Takusa going this far. None of us could. Do you have any idea where Takusa would take her?"

"He wouldn't be stupid enough to take her to one of his homes or places of business, because regardless of how he feels about Charlene. She is well-known and he wouldn't want to bring the American Embassy down on his head, or cause Japan any embarrassment."

"I agree. Takusa is a lot of things but a killer I don't think so." Abe sighed and ran a hand through his hair. He pushed his glasses up on his nose. "I think I might know where he took her."

Kane stared at Abe. "Nonie? What? How could you know?"

"I know, because William Alfred, Charlene's father, entrusted some information to me that he didn't want Charlene to find out about by reading it in those files. I haven't had the chance to tell her because, well, she's been so happy lately."

"What the hell is it?" Kane asked his patients beyond thin for long speeches. They should be moving, if he had any idea where his father would be keeping Charlene.

"Come on, we're wasting time standing here!" Abe released a frustrated curse. "I will fill you in on everything in the car."

"Stu-san, I'll get one of the band members to take you to the hospital." Kane said.

"There is no fucking way I'm allowing you two to deal with Takusa and his men alone. This is what I get paid for and even if I didn't, you're my friend, and I got your back."

♪

Charlene swatted at whatever putrid smell was beneath her nose. She coughed and sputtered into awareness. Bitter bile came up and burned the back of her throat and she gagged.

"Leave me alone," she moaned.

"Here, is some water, I need you to take a sip, it will help clear your throat. The Chloroform should be wearing off soon. I apologize for this unorthodox method of bringing you here, but I couldn't chance you refusing to meet with me, for it was not an option. I need to speak with you, without Kane and without your guard dog lawyer's interference."

"Takusa-san?" Charlene scowled managing to pen her eyes. The lids felt as if they were weighted and the effort left her panting. She came up on her elbow and took the bottled water from his hand and drink greedily.

"Careful now," Takusa tugged at the bottle. "Too much, too fast will only make you nauseated."

"Where are we?" She asked noting that wherever they were, they were up very high. The light of Tokyo twinkled all around them, the view familiar, yet there were so many sky-high buildings in the city she could be on top of any one of them.

"Don't just stand there gentlemen, help the woman to her feet," he barked orders. "Also one of you give her your jacket, there's a bit of a chill in the air tonight."

Without hesitation they did as they were told.

Charlene swooned on her feet and on of the men caught her against his chest until she gained her bearings, her head was killing her and her empty stomach heaved, causing her to gag and the water she just drank came back up.

As she righted herself and tried to retain some of her dignity, she accepted the oversized jacket as the man placed it over her shoulders. She held it close and prayed the shivering would start soon. It wasn't from the cold air of the night as much as from the fear of the unknown, for Takusa was not one easy to read.

"Are you okay?" Takusa asked in a clipped voice.

"As if you care!" Charlene's eyes narrowed on his face. "Just tell me, where I am and why am I here?"

"Obviously, you are on the rooftop of a building; *your*, hotel building to be exact," Takusa informed her.

She kept her eyes focused on his thin frame. He stood a few feet away, his thin frame stooped over at the shoulder in a relaxed stance with his hands shoved deeply in his trouser pockets. There were tired pockets around his dark eyes and he seemed to have aged since the last time she saw him.

"Why am I here?" she asked once more. The wind whistled in her ears and encompassed them. With shaky hands she tucked her hair inside the jacket and pulled it tightly about her shoulders.

"Take a look at this view. Isn't it beautiful? This was the last thing he would have seen. Not, the face of his wife, because she was out at an award ceremony accepting her accolades." Takusa sighed. "This is where it all began and ended. The place where all our lives became intertwined."

Her gaze collided with his. "Why would you imagine I would want to be up here? You and everyone else in Japan that keeps up with the news, knows this is where Jason chose to end his life."

"Exactly. That is why I brought you here." Takusa looked back at her, his eyes accusing. For a long moment they didn't say anything, but she knew there was much that needed to be said.

"So this is about Jason and not Kane?" She asked in surprise.

"Both, actually." Takusa announced. "All my life I have been surround by lying deceitful women whom only thought about themselves and made decisions that fitted their own selfish motives. The one and only woman I have loved in my entire life, was like yourself and American. She was Caucasian and beautiful. An heiress to her fashion designer mother's fortune attending school here on an exchange program—"

"Excuse me, but I'm tired, hungry, have a headache and cranky as hell from being accosted, so if you don't mind, I'm not interested in your love life." Charlene's voice was cold and exact.

To her surprise Takusa chuckled. "Beautiful, passionate, talented, and to the

J-Pop Love Song

point. I can see why Jason and Kane would find you hard to resist. Forgive me for saying, Alfred-san, but I must insist that you hear me out. I've waited years for you to return to Japan and to get this opportunity to have this conversation with you."

Charlene crossed her arms protectively beneath her breast. "Then by all means have your say, but is there anyway I can get the cliff notes version of your life story? After all, I already know most of it. Like you're in up to your ass in debt to the Yakuza, and the fact that Kane is your son, also that you need him and his money more then he need you."

Takusa nodded and laughed aloud. "You are something else. I should have known you wouldn't be standing up here like a simpering female whimpering and begging me for your release. That's why I knew that keeping you out of my son's life was imperative for my plans for his future to come to pass. You have a gift to wield much power over the men that grace your presence. Even now Kane is obsessively protective of you. The seventeen heated messages he's left in my voicemail throughout the day prove my greatest fear. He is no longer under my control, but yours."

"If that is true why did you allow things to progress this far with Kane getting involved with *Blu's Diary?*"

"So that we may get to this point and I also hope that the years since Jason's death had been physically unkind to you, since you seemed to have become a recluse of sorts. Then that first day I saw you up close and in person, I believe you had thrived from Jason's death, because you seemed more vibrant, lovely and alive." Takusa splayed his hands wide at her. "You see I met you once back when you were married to Jason. I wasn't as important as I am now, but I knew I had to get through you to get to Jason, because he allowed you to run his career. On first meeting him I realized he was useless without you. In many ways we are the same. You created the legend Jason James is today, as I created the legend "Kane" will become some day."

Charlene cocked her head to the side in question, "So this is why I am here? You felt I slighted you in someway years ago and you want revenge? To show me how powerful you've become, or what?"

"May I finish the telling of my story Alfred-san, I assure you by the end all things will be clear."

"By all means," she said sarcastically. "It's not like leaving, is another one of my options."

"No, you are free to leave at anytime. I brought you here against your will, however I have no intentions of keeping you here under the same duress. Go if you wish, but if you do you will never know the reasoning behind all that the things I do. I'm sure if nothing else, you have to be curious as to why I have handled my relationship with Kane the way I have all these years. Don't you want to know why I molded my son to be the image of your dead husband?"

"Greed and power."

"To some extent."

"Then why?"

"The American heiress I fell in love with left me because her season long fling with this Japanese young man working two jobs to pay his student loans. I meant absolutely nothing to her. What I didn't know was even though she had left school and left Tokyo, she didn't leave Japan until nine months later. Being Catholic there was no way she could return home unwed with a half-breed baby. Not in back in the sixties, those types of things just weren't done."

"What are you saying?"

"She thought so little of me as a man, that instead of bringing my son to me, so that I could work harder and give him the life he deserved and be the father I could have been, she abandon him at some Catholic orphanage in Kagoshima. Years later I ran into her at an opera in New York, with her husband and gave her my business card I wanted her to see I was on my way to being somebody more wealthy and more powerful then her father's old money could every make him." Takusa bitterness was etched on his face. "She had the audacity to call and ask me to dine with her. I did, because in many ways my love and anger for her, is what gave me the will to mow down all obstacles."

"It was during this meeting she told you about your child?"

"Yes. She gave me written permission to have her records opened up at the nursery so that I could know what my son's name was, in hopes to find out what happened to him. So you can imagine my surprise once I found out that the well known Japanese rock star, your husband, Jason James was my son."

Charlene's eyes grew wide in stunned disbelief. That meant Kane and Jason half-brothers. "Oh, God," she moaned, closing her eyes, swaying on her feet. The bodyguard beside her once again came to her rescue.

"My sentiments exact, if I believed one existed," Takusa murmured.

"Did Jason ever know or did you find out after his death?"

"He knew. I contacted him as soon as I found out and showed him the proof because he thought I was lying because I wanted to take him from you and oversee his career myself. He refused to let you go, he would always say without you in his life he would be nothing. I knew that wasn't completely true." Takusa said, sweeping his hand through his windswept hair.

"With my abilities, I knew I could make a difference in his life, like I have for Kane these past years. Jason would have been my first big success, if only he was willing to severe all ties with you, and all he associated with from the American music scene, I could get him clean and sober. I knew as long as my son had ties to those who enabled his destructive behavior, he would never reach his musical potential."

"Trust me I know from experience, Jason would never have reached the status of Kane if he hadn't died. Dying early in the middle of a successful career run in a tragic way is what made Jason a legend."

"It also made you a very wealthy woman," Takusa sneered.

"Excuse me, but it's not like I didn't come from a wealthy family myself, something you would have known if you had done your research. It was never about the money with Jason, it was about the fact that he was needy as hell and I needed someone to need me. *I* wrote the songs for him because I loved him. *I'm* the one who stayed up for three days straight while he sobered up long enough to do his next gig. *I'm* the one who stood by and took the cheating and the lying because I knew if I left him he would do something stupid. He had threatened to kill himself numerous times!"

"Is that why he finally did it, Alfred-san? Did you walk out of his life that night and he felt all was lost? Did you allow him to make you his entire world and then take it all from him?" Takusa demanded.

"No!" Charlene yelled back. "HE let *me* down that night! He snatched *my* world from me when he chose to die. I was to the one who faced the press and my peers when the story and the photos emerged of the underage female and male he shared a bed with!

"That turned out to be a hoax." Takusa reminded her coldly.

"Which part," she shot back. "The fact that they were not underage or the fact that there were drugs out on the table in the hotel room and his face, body, tattoos showing me and the world he'd really been taking drugs and fucking two complete strangers?"

Takusa had the nerve to look stricken at her outburst, but she wasn't finished. "I was pissed and I left him alone that night. I was getting tired of him slowly killing me. Hell, I don't even know what happened to send him over the edge. He'd been clean and sober up to that point, and I warned him if he blew it one more time it was over."

"He kept saying he was setup, that someone had drugged him, and that he'd never seen those kids in his life. That he didn't remember what had happened. We argued, he begged me to stay and I told I him I couldn't deal with anymore that night and I had to be at the banquet. I told him to hold his head up and be a man for once and show the entire world he had nothing to hide. He couldn't, he went downstairs to the hotel bar and I left. No matter what, he knew I wouldn't really walk out of his life forever."

"Jason couldn't have been that weak, tell me you don't believe that's why he did it." Takusa demanded.

Charlene didn't know why it was so important to him, but Takusa had to face the harsh truth. She had all those years. "I know you want to make me out to be the person coming between you and all your dreams, Takusa-san, but that isn't the case. I left Jason to go to a banquet. He knew I was coming back so we could talk about everything. I didn't know if he was lying or not about being set up at the time, but after he died and the truth gradually came out and it was only then I began to wonder—"

"What have I done?" Takusa wailed backing up until he was doubled over against the opened concreted railing. "I killed my first born son."

"What—Kane!" Charlene had never been so happy to see someone in her entire life. She rushed forward dropping the jacket from her shoulders in her haste. Kane swept her up in his arms and they kissed, cried and tried to speak at the same time. She felt as if his hands where everywhere on her body as he assured himself of her safety.

"Charlene, I was horrified that I hadn't gotten here in time." Kane murmured against her lips.

"I'm fine. I was so scared. How did you find me?" She asked pulling back to look up at him. He kept his hold on her. Cupping her face in his hands, his eyes searched her face as if he was memorizing her. "You're shaking. Kane, I'm fine, really."

"The baby?"

"*We're* fine."

Kane saw Takusa and she could swear he released a growl from the back of his throat as he moved with outstretched hands towards his father. Stuart and Abe assured that the Takusa's men stayed out of it. This was between father and son.

Charlene watched in horror as Kane grabbed Takusa by the lapels and shook the aging man. Pushing his upper body through the opening in the concrete that allowed access to a thin workman's walkway and a drop from one of the tallest hotels in Tokyo.

"Kane! Don't!" Charlene screamed, scared for the both of them.

"*Baka-janai*, are you stupid or what? What the hell is wrong with you?" He bellowed. "*Kichigai!* You're crazy! *Mo owari-da!* It's over! You hear me? Charlene is my wife now and there is nothing you could do to us anymore. It's fucking over!"

"Baby, please!" Charlene cried. "Come away from the ledge, please, I couldn't bear it if something happens to you."

"I'm so sorry, Son, I was wrong...wrong about everything." Takusa wept.

Kane eased his hold on Takusa and pulled him up to his feet backing away from him. Charlene hurried to his side and wrapped her hands around his waist. "Kane, Jason was your half brother."

Kane breathing heavy looked into her eyes, his hand buried in her hair. "I know. Abe filled us in on everything in the car. Your father told him to tell us when the time was right. We weren't sure that Takusa knew, for this information was gather from elsewhere."

"He found out and told Jason," she explained. "He blamed me for Jason's suicide, but it wasn't my fault, I swear I wasn't going to leave him, even though I knew I should have. I was just gone for that evening and I returned as soon as it was over, to find I was too late."

She felt soothed by Kane's capable fingers wiping the tears from her face. His beautiful brown eyes looked into hers with love and longing. "We've discussed this and I don't care if he was my brother. I feel the same way I did before. He was a weak man and a fool to choose death over you."

"I was so scared I wouldn't see you again," she admitted losing all the bravado she showed when she was alone with Takusa and his men.

"I was horrified I would be too late. I didn't want to believe he would intentionally hurt you, but anything could have happened to harm you or the baby. I love you."

She didn't say another word. He knew. She clung, devouring his lips and soaking up his warmth, they held each other for a long moment and he kissed her again. The present was all that mattered to them, this moment; each knowing the other was safe.

"I'm don't know how much of the show you got to see, but I sang just for you tonight," he whispered.

"I saw enough to know, that I am the luckiest, most loved Black woman in all of Japan," she said in a husky voice roughened by emotions, then once more his mouth was on hers, hot and insistent.

"*Gomen-ne*, I wanted to say I'm sorry, to the both of you." Takusa interrupted them.

Kane reluctantly lifted his mouth, to stare over at his father. "Are you? Do you have any idea what you've done tonight? Charlene is carrying your first grandchild!"

Takusa turned pale under the moonlight and surrounding rooftop lighting. "I...I had no idea! Why didn't you tell me?"

"Why should I? So you would have something else to threaten me with? It wasn't enough that you tried to ruin my life, but that of your own daughter. When is it ever enough for you?" Kane demanded, his face contorted in anger and mistrust.

"I'm finished." Takusa released a weary sigh. "I'm tired. Do to me what you will. You can have me arrested and destroy all I have built. I don't care anymore. I don't have any one to leave all of this to, so why does it even matter? I killed your brother, and now I made you despise me."

"What do you mean *you* killed Jason?" It was Charlene's turn to demand answers.

"I...it was I that set up the hotel tryst with Jason and the two that were in the picture. They drugged his drink, stripped off all his clothing and took those pictures," Takusa confessed. "If I knew Jason had such a weak constitution, I wouldn't have done such a thing to him."

"*Sensei—*" Kane whispered.

"My God," Charlene cried. "*Why?* Why would you do such a thing to your own son?"

"Because I wanted him to divorce you. He wanted all I had to offer, but he didn't want to give you up. I believed you were the one bringing his down, making him weak. So I came up with an idea of making *you* leave *him*. I just wanted him to be *my* son again."

It was too much to take in, but Charlene had to hear it all. "So, all this time you thought *I* was the cause of all of Jason's problems, in spite of the fact that *I* was the one who kept him clean, and then you believed I was trying to do the same thing to Kane?"

Takusa nodded slowly. "Yes."

Kane folded his arms over his chest. He regarded the man whom he had honored for so long with contempt. "What about you and my mother? How long have you known that I was your son and why didn't you tell me the truth?"

A little of Takusa's bluster came to the fore. "As much as you would like to think the man you thought was your father was a paragon of virtue, in reality he was very cruel and completely disrespected your mother and her love for him. We were friends in school, she helped me get through my broken heart with Jason's mother."

"You were always lovers?"

"No, it was one time, after she found out her husband's mistress had a child by him. The one thing she wanted more then anything in this world was a child, yet he told her he couldn't have children and because of his infidelity she insisted he wore protection those rare times he actually touched her. When she found about the child, she was upset and I was there. I didn't know you were mine until she committed suicide."

"How do I know that's the truth," Kane eyed him warily.

"After all I have revealed, why would I lie now?" Takusa asked wearily. "If you want proof, contact her lawyers. They gave me a letter from her; I still have it in my safety deposit box. She wrote that you were my son. She asked me to raise you in a good family and not to leave you in the care of her husband because of his cruelty. After finding you had run away the day of her funeral, I realized she most likely was telling the truth. The one thing she asked of me was that I never tell you the truth. She didn't want you to think any more ill of her then you probably already did for committing suicide."

Tears fell down Kane's face and he brusquely wiped them away with his hand. "Did..." he cleared the lump in the back of his throat. "Did she say why? Why she left me?"

Charlene tightened her hold on his hand.

"Yuza-kun, your mother suffered from *fibromyalgia*. She died from neglect because no matter how many doctors she went to, they always told her it was all in her head. That she was only trying to get attention from her husband to save her marriage. So they gave her sleeping pills instead. It had nothing to do with you. Living just got to be too much for her."

Kane nodded. "*Sokka*. I see."

Takusa sighed. "So, I'm going to be a grandfather. Well, hopefully, one day, you two will allow me to be a part of your lives. That is after I put wrong to right."

"I don't—" Kane began, not in a forgiving mood.

"Anything is possible when it comes to family, Takusa-san." Charlene jumped in before Kane could say something he might regret.

"Charlie-chan," Kane's tone was tinged with rage. "Do you know what you're saying? Look at all that he has done to *you*. To both Jason and myself!"

Charlene laid an understanding hand on his. "Baby, I'm not saying I condone what your father has done, but he *is* your father and for better or worse he has honored the promise he made to your mother, which doesn't make him that much of a monster. Maybe Takusa-san was a little overzealous in trying to protect you and Jason, and I can't fault him for that." She felt the tension slowly drain from her lover and smiled reassuringly.

Turning back to a chastened Takusa, Charlene's gaze hardened. "Make no mistake Takusa-san, I'm not quite ready to make nice yet. You drove your own son to suicide, because you couldn't accept that I wasn't a nice Japanese girl. You caused me years of grief, blaming myself for not having been there when I should have, and worse, having to live with the scandal."

Takusa lowered his head in shame.

"Maybe now you will listen to the plan that Kane and I had discussed prior to your blackmail threat. In spite of what you may be thinking, he has always shown concern and a loyalty for you that given the circumstances is truly amazing. We're both upset, but I still would like to believe that we can get through this entire mess and hopefully begin to discuss taking Takusa Entertainment Group from a domestic business to an international conglomerate."

"The police are here," Abe announced.

Takusa chuckled and shook his head. "I said from the beginning you were a shrewd business woman, Alfred-san."

J-Pop Love Song

"That she is," Kane pressed a kiss to her temple.

Charlene smiled at the backhanded compliment from her former nemesis. "Let's just say, like you I make better a better partner than enemy." She looked at her manager. "Abe, will you make sure my new *father-in-law* has the best representation. I believe all of this can be made into one big misunderstanding. Don't you?"

"I suppose miracles can happen," Abe arched an eyebrow.

"We're proof of that," Kane finally relaxed enough to smile at her while placing his free hand on her stomach. "We are going to the hospital to get Charlene looked over."

"I'm fine," Charlene protested.

"Humor me. It's been a long birthday."

"I've made a mess of your birthday, haven't I?" Takusa frowned.

"You have a lot to make up for...*Father*." Kane glared at Takusa, still not fully trusting him.

"I will do all that you ask, *Son*." Takusa promised.

"Starting with Arisa." Charlene stated firmly.

Kane nodded. "Indeed. You will release Arisa's trust fund to her. Also, you will give her the huge wedding her she deserves for being a loving daughter to you all these years."

As he was lead away by the police, he said, "It will be as you wish, my Son."

As they all made their way to the rooftop elevator, Kane and Charlene lingered behind looking out over the breathtaking view of Tokyo.

"Is the thought of Jason still a painful memory?"

"No, I think finally we are all at peace, including him. I know that Jason didn't die because of anything I did or said. Maybe if he had turned to me instead of drugs and alcohol, he'd still be here. All we can do now is move forward."

"The media is going to be in a frenzy with everything that's happened this night."

"Yup, but you know what. We are shutting off all phones and we're going to test that theory of hotel living for the remainder of the week. Abe will handle things. He thrives on damage control, that's how we met after all."

"What about one of our homes here in Tokyo with a nice view like this one. Say a four bedroom apartment in the midst of everything, what do you think, Charlie-chan?"

"Will you be there?" She asked.

"Most definitely."

"Then wherever you are, I will call it *home*."

"*So-dana!* That's right, Charlene Kaneishi-san."

"Oh I forgot, I have a birthday present for you." Charlene stated as they stepped into the now empty elevator. She reached into her jacket pocket, happy to find the precious photo was still there. "I made a special trip this afternoon to get an updated picture of our baby. The doctor said it's hard to be sure this early in the pregnancy and suggested I ask my doctor again at twenty weeks, but from what she could tell it looks like there's a good chance we're having a boy." She nestled into him.

"Oh, Charlie-chan," Kane stared at the picture in awe. He maneuvered her until her back was against the wall. "I have no idea what I'm suppose to be looking for but if this is what I think it is, this is definitely going to be *my son*."

Charlene stared at where his finger was pointing and laughingly poked him in the ribs, shaking her head. "That's his knee, Kane."

"If you say so." He pressed her against the elevator wall with his hard body and nuzzled the size of her neck. "Can you feel my...*knee?*"

"Not quite."

He lifted her so that she straddled his hips and her butt was on the handrail of the elevator wall. The hard ridge of his cock pressed against her heated vagina. She released a long shuddering moan as he ground his hips against hers.

"How about now?"

"Oh yeah," she breathed heavily into his open mouth.

Charlene's fingers worked to open the buckle of his wide belt and unsnap his jeans. The heels of her feet nestled just above his firm buttocks before she glided down the sides of his legs with hers and her feet touched the floor.

"Please allow me, *Birthday Boy*."

Pushing him back a little, she sank to her knees while easing his zipper down. Freeing his erection, her hands pumped and squeezed before her tongue snaked out to lick the weeping pearl drop at the tip before she took him into her mouth.

Kane groaned, a man in ecstasy. With one hand he buried it in the braided mass of her hair. With the other he placed the picture in the inner pocket of his jacket, over his heart and then leaned over to the side he reached out hit the red "stop" button. The emergency bell rang as the elevator stopped.

"What if we're being watched? Kane managed to pant between clenched teeth. His eyes closed and beads of moisture rested on his brow.

Charlene released him with a loud wet pop. She looked up at him with passion filled eyes, breathing in his wonderful masculine scent. "We've already broken several taboos by being together."

Kane grinned and winked. "*So-dane*. I guess so."

"*Yokatta?*" she asked. "You like that?"

"*Un*, yes, I *like* it very much." He bit down on his bottom lip. ", you look like you're having a good time."

"*Un*, yes." Charlene went back to the task at hand, sucking, tugging, licking and stroking him with her hand. As she felt his stomach muscles clench she paused to say, "*Tanoshii-yo*, I'm having fun. You know I read someplace that sperm is a great source of protein on a pinch and I'm very hungry."

Kane cursed softly and she smiled knowing he was almost there and she withdrew.

Once he found his voice again he said, "*Honto*, really?" A mischievous grin came to his lips. "Well, I read in both Japanese and English, that it's rude to speak with your mouth full."

She arched an eyebrow at him. Her eyes wide with feigned innocence. "So what are you saying?"

"Stop being rude, your much needed *protein* awaits." He winked and added, "Bay-bee. *Kimi no vanilla*."

She narrowed her eyes at him and went back to what she was doing, this time

J-Pop Love Song

allowing Kane to peak, gain relief and bring him to his knees. Charlene felt vindicated until Kane returned the favor.

Overhead a crackling voice came over the intercom and a soft female voice said in polite Japanese, "*Suminasen*, excuse me, the elevator reading shows no computer errors, upon completion, please release the button so that the elevator may proceed, thank you."

Both Charlene and Kane groaned and said in unison, "I hope that's a automatic message machine." The giggling couple straightened out their clothing and pressed the button, stealing more kisses until they reached their floor.

The elevator door opened and before they stepped out the intercom crackled again and the same voice said, "Congratulations on your marriage Kane-san, and *arigato*, thanks for the great performance tonight! Happy Birthday!"

They looked at each other in shock. The elevator doors closed.

"Why are you looking like that? You wondering if Abe will have to clean up this *indiscretion* too?"

"No, I was wondering, which *performance* do you think she was thanking me for?" Kane winked and gave her one of his infamous dimpled grins.

♪

ABOUT THE AUTHOR

Alabama native Shiree McCarver is a freelance writer, poet and lyricist. She has a great love of karaoke, history, music, folk and urban myths and paranormal occurances in which she has a gift of utilizing in her stories. Shiree writes because the characters in her head won't let her sleep like sane people and she loves hearing from her readers!

To learn more about Shiree, visit her website:
http://www.shireemccarver.com
Email Shiree at: shireemccarver@yahoo.com